Top Cow Productions Presents...

Fine Print Volume 1

Created by Stjepan Sejic

Published by Top Cow Productions, Inc.
Los Angeles

Top Cow Productions Presents...

Volume 1

Stjepan Sejic
Creator, Artist, and Writer

Stjepan Sejic
Cover Art and Logo Design

Ryan Cady
Editor

Vincent Valentine
Production

For Top Cow Productions, Inc.
For Top Cow Productions, Inc.
Marc Silvestri - CEO
Matt Hawkins - President & COO
Elena Salcedo - Vice President of Operations
Vincent Valentine - Production Manager

IMAGE COMICS, INC. • **Todd McFarlane:** President • **Jim Valentino:** Vice President • **Marc Silvestri:** Chief Executive Officer • **Erik Larsen:** Chief Financial Officer • **Robert Kirkman:** Chief Operating Officer • **Eric Stephenson:** Publisher / Chief Creative Officer • **Nicole Lapalme:** Controller • **Leanna Caunter:** Accounting Analyst • **Sue Korpela:** Accounting & HR Manager • **Marla Eizik:** Talent Liaison • **Jeff Boison:** Director of Sales & Publishing Planning • **Dirk Wood:** Director of International Sales & Licensing • **Alex Cox:** Director of Direct Market Sales • **Chloe Ramos:** Book Market & Library Sales Manager • **Emilio Bautista:** Digital Sales Coordinator • **Jon Schlaffman:** Specialty Sales Coordinator • **Kat Salazar:** Director of PR & Marketing • **Drew Fitzgerald:** Marketing Content Associate • **Heather Doornink:** Production Director • **Drew Gill:** Art Director • **Hilary DiLoreto:** Print Manager • **Tricia Ramos:** Traffic Manager • **Melissa Gifford:** Content Manager • **Erika Schnatz:** Senior Production Artist • **Ryan Brewer:** Production Artist • **Deanna Phelps:** Production Artist • **IMAGECOMICS.COM**

To find the comic shop nearest you, call:
1-888-COMICBOOK
Want more info? Check out:
www.topcow.com
for news & exclusive Top Cow merchandise!

Fine Print, Volume 1.
ISBN: 978-1-5343-2070-3

Prologue

The butterfly that started the storm

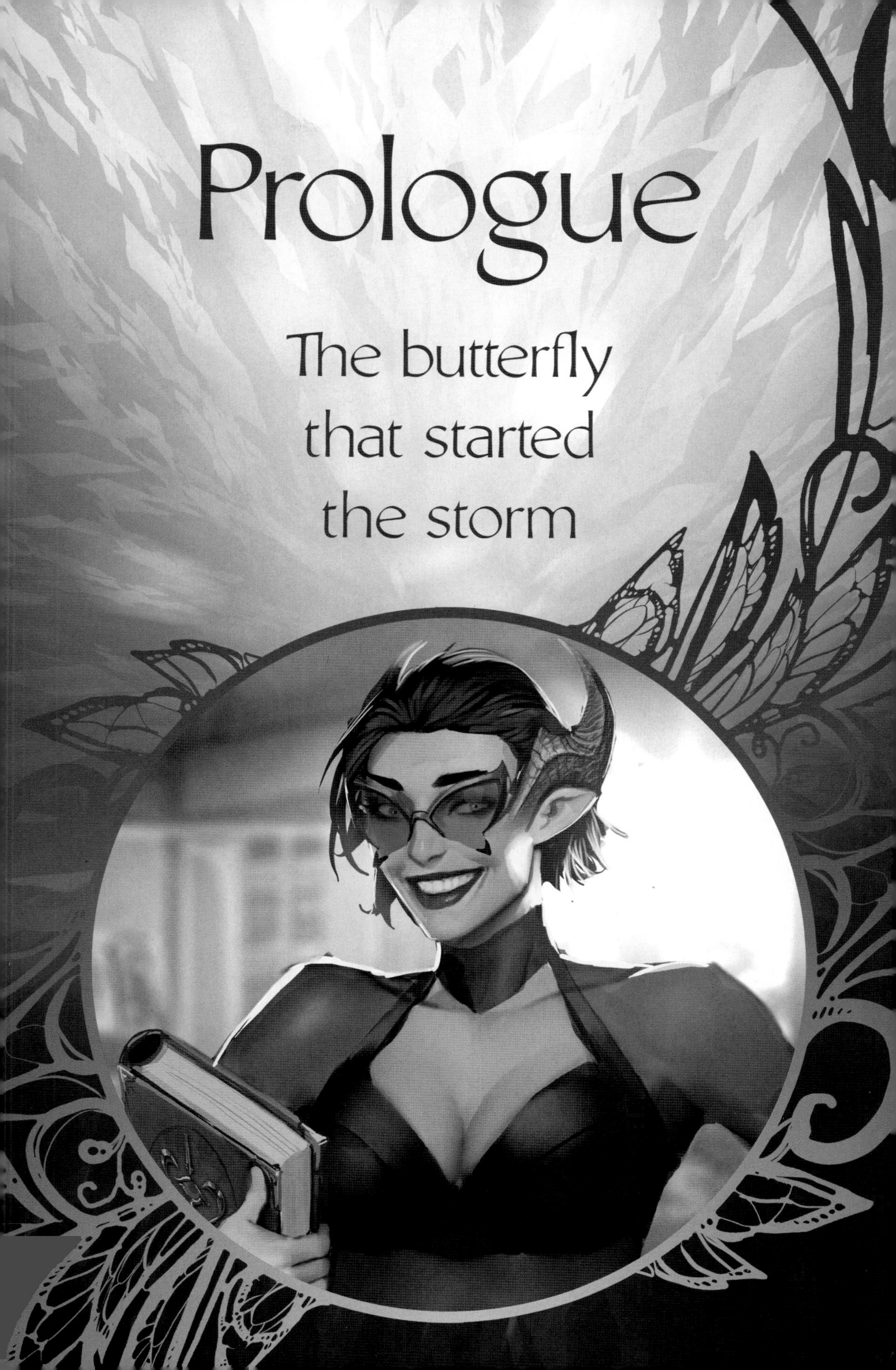

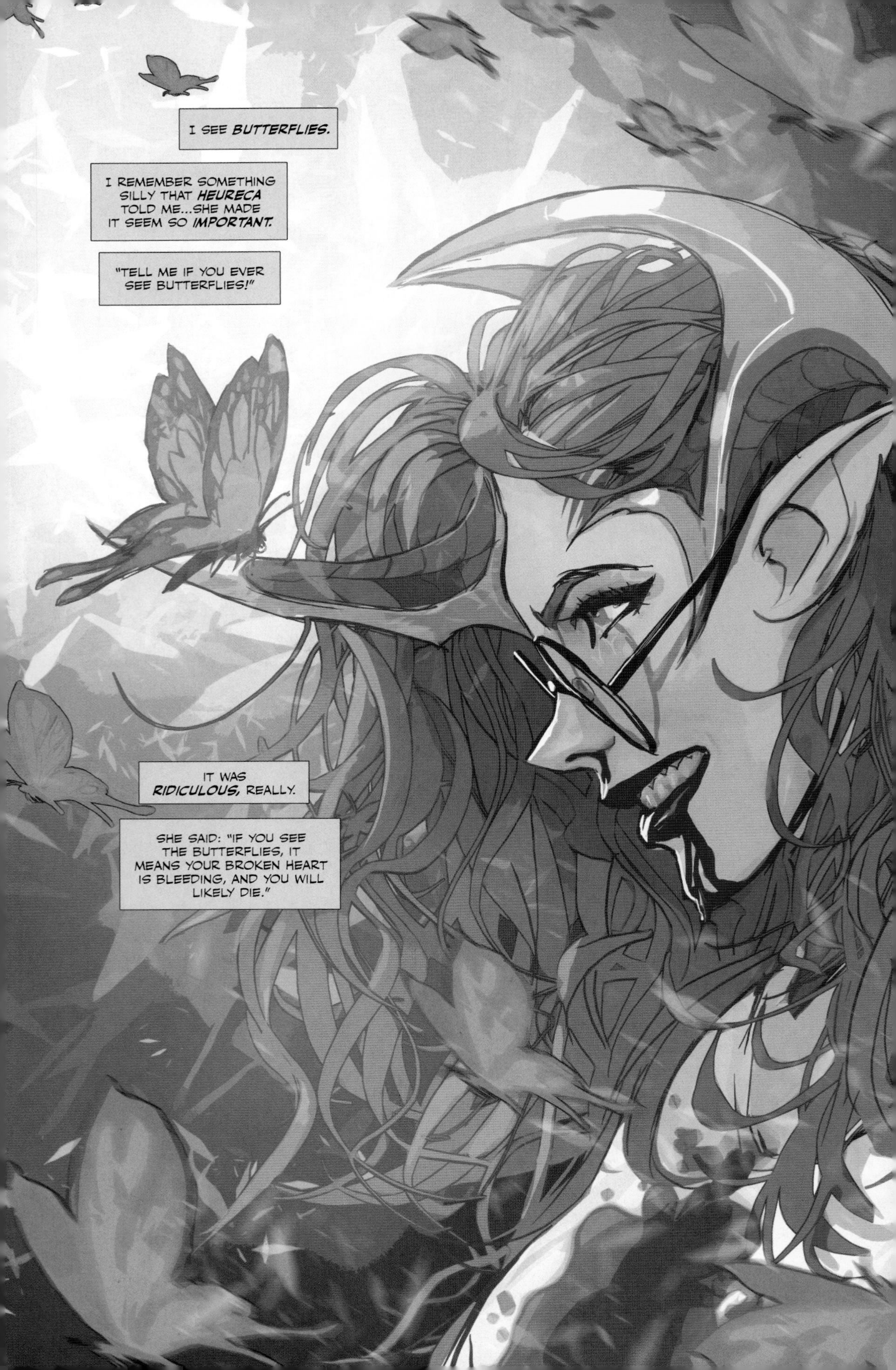
I SEE *BUTTERFLIES.*
I REMEMBER SOMETHING SILLY THAT *HEURECA* TOLD ME...SHE MADE IT SEEM SO *IMPORTANT.*
"TELL ME IF YOU EVER SEE BUTTERFLIES!"
IT WAS *RIDICULOUS,* REALLY.
SHE SAID: "IF YOU SEE THE BUTTERFLIES, IT MEANS YOUR BROKEN HEART IS BLEEDING, AND YOU WILL LIKELY DIE."

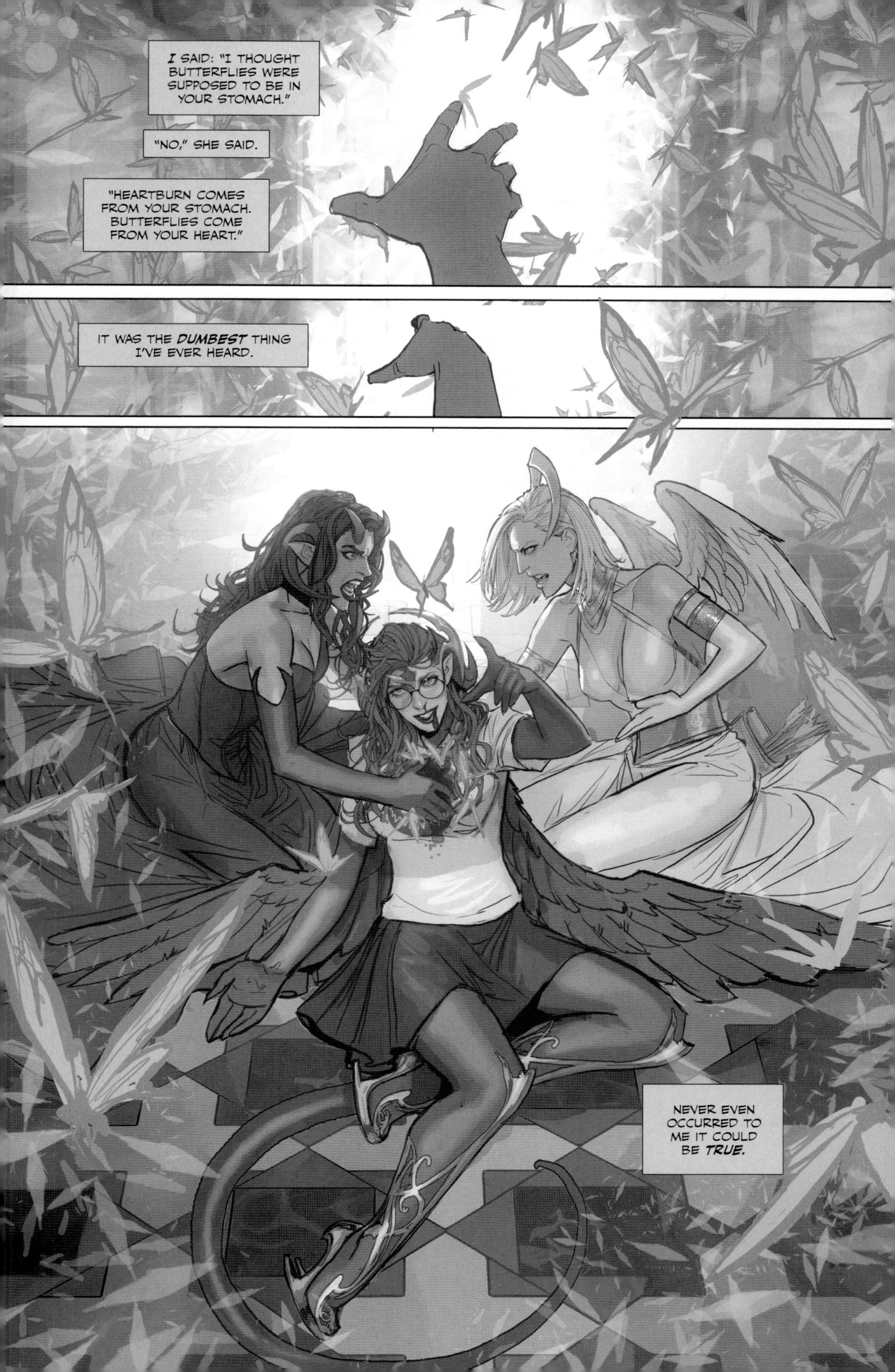
I SAID: "I THOUGHT BUTTERFLIES WERE SUPPOSED TO BE IN YOUR STOMACH."
"NO," SHE SAID.
"HEARTBURN COMES FROM YOUR STOMACH. BUTTERFLIES COME FROM YOUR HEART."
IT WAS THE DUMBEST THING I'VE EVER HEARD.
NEVER EVEN OCCURRED TO ME IT COULD BE TRUE.

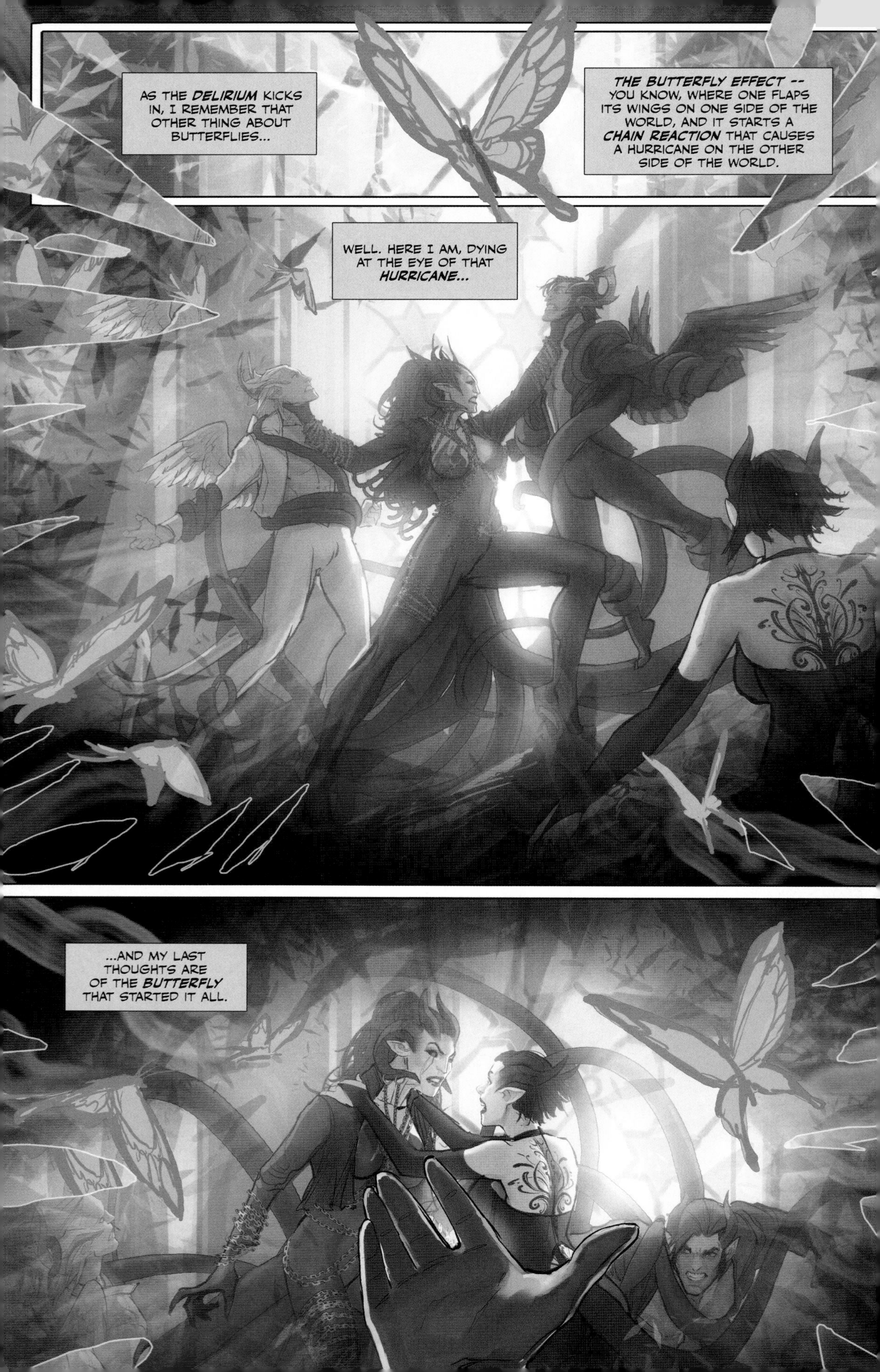
AS THE *DELIRIUM* KICKS IN, I REMEMBER THAT OTHER THING ABOUT BUTTERFLIES...
THE BUTTERFLY EFFECT -- YOU KNOW, WHERE ONE FLAPS ITS WINGS ON ONE SIDE OF THE WORLD, AND IT STARTS A *CHAIN REACTION* THAT CAUSES A HURRICANE ON THE OTHER SIDE OF THE WORLD.
WELL. HERE I AM, DYING AT THE EYE OF THAT *HURRICANE*...
...AND MY LAST THOUGHTS ARE OF THE *BUTTERFLY* THAT STARTED IT ALL.

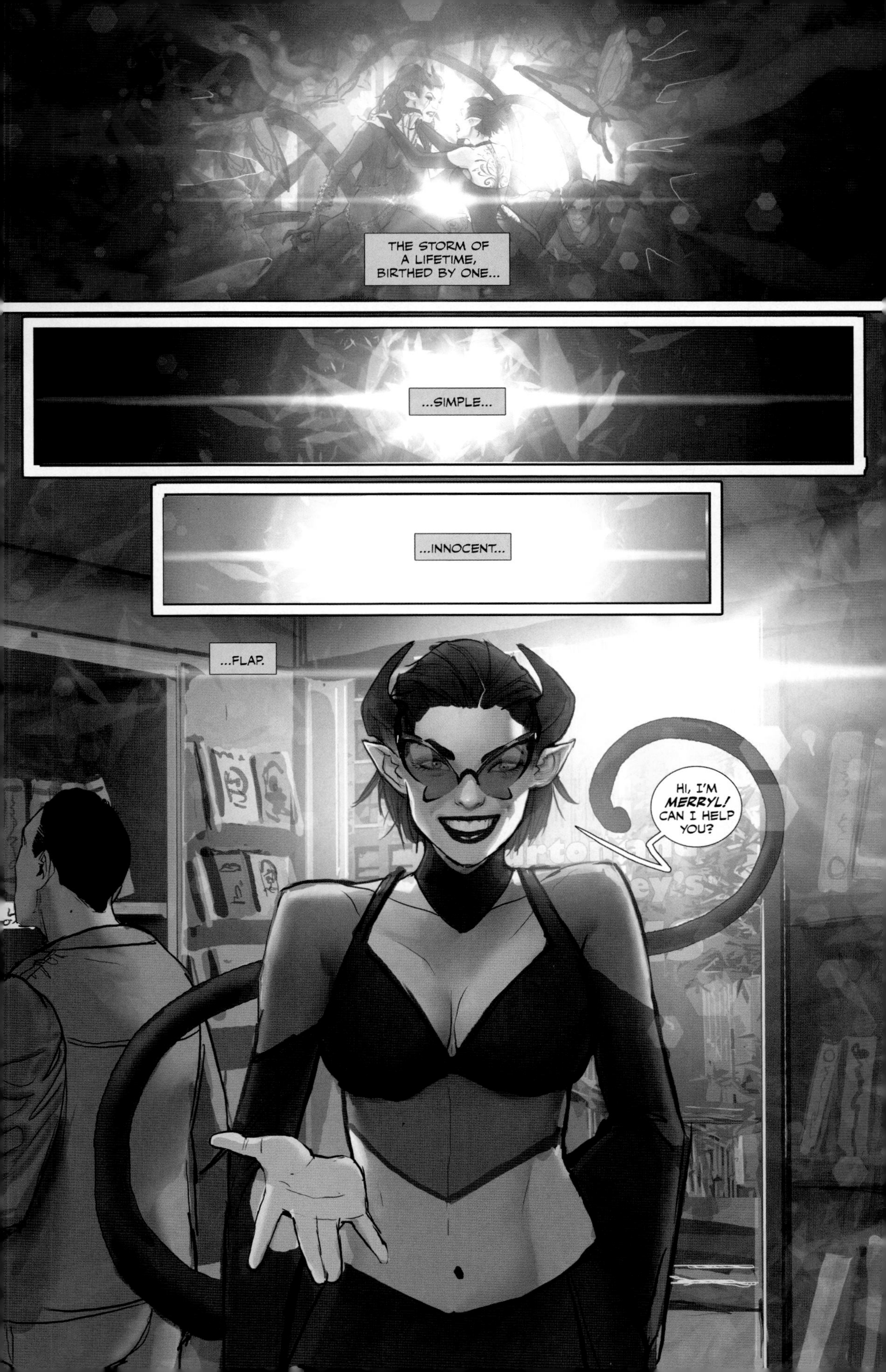
THE STORM OF A LIFETIME, BIRTHED BY ONE...
...SIMPLE...
...INNOCENT...
...FLAP.
HI, I'M MERRYL! CAN I HELP YOU?

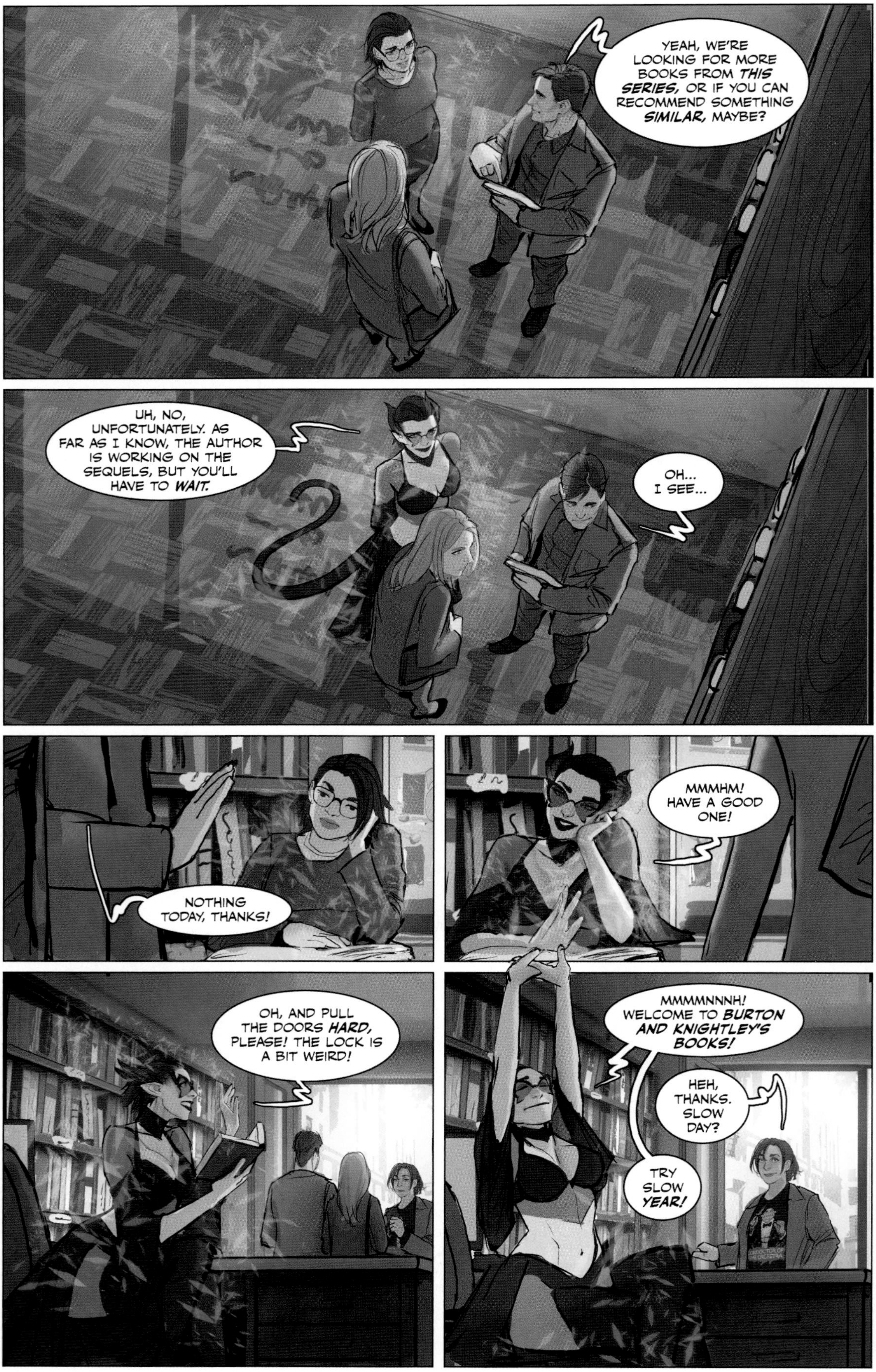
YEAH, WE'RE LOOKING FOR MORE BOOKS FROM *THIS SERIES,* OR IF YOU CAN RECOMMEND SOMETHING *SIMILAR,* MAYBE?
UH, NO, UNFORTUNATELY. AS FAR AS I KNOW, THE AUTHOR IS WORKING ON THE SEQUELS, BUT YOU'LL HAVE TO *WAIT.*
OH... I SEE...
NOTHING TODAY, THANKS!
MMMHM! HAVE A GOOD ONE!
OH, AND PULL THE DOORS *HARD,* PLEASE! THE LOCK IS A BIT WEIRD!
MMMMNNNH! WELCOME TO *BURTON AND KNIGHTLEY'S BOOKS!*
HEH, THANKS. SLOW DAY?
TRY SLOW *YEAR!*

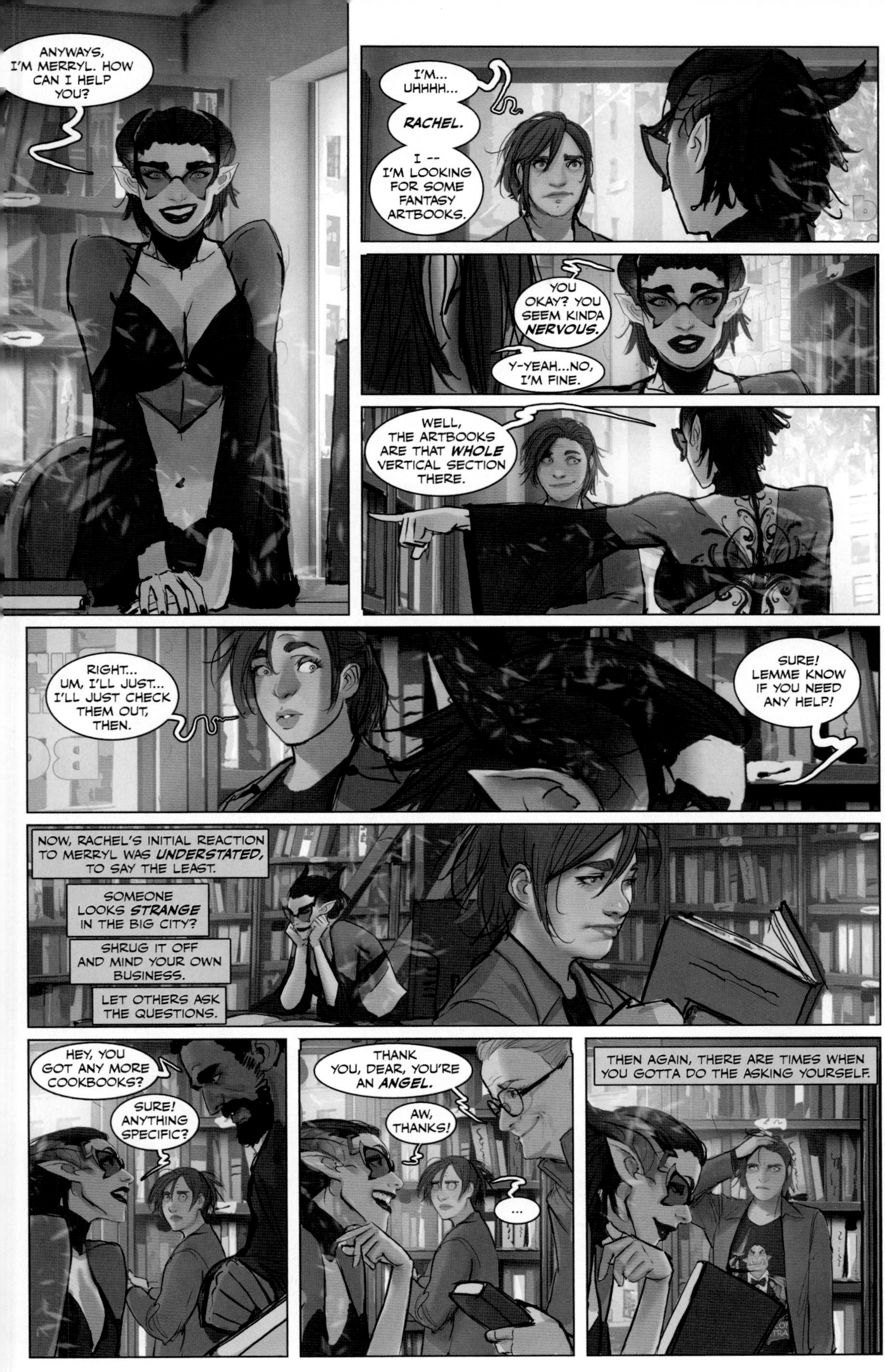
ANYWAYS, I'M MERRYL. HOW CAN I HELP YOU?
I'M... UHHHH...
RACHEL.
I -- I'M LOOKING FOR SOME FANTASY ARTBOOKS.
YOU OKAY? YOU SEEM KINDA NERVOUS.
Y-YEAH...NO, I'M FINE.
WELL, THE ARTBOOKS ARE THAT WHOLE VERTICAL SECTION THERE.
RIGHT... UM, I'LL JUST... I'LL JUST CHECK THEM OUT, THEN.
SURE! LEMME KNOW IF YOU NEED ANY HELP!
NOW, RACHEL'S INITIAL REACTION TO MERRYL WAS UNDERSTATED, TO SAY THE LEAST.
SOMEONE LOOKS STRANGE IN THE BIG CITY?
SHRUG IT OFF AND MIND YOUR OWN BUSINESS.
LET OTHERS ASK THE QUESTIONS.
HEY, YOU GOT ANY MORE COOKBOOKS?
SURE! ANYTHING SPECIFIC?
THANK YOU, DEAR, YOU'RE AN ANGEL.
AW, THANKS!
...
THEN AGAIN, THERE ARE TIMES WHEN YOU GOTTA DO THE ASKING YOURSELF.

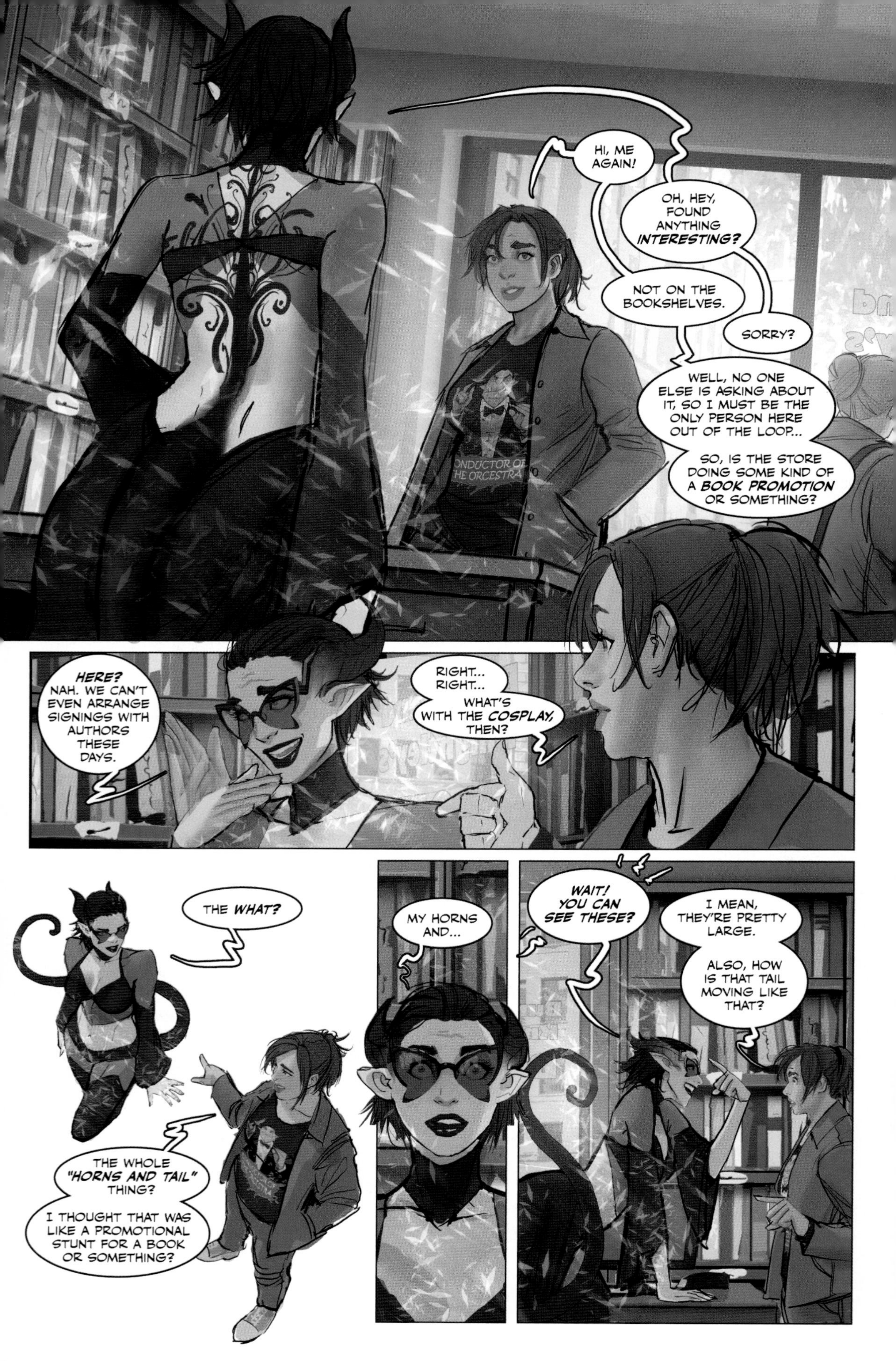
HI, ME AGAIN!
OH, HEY, FOUND ANYTHING *INTERESTING?*
NOT ON THE BOOKSHELVES.
SORRY?
WELL, NO ONE ELSE IS ASKING ABOUT IT, SO I MUST BE THE ONLY PERSON HERE OUT OF THE LOOP...
SO, IS THE STORE DOING SOME KIND OF A *BOOK PROMOTION* OR SOMETHING?
CONDUCTOR OF THE ORCESTRA
HERE? NAH. WE CAN'T EVEN ARRANGE SIGNINGS WITH AUTHORS THESE DAYS.
RIGHT... RIGHT...
WHAT'S WITH THE *COSPLAY,* THEN?
THE *WHAT?*
THE WHOLE *"HORNS AND TAIL"* THING?
I THOUGHT THAT WAS LIKE A PROMOTIONAL STUNT FOR A BOOK OR SOMETHING?
MY HORNS AND...
WAIT! YOU CAN SEE THESE?
I MEAN, THEY'RE PRETTY LARGE.
ALSO, HOW IS THAT TAIL MOVING LIKE THAT?

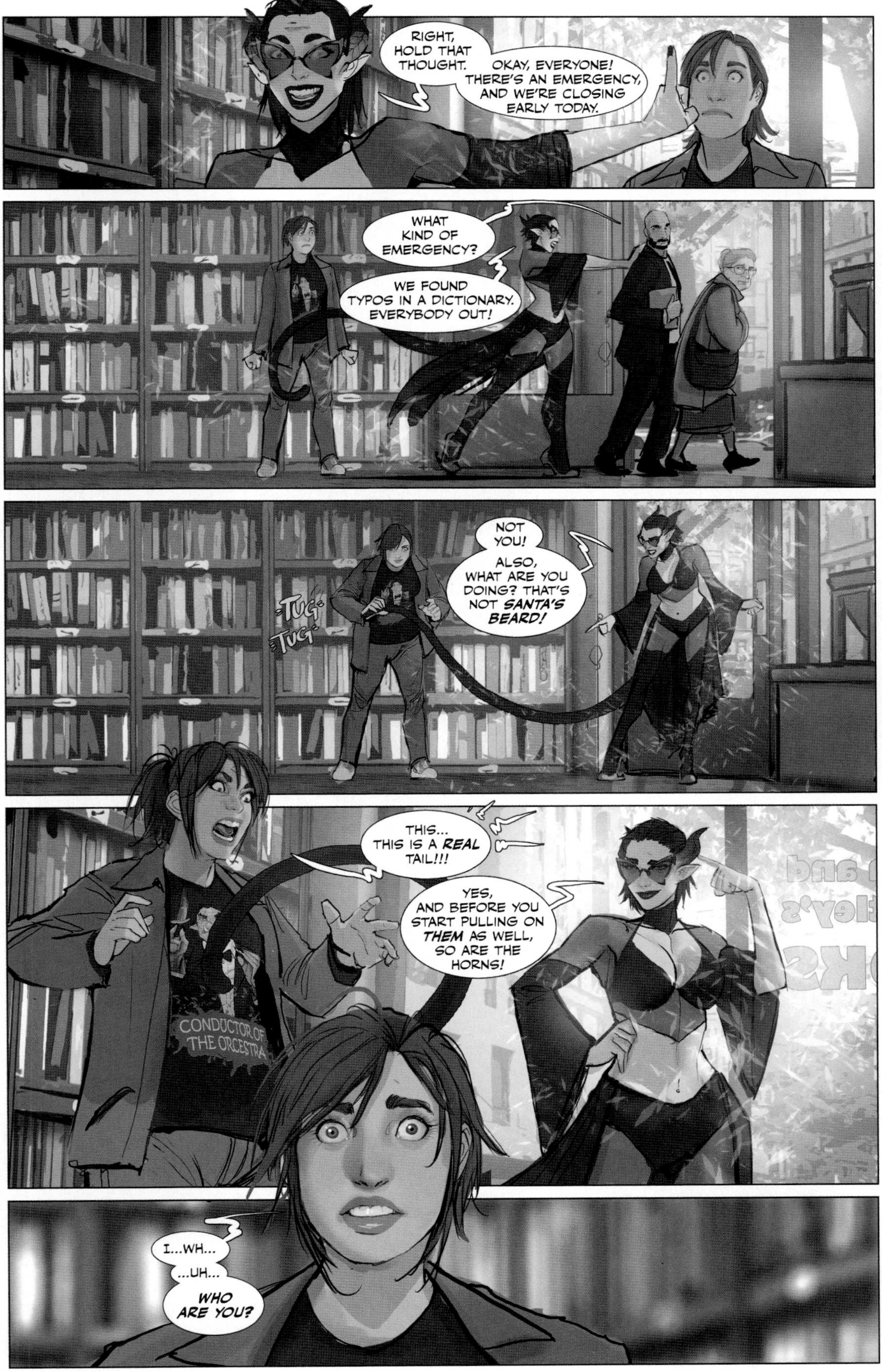
RIGHT, HOLD THAT THOUGHT.
OKAY, EVERYONE! THERE'S AN EMERGENCY, AND WE'RE CLOSING EARLY TODAY.
WHAT KIND OF EMERGENCY?
WE FOUND TYPOS IN A DICTIONARY. EVERYBODY OUT!
NOT YOU!
ALSO, WHAT ARE YOU DOING? THAT'S NOT SANTA'S BEARD!
TUG
TUG
THIS... THIS IS A REAL TAIL!!!
YES, AND BEFORE YOU START PULLING ON THEM AS WELL, SO ARE THE HORNS!
CONDUCTOR OF THE ORCESTRA
I...WH...
...UH...
WHO ARE YOU?

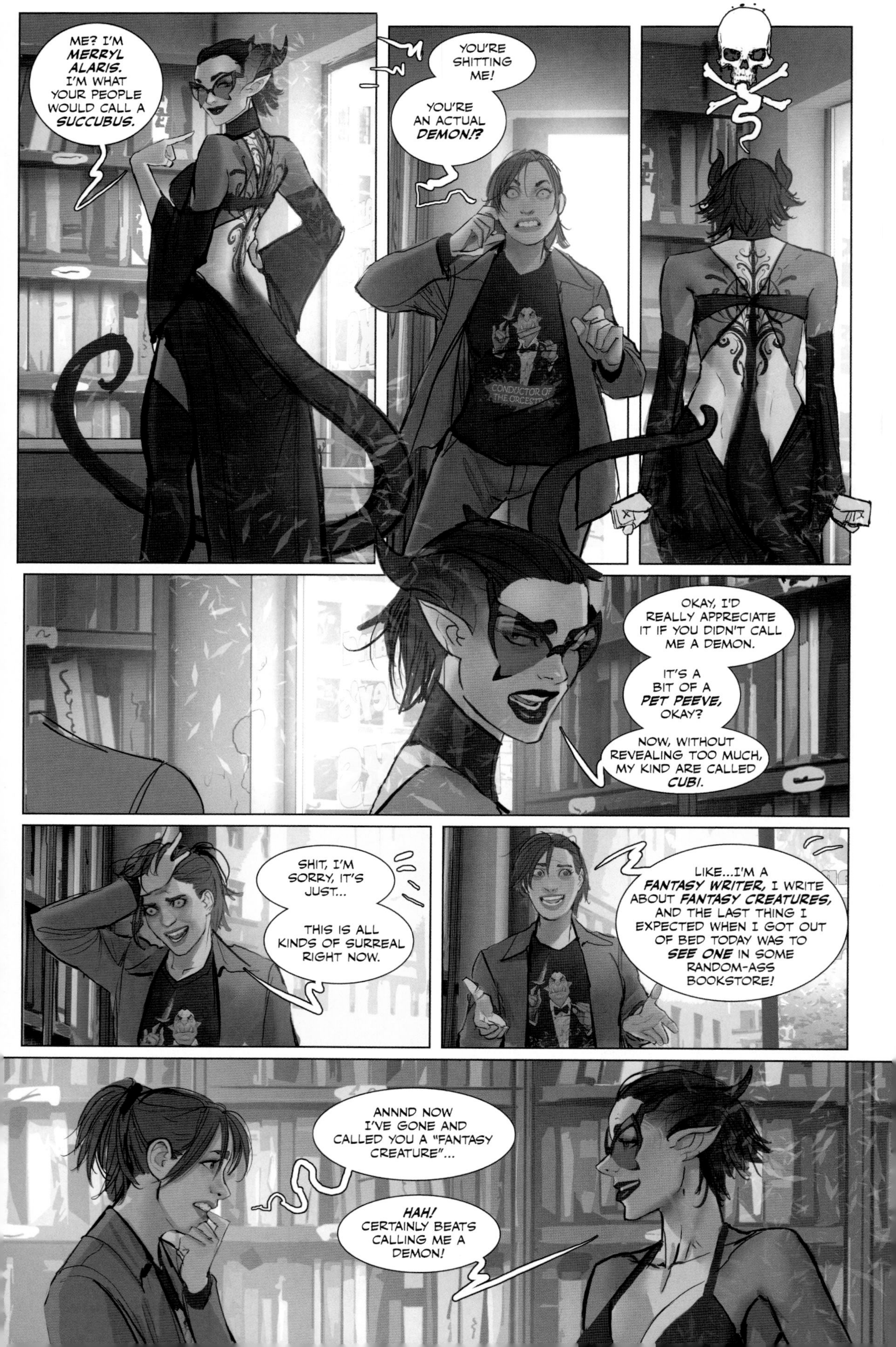
ME? I'M MERRYL ALARIS. I'M WHAT YOUR PEOPLE WOULD CALL A SUCCUBUS.
YOU'RE SHITTING ME!
YOU'RE AN ACTUAL DEMON!?
CONDUCTOR OF THE ORCESTR
OKAY, I'D REALLY APPRECIATE IT IF YOU DIDN'T CALL ME A DEMON.
IT'S A BIT OF A PET PEEVE, OKAY?
NOW, WITHOUT REVEALING TOO MUCH, MY KIND ARE CALLED CUBI.
SHIT, I'M SORRY, IT'S JUST...
THIS IS ALL KINDS OF SURREAL RIGHT NOW.
LIKE...I'M A FANTASY WRITER, I WRITE ABOUT FANTASY CREATURES, AND THE LAST THING I EXPECTED WHEN I GOT OUT OF BED TODAY WAS TO SEE ONE IN SOME RANDOM-ASS BOOKSTORE!
ANNND NOW I'VE GONE AND CALLED YOU A "FANTASY CREATURE"...
HAH! CERTAINLY BEATS CALLING ME A DEMON!

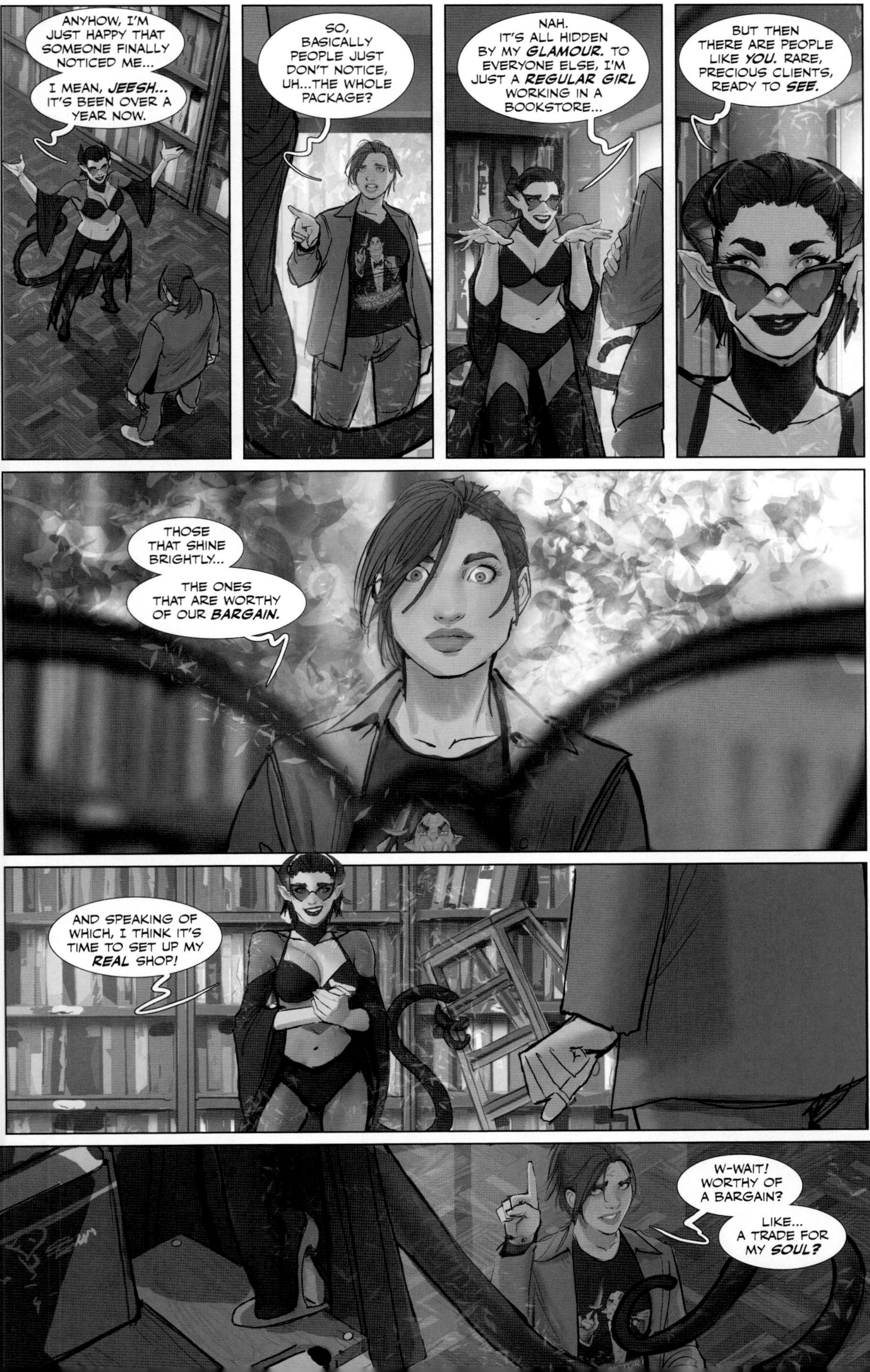
ANYHOW, I'M JUST HAPPY THAT SOMEONE FINALLY NOTICED ME...
I MEAN, JEESH... IT'S BEEN OVER A YEAR NOW.
SO, BASICALLY PEOPLE JUST DON'T NOTICE, UH...THE WHOLE PACKAGE?
NAH. IT'S ALL HIDDEN BY MY GLAMOUR. TO EVERYONE ELSE, I'M JUST A REGULAR GIRL WORKING IN A BOOKSTORE...
BUT THEN THERE ARE PEOPLE LIKE YOU. RARE, PRECIOUS CLIENTS, READY TO SEE.
THOSE THAT SHINE BRIGHTLY...
THE ONES THAT ARE WORTHY OF OUR BARGAIN.
AND SPEAKING OF WHICH, I THINK IT'S TIME TO SET UP MY REAL SHOP!
W-WAIT! WORTHY OF A BARGAIN?
LIKE... A TRADE FOR MY SOUL?

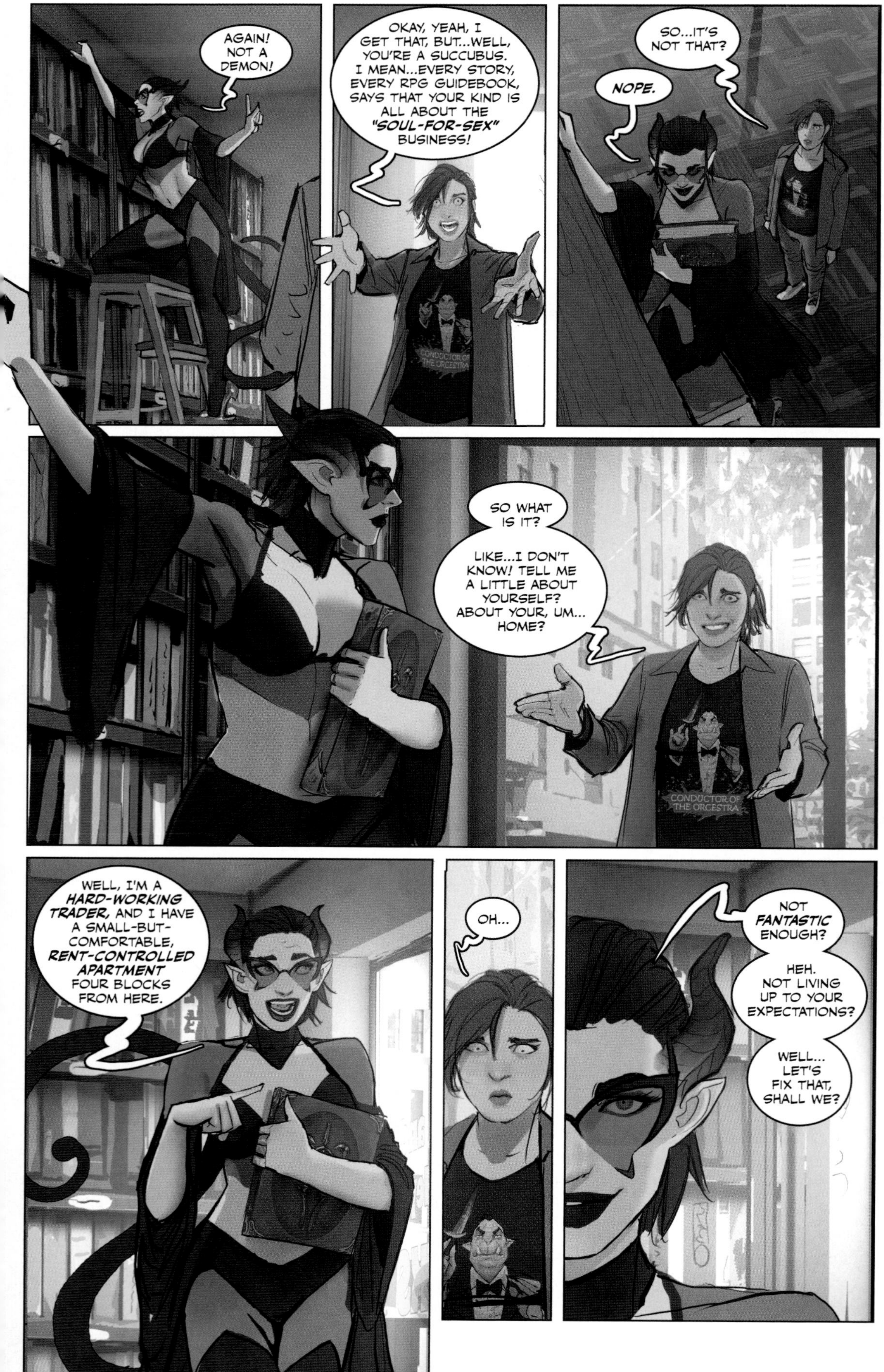
AGAIN! NOT A DEMON!
OKAY, YEAH, I GET THAT, BUT...WELL, YOU'RE A SUCCUBUS. I MEAN...EVERY STORY, EVERY RPG GUIDEBOOK, SAYS THAT YOUR KIND IS ALL ABOUT THE "SOUL-FOR-SEX" BUSINESS!
CONDUCTOR OF THE ORCESTRA
SO...IT'S NOT THAT?
NOPE.
SO WHAT IS IT?
LIKE...I DON'T KNOW! TELL ME A LITTLE ABOUT YOURSELF? ABOUT YOUR, UM... HOME?
CONDUCTOR OF THE ORCESTRA
WELL, I'M A HARD-WORKING TRADER, AND I HAVE A SMALL-BUT-COMFORTABLE, RENT-CONTROLLED APARTMENT FOUR BLOCKS FROM HERE.
OH...
NOT FANTASTIC ENOUGH?
HEH. NOT LIVING UP TO YOUR EXPECTATIONS?
WELL... LET'S FIX THAT, SHALL WE?

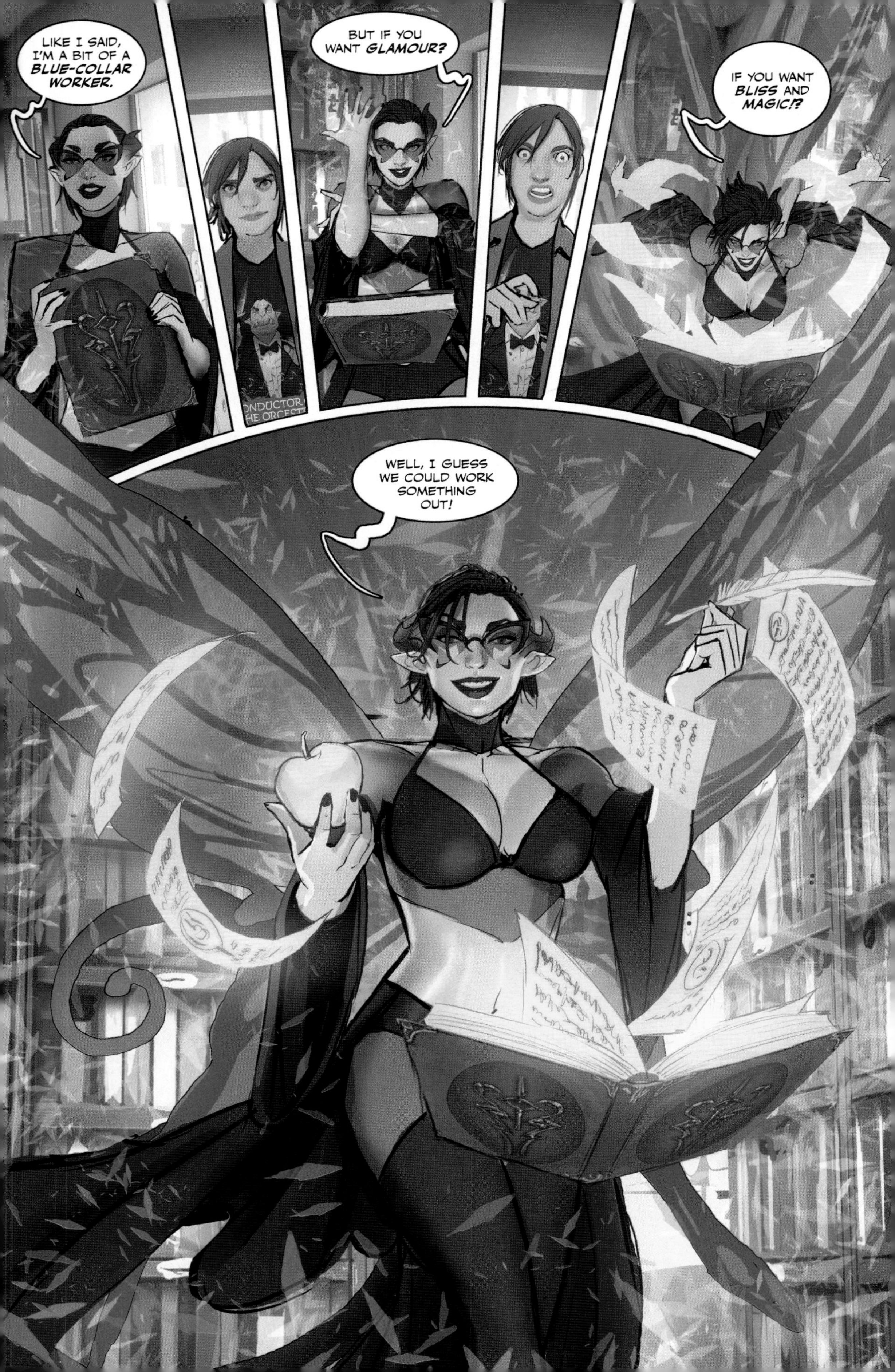
LIKE I SAID, I'M A BIT OF A BLUE-COLLAR WORKER.
BUT IF YOU WANT GLAMOUR?
IF YOU WANT BLISS AND MAGIC!?
WELL, I GUESS WE COULD WORK SOMETHING OUT!

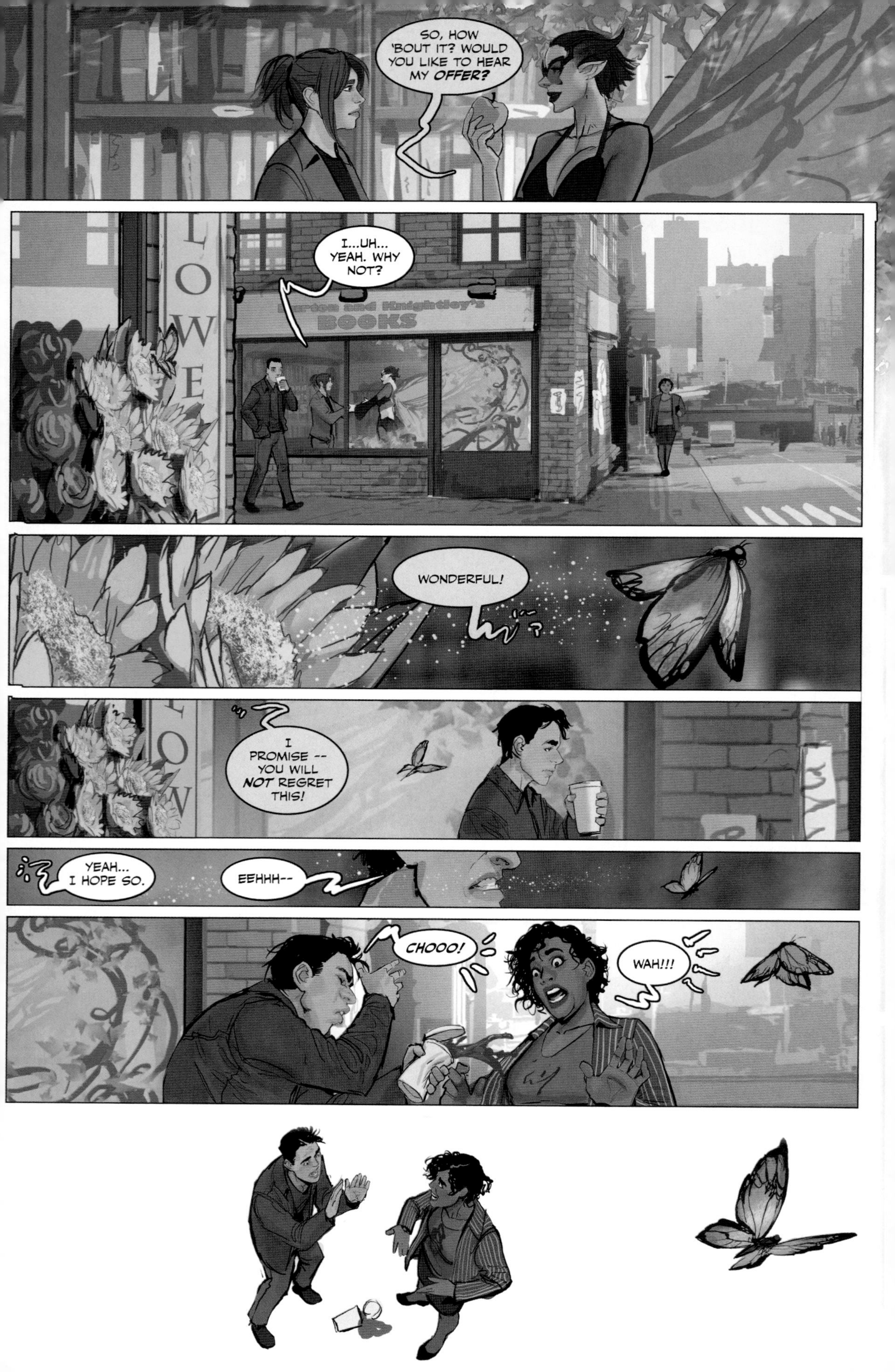
SO, HOW 'BOUT IT? WOULD YOU LIKE TO HEAR MY *OFFER?*
I...UH... YEAH. WHY NOT?
Knightley's
BOOKS
WONDERFUL!
I PROMISE -- YOU WILL *NOT* REGRET THIS!
YEAH... I HOPE SO.
EEHHH--
CHOOO!
WAH!!!

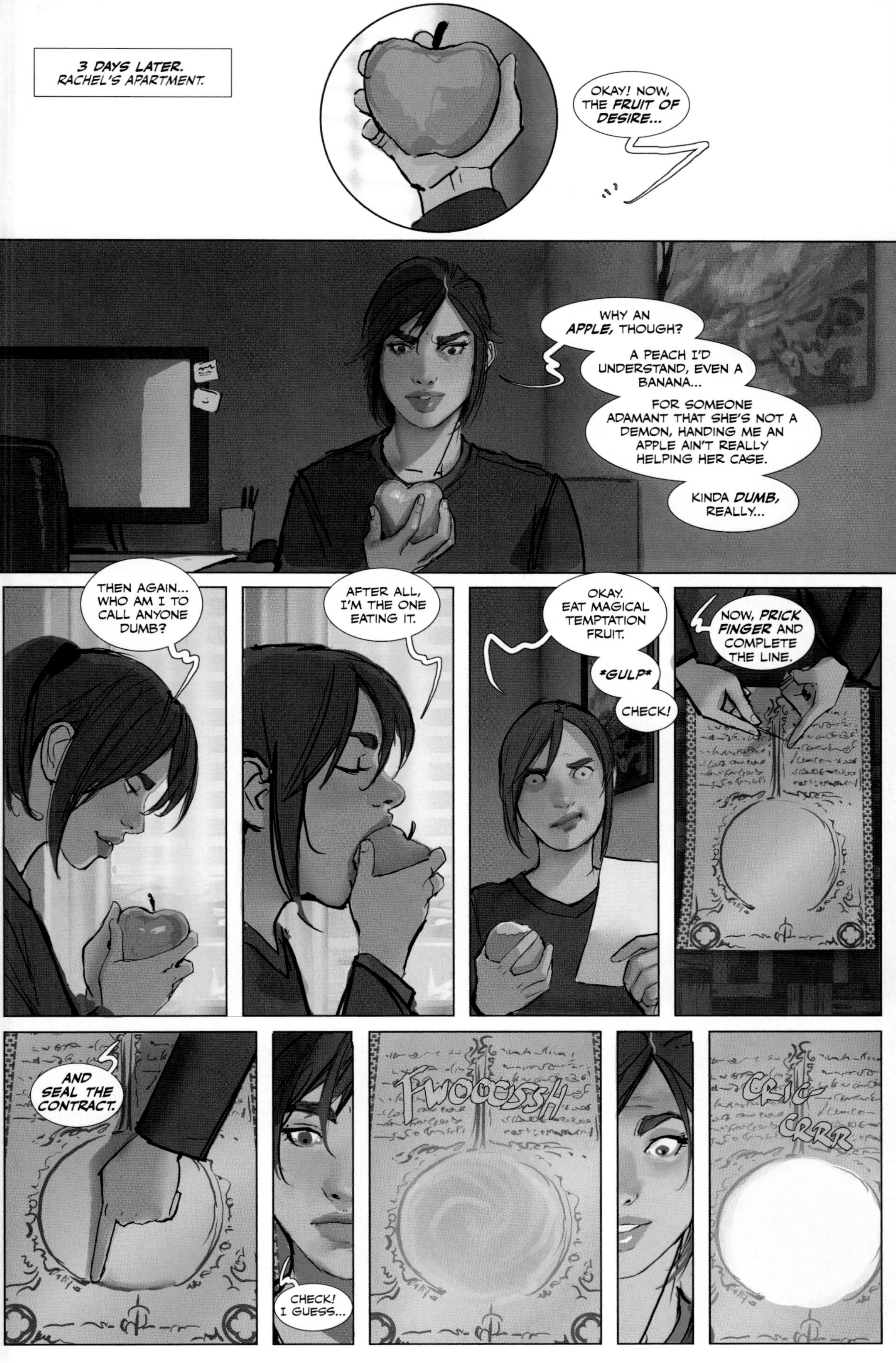
3 DAYS LATER. RACHEL'S APARTMENT.
OKAY! NOW, THE FRUIT OF DESIRE...
WHY AN APPLE, THOUGH?
A PEACH I'D UNDERSTAND, EVEN A BANANA...
FOR SOMEONE ADAMANT THAT SHE'S NOT A DEMON, HANDING ME AN APPLE AIN'T REALLY HELPING HER CASE.
KINDA DUMB, REALLY...
THEN AGAIN... WHO AM I TO CALL ANYONE DUMB?
AFTER ALL, I'M THE ONE EATING IT.
OKAY. EAT MAGICAL TEMPTATION FRUIT.
GULP
CHECK!
NOW, PRICK FINGER AND COMPLETE THE LINE.
AND SEAL THE CONTRACT.
CHECK! I GUESS...
FWOOOSSH
CRIC-CRRR

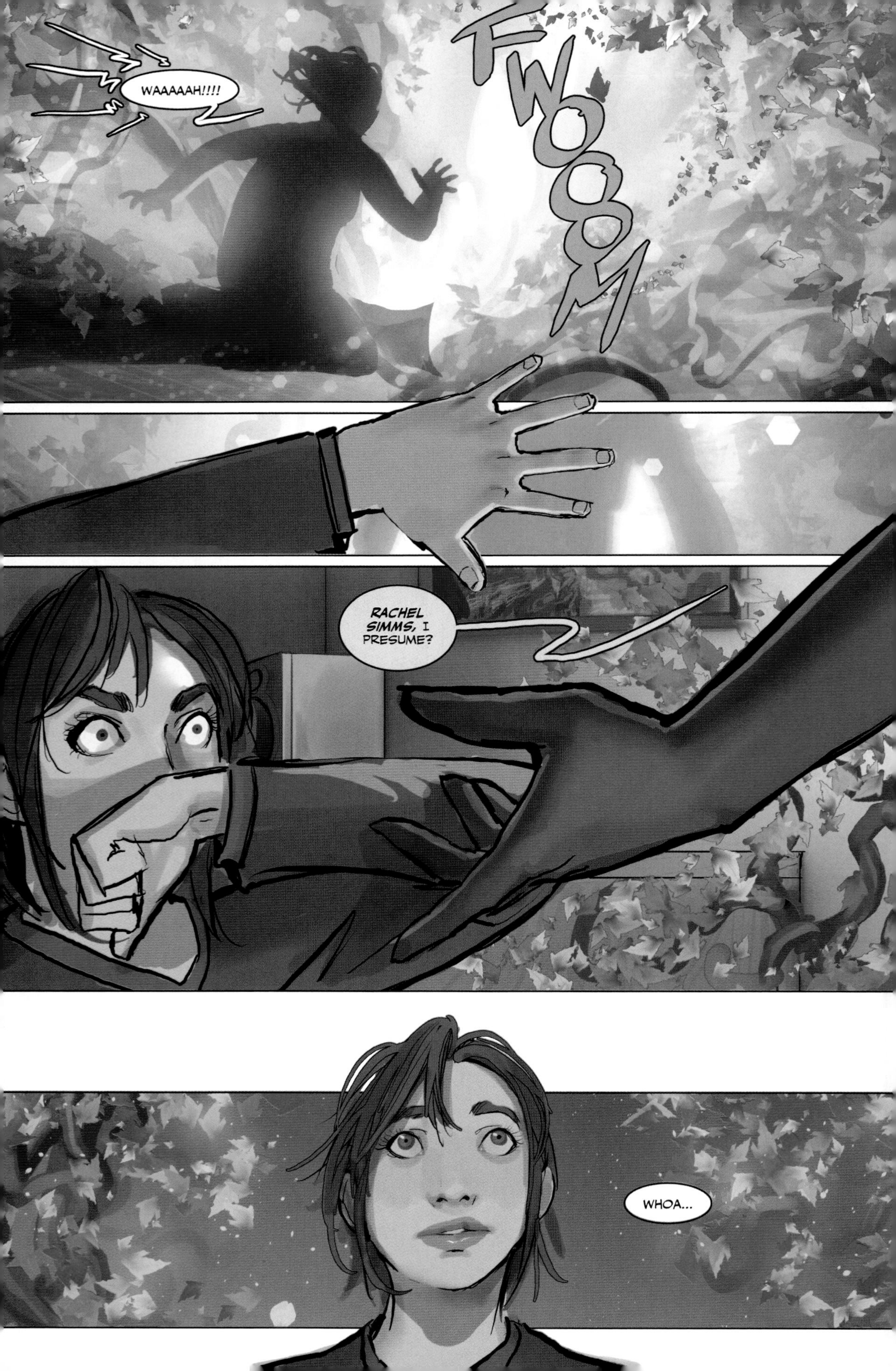
WAAAAAH!!!!
FWOOOM
RACHEL SIMMS, I PRESUME?
WHOA...

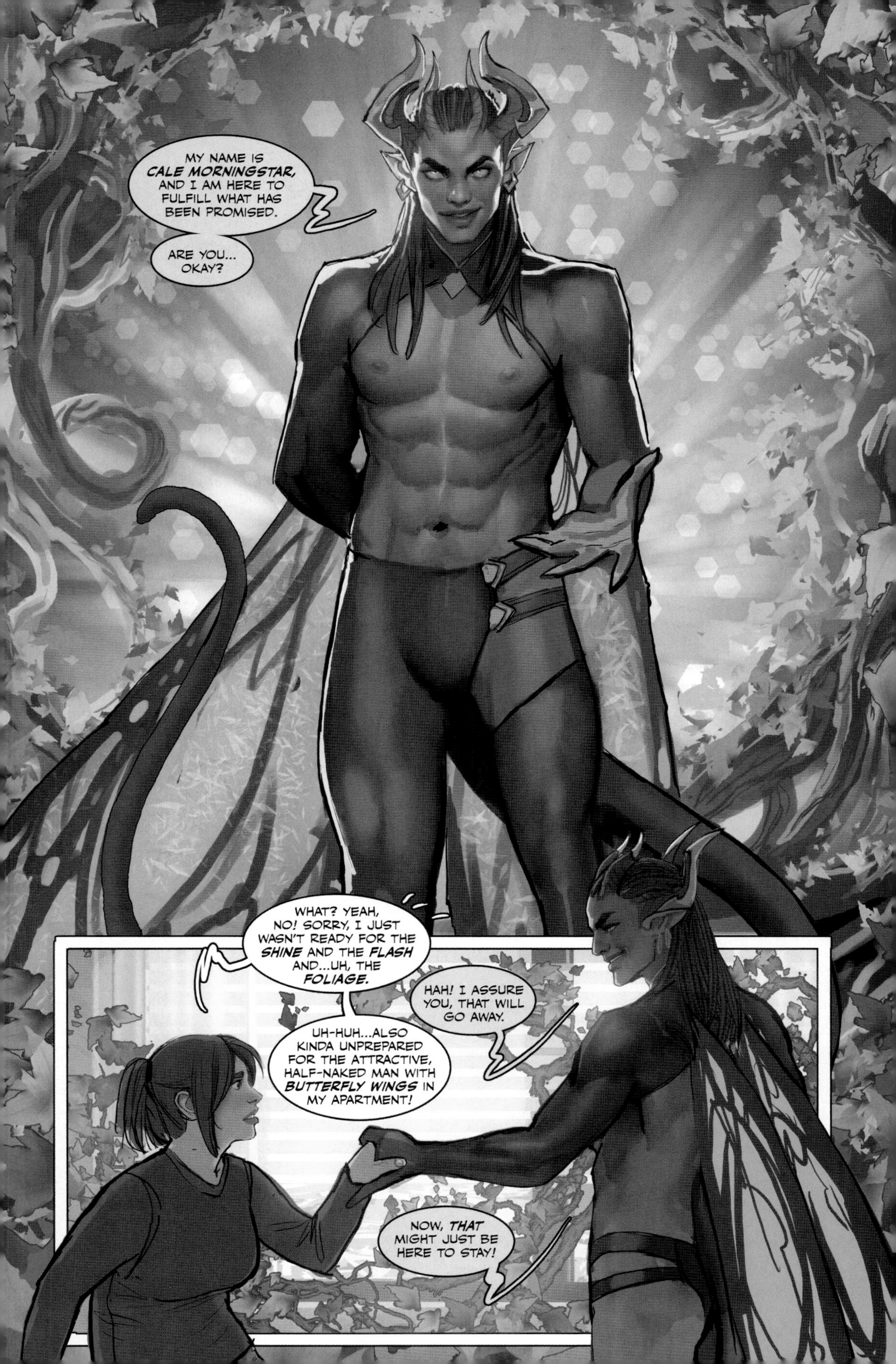
MY NAME IS CALE MORNINGSTAR, AND I AM HERE TO FULFILL WHAT HAS BEEN PROMISED.
ARE YOU... OKAY?
WHAT? YEAH, NO! SORRY, I JUST WASN'T READY FOR THE SHINE AND THE FLASH AND...UH, THE FOLIAGE.
HAH! I ASSURE YOU, THAT WILL GO AWAY.
UH-HUH...ALSO KINDA UNPREPARED FOR THE ATTRACTIVE, HALF-NAKED MAN WITH BUTTERFLY WINGS IN MY APARTMENT!
NOW, THAT MIGHT JUST BE HERE TO STAY!

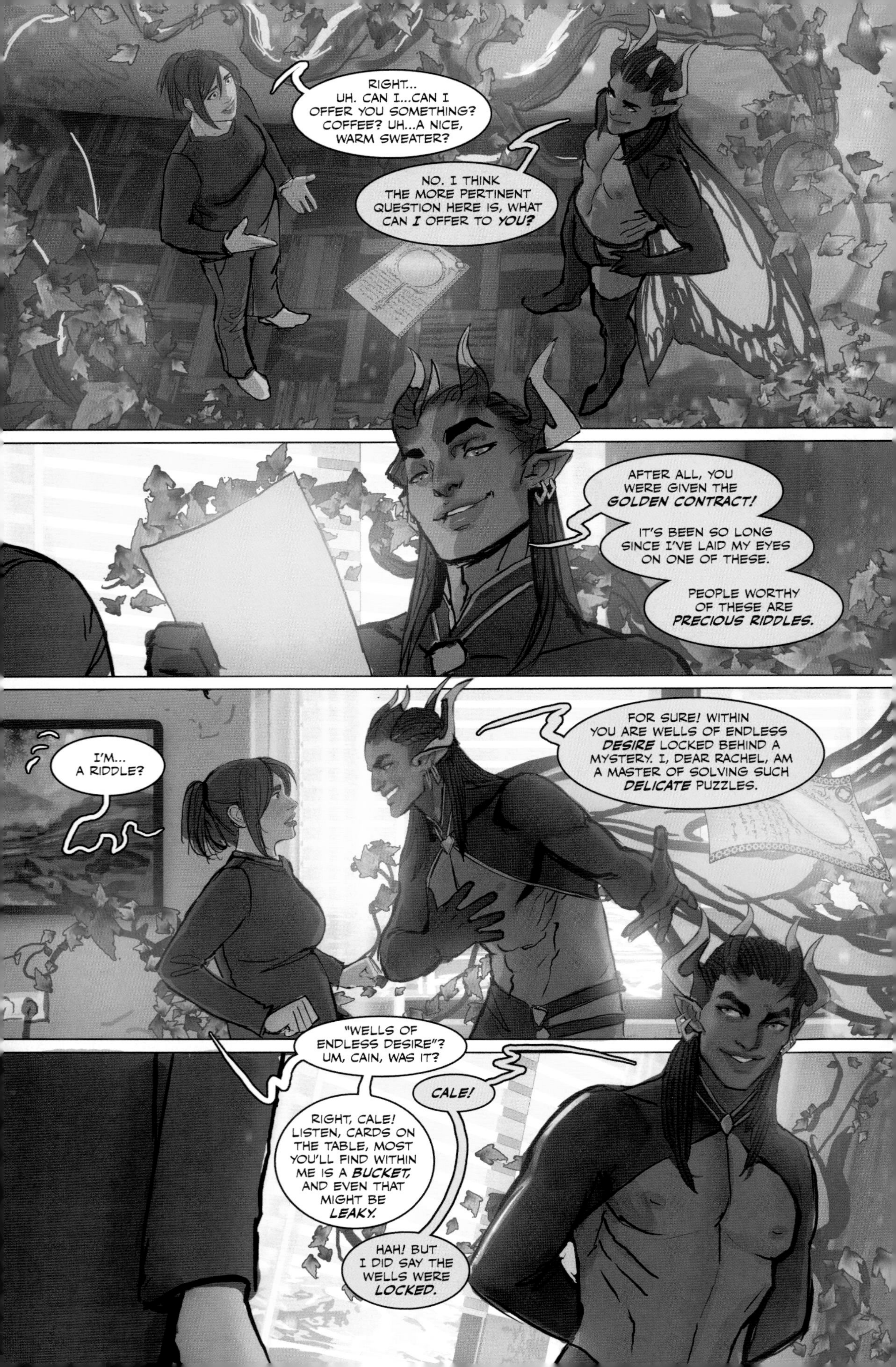
RIGHT... UH. CAN I...CAN I OFFER YOU SOMETHING? COFFEE? UH...A NICE, WARM SWEATER?
NO. I THINK THE MORE PERTINENT QUESTION HERE IS, WHAT CAN *I* OFFER TO *YOU?*
AFTER ALL, YOU WERE GIVEN THE ***GOLDEN CONTRACT!***
IT'S BEEN SO LONG SINCE I'VE LAID MY EYES ON ONE OF THESE.
PEOPLE WORTHY OF THESE ARE ***PRECIOUS RIDDLES.***
I'M... A RIDDLE?
FOR SURE! WITHIN YOU ARE WELLS OF ENDLESS ***DESIRE*** LOCKED BEHIND A MYSTERY. I, DEAR RACHEL, AM A MASTER OF SOLVING SUCH ***DELICATE*** PUZZLES.
"WELLS OF ENDLESS DESIRE"? UM, CAIN, WAS IT?
CALE!
RIGHT, CALE! LISTEN, CARDS ON THE TABLE, MOST YOU'LL FIND WITHIN ME IS A ***BUCKET,*** AND EVEN THAT MIGHT BE ***LEAKY.***
HAH! BUT I DID SAY THE WELLS WERE ***LOCKED.***

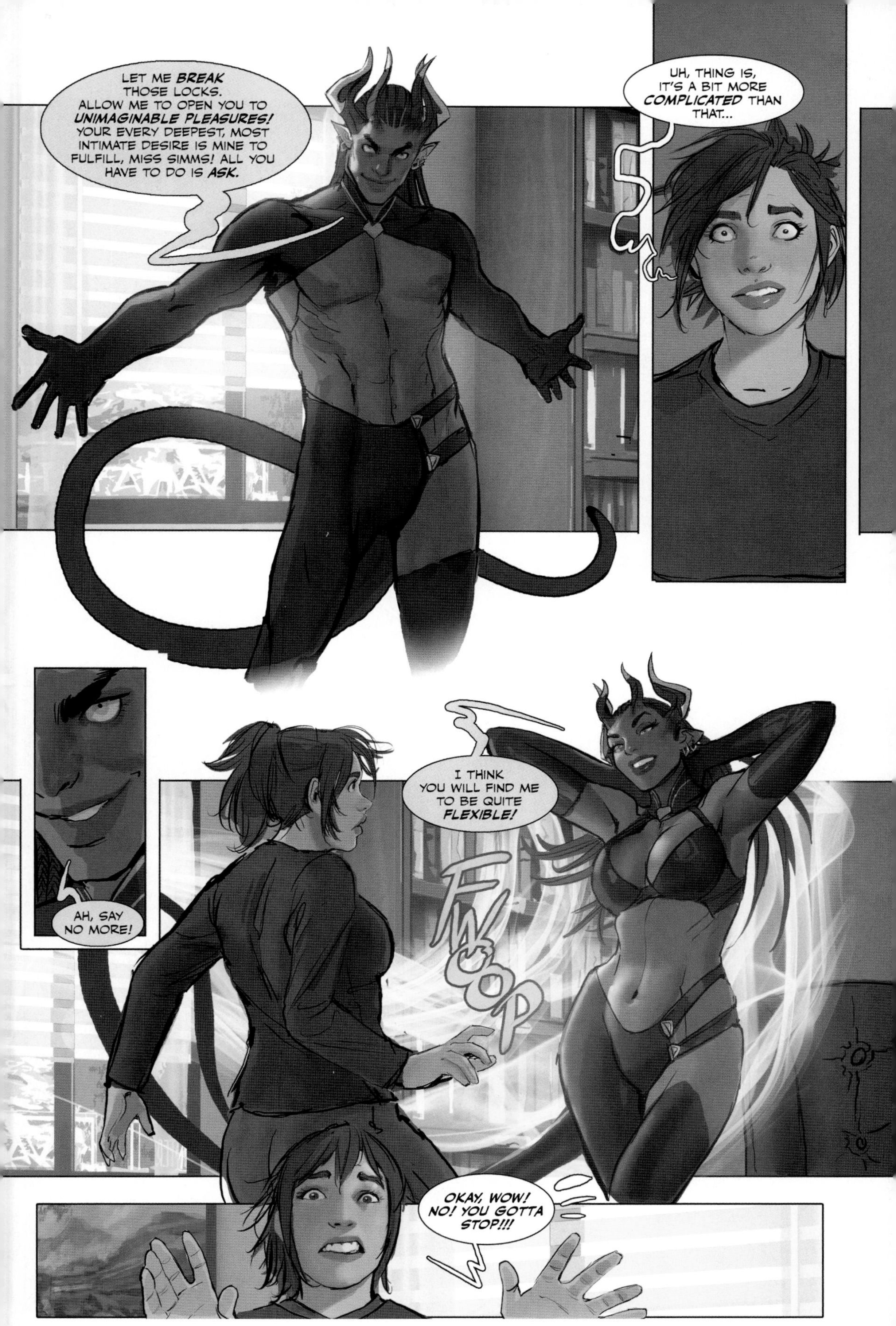

LET ME BREAK THOSE LOCKS. ALLOW ME TO OPEN YOU TO UNIMAGINABLE PLEASURES! YOUR EVERY DEEPEST, MOST INTIMATE DESIRE IS MINE TO FULFILL, MISS SIMMS! ALL YOU HAVE TO DO IS ASK.
UH, THING IS, IT'S A BIT MORE COMPLICATED THAN THAT...
AH, SAY NO MORE!
I THINK YOU WILL FIND ME TO BE QUITE FLEXIBLE!
FWOOP
OKAY, WOW! NO! YOU GOTTA STOP!!!

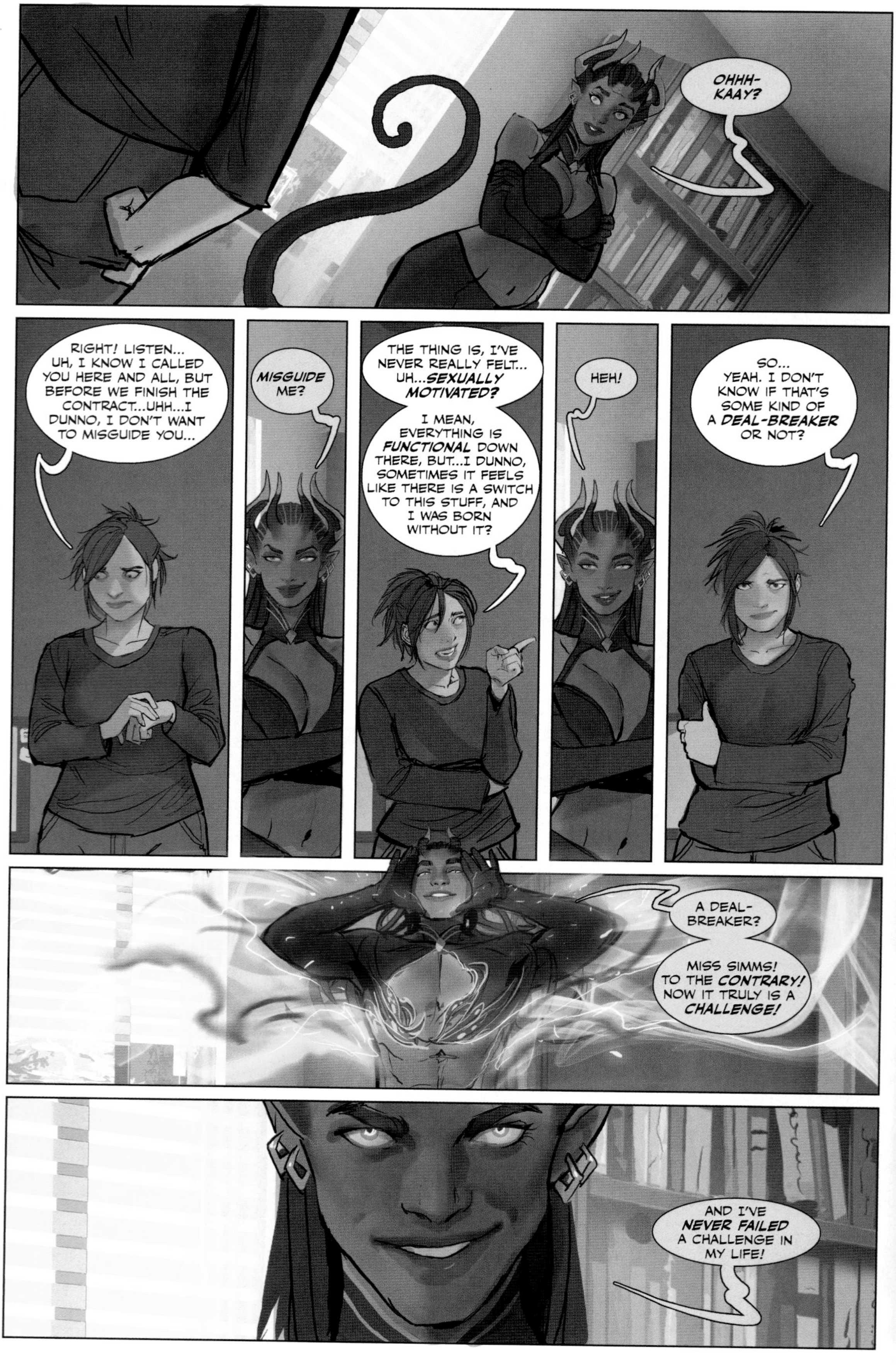
OHHH-KAAY?
RIGHT! LISTEN... UH, I KNOW I CALLED YOU HERE AND ALL, BUT BEFORE WE FINISH THE CONTRACT...UHH...I DUNNO, I DON'T WANT TO MISGUIDE YOU...
MISGUIDE ME?
THE THING IS, I'VE NEVER REALLY FELT... UH...SEXUALLY MOTIVATED?
I MEAN, EVERYTHING IS FUNCTIONAL DOWN THERE, BUT...I DUNNO, SOMETIMES IT FEELS LIKE THERE IS A SWITCH TO THIS STUFF, AND I WAS BORN WITHOUT IT?
HEH!
SO... YEAH. I DON'T KNOW IF THAT'S SOME KIND OF A DEAL-BREAKER OR NOT?
A DEAL-BREAKER?
MISS SIMMS! TO THE CONTRARY! NOW IT TRULY IS A CHALLENGE!
AND I'VE NEVER FAILED A CHALLENGE IN MY LIFE!

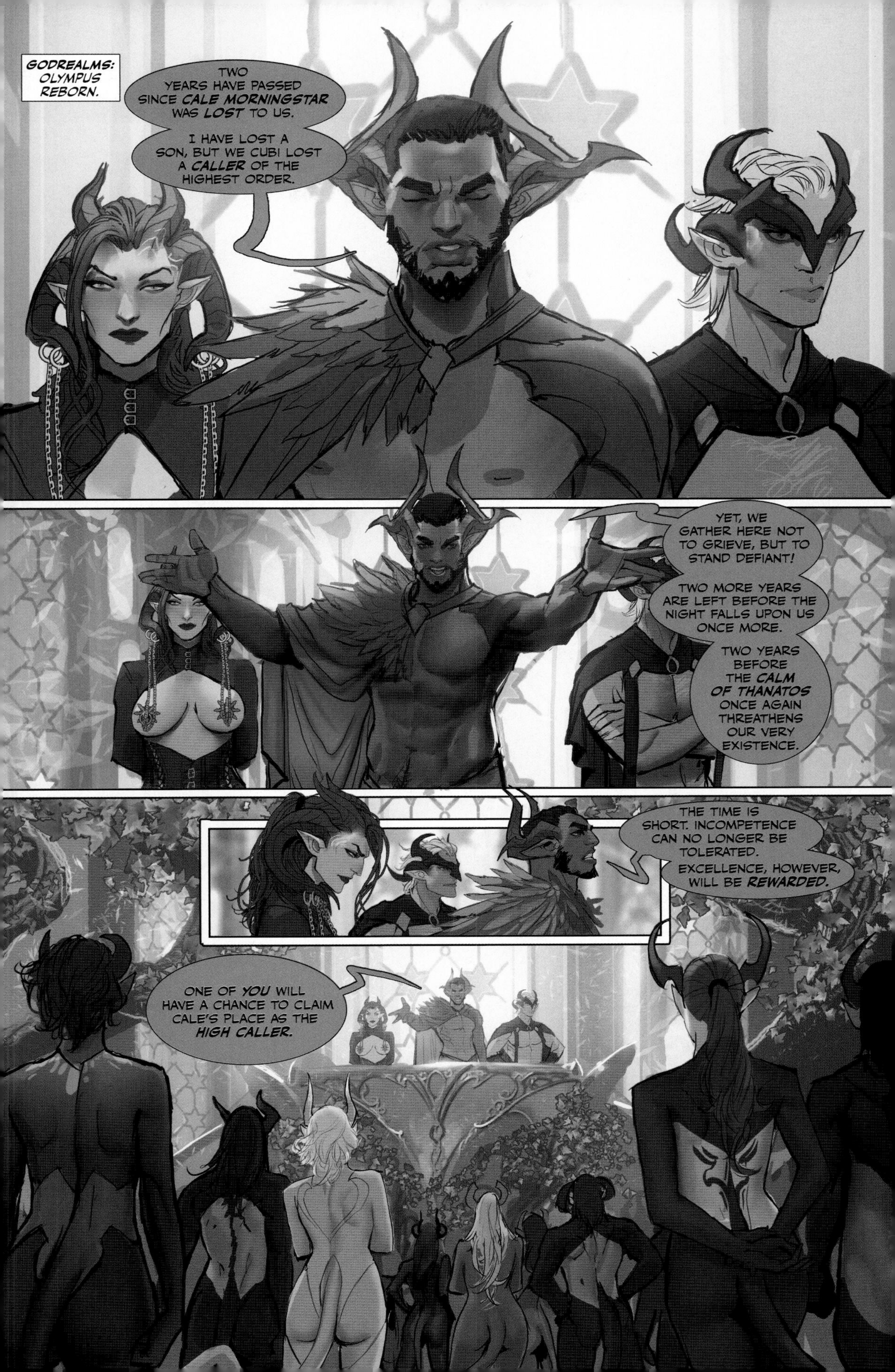
GODREALMS: OLYMPUS REBORN.
TWO YEARS HAVE PASSED SINCE CALE MORNINGSTAR WAS LOST TO US.
I HAVE LOST A SON, BUT WE CUBI LOST A CALLER OF THE HIGHEST ORDER.
YET, WE GATHER HERE NOT TO GRIEVE, BUT TO STAND DEFIANT!
TWO MORE YEARS ARE LEFT BEFORE THE NIGHT FALLS UPON US ONCE MORE.
TWO YEARS BEFORE THE CALM OF THANATOS ONCE AGAIN THREATHENS OUR VERY EXISTENCE.
THE TIME IS SHORT. INCOMPETENCE CAN NO LONGER BE TOLERATED.
EXCELLENCE, HOWEVER, WILL BE REWARDED.
ONE OF YOU WILL HAVE A CHANCE TO CLAIM CALE'S PLACE AS THE HIGH CALLER.

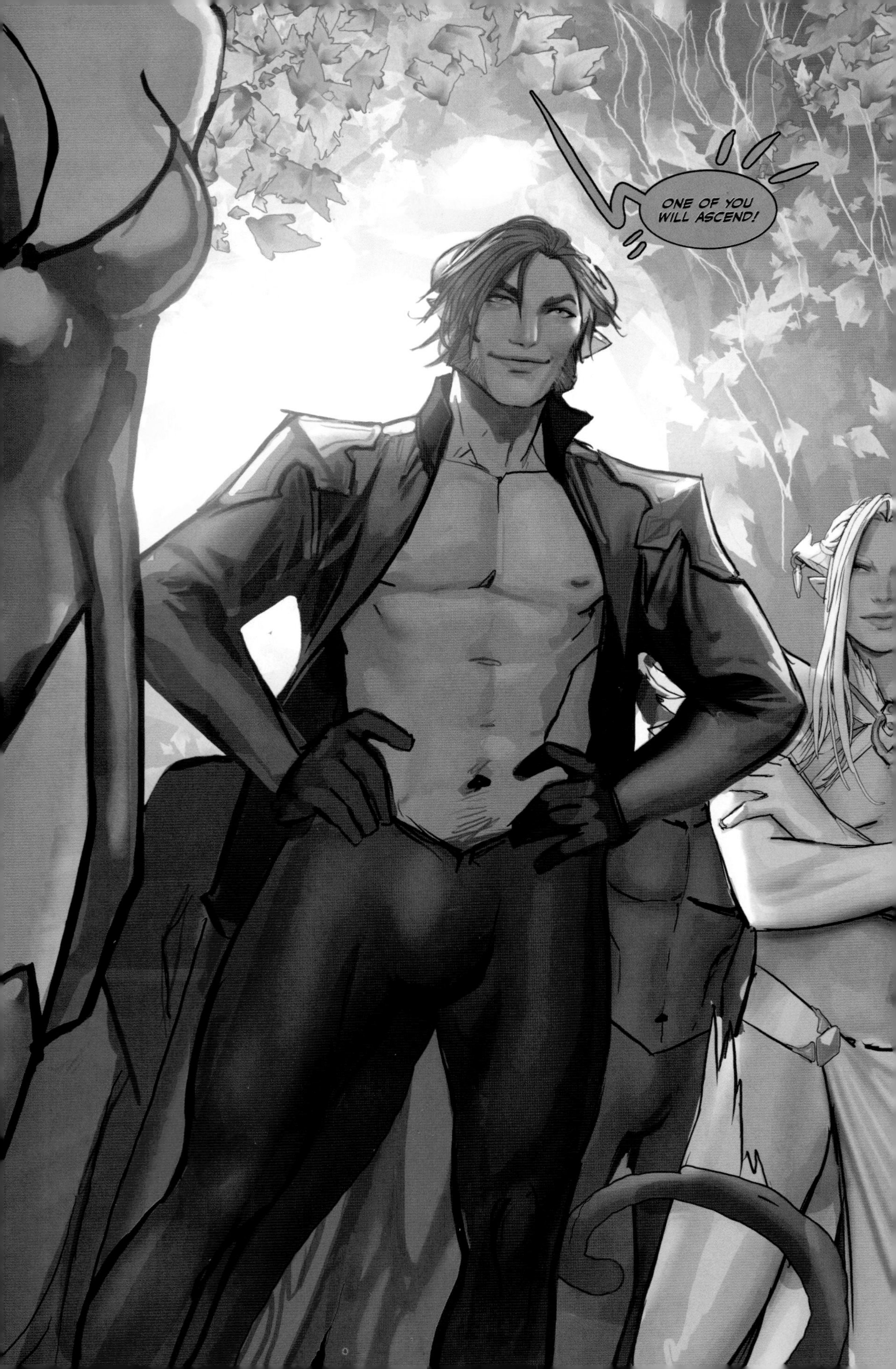
ONE OF YOU WILL ASCEND!

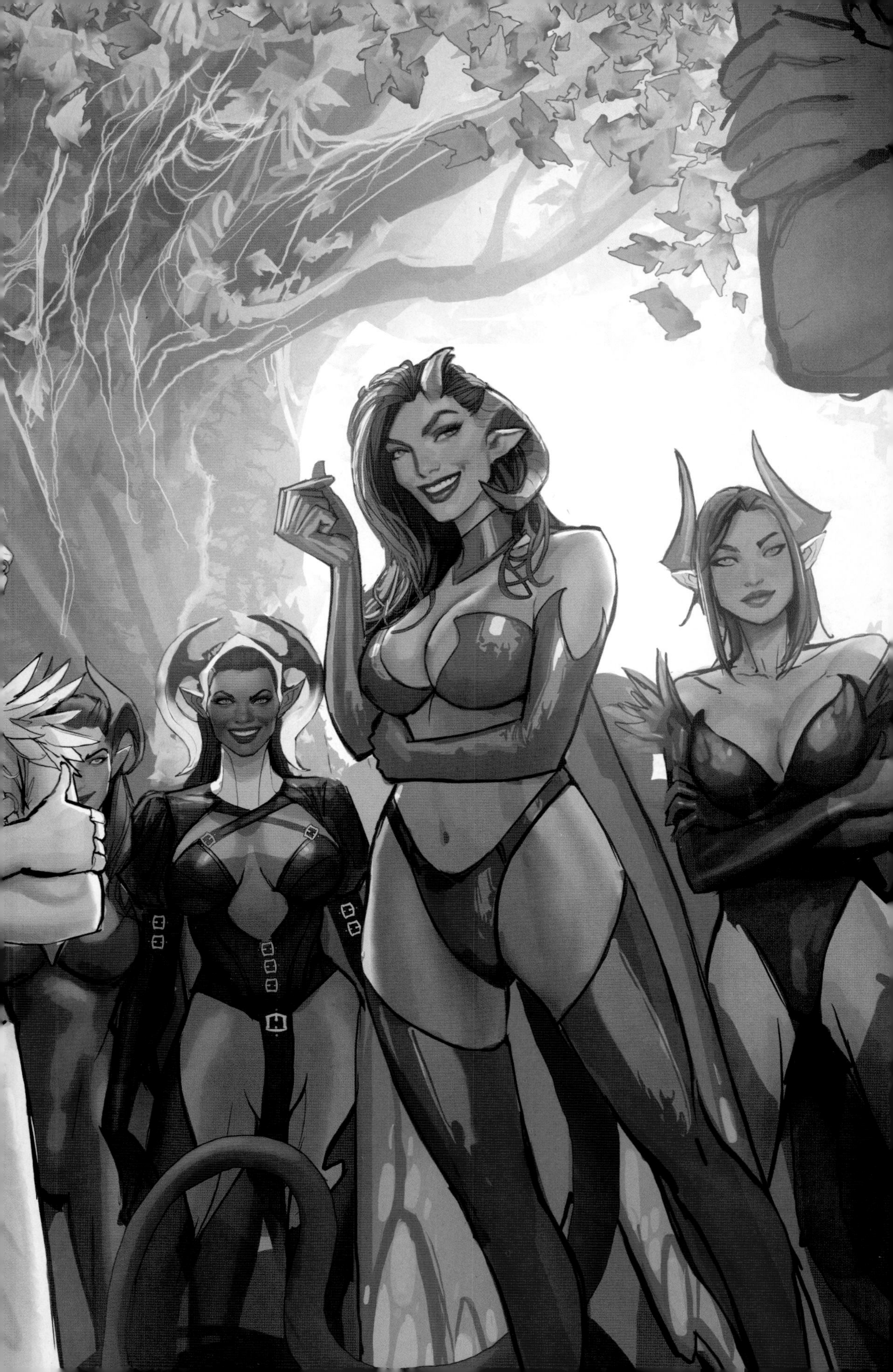

Chapter 1

The one that got away

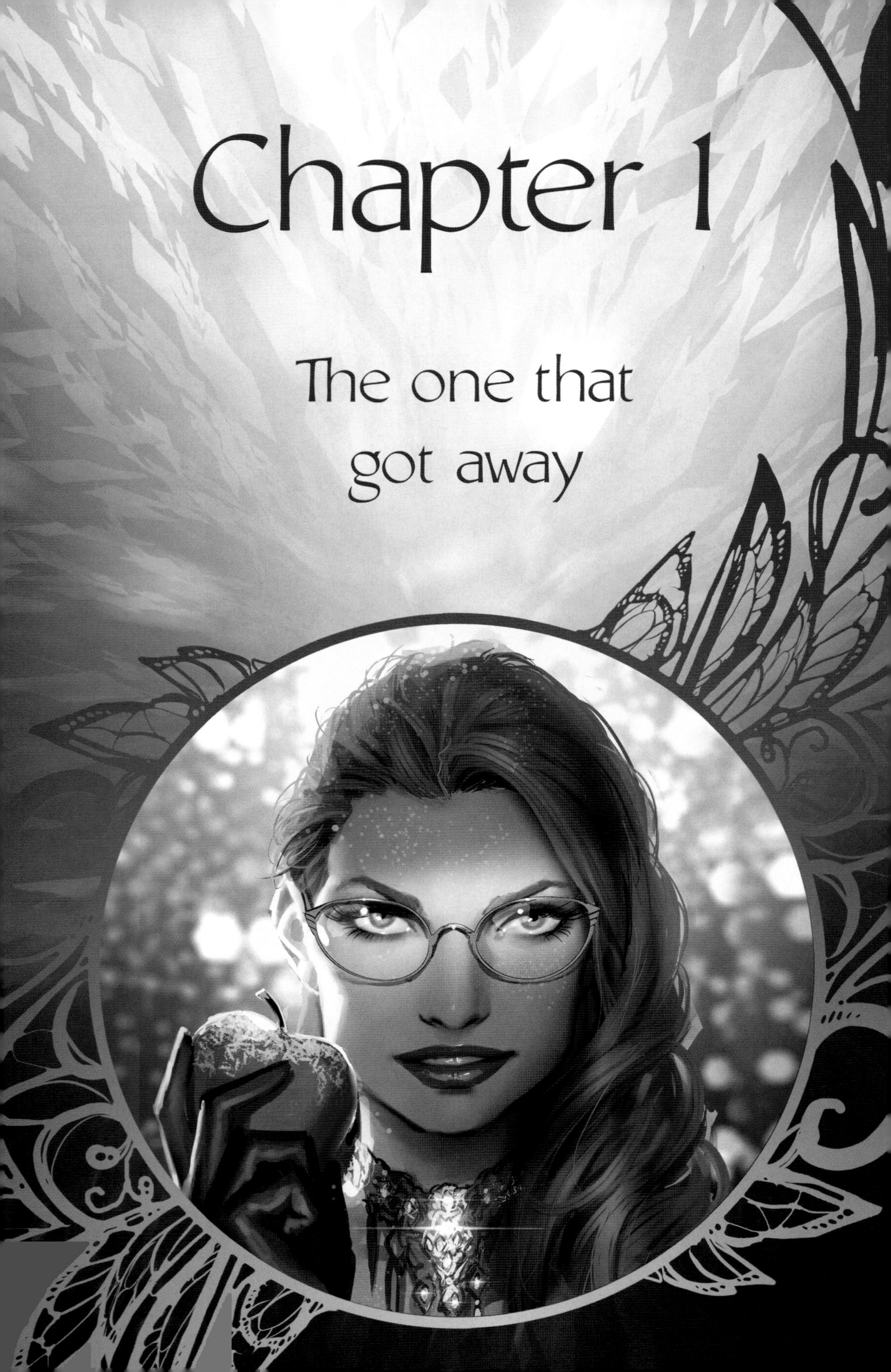

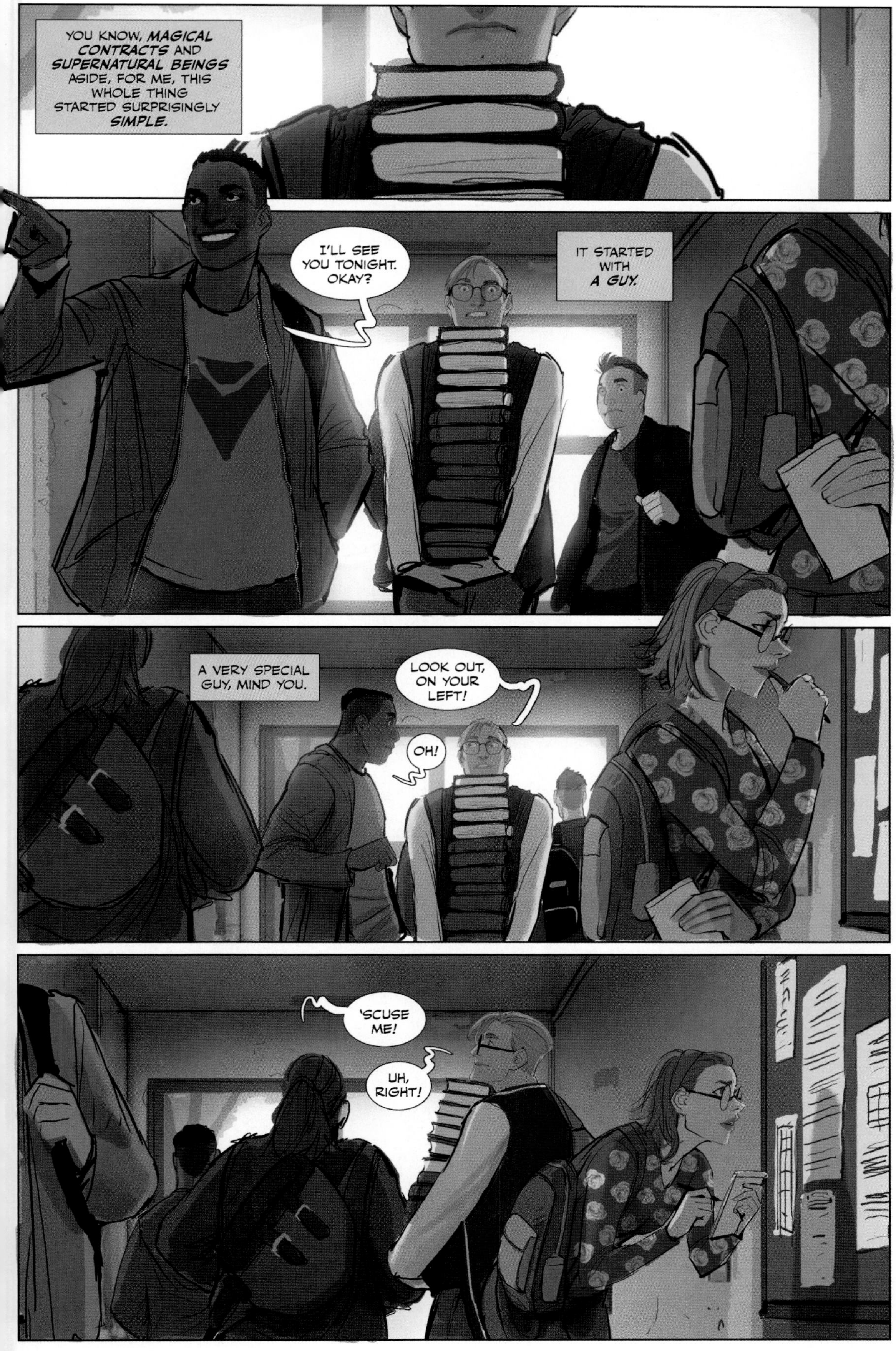
YOU KNOW, MAGICAL CONTRACTS AND SUPERNATURAL BEINGS ASIDE, FOR ME, THIS WHOLE THING STARTED SURPRISINGLY SIMPLE.
I'LL SEE YOU TONIGHT. OKAY?
IT STARTED WITH A GUY.
A VERY SPECIAL GUY, MIND YOU.
LOOK OUT, ON YOUR LEFT!
OH!
'SCUSE ME!
UH, RIGHT!

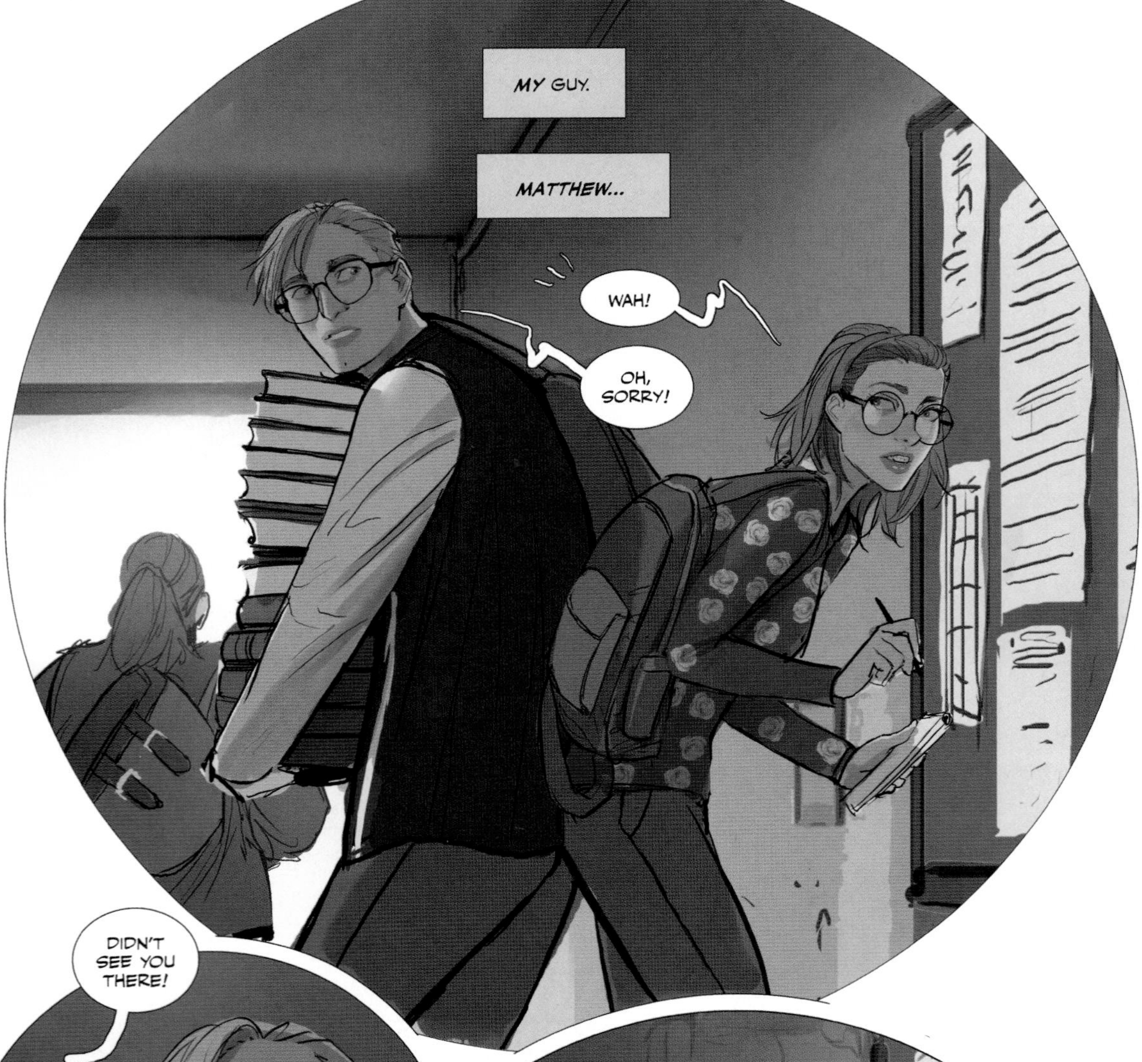
MY GUY.
MATTHEW...
WAH!
OH, SORRY!

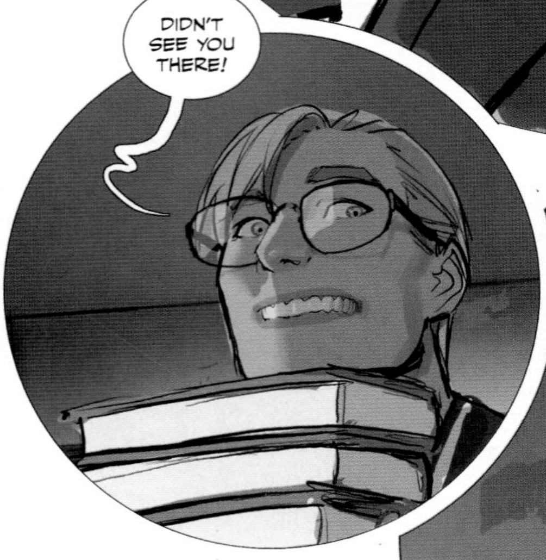
DIDN'T SEE YOU THERE!

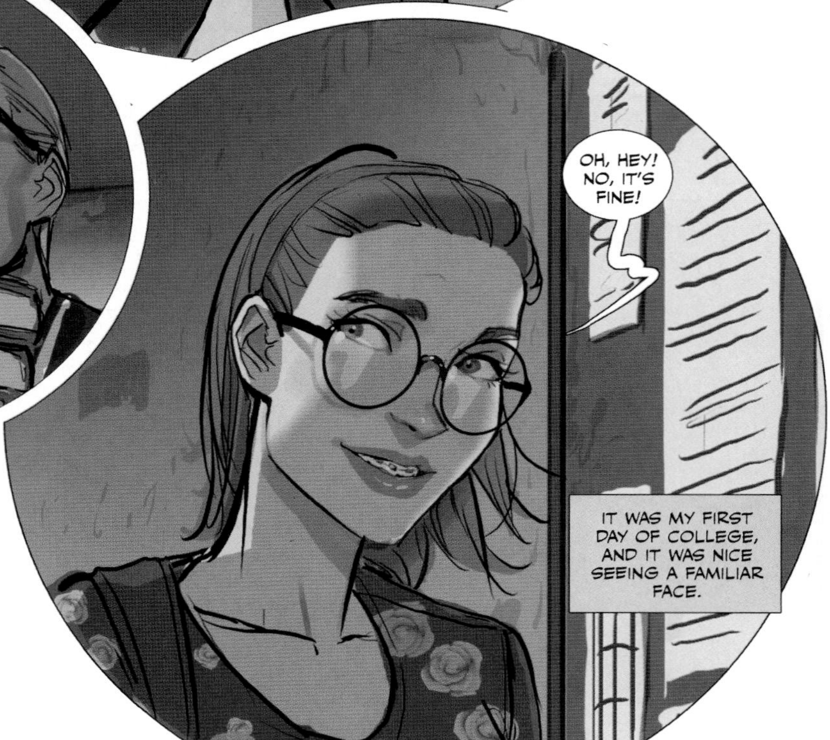
OH, HEY! NO, IT'S FINE!
IT WAS MY FIRST DAY OF COLLEGE, AND IT WAS NICE SEEING A FAMILIAR FACE.

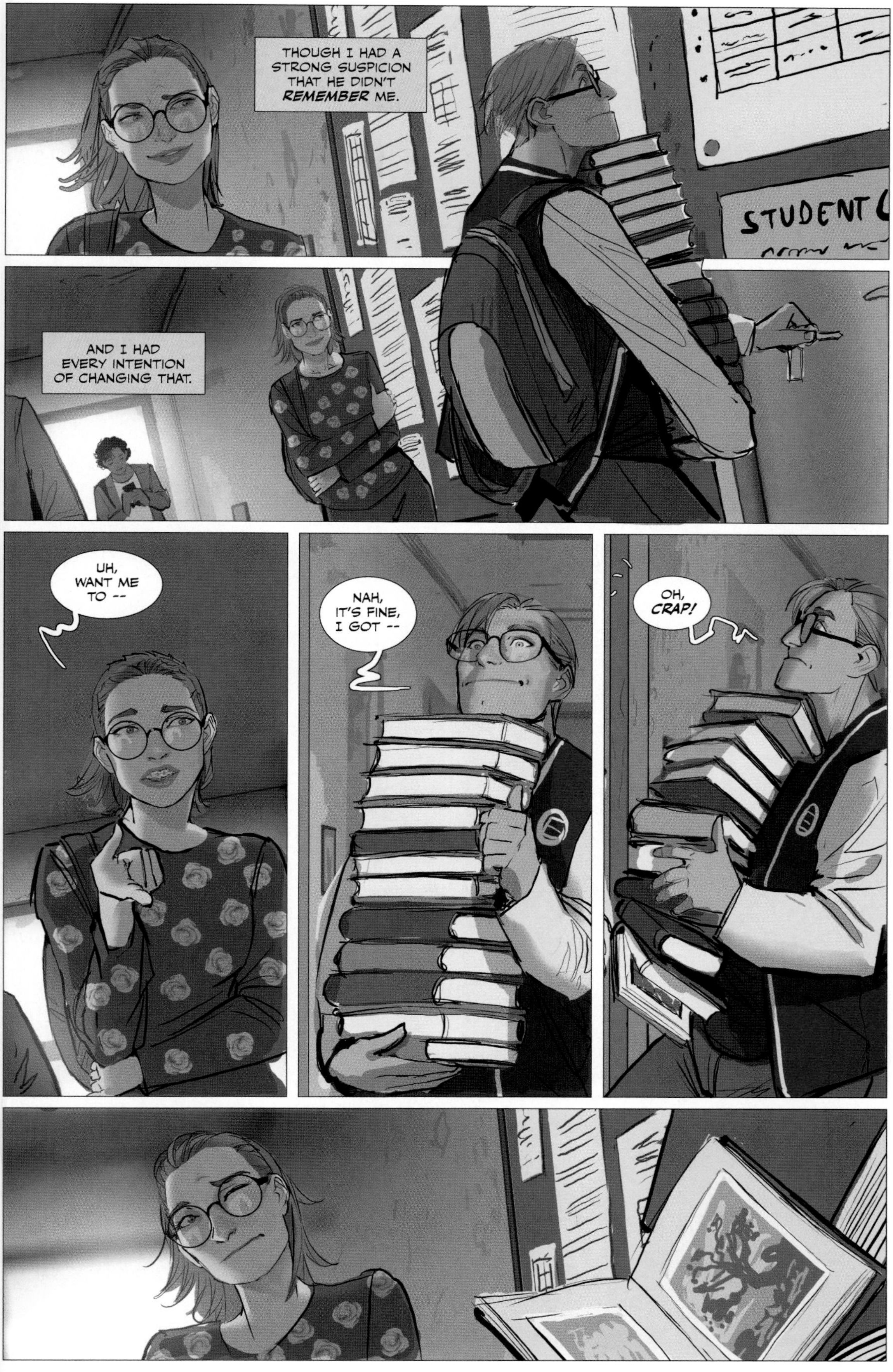
THOUGH I HAD A STRONG SUSPICION THAT HE DIDN'T *REMEMBER* ME.
STUDENT
AND I HAD EVERY INTENTION OF CHANGING THAT.
UH, WANT ME TO --
NAH, IT'S FINE, I GOT --
OH, *CRAP!*

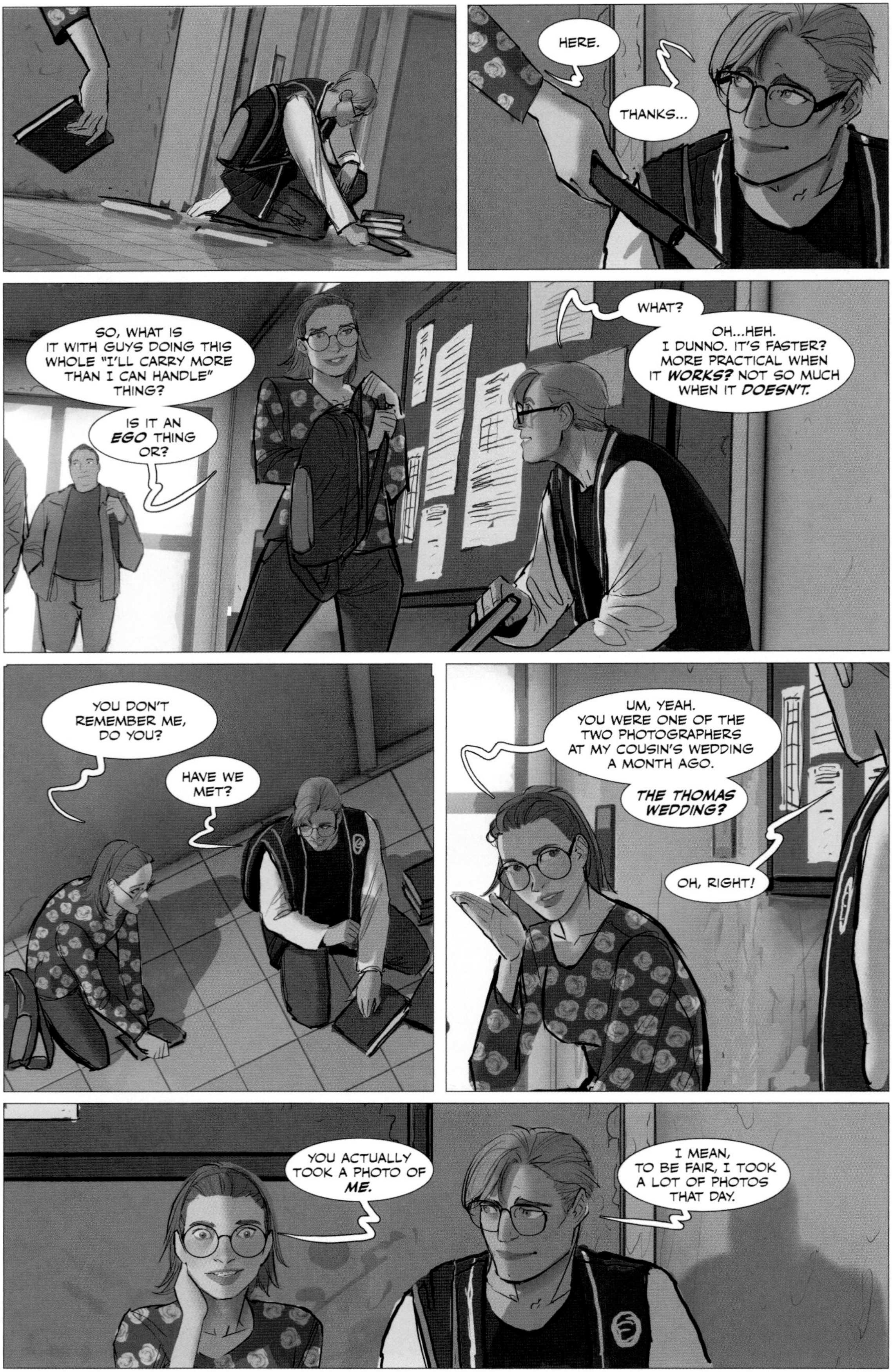
HERE.
THANKS...
SO, WHAT IS IT WITH GUYS DOING THIS WHOLE "I'LL CARRY MORE THAN I CAN HANDLE" THING?
IS IT AN EGO THING OR?
WHAT?
OH...HEH. I DUNNO. IT'S FASTER? MORE PRACTICAL WHEN IT WORKS? NOT SO MUCH WHEN IT DOESN'T.
YOU DON'T REMEMBER ME, DO YOU?
HAVE WE MET?
UM, YEAH. YOU WERE ONE OF THE TWO PHOTOGRAPHERS AT MY COUSIN'S WEDDING A MONTH AGO.
THE THOMAS WEDDING?
OH, RIGHT!
YOU ACTUALLY TOOK A PHOTO OF ME.
I MEAN, TO BE FAIR, I TOOK A LOT OF PHOTOS THAT DAY.

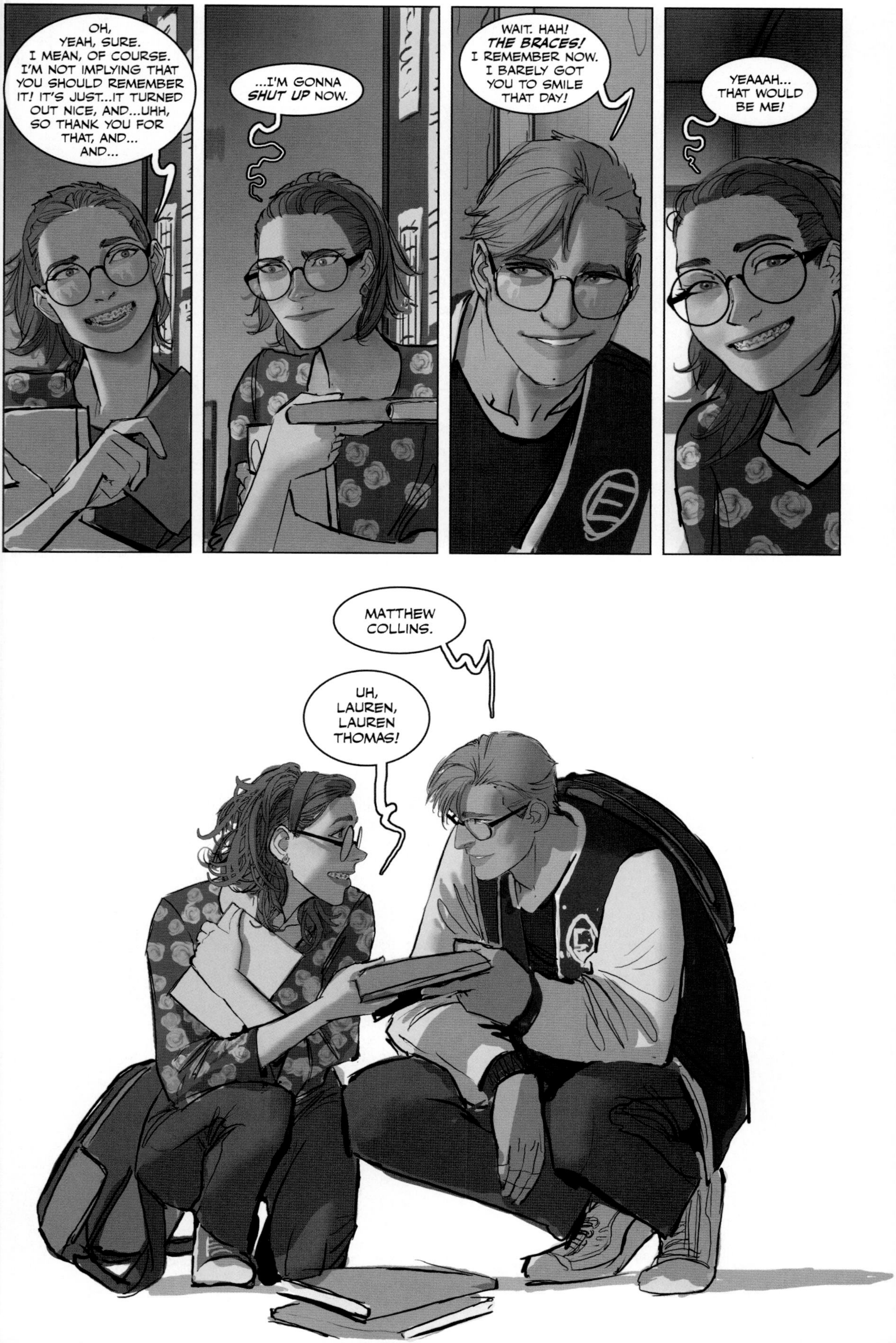
OH, YEAH, SURE. I MEAN, OF COURSE. I'M NOT IMPLYING THAT YOU SHOULD REMEMBER IT! IT'S JUST...IT TURNED OUT NICE, AND...UHH, SO THANK YOU FOR THAT, AND... AND...
...I'M GONNA *SHUT UP* NOW.
WAIT. HAH! *THE BRACES!* I REMEMBER NOW. I BARELY GOT YOU TO SMILE THAT DAY!
YEAAAH... THAT WOULD BE ME!
MATTHEW COLLINS.
UH, LAUREN, LAUREN THOMAS!

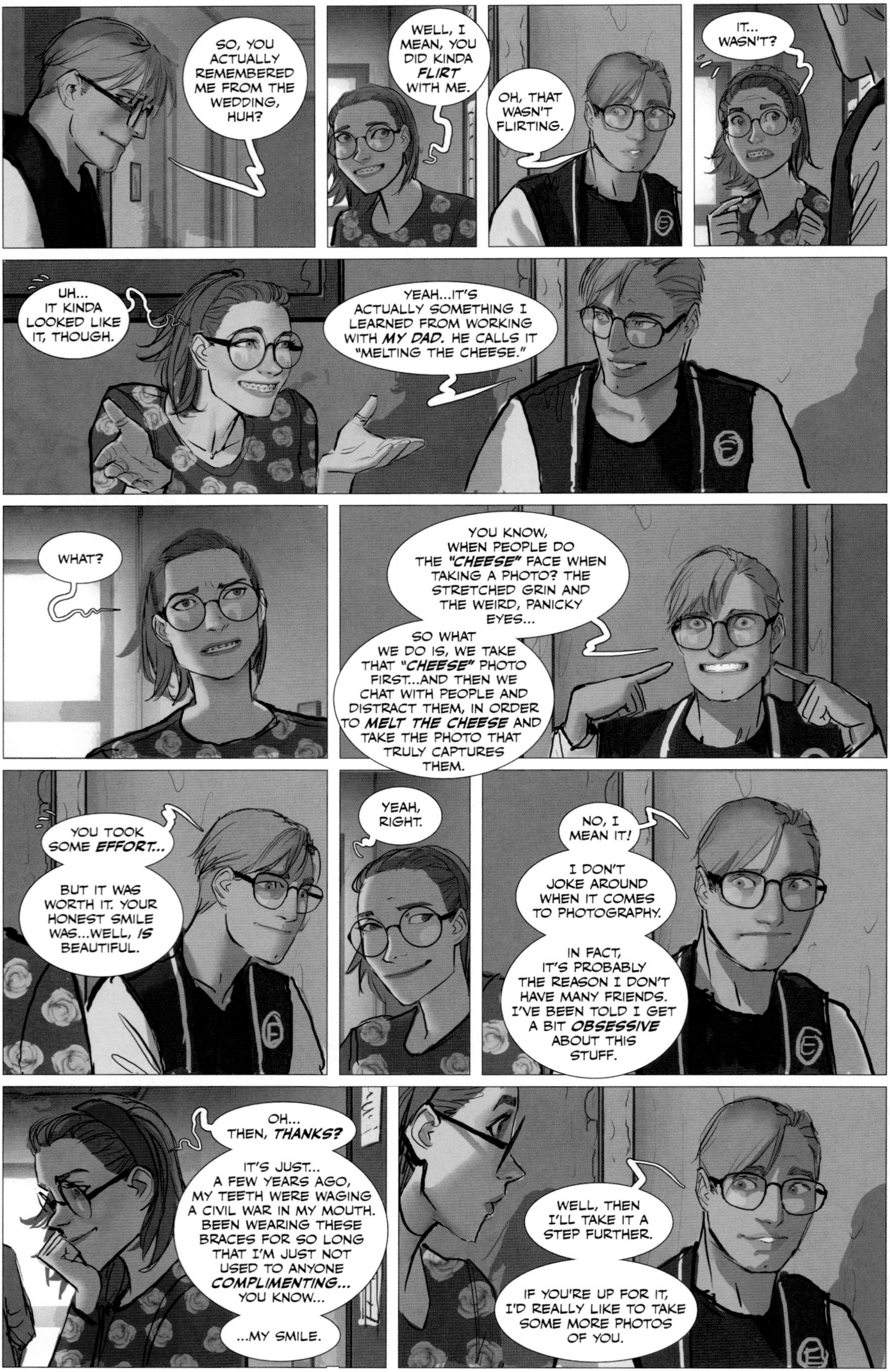
SO, YOU ACTUALLY REMEMBERED ME FROM THE WEDDING, HUH?
WELL, I MEAN, YOU DID KINDA FLIRT WITH ME.
OH, THAT WASN'T FLIRTING.
IT... WASN'T?
UH... IT KINDA LOOKED LIKE IT, THOUGH.
YEAH...IT'S ACTUALLY SOMETHING I LEARNED FROM WORKING WITH MY DAD. HE CALLS IT "MELTING THE CHEESE."
WHAT?
YOU KNOW, WHEN PEOPLE DO THE "CHEESE" FACE WHEN TAKING A PHOTO? THE STRETCHED GRIN AND THE WEIRD, PANICKY EYES...
SO WHAT WE DO IS, WE TAKE THAT "CHEESE" PHOTO FIRST...AND THEN WE CHAT WITH PEOPLE AND DISTRACT THEM, IN ORDER TO MELT THE CHEESE AND TAKE THE PHOTO THAT TRULY CAPTURES THEM.
YOU TOOK SOME EFFORT...
BUT IT WAS WORTH IT. YOUR HONEST SMILE WAS...WELL, IS BEAUTIFUL.
YEAH, RIGHT.
NO, I MEAN IT!
I DON'T JOKE AROUND WHEN IT COMES TO PHOTOGRAPHY.
IN FACT, IT'S PROBABLY THE REASON I DON'T HAVE MANY FRIENDS. I'VE BEEN TOLD I GET A BIT OBSESSIVE ABOUT THIS STUFF.
OH... THEN, THANKS?
IT'S JUST... A FEW YEARS AGO, MY TEETH WERE WAGING A CIVIL WAR IN MY MOUTH. BEEN WEARING THESE BRACES FOR SO LONG THAT I'M JUST NOT USED TO ANYONE COMPLIMENTING... YOU KNOW...
...MY SMILE.
WELL, THEN I'LL TAKE IT A STEP FURTHER.
IF YOU'RE UP FOR IT, I'D REALLY LIKE TO TAKE SOME MORE PHOTOS OF YOU.

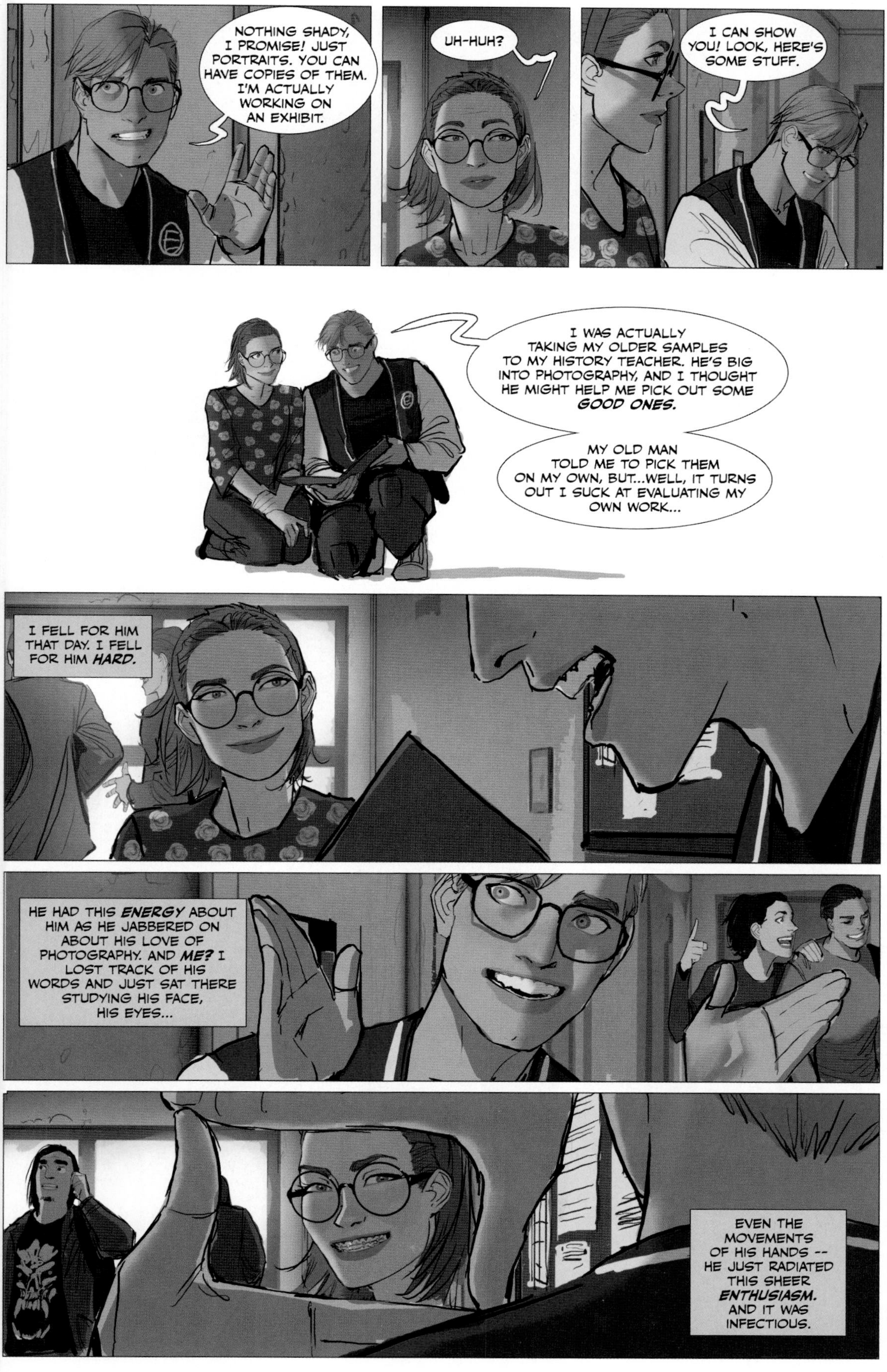
NOTHING SHADY, I PROMISE! JUST PORTRAITS. YOU CAN HAVE COPIES OF THEM. I'M ACTUALLY WORKING ON AN EXHIBIT.
UH-HUH?
I CAN SHOW YOU! LOOK, HERE'S SOME STUFF.
I WAS ACTUALLY TAKING MY OLDER SAMPLES TO MY HISTORY TEACHER. HE'S BIG INTO PHOTOGRAPHY, AND I THOUGHT HE MIGHT HELP ME PICK OUT SOME ***GOOD ONES.***
MY OLD MAN TOLD ME TO PICK THEM ON MY OWN, BUT...WELL, IT TURNS OUT I SUCK AT EVALUATING MY OWN WORK...
I FELL FOR HIM THAT DAY. I FELL FOR HIM ***HARD.***
HE HAD THIS ***ENERGY*** ABOUT HIM AS HE JABBERED ON ABOUT HIS LOVE OF PHOTOGRAPHY. AND ***ME?*** I LOST TRACK OF HIS WORDS AND JUST SAT THERE STUDYING HIS FACE, HIS EYES...
EVEN THE MOVEMENTS OF HIS HANDS -- HE JUST RADIATED THIS SHEER ***ENTHUSIASM.*** AND IT WAS INFECTIOUS.

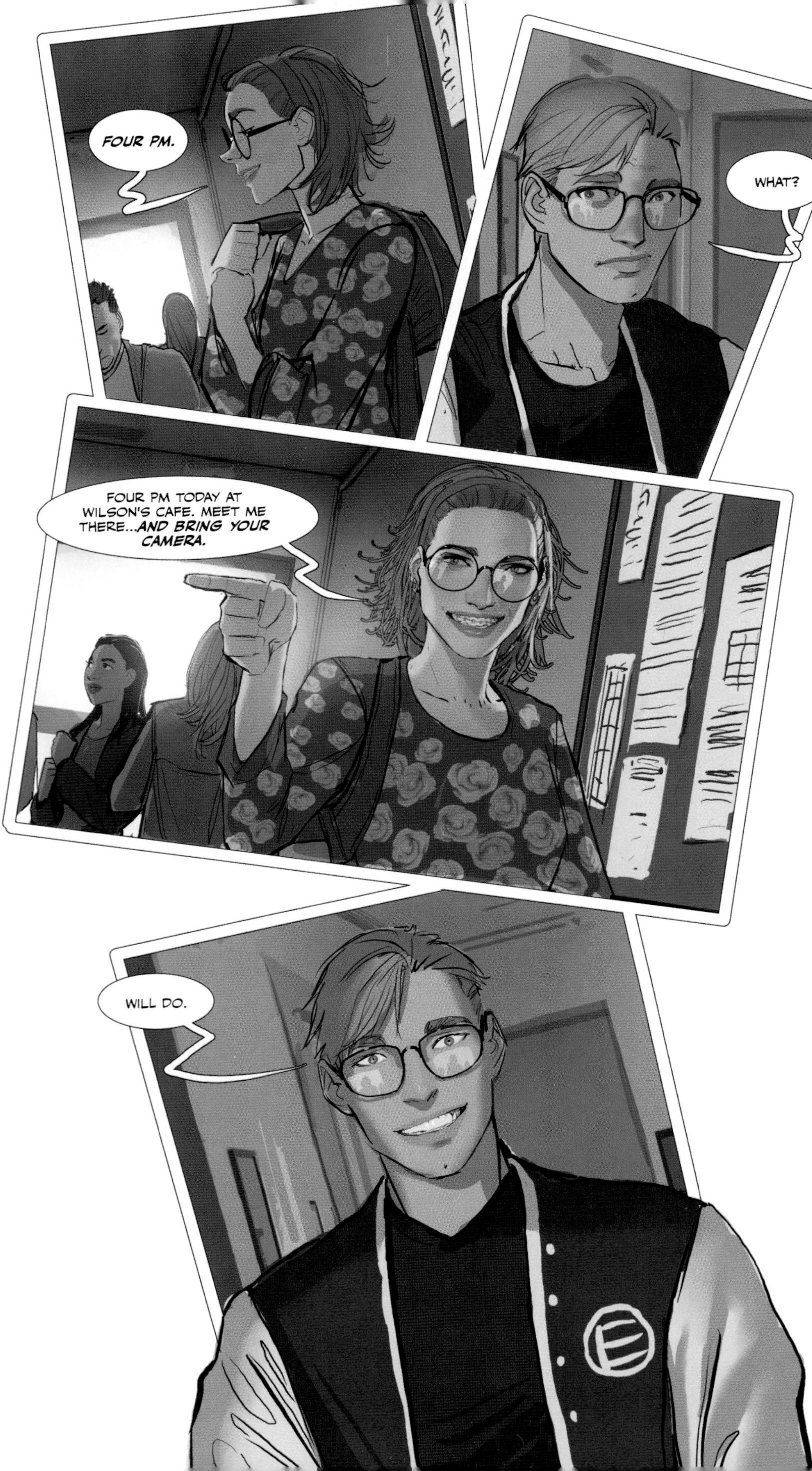
FOUR PM.
WHAT?
FOUR PM TODAY AT WILSON'S CAFE. MEET ME THERE...AND BRING YOUR CAMERA.
WILL DO.

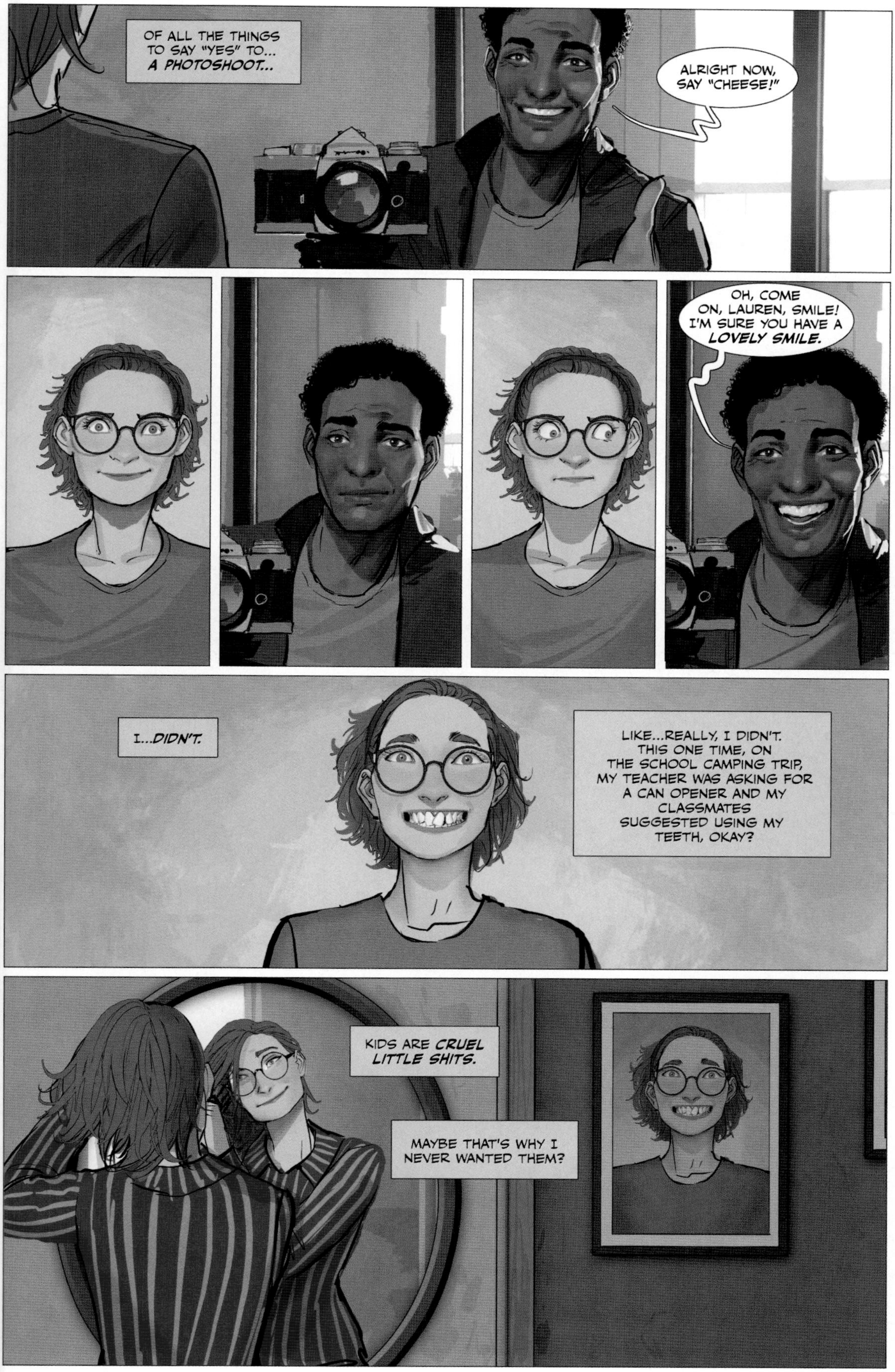

OF ALL THE THINGS TO SAY "YES" TO... *A PHOTOSHOOT...*
ALRIGHT NOW, SAY "CHEESE!"
OH, COME ON, LAUREN, SMILE! I'M SURE YOU HAVE A *LOVELY SMILE.*
I...*DIDN'T.*
LIKE...REALLY, I DIDN'T. THIS ONE TIME, ON THE SCHOOL CAMPING TRIP, MY TEACHER WAS ASKING FOR A CAN OPENER AND MY CLASSMATES SUGGESTED USING MY TEETH, OKAY?
KIDS ARE *CRUEL LITTLE SHITS.*
MAYBE THAT'S WHY I NEVER WANTED THEM?

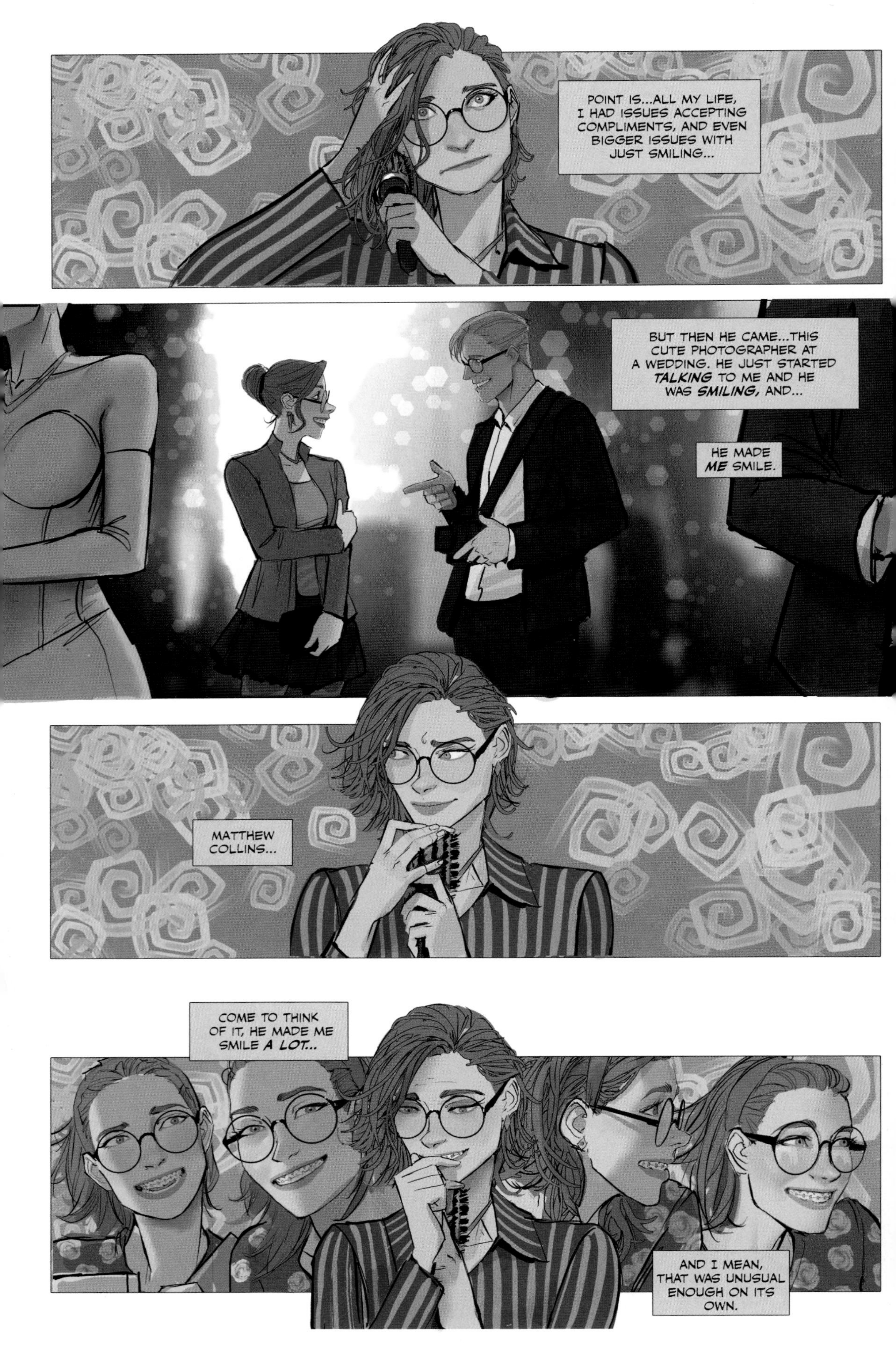
POINT IS...ALL MY LIFE, I HAD ISSUES ACCEPTING COMPLIMENTS, AND EVEN BIGGER ISSUES WITH JUST SMILING...
BUT THEN HE CAME...THIS CUTE PHOTOGRAPHER AT A WEDDING. HE JUST STARTED TALKING TO ME AND HE WAS SMILING, AND...
HE MADE ME SMILE.
MATTHEW COLLINS...
COME TO THINK OF IT, HE MADE ME SMILE A LOT...
AND I MEAN, THAT WAS UNUSUAL ENOUGH ON ITS OWN.

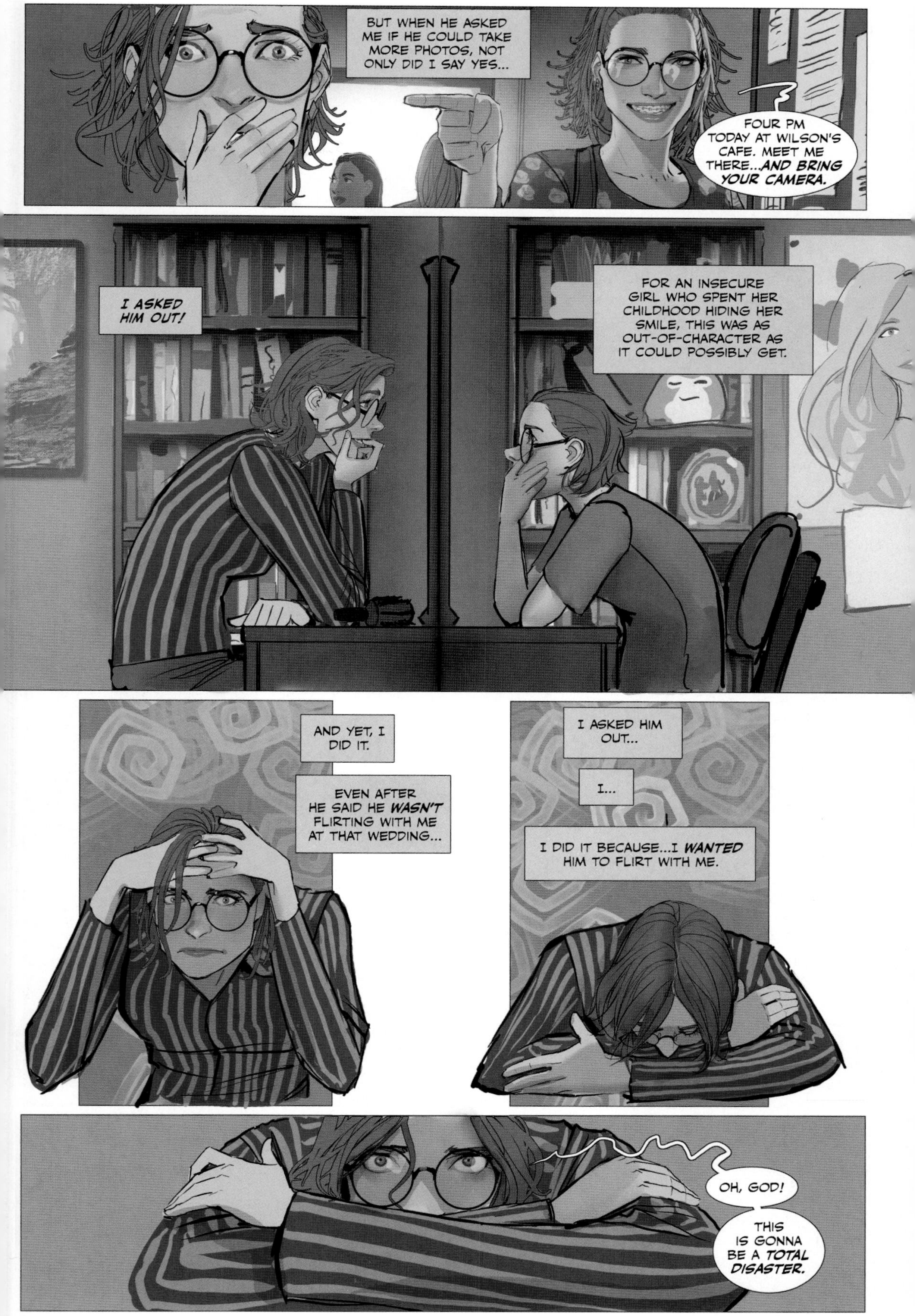
BUT WHEN HE ASKED ME IF HE COULD TAKE MORE PHOTOS, NOT ONLY DID I SAY YES...
FOUR PM TODAY AT WILSON'S CAFE. MEET ME THERE...*AND BRING YOUR CAMERA.*
I ASKED HIM OUT!
FOR AN INSECURE GIRL WHO SPENT HER CHILDHOOD HIDING HER SMILE, THIS WAS AS OUT-OF-CHARACTER AS IT COULD POSSIBLY GET.
AND YET, I DID IT.
EVEN AFTER HE SAID HE *WASN'T* FLIRTING WITH ME AT THAT WEDDING...
I ASKED HIM OUT...
I...
I DID IT BECAUSE...I *WANTED* HIM TO FLIRT WITH ME.
OH, GOD!
THIS IS GONNA BE A *TOTAL DISASTER.*

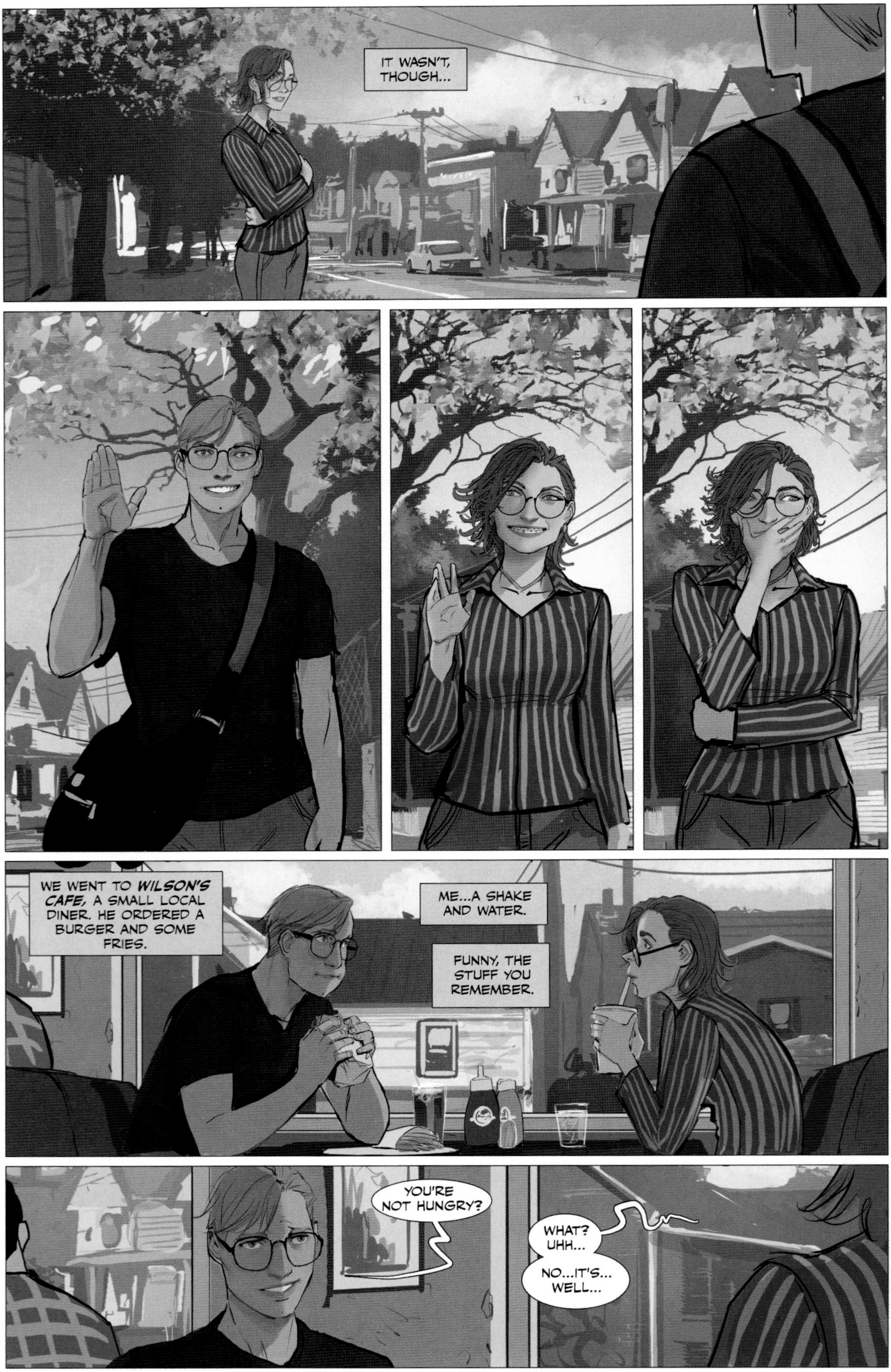
IT WASN'T, THOUGH...
WE WENT TO *WILSON'S CAFE,* A SMALL LOCAL DINER. HE ORDERED A BURGER AND SOME FRIES.
ME...A SHAKE AND WATER.
FUNNY, THE STUFF YOU REMEMBER.
YOU'RE NOT HUNGRY?
WHAT? UHH...
NO...IT'S... WELL...

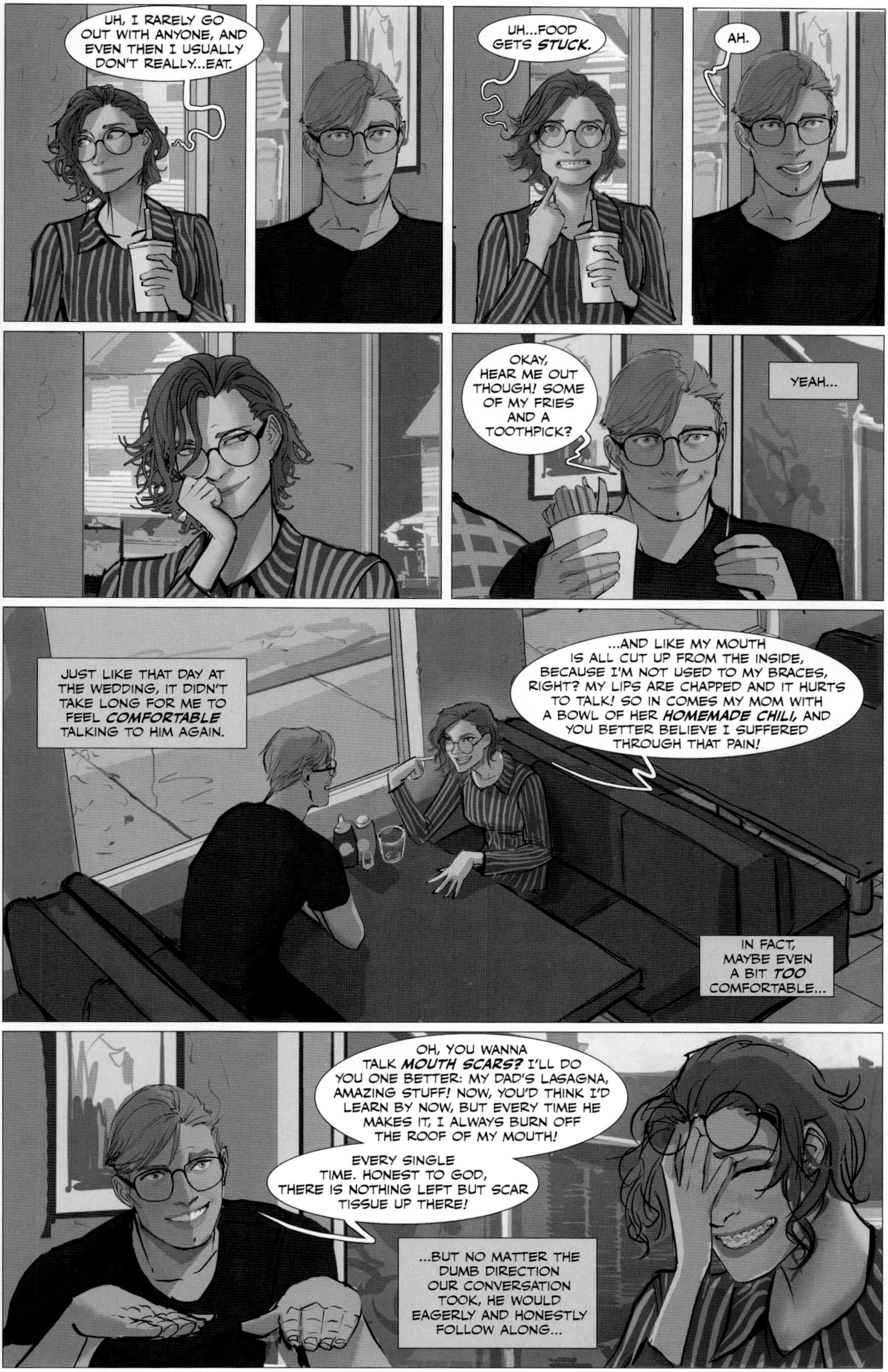
UH, I RARELY GO OUT WITH ANYONE, AND EVEN THEN I USUALLY DON'T REALLY...EAT.
UH...FOOD GETS STUCK.
AH.
OKAY, HEAR ME OUT THOUGH! SOME OF MY FRIES AND A TOOTHPICK?
YEAH...
JUST LIKE THAT DAY AT THE WEDDING, IT DIDN'T TAKE LONG FOR ME TO FEEL COMFORTABLE TALKING TO HIM AGAIN.
...AND LIKE MY MOUTH IS ALL CUT UP FROM THE INSIDE, BECAUSE I'M NOT USED TO MY BRACES, RIGHT? MY LIPS ARE CHAPPED AND IT HURTS TO TALK! SO IN COMES MY MOM WITH A BOWL OF HER HOMEMADE CHILI, AND YOU BETTER BELIEVE I SUFFERED THROUGH THAT PAIN!
IN FACT, MAYBE EVEN A BIT TOO COMFORTABLE...
OH, YOU WANNA TALK MOUTH SCARS? I'LL DO YOU ONE BETTER: MY DAD'S LASAGNA, AMAZING STUFF! NOW, YOU'D THINK I'D LEARN BY NOW, BUT EVERY TIME HE MAKES IT, I ALWAYS BURN OFF THE ROOF OF MY MOUTH!
EVERY SINGLE TIME. HONEST TO GOD, THERE IS NOTHING LEFT BUT SCAR TISSUE UP THERE!
...BUT NO MATTER THE DUMB DIRECTION OUR CONVERSATION TOOK, HE WOULD EAGERLY AND HONESTLY FOLLOW ALONG...

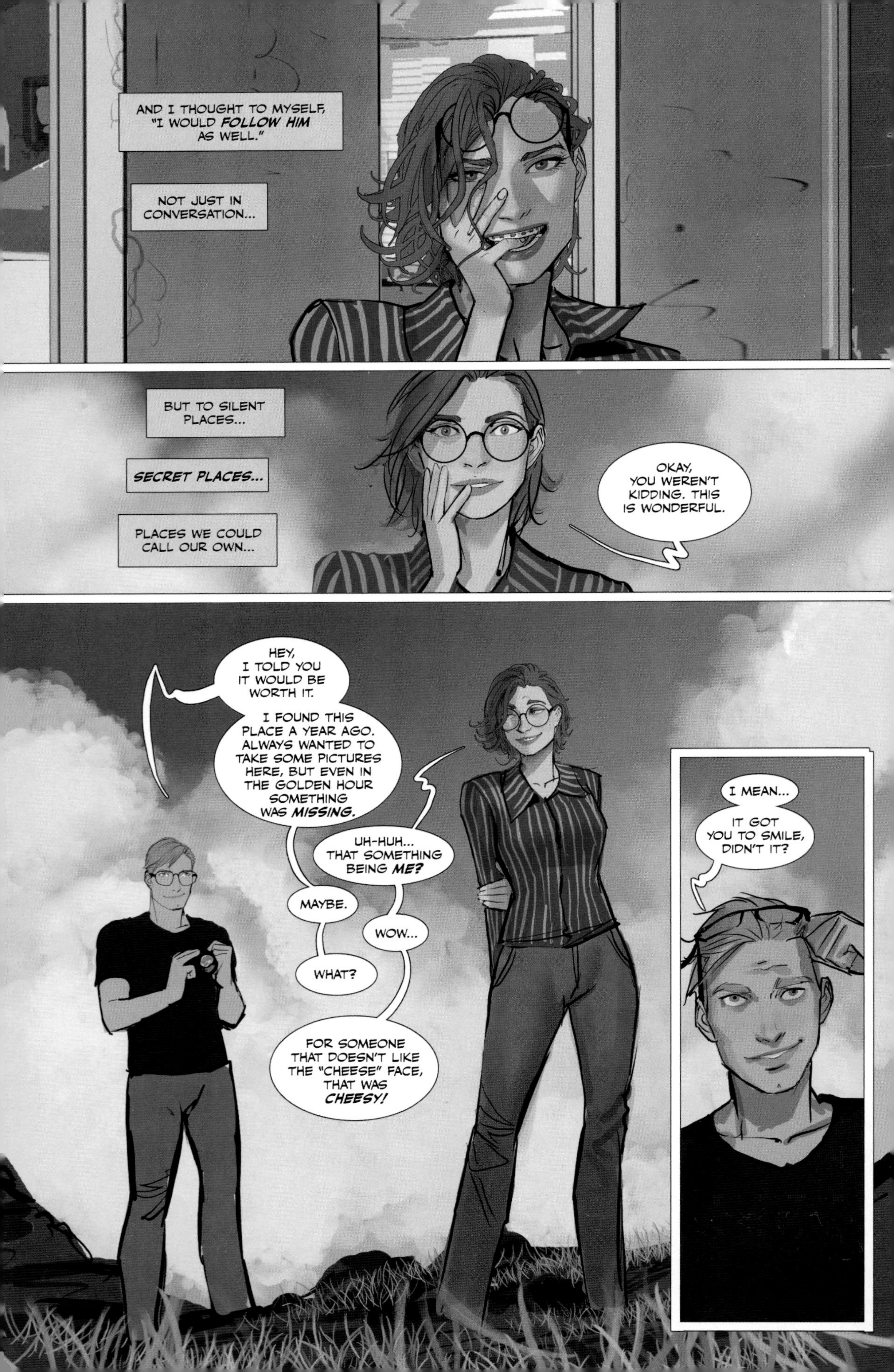
AND I THOUGHT TO MYSELF, "I WOULD *FOLLOW HIM* AS WELL."
NOT JUST IN CONVERSATION...
BUT TO SILENT PLACES...
SECRET PLACES...
PLACES WE COULD CALL OUR OWN...
OKAY, YOU WEREN'T KIDDING. THIS IS WONDERFUL.
HEY, I TOLD YOU IT WOULD BE WORTH IT.
I FOUND THIS PLACE A YEAR AGO. ALWAYS WANTED TO TAKE SOME PICTURES HERE, BUT EVEN IN THE GOLDEN HOUR SOMETHING WAS *MISSING*.
UH-HUH... THAT SOMETHING BEING *ME?*
MAYBE.
WOW...
WHAT?
FOR SOMEONE THAT DOESN'T LIKE THE "CHEESE" FACE, THAT WAS *CHEESY!*
I MEAN...
IT GOT YOU TO SMILE, DIDN'T IT?

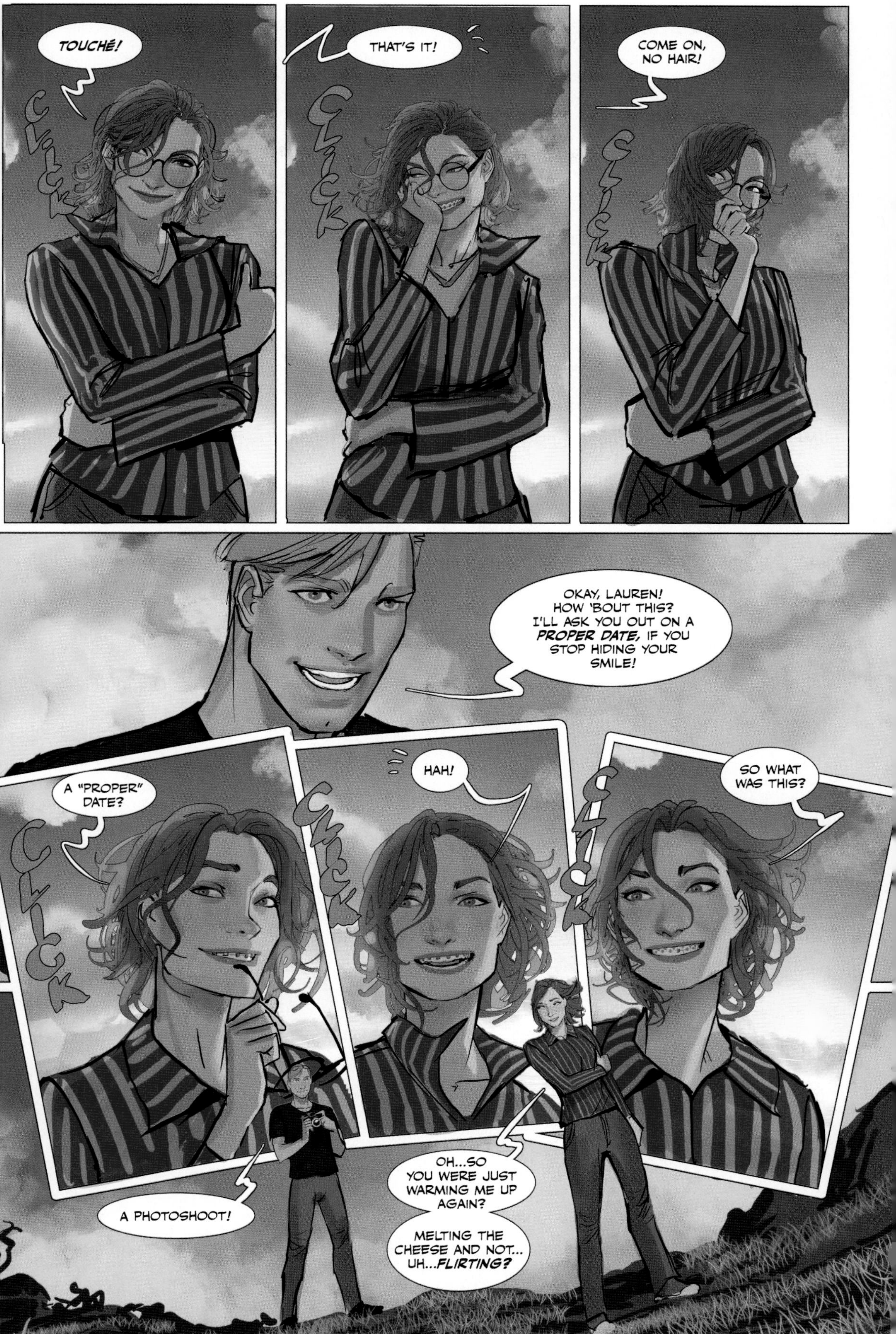
TOUCHÉ!
CLICK
THAT'S IT!
CLICK
COME ON, NO HAIR!
CLICK
OKAY, LAUREN! HOW 'BOUT THIS? I'LL ASK YOU OUT ON A PROPER DATE, IF YOU STOP HIDING YOUR SMILE!
A "PROPER" DATE?
CLICK
HAH!
CLICK
SO WHAT WAS THIS?
CLICK
A PHOTOSHOOT!
OH...SO YOU WERE JUST WARMING ME UP AGAIN?
MELTING THE CHEESE AND NOT... UH...FLIRTING?

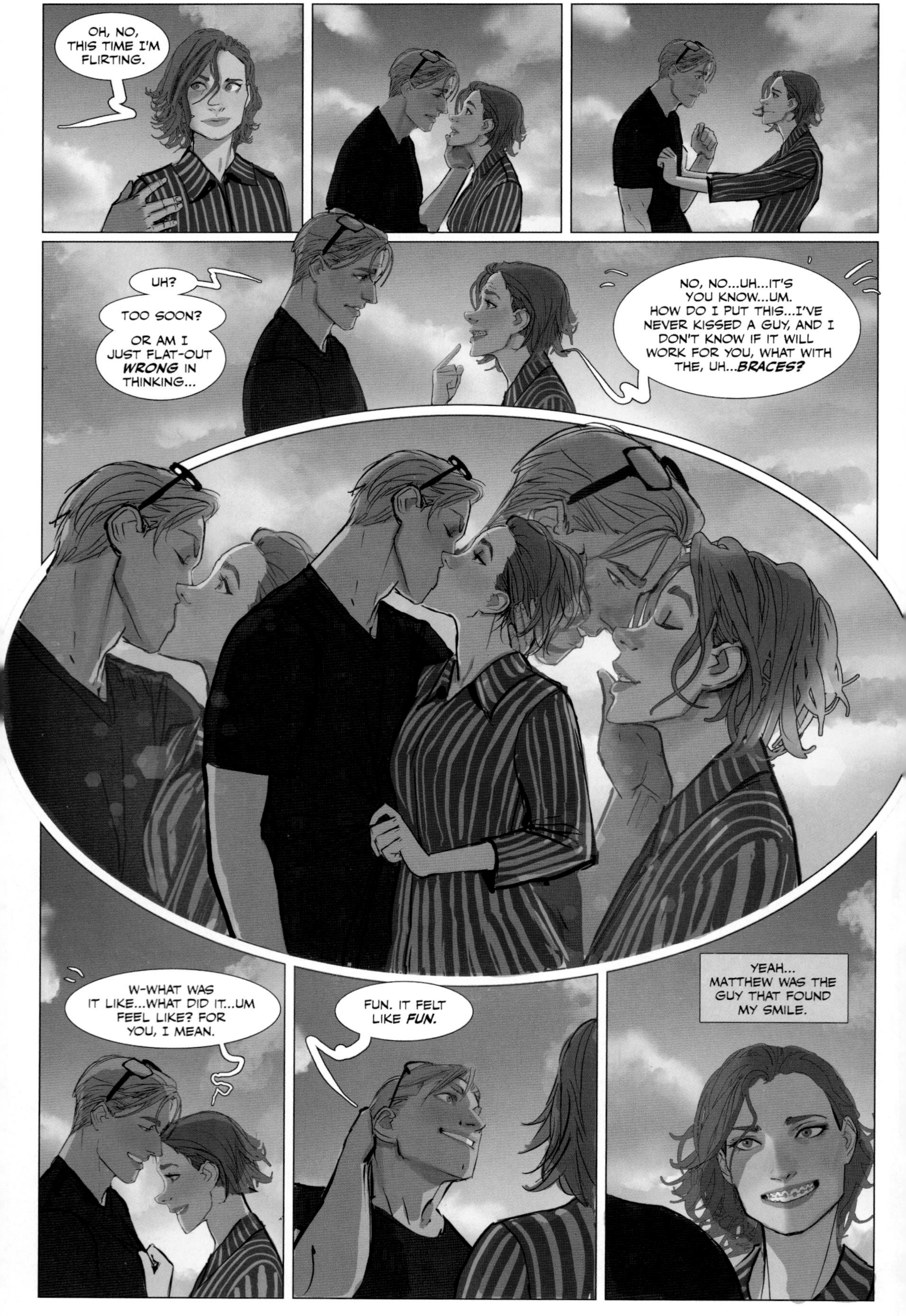
OH, NO, THIS TIME I'M FLIRTING.
UH?
TOO SOON?
OR AM I JUST FLAT-OUT *WRONG* IN THINKING...
NO, NO...UH...IT'S YOU KNOW...UM. HOW DO I PUT THIS...I'VE NEVER KISSED A GUY, AND I DON'T KNOW IF IT WILL WORK FOR YOU, WHAT WITH THE, UH...*BRACES?*
W-WHAT WAS IT LIKE...WHAT DID IT...UM FEEL LIKE? FOR YOU, I MEAN.
FUN. IT FELT LIKE *FUN.*
YEAH... MATTHEW WAS THE GUY THAT FOUND MY SMILE.

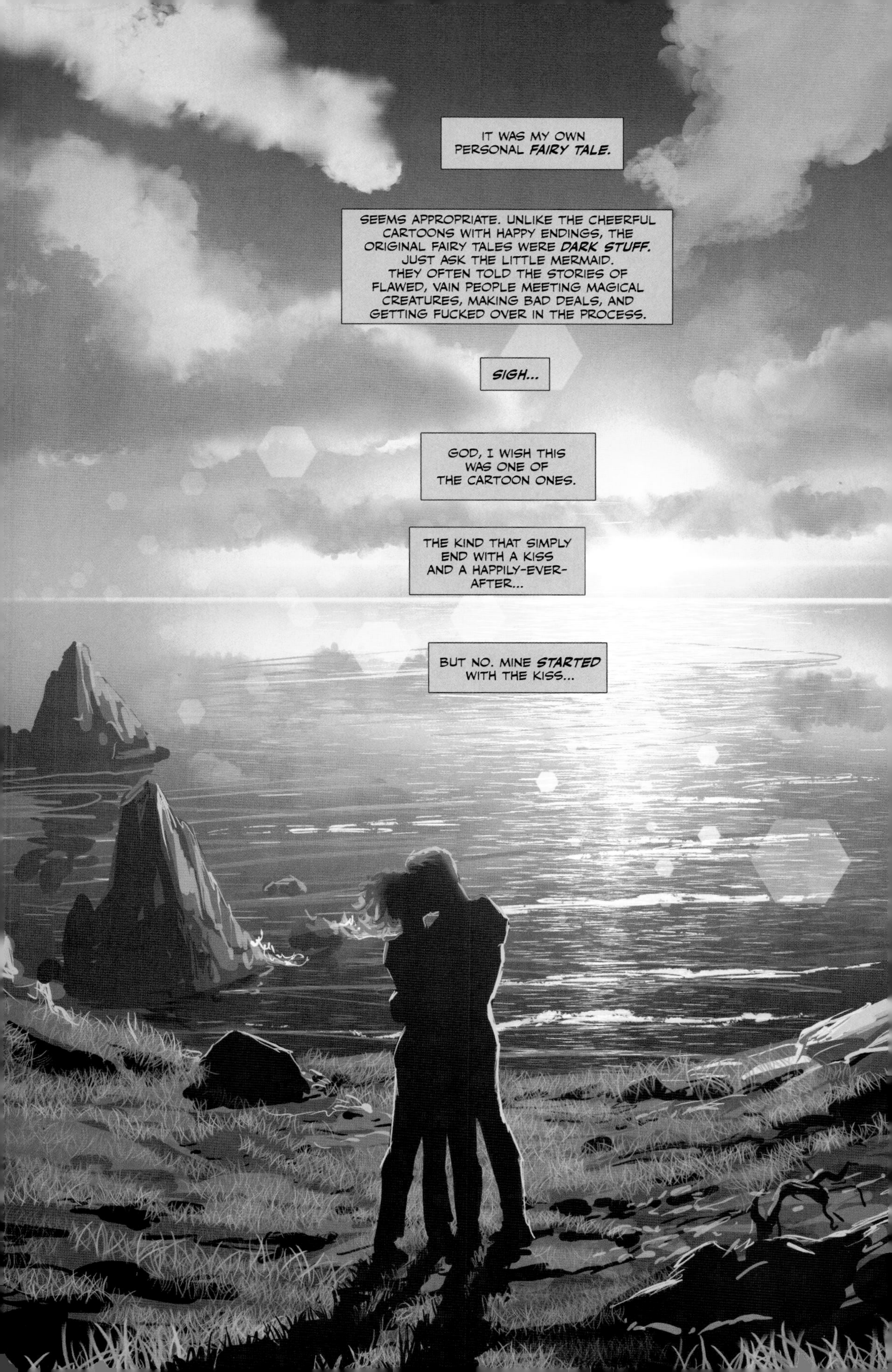
IT WAS MY OWN PERSONAL FAIRY TALE.
SEEMS APPROPRIATE. UNLIKE THE CHEERFUL CARTOONS WITH HAPPY ENDINGS, THE ORIGINAL FAIRY TALES WERE DARK STUFF. JUST ASK THE LITTLE MERMAID. THEY OFTEN TOLD THE STORIES OF FLAWED, VAIN PEOPLE MEETING MAGICAL CREATURES, MAKING BAD DEALS, AND GETTING FUCKED OVER IN THE PROCESS.
SIGH...
GOD, I WISH THIS WAS ONE OF THE CARTOON ONES.
THE KIND THAT SIMPLY END WITH A KISS AND A HAPPILY-EVER-AFTER...
BUT NO. MINE STARTED WITH THE KISS...

AS FOR THE HAPPILY-EVER-AFTER PART?
I MISSED IT BY A MILE.
SEE, I HAD MY WONDERFUL SUNSET, BUT ME?
MMMMHMMM...
I WAS SHOOTING FOR THE MOON.
BUT THE THING YOU LEARN WHEN YOU REACH THE MOON IS...IT'S COLD, ITS GLOW IS ALL FAKE, AND YOU FIND YOURSELF GASPING FOR AIR THAT'S JUST NOT THERE.

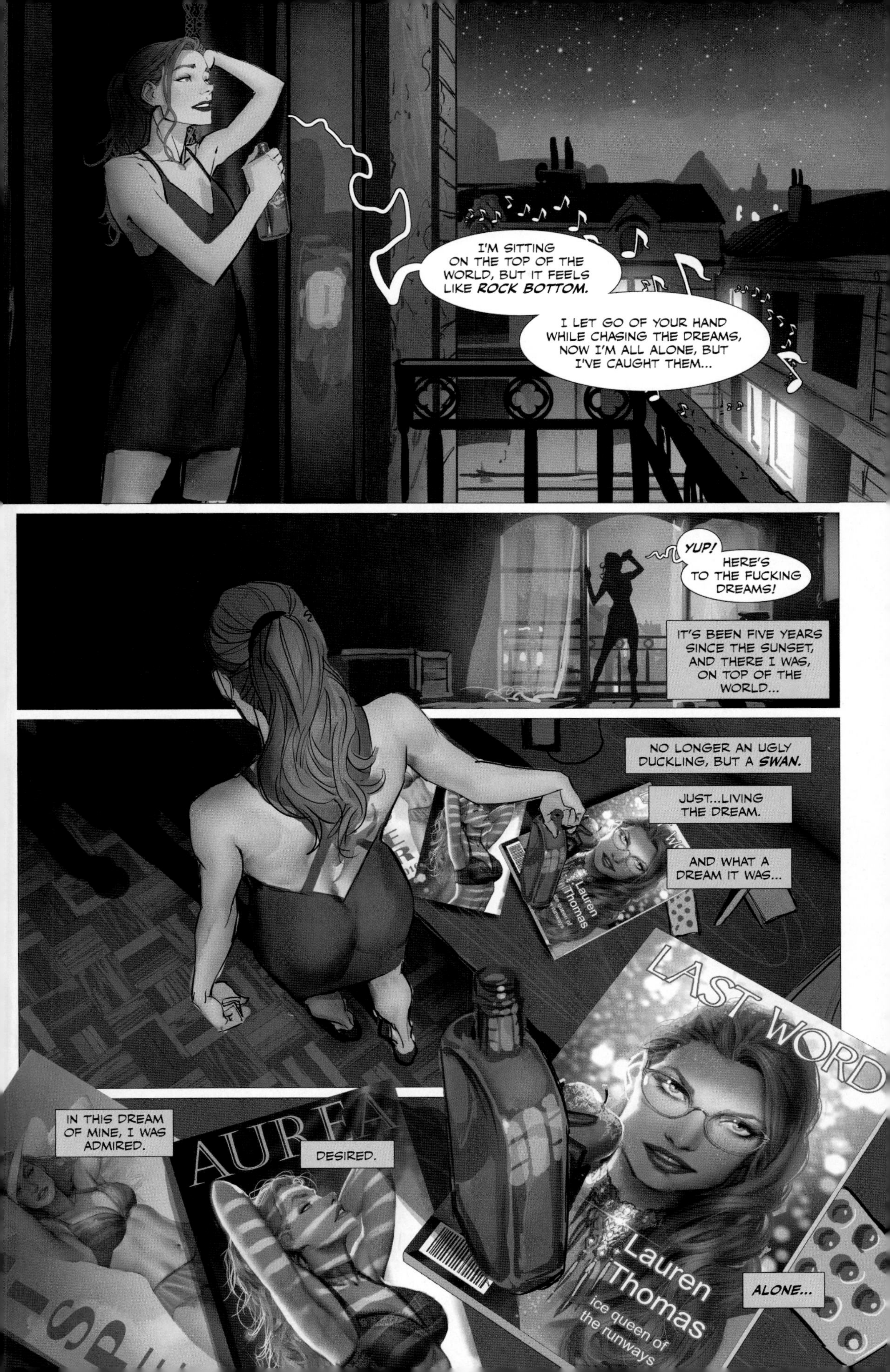

I'M SITTING ON THE TOP OF THE WORLD, BUT IT FEELS LIKE *ROCK BOTTOM.*
I LET GO OF YOUR HAND WHILE CHASING THE DREAMS, NOW I'M ALL ALONE, BUT I'VE CAUGHT THEM...
YUP! HERE'S TO THE FUCKING DREAMS!
IT'S BEEN FIVE YEARS SINCE THE SUNSET, AND THERE I WAS, ON TOP OF THE WORLD...
NO LONGER AN UGLY DUCKLING, BUT A *SWAN.*
JUST...LIVING THE DREAM.
AND WHAT A DREAM IT WAS...
LAST WORD
Lauren Thomas
ice queen of the runways
IN THIS DREAM OF MINE, I WAS ADMIRED.
AUREA
DESIRED.
ALONE...

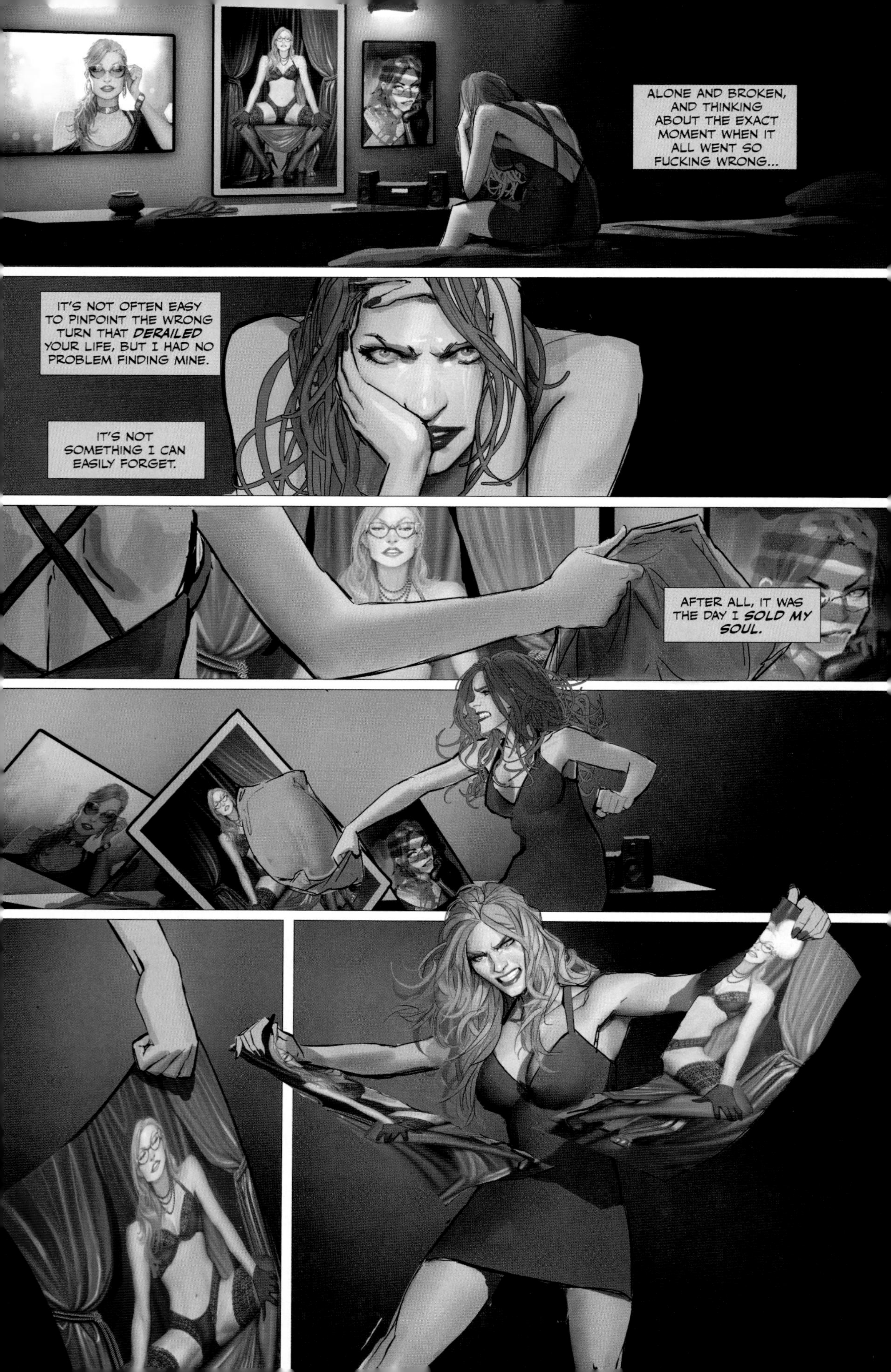
ALONE AND BROKEN, AND THINKING ABOUT THE EXACT MOMENT WHEN IT ALL WENT SO FUCKING WRONG...
IT'S NOT OFTEN EASY TO PINPOINT THE WRONG TURN THAT *DERAILED* YOUR LIFE, BUT I HAD NO PROBLEM FINDING MINE.
IT'S NOT SOMETHING I CAN EASILY FORGET.
AFTER ALL, IT WAS THE DAY I *SOLD MY SOUL.*

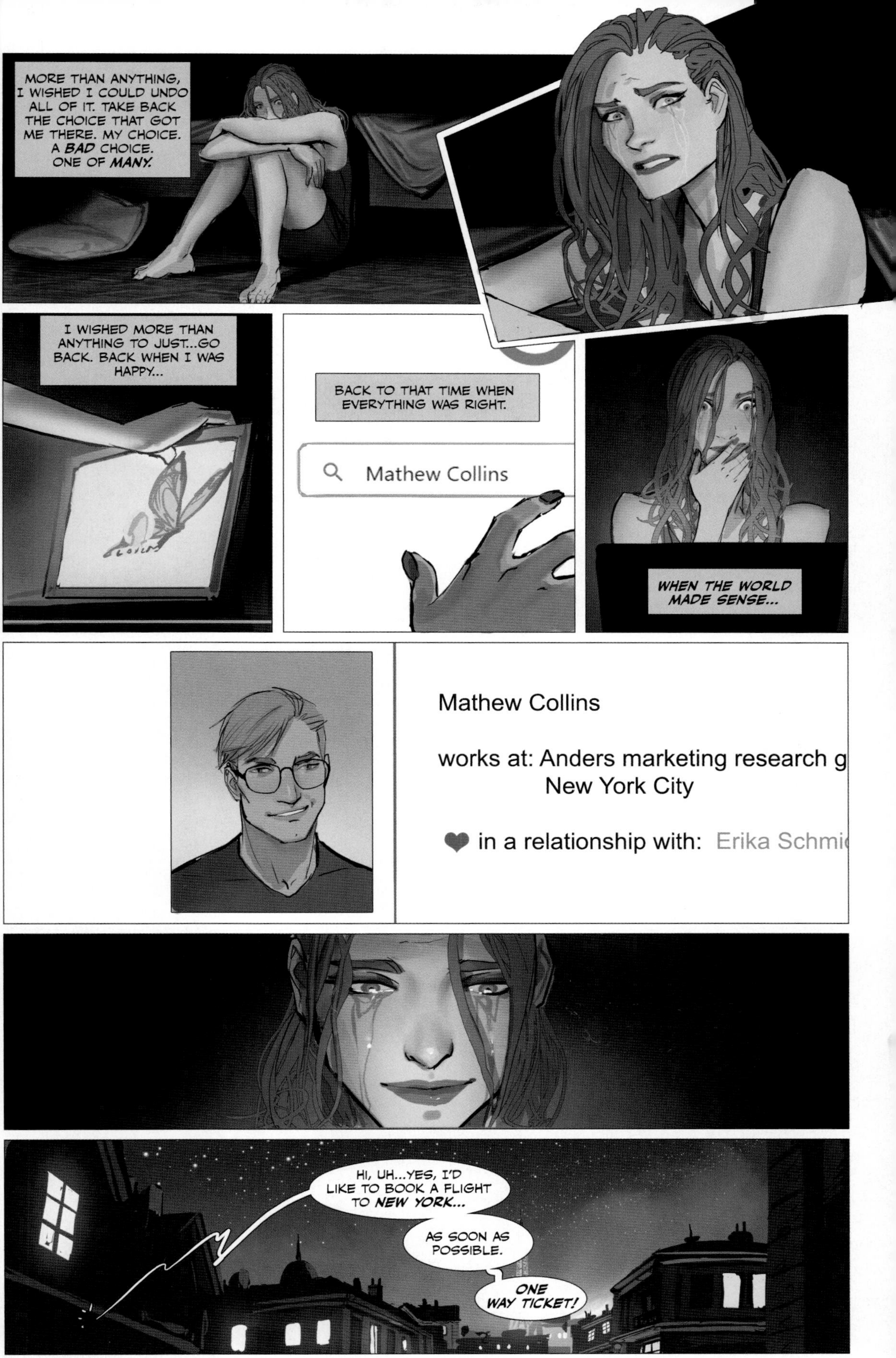
MORE THAN ANYTHING, I WISHED I COULD UNDO ALL OF IT. TAKE BACK THE CHOICE THAT GOT ME THERE. MY CHOICE. A BAD CHOICE. ONE OF MANY.
I WISHED MORE THAN ANYTHING TO JUST...GO BACK. BACK WHEN I WAS HAPPY...
BACK TO THAT TIME WHEN EVERYTHING WAS RIGHT.
Mathew Collins
WHEN THE WORLD MADE SENSE...
Mathew Collins
works at: Anders marketing research g
New York City
in a relationship with: Erika Schmi
HI, UH...YES, I'D LIKE TO BOOK A FLIGHT TO NEW YORK...
AS SOON AS POSSIBLE.
ONE WAY TICKET!

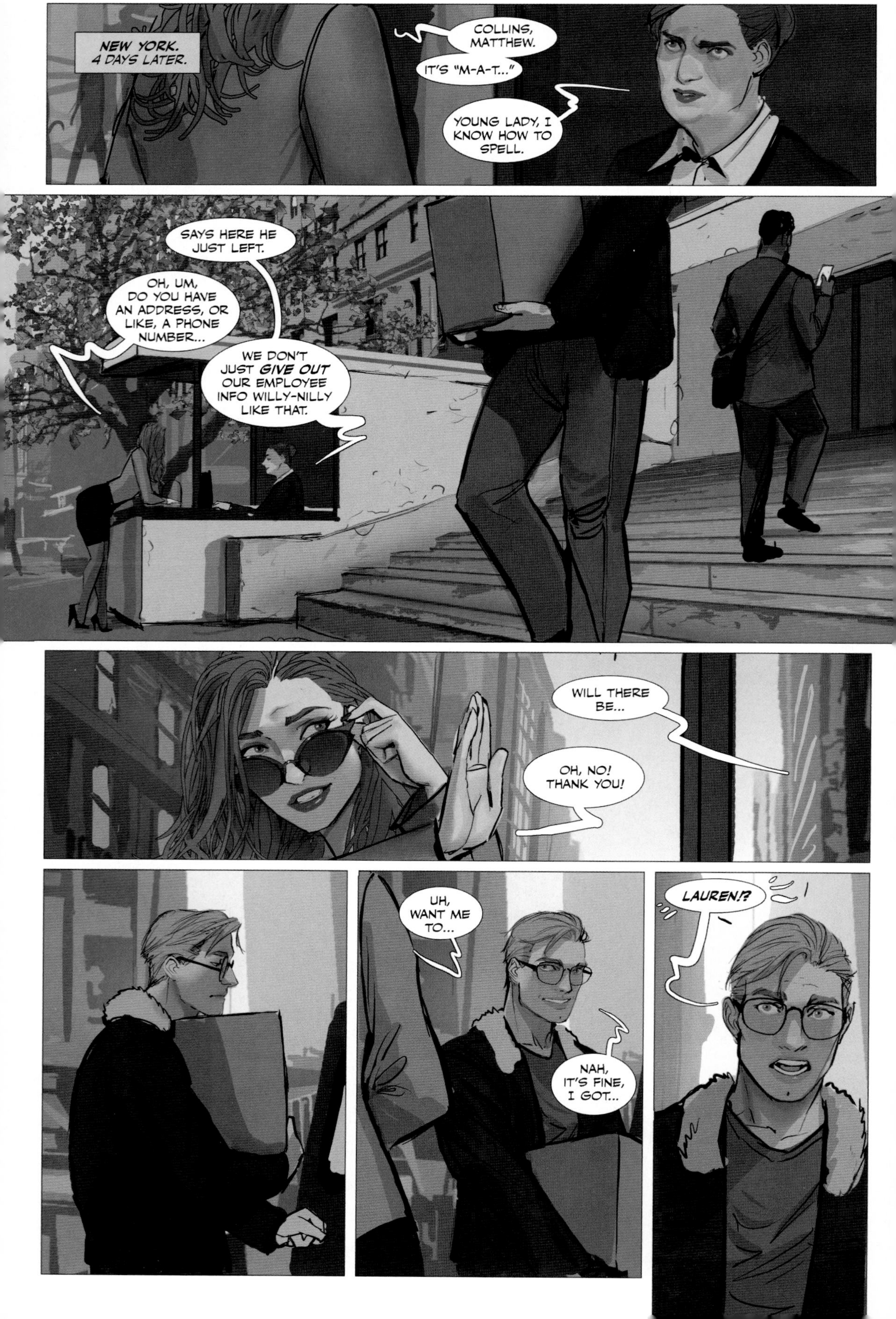
NEW YORK.
4 DAYS LATER.
COLLINS, MATTHEW.
IT'S "M-A-T..."
YOUNG LADY, I KNOW HOW TO SPELL.
SAYS HERE HE JUST LEFT.
OH, UM, DO YOU HAVE AN ADDRESS, OR LIKE, A PHONE NUMBER...
WE DON'T JUST GIVE OUT OUR EMPLOYEE INFO WILLY-NILLY LIKE THAT.
WILL THERE BE...
OH, NO! THANK YOU!
UH, WANT ME TO...
NAH, IT'S FINE, I GOT...
LAUREN!?

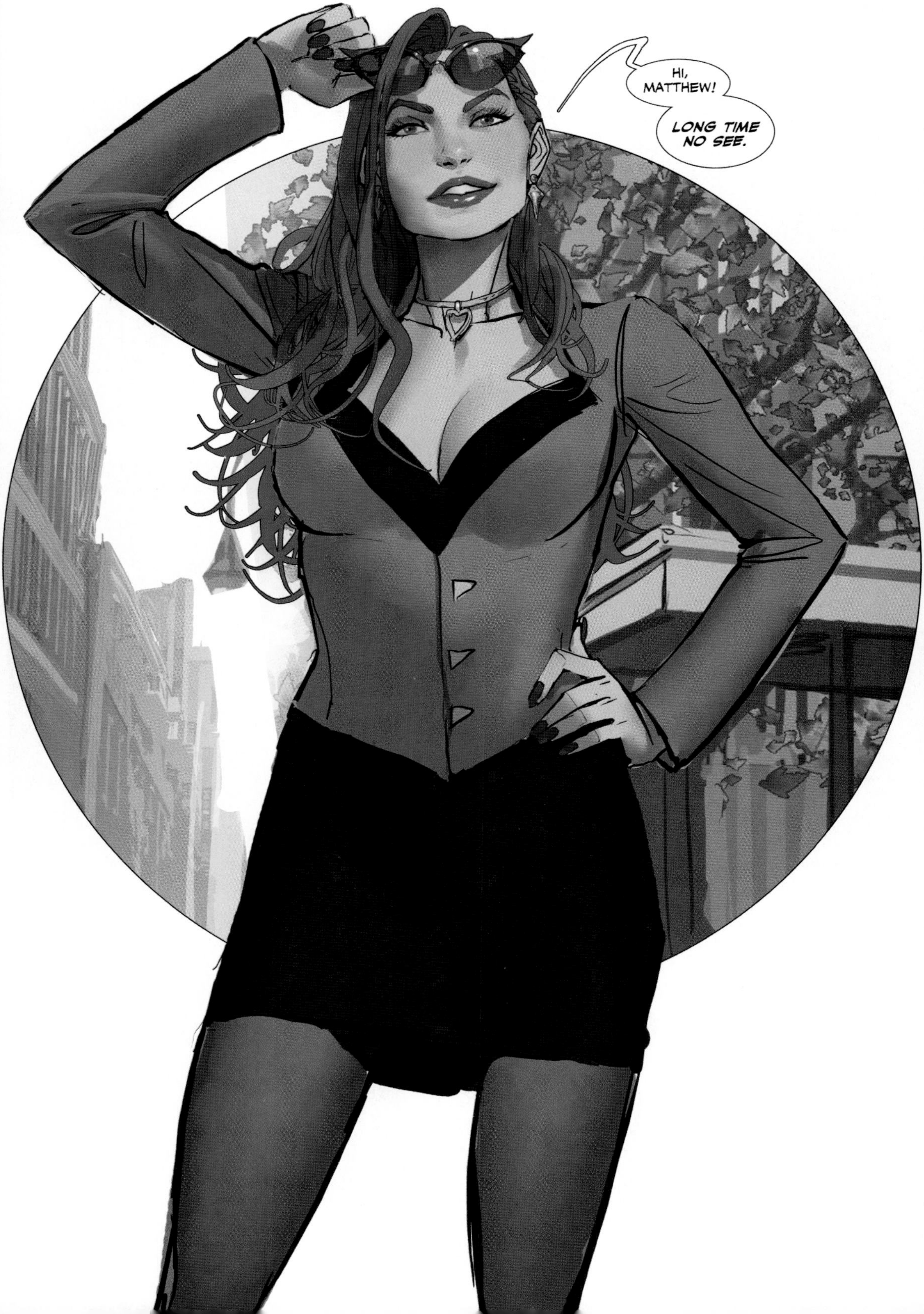
HI, MATTHEW!
LONG TIME NO SEE.

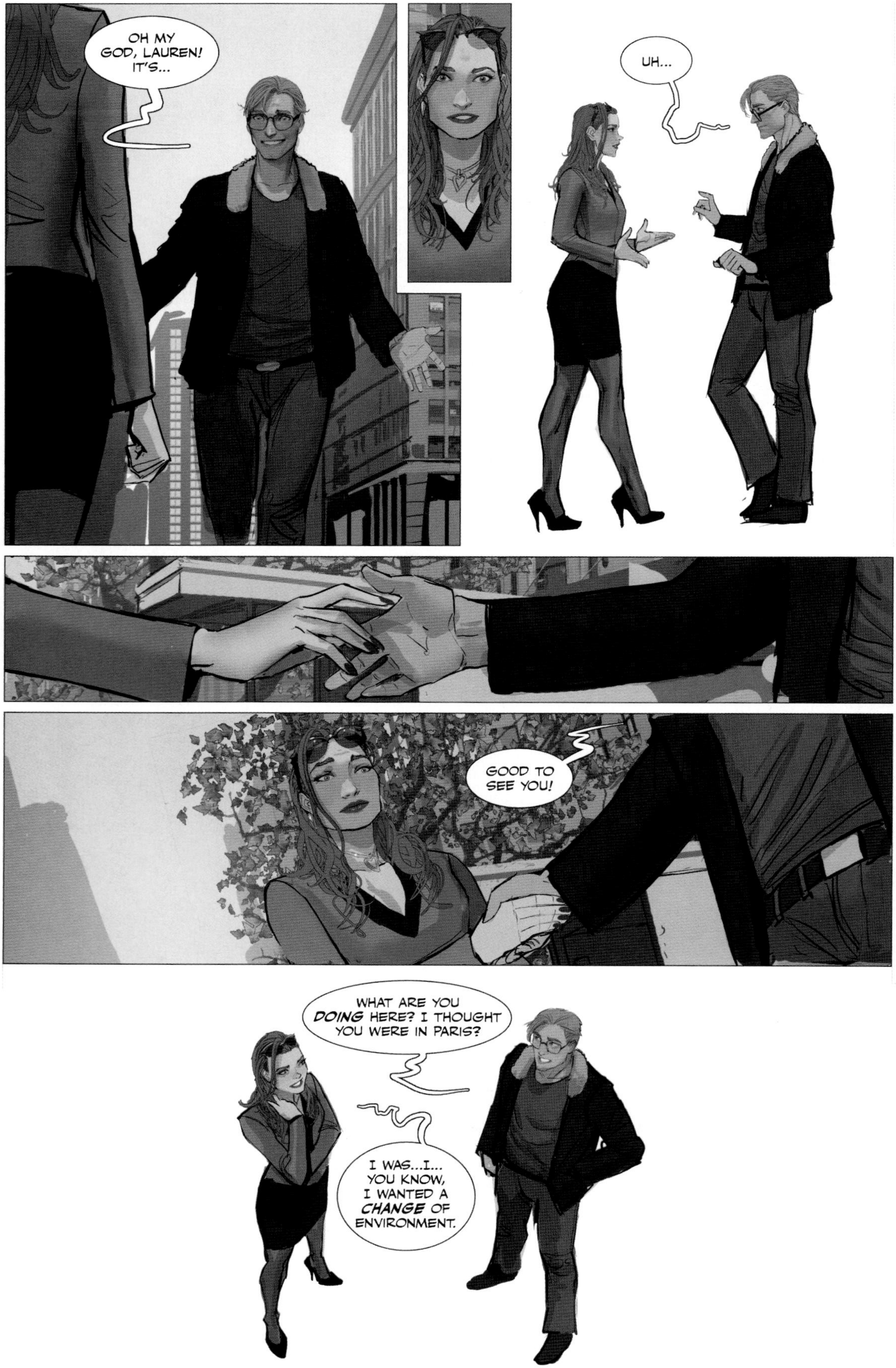
OH MY GOD, LAUREN! IT'S...
UH...
GOOD TO SEE YOU!
WHAT ARE YOU *DOING* HERE? I THOUGHT YOU WERE IN PARIS?
I WAS...I... YOU KNOW, I WANTED A *CHANGE* OF ENVIRONMENT.

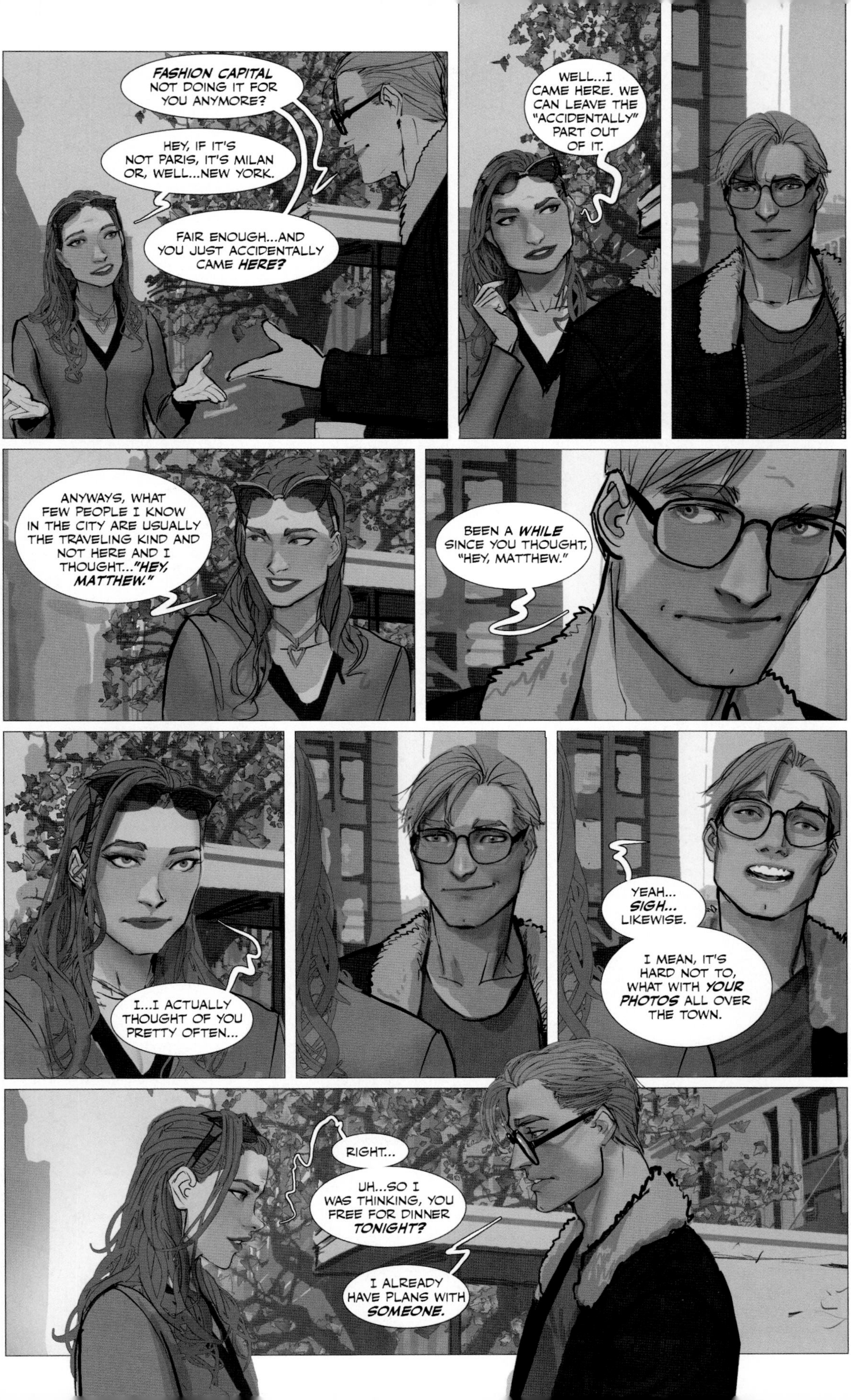
FASHION CAPITAL NOT DOING IT FOR YOU ANYMORE?
HEY, IF IT'S NOT PARIS, IT'S MILAN OR, WELL...NEW YORK.
FAIR ENOUGH...AND YOU JUST ACCIDENTALLY CAME HERE?
WELL...I CAME HERE. WE CAN LEAVE THE "ACCIDENTALLY" PART OUT OF IT.
ANYWAYS, WHAT FEW PEOPLE I KNOW IN THE CITY ARE USUALLY THE TRAVELING KIND AND NOT HERE AND I THOUGHT..."HEY, MATTHEW."
BEEN A WHILE SINCE YOU THOUGHT, "HEY, MATTHEW."
I...I ACTUALLY THOUGHT OF YOU PRETTY OFTEN...
YEAH... SIGH... LIKEWISE.
I MEAN, IT'S HARD NOT TO, WHAT WITH YOUR PHOTOS ALL OVER THE TOWN.
RIGHT...
UH...SO I WAS THINKING, YOU FREE FOR DINNER TONIGHT?
I ALREADY HAVE PLANS WITH SOMEONE.

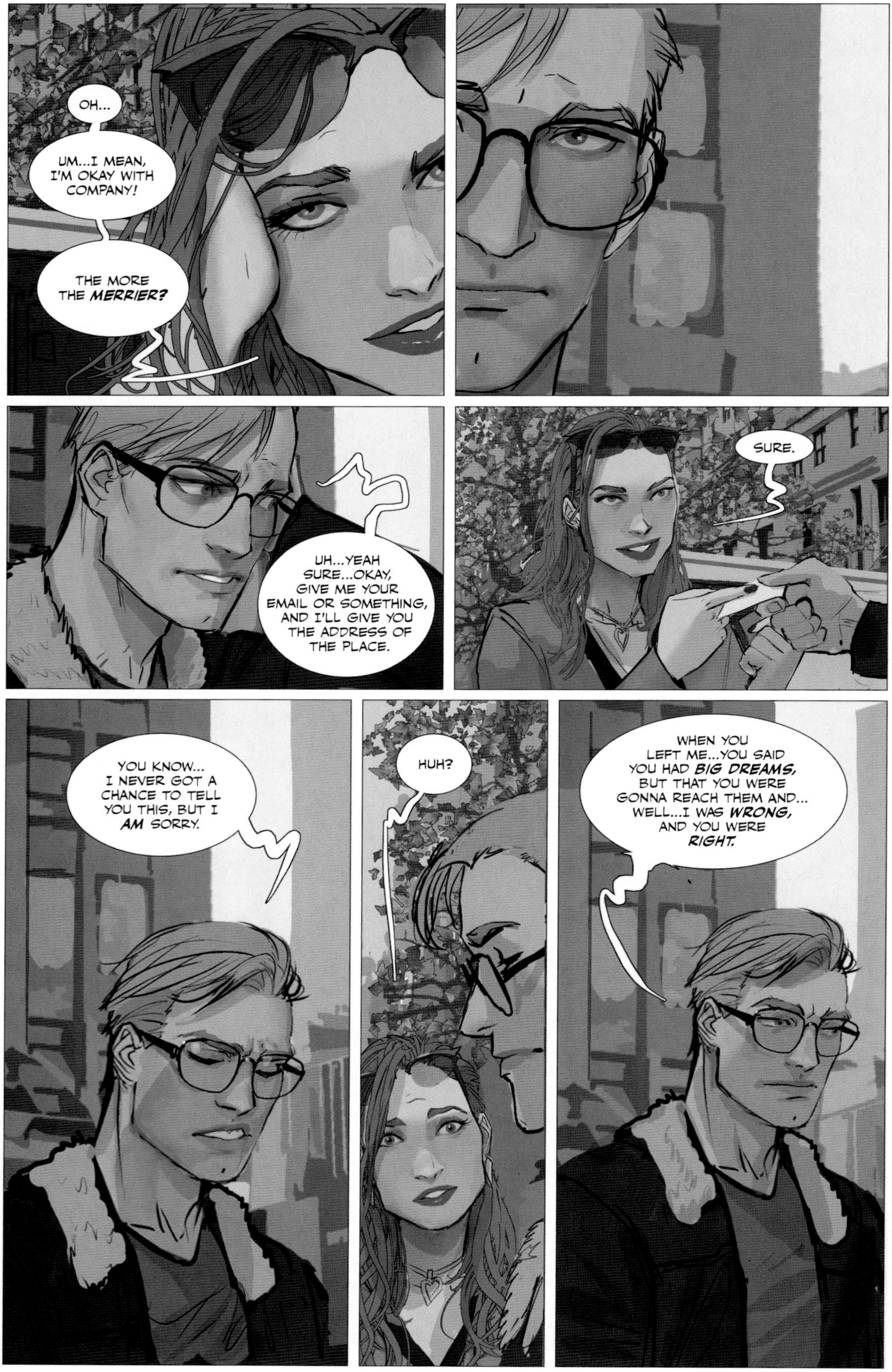
OH...
UM...I MEAN, I'M OKAY WITH COMPANY!
THE MORE THE *MERRIER?*
UH...YEAH SURE...OKAY, GIVE ME YOUR EMAIL OR SOMETHING, AND I'LL GIVE YOU THE ADDRESS OF THE PLACE.
SURE.
YOU KNOW... I NEVER GOT A CHANCE TO TELL YOU THIS, BUT I *AM* SORRY.
HUH?
WHEN YOU LEFT ME...YOU SAID YOU HAD *BIG DREAMS,* BUT THAT YOU WERE GONNA REACH THEM AND... WELL...I WAS *WRONG,* AND YOU WERE *RIGHT.*

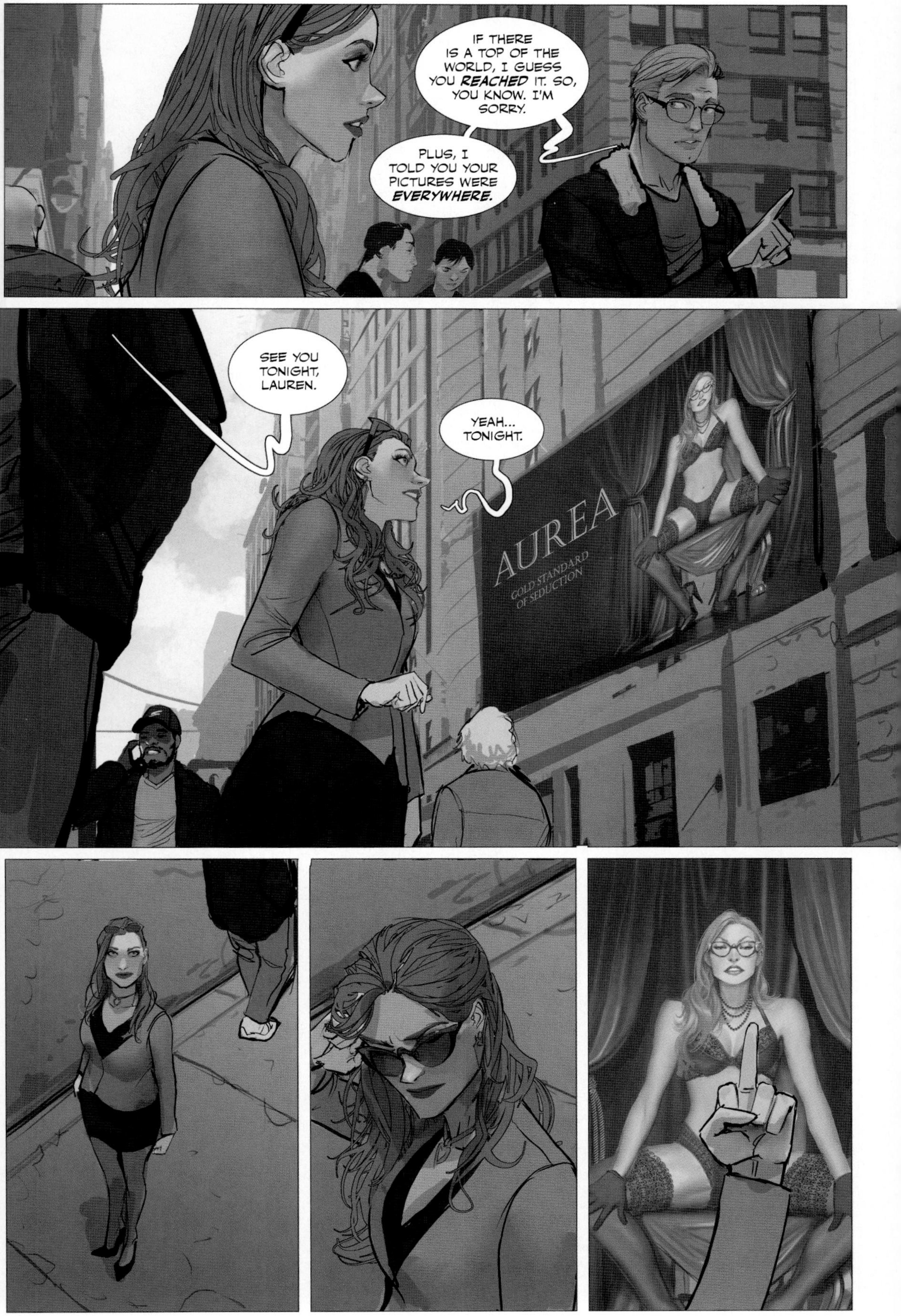
IF THERE IS A TOP OF THE WORLD, I GUESS YOU REACHED IT. SO, YOU KNOW. I'M SORRY.
PLUS, I TOLD YOU YOUR PICTURES WERE EVERYWHERE.
SEE YOU TONIGHT, LAUREN.
YEAH... TONIGHT.
AUREA
GOLD STANDARD OF SEDUCTION

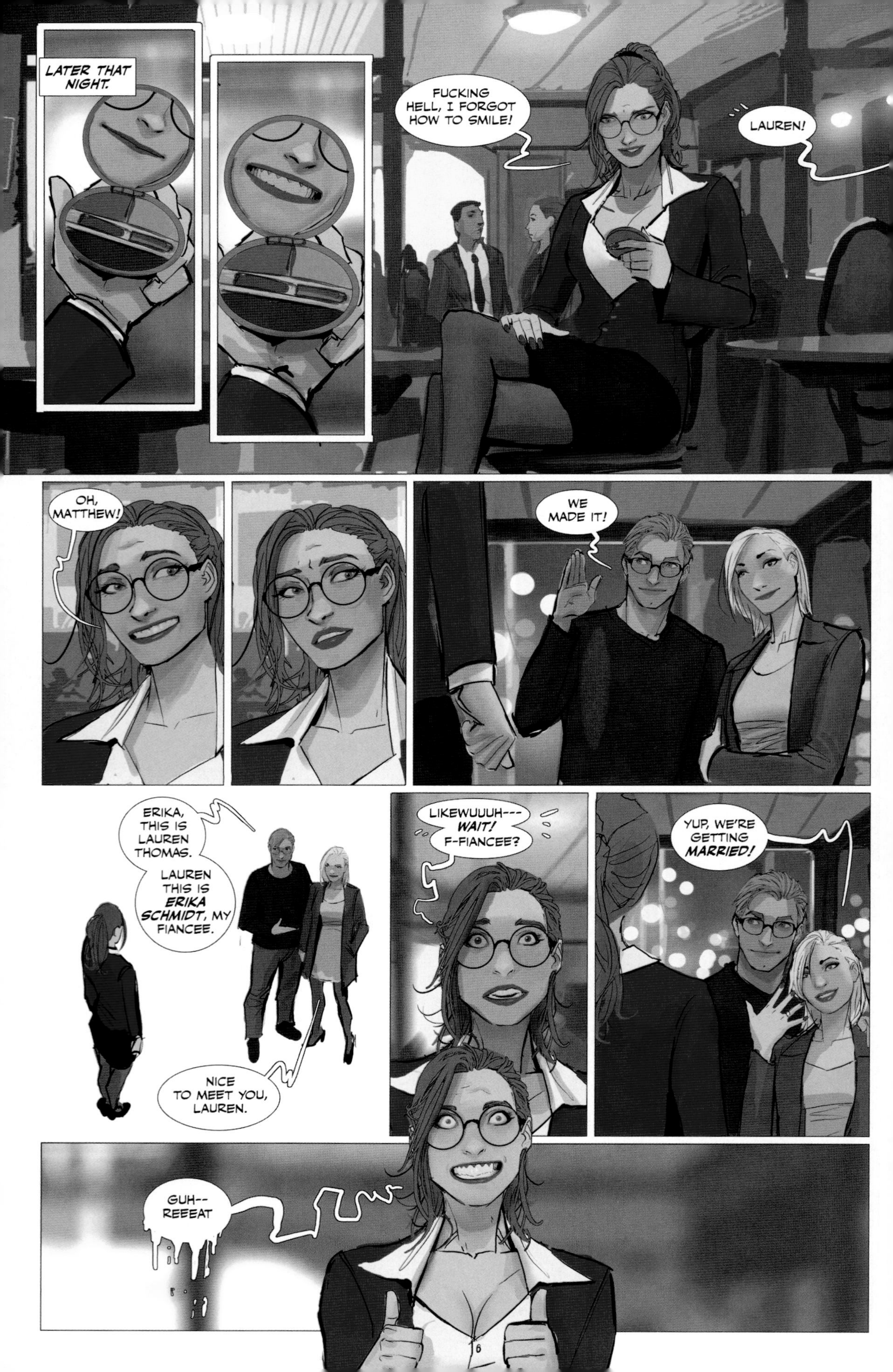
LATER THAT NIGHT.
FUCKING HELL, I FORGOT HOW TO SMILE!
LAUREN!
OH, MATTHEW!
WE MADE IT!
ERIKA, THIS IS LAUREN THOMAS.
LAUREN THIS IS ERIKA SCHMIDT, MY FIANCEE.
NICE TO MEET YOU, LAUREN.
LIKEWUUUH--- WAIT! F-FIANCEE?
YUP, WE'RE GETTING MARRIED!
GUH-- REEEAT

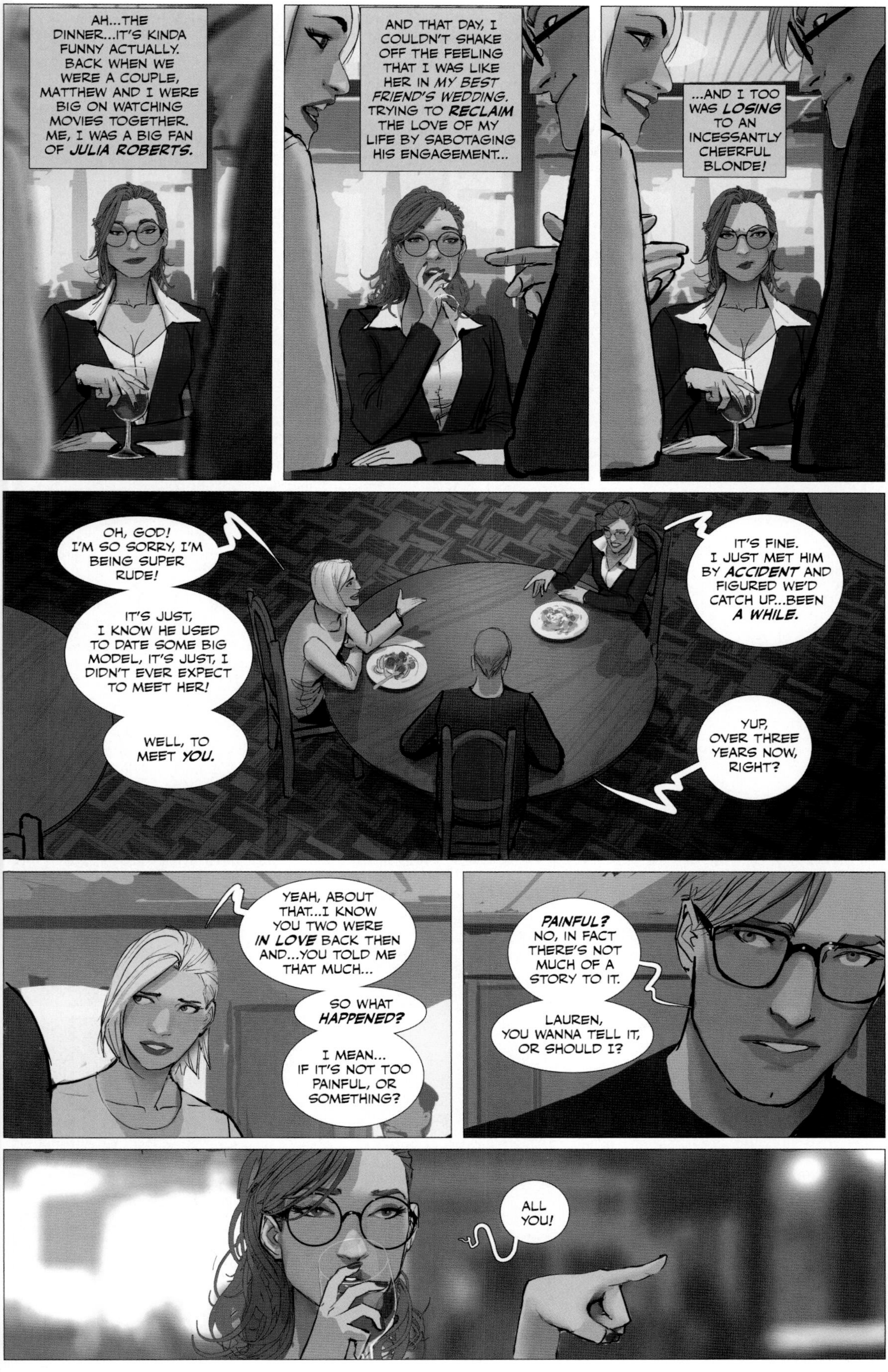
AH...THE DINNER...IT'S KINDA FUNNY ACTUALLY. BACK WHEN WE WERE A COUPLE, MATTHEW AND I WERE BIG ON WATCHING MOVIES TOGETHER. ME, I WAS A BIG FAN OF *JULIA ROBERTS.*
AND THAT DAY, I COULDN'T SHAKE OFF THE FEELING THAT I WAS LIKE HER IN *MY BEST FRIEND'S WEDDING.* TRYING TO ***RECLAIM*** THE LOVE OF MY LIFE BY SABOTAGING HIS ENGAGEMENT...
...AND I TOO WAS ***LOSING*** TO AN INCESSANTLY CHEERFUL BLONDE!
OH, GOD! I'M SO SORRY, I'M BEING SUPER RUDE!
IT'S JUST, I KNOW HE USED TO DATE SOME BIG MODEL, IT'S JUST, I DIDN'T EVER EXPECT TO MEET HER!
WELL, TO MEET ***YOU.***
IT'S FINE. I JUST MET HIM BY ***ACCIDENT*** AND FIGURED WE'D CATCH UP...BEEN ***A WHILE.***
YUP, OVER THREE YEARS NOW, RIGHT?
YEAH, ABOUT THAT...I KNOW YOU TWO WERE ***IN LOVE*** BACK THEN AND...YOU TOLD ME THAT MUCH...
SO WHAT ***HAPPENED?***
I MEAN... IF IT'S NOT TOO PAINFUL, OR SOMETHING?
PAINFUL? NO, IN FACT THERE'S NOT MUCH OF A STORY TO IT.
LAUREN, YOU WANNA TELL IT, OR SHOULD I?
ALL YOU!

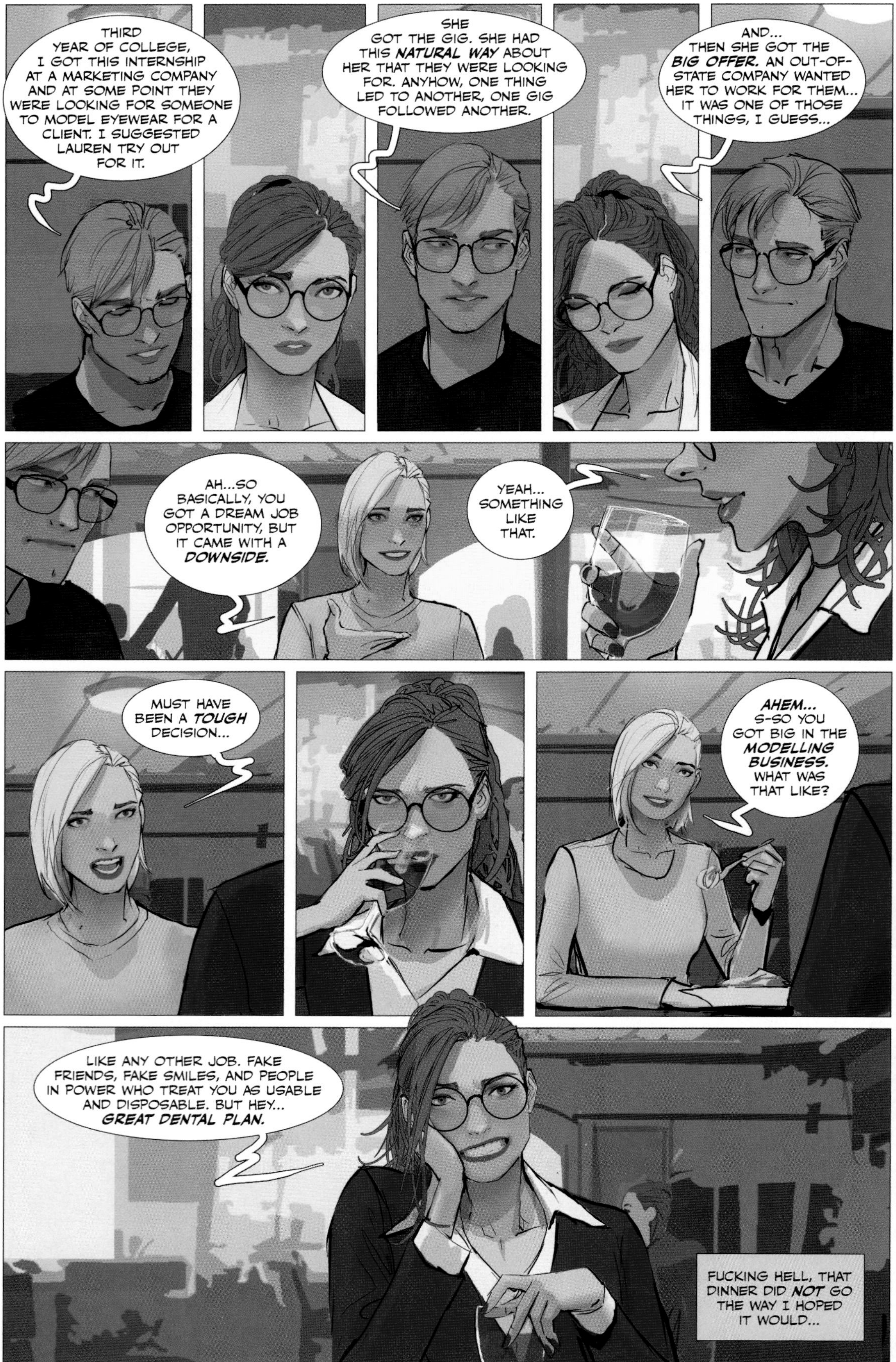
THIRD YEAR OF COLLEGE, I GOT THIS INTERNSHIP AT A MARKETING COMPANY AND AT SOME POINT THEY WERE LOOKING FOR SOMEONE TO MODEL EYEWEAR FOR A CLIENT. I SUGGESTED LAUREN TRY OUT FOR IT.
SHE GOT THE GIG. SHE HAD THIS NATURAL WAY ABOUT HER THAT THEY WERE LOOKING FOR. ANYHOW, ONE THING LED TO ANOTHER, ONE GIG FOLLOWED ANOTHER.
AND... THEN SHE GOT THE BIG OFFER. AN OUT-OF-STATE COMPANY WANTED HER TO WORK FOR THEM... IT WAS ONE OF THOSE THINGS, I GUESS...
AH...SO BASICALLY, YOU GOT A DREAM JOB OPPORTUNITY, BUT IT CAME WITH A DOWNSIDE.
YEAH... SOMETHING LIKE THAT.
MUST HAVE BEEN A TOUGH DECISION...
AHEM... S-SO YOU GOT BIG IN THE MODELLING BUSINESS. WHAT WAS THAT LIKE?
LIKE ANY OTHER JOB. FAKE FRIENDS, FAKE SMILES, AND PEOPLE IN POWER WHO TREAT YOU AS USABLE AND DISPOSABLE. BUT HEY... GREAT DENTAL PLAN.
FUCKING HELL, THAT DINNER DID NOT GO THE WAY I HOPED IT WOULD...

I REMEMBER THAT NIGHT, ALONE IN A HOTEL ROOM, JUST CHEWING ON THE EVENTS OF IT ALL.

DROWNING IN SELF-PITY AND SEETHING WITH ANGER...

THIS FUCKING GIRL!

THIS ERIKA SCHMIDT...

I HATED HER! I HATED HER BECAUSE SHE WAS EVERYTHING I WAS NOT...

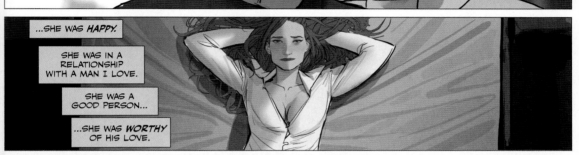

...SHE WAS HAPPY.

SHE WAS IN A RELATIONSHIP WITH A MAN I LOVE.

SHE WAS A GOOD PERSON...

...SHE WAS WORTHY OF HIS LOVE.

AND ME...I WAS NOW THE OTHER WOMAN. SCHEMING, PLANNING, CONNIVING...

...I WAS AN ANGRY BITCH WITH A FAKE SMILE.

BUT I WAS ALSO A STUBBORN BITCH!

I TOOK MY MEDICINE, BITTER THOUGH IT WAS, AND I BOUNCED BACK!

AFTER ALL, MAMA THOMAS DIDN'T RAISE A QUITTER.

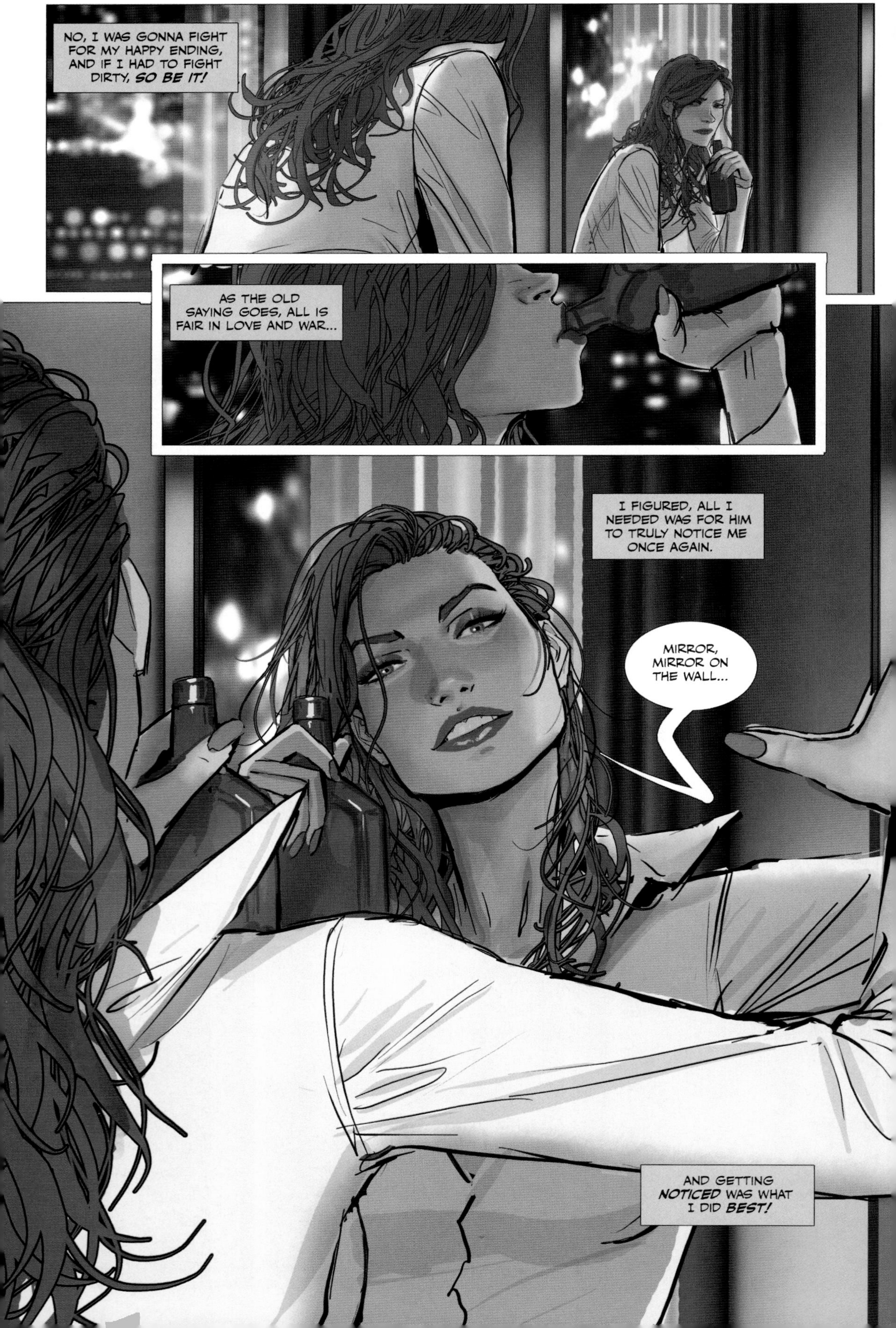
NO, I WAS GONNA FIGHT FOR MY HAPPY ENDING, AND IF I HAD TO FIGHT DIRTY, *SO BE IT!*
AS THE OLD SAYING GOES, ALL IS FAIR IN LOVE AND WAR...
I FIGURED, ALL I NEEDED WAS FOR HIM TO TRULY NOTICE ME ONCE AGAIN.
MIRROR, MIRROR ON THE WALL...
AND GETTING *NOTICED* WAS WHAT I DID *BEST!*

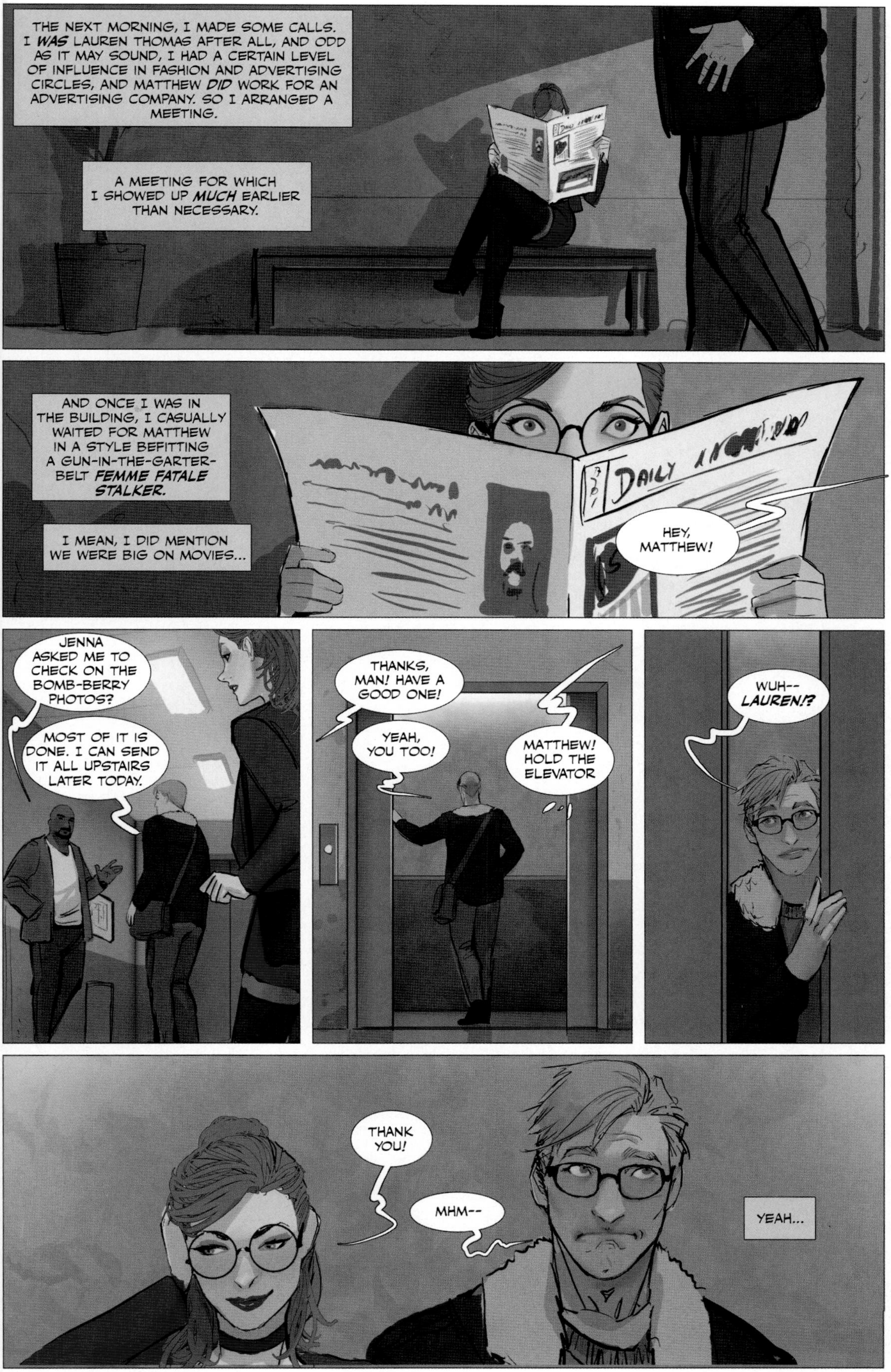
THE NEXT MORNING, I MADE SOME CALLS. I *WAS* LAUREN THOMAS AFTER ALL, AND ODD AS IT MAY SOUND, I HAD A CERTAIN LEVEL OF INFLUENCE IN FASHION AND ADVERTISING CIRCLES, AND MATTHEW *DID* WORK FOR AN ADVERTISING COMPANY. SO I ARRANGED A MEETING.
A MEETING FOR WHICH I SHOWED UP *MUCH* EARLIER THAN NECESSARY.
AND ONCE I WAS IN THE BUILDING, I CASUALLY WAITED FOR MATTHEW IN A STYLE BEFITTING A GUN-IN-THE-GARTER-BELT *FEMME FATALE STALKER.*
I MEAN, I DID MENTION WE WERE BIG ON MOVIES...
DAILY
HEY, MATTHEW!
JENNA ASKED ME TO CHECK ON THE BOMB-BERRY PHOTOS?
MOST OF IT IS DONE. I CAN SEND IT ALL UPSTAIRS LATER TODAY.
THANKS, MAN! HAVE A GOOD ONE!
YEAH, YOU TOO!
MATTHEW! HOLD THE ELEVATOR
WUH-- *LAUREN!?*
THANK YOU!
MHM--
YEAH...

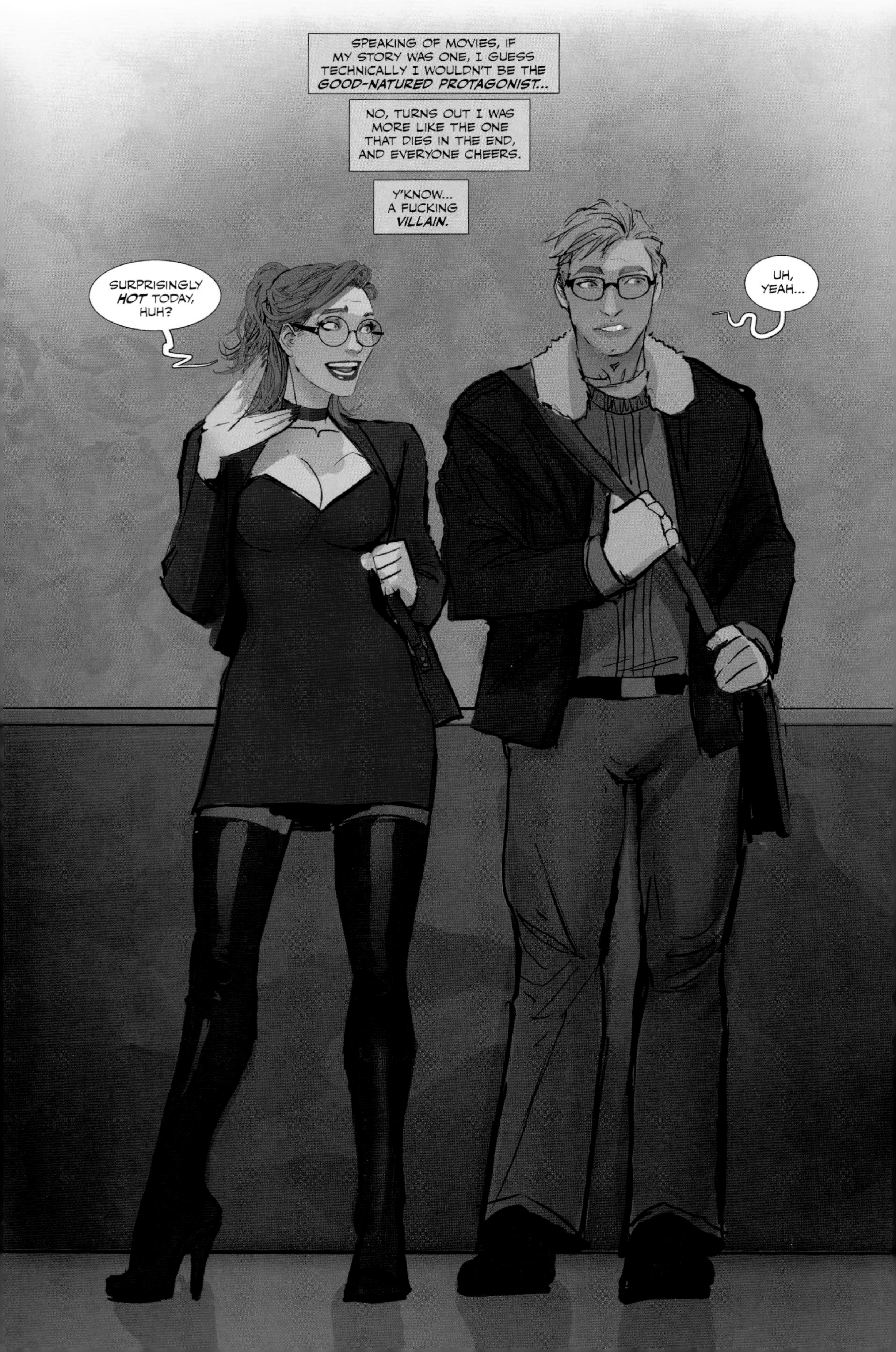
SPEAKING OF MOVIES, IF MY STORY WAS ONE, I GUESS TECHNICALLY I WOULDN'T BE THE ***GOOD-NATURED PROTAGONIST...***
NO, TURNS OUT I WAS MORE LIKE THE ONE THAT DIES IN THE END, AND EVERYONE CHEERS.
Y'KNOW... A FUCKING ***VILLAIN.***
SURPRISINGLY ***HOT*** TODAY, HUH?
UH, YEAH...

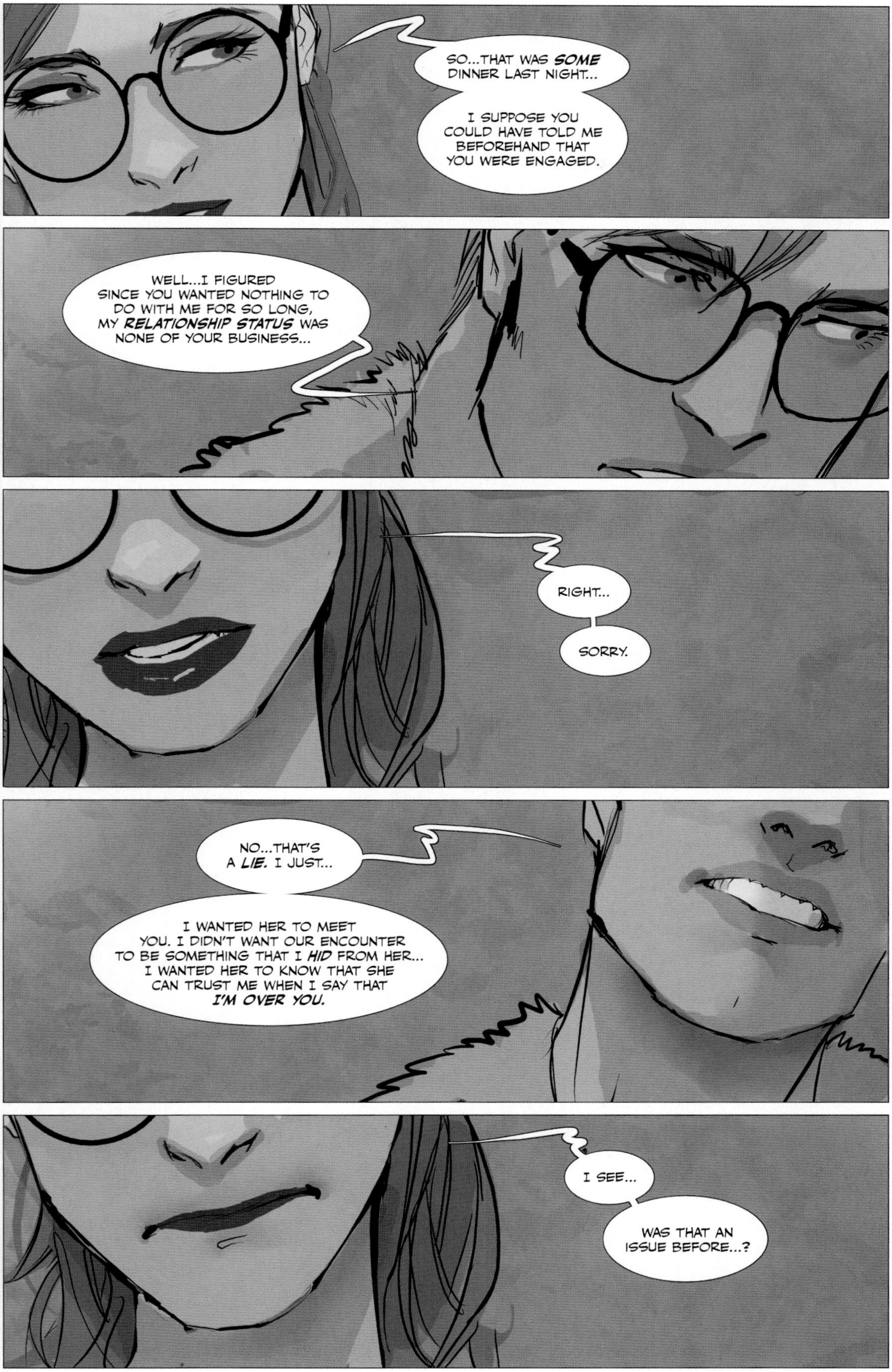
SO...THAT WAS SOME DINNER LAST NIGHT...
I SUPPOSE YOU COULD HAVE TOLD ME BEFOREHAND THAT YOU WERE ENGAGED.
WELL...I FIGURED SINCE YOU WANTED NOTHING TO DO WITH ME FOR SO LONG, MY RELATIONSHIP STATUS WAS NONE OF YOUR BUSINESS...
RIGHT...
SORRY.
NO...THAT'S A LIE. I JUST...
I WANTED HER TO MEET YOU. I DIDN'T WANT OUR ENCOUNTER TO BE SOMETHING THAT I HID FROM HER... I WANTED HER TO KNOW THAT SHE CAN TRUST ME WHEN I SAY THAT I'M OVER YOU.
I SEE...
WAS THAT AN ISSUE BEFORE...?

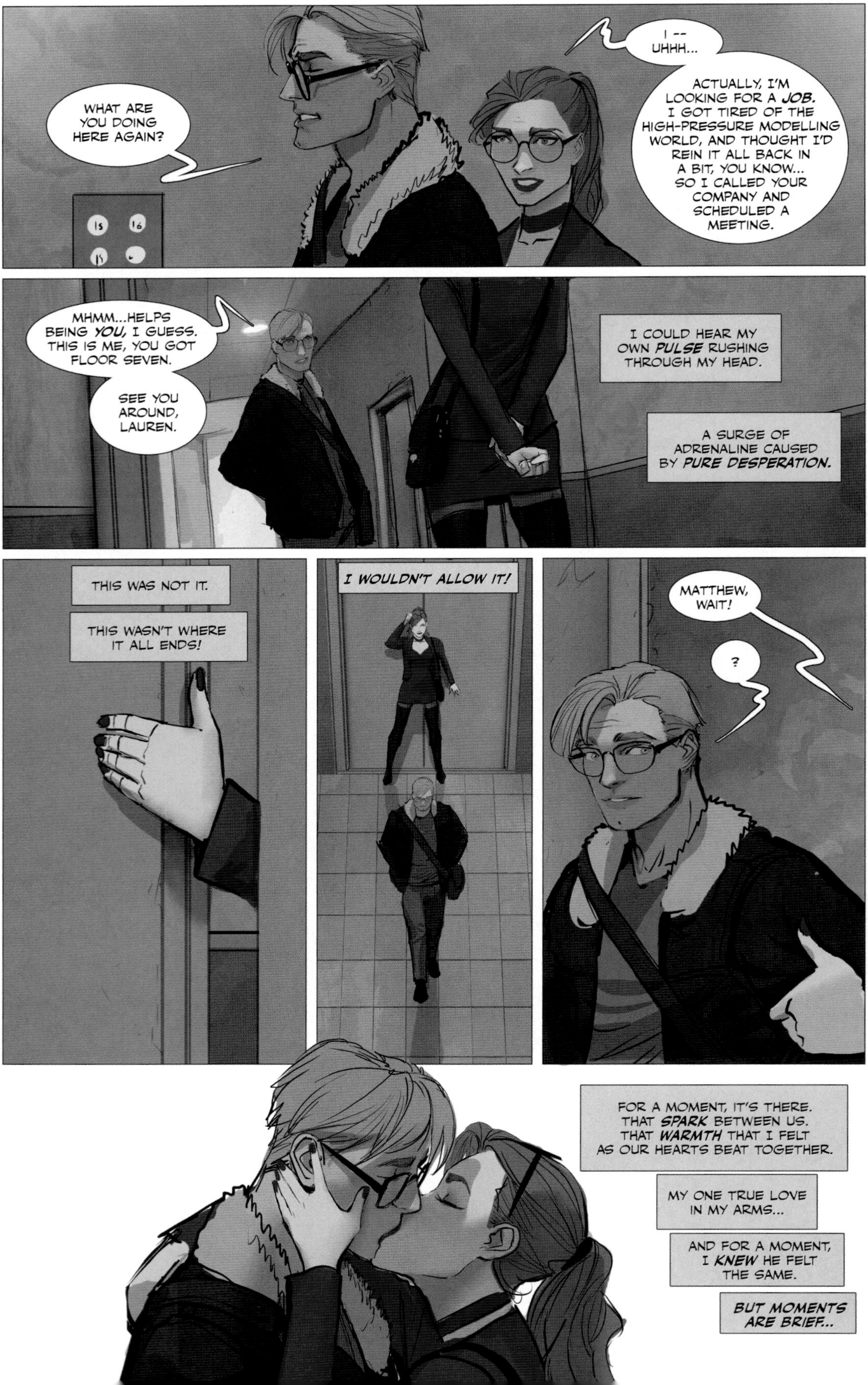
WHAT ARE YOU DOING HERE AGAIN?
I -- UHHH...
ACTUALLY, I'M LOOKING FOR A JOB. I GOT TIRED OF THE HIGH-PRESSURE MODELLING WORLD, AND THOUGHT I'D REIN IT ALL BACK IN A BIT, YOU KNOW... SO I CALLED YOUR COMPANY AND SCHEDULED A MEETING.
MHMM...HELPS BEING YOU, I GUESS. THIS IS ME, YOU GOT FLOOR SEVEN.
SEE YOU AROUND, LAUREN.
I COULD HEAR MY OWN PULSE RUSHING THROUGH MY HEAD.
A SURGE OF ADRENALINE CAUSED BY PURE DESPERATION.
THIS WAS NOT IT.
THIS WASN'T WHERE IT ALL ENDS!
I WOULDN'T ALLOW IT!
MATTHEW, WAIT!
?
FOR A MOMENT, IT'S THERE. THAT SPARK BETWEEN US. THAT WARMTH THAT I FELT AS OUR HEARTS BEAT TOGETHER.
MY ONE TRUE LOVE IN MY ARMS...
AND FOR A MOMENT, I KNEW HE FELT THE SAME.
BUT MOMENTS ARE BRIEF...

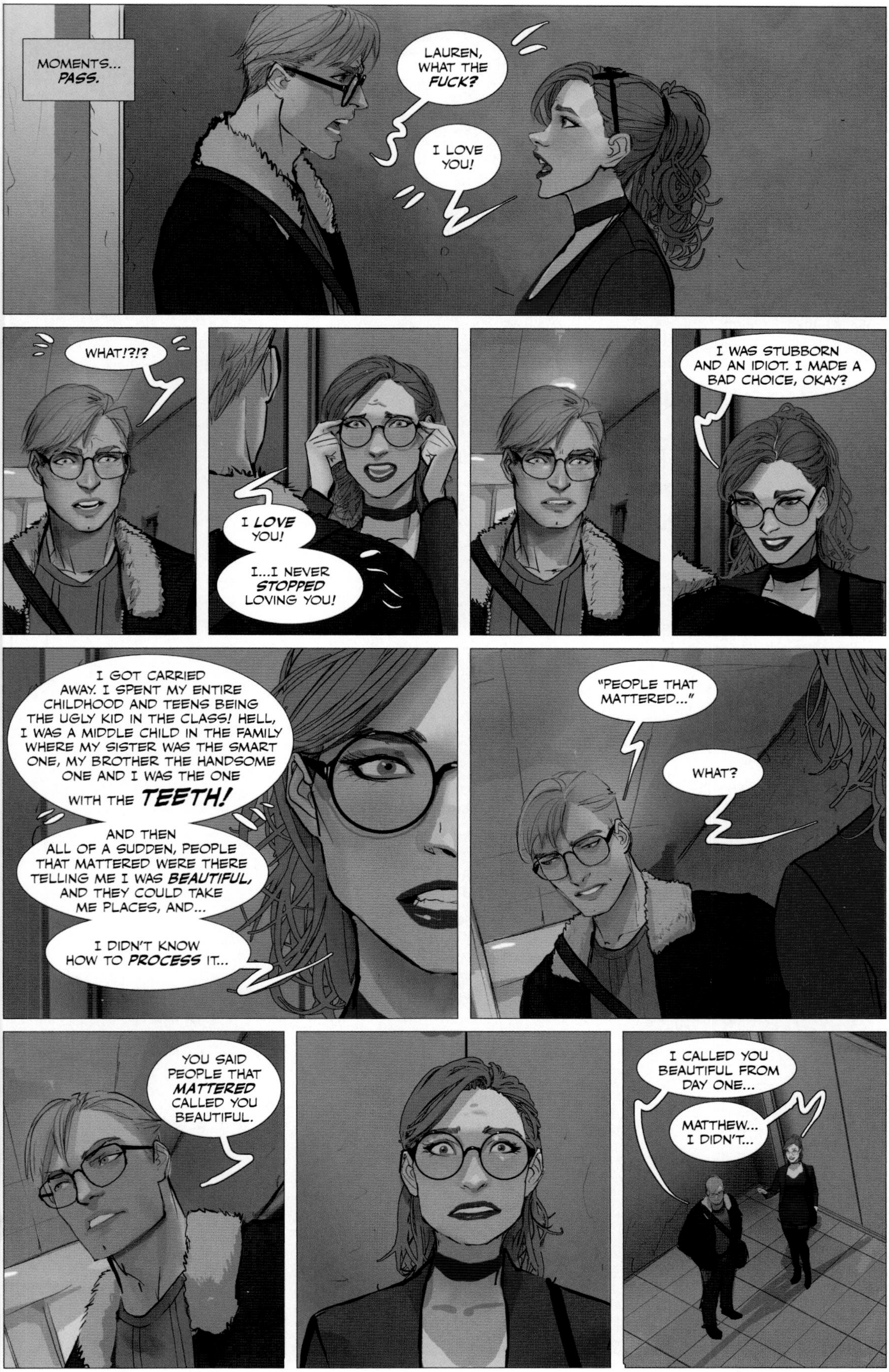

MOMENTS... PASS.
LAUREN, WHAT THE FUCK?
I LOVE YOU!
WHAT!?!?
I LOVE YOU!
I...I NEVER STOPPED LOVING YOU!
I WAS STUBBORN AND AN IDIOT. I MADE A BAD CHOICE, OKAY?
I GOT CARRIED AWAY. I SPENT MY ENTIRE CHILDHOOD AND TEENS BEING THE UGLY KID IN THE CLASS! HELL, I WAS A MIDDLE CHILD IN THE FAMILY WHERE MY SISTER WAS THE SMART ONE, MY BROTHER THE HANDSOME ONE AND I WAS THE ONE WITH THE TEETH!
AND THEN ALL OF A SUDDEN, PEOPLE THAT MATTERED WERE THERE TELLING ME I WAS BEAUTIFUL, AND THEY COULD TAKE ME PLACES, AND...
I DIDN'T KNOW HOW TO PROCESS IT...
"PEOPLE THAT MATTERED..."
WHAT?
YOU SAID PEOPLE THAT MATTERED CALLED YOU BEAUTIFUL.
I CALLED YOU BEAUTIFUL FROM DAY ONE...
MATTHEW... I DIDN'T...

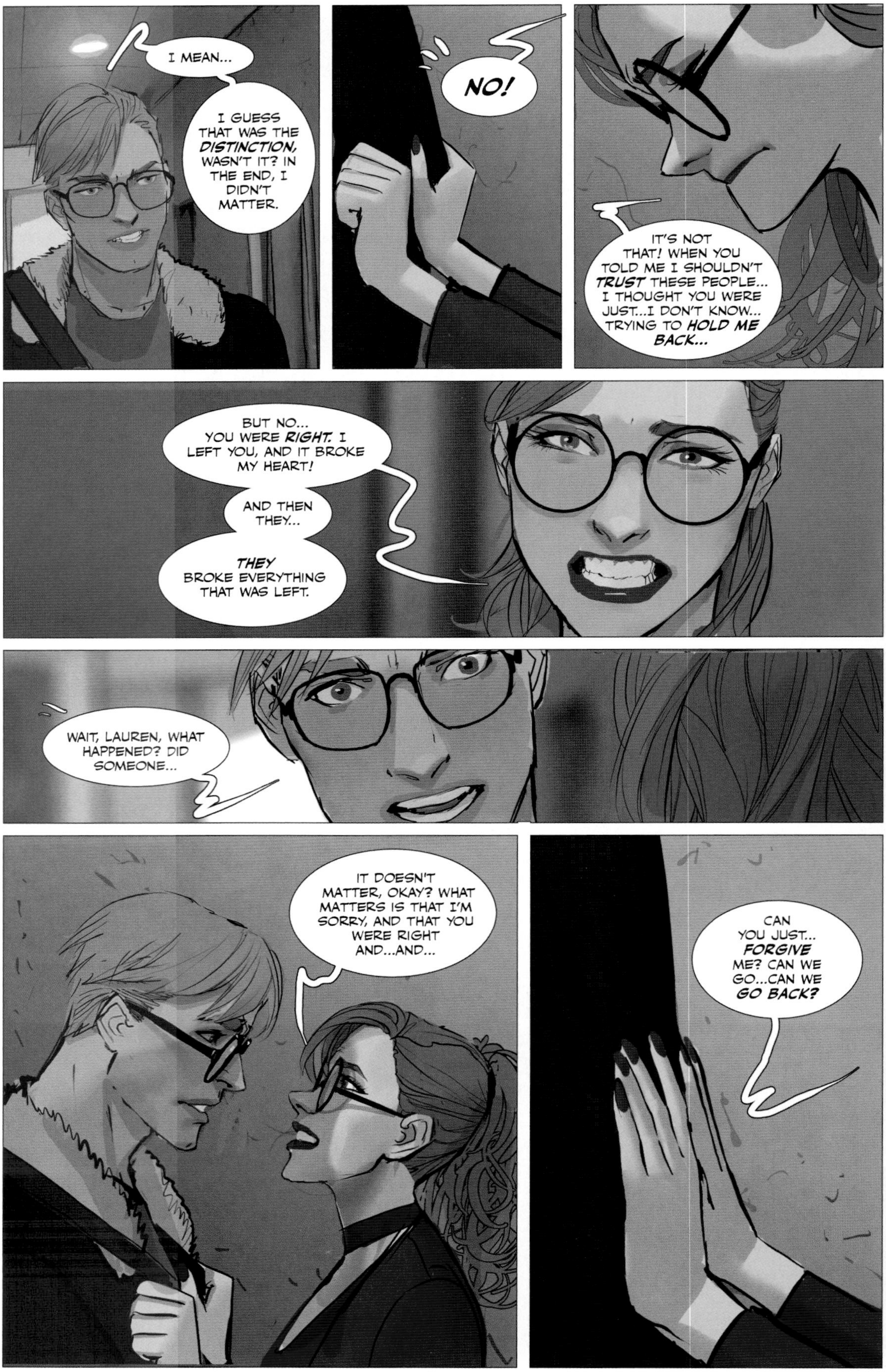
I MEAN...
I GUESS THAT WAS THE *DISTINCTION*, WASN'T IT? IN THE END, I DIDN'T MATTER.
NO!
IT'S NOT THAT! WHEN YOU TOLD ME I SHOULDN'T *TRUST* THESE PEOPLE... I THOUGHT YOU WERE JUST...I DON'T KNOW... TRYING TO *HOLD ME BACK...*
BUT NO... YOU WERE *RIGHT*. I LEFT YOU, AND IT BROKE MY HEART!
AND THEN THEY...
THEY BROKE EVERYTHING THAT WAS LEFT.
WAIT, LAUREN, WHAT HAPPENED? DID SOMEONE...
IT DOESN'T MATTER, OKAY? WHAT MATTERS IS THAT I'M SORRY, AND THAT YOU WERE RIGHT AND...AND...
CAN YOU JUST... *FORGIVE* ME? CAN WE GO...CAN WE *GO BACK?*

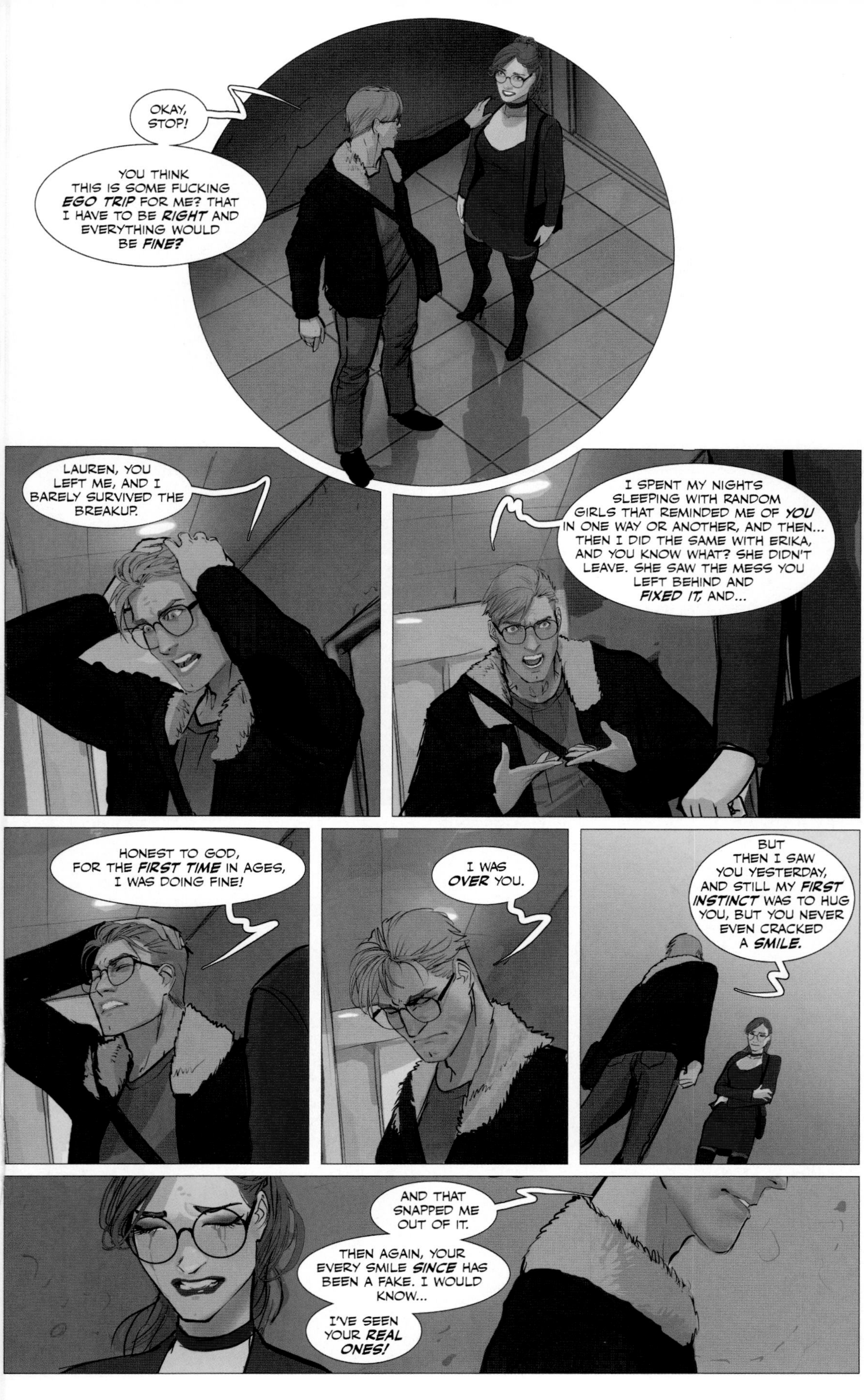
OKAY, STOP!
YOU THINK THIS IS SOME FUCKING EGO TRIP FOR ME? THAT I HAVE TO BE RIGHT AND EVERYTHING WOULD BE FINE?
LAUREN, YOU LEFT ME, AND I BARELY SURVIVED THE BREAKUP.
I SPENT MY NIGHTS SLEEPING WITH RANDOM GIRLS THAT REMINDED ME OF YOU IN ONE WAY OR ANOTHER, AND THEN... THEN I DID THE SAME WITH ERIKA, AND YOU KNOW WHAT? SHE DIDN'T LEAVE. SHE SAW THE MESS YOU LEFT BEHIND AND FIXED IT, AND...
HONEST TO GOD, FOR THE FIRST TIME IN AGES, I WAS DOING FINE!
I WAS OVER YOU.
BUT THEN I SAW YOU YESTERDAY, AND STILL MY FIRST INSTINCT WAS TO HUG YOU, BUT YOU NEVER EVEN CRACKED A SMILE.
AND THAT SNAPPED ME OUT OF IT.
THEN AGAIN, YOUR EVERY SMILE SINCE HAS BEEN A FAKE. I WOULD KNOW...
I'VE SEEN YOUR REAL ONES!

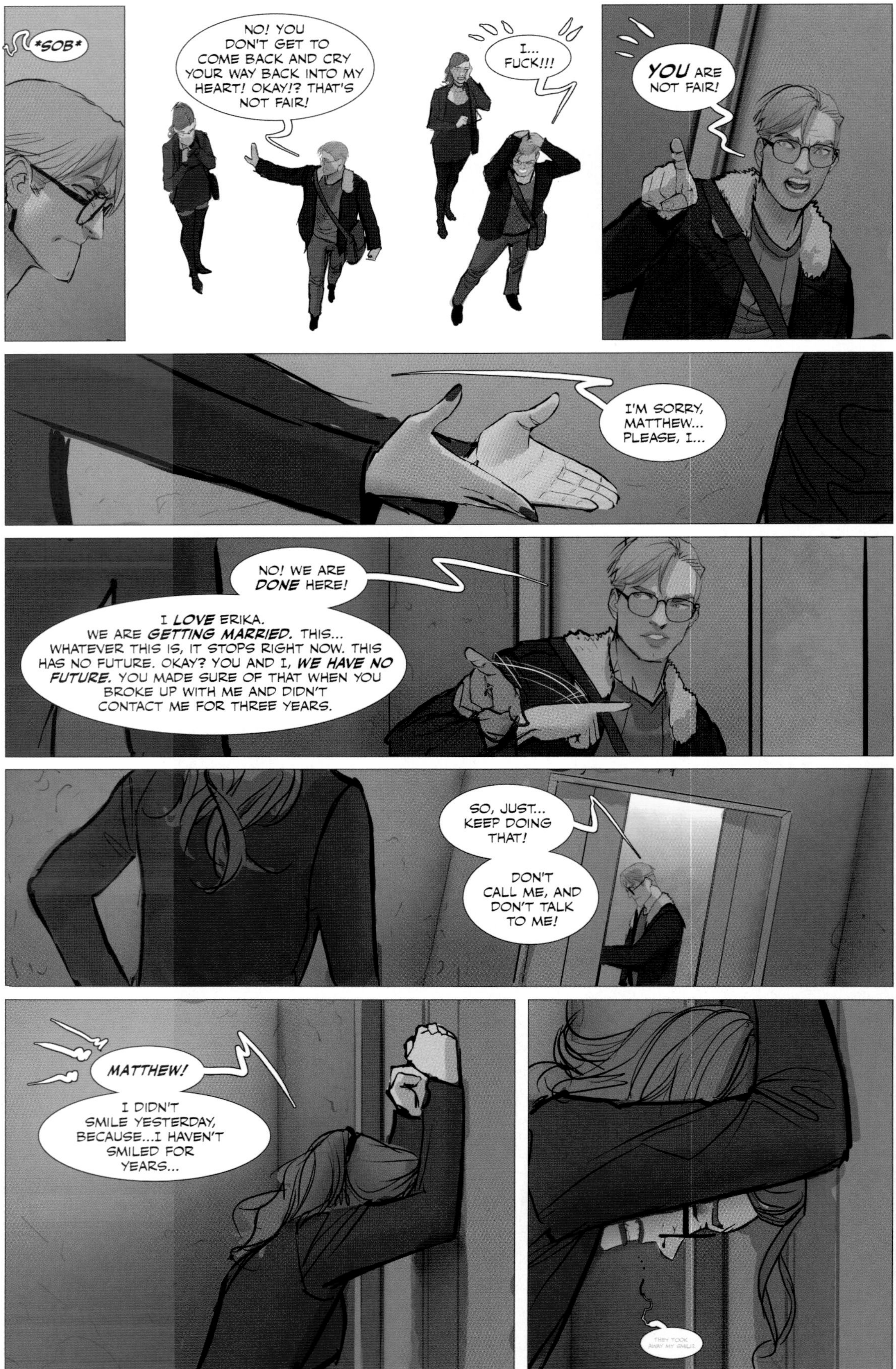
SOB
NO! YOU DON'T GET TO COME BACK AND CRY YOUR WAY BACK INTO MY HEART! OKAY!? THAT'S NOT FAIR!
I... FUCK!!!
YOU ARE NOT FAIR!
I'M SORRY, MATTHEW... PLEASE, I...
NO! WE ARE DONE HERE!
I LOVE ERIKA. WE ARE GETTING MARRIED. THIS... WHATEVER THIS IS, IT STOPS RIGHT NOW. THIS HAS NO FUTURE. OKAY? YOU AND I, WE HAVE NO FUTURE. YOU MADE SURE OF THAT WHEN YOU BROKE UP WITH ME AND DIDN'T CONTACT ME FOR THREE YEARS.
SO, JUST... KEEP DOING THAT!
DON'T CALL ME, AND DON'T TALK TO ME!
MATTHEW!
I DIDN'T SMILE YESTERDAY, BECAUSE...I HAVEN'T SMILED FOR YEARS...
...
THEY TOOK AWAY MY SMILE.

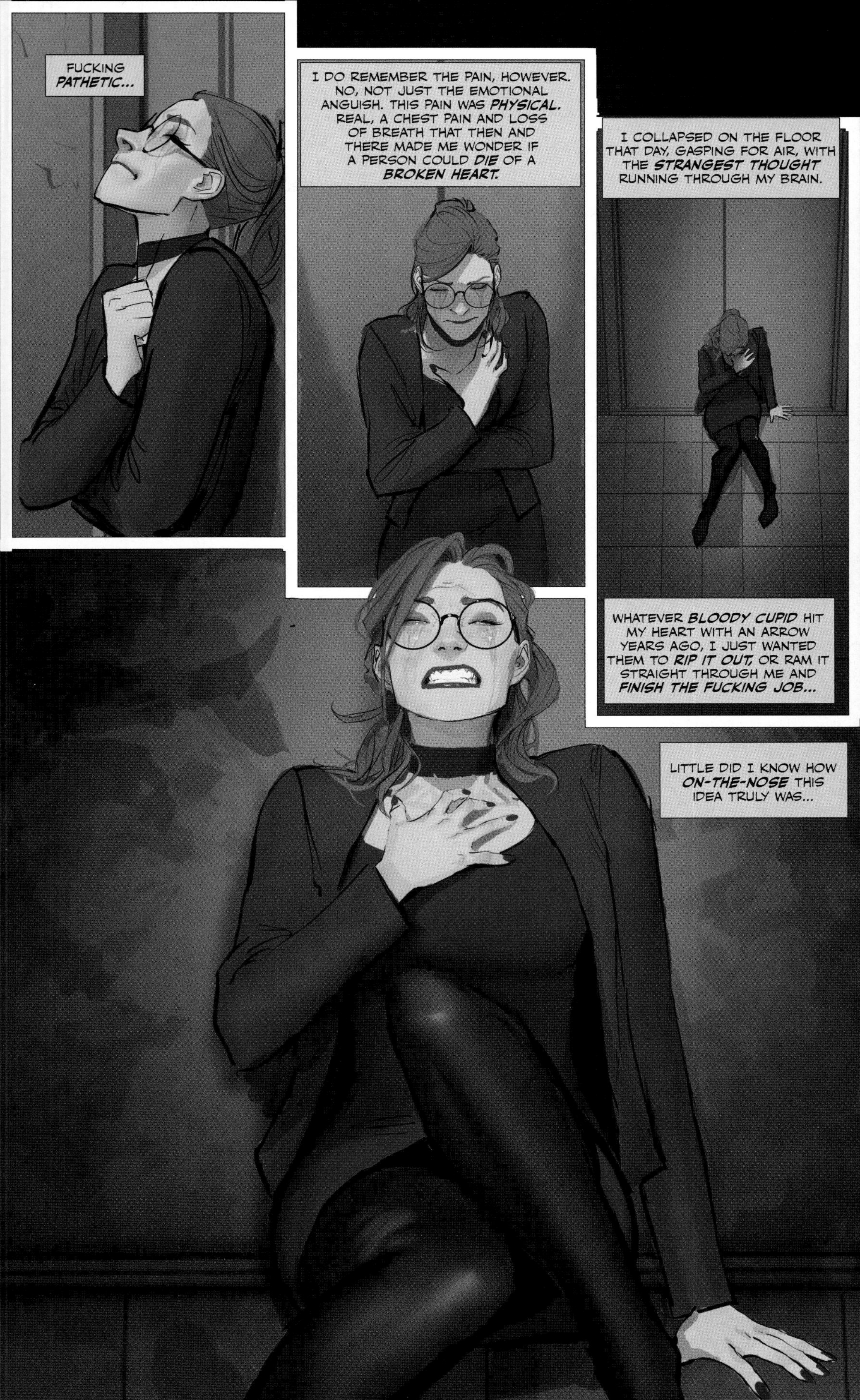
FUCKING PATHETIC...
I DO REMEMBER THE PAIN, HOWEVER. NO, NOT JUST THE EMOTIONAL ANGUISH. THIS PAIN WAS PHYSICAL. REAL, A CHEST PAIN AND LOSS OF BREATH THAT THEN AND THERE MADE ME WONDER IF A PERSON COULD DIE OF A BROKEN HEART.
I COLLAPSED ON THE FLOOR THAT DAY, GASPING FOR AIR, WITH THE STRANGEST THOUGHT RUNNING THROUGH MY BRAIN.
WHATEVER BLOODY CUPID HIT MY HEART WITH AN ARROW YEARS AGO, I JUST WANTED THEM TO RIP IT OUT, OR RAM IT STRAIGHT THROUGH ME AND FINISH THE FUCKING JOB...
LITTLE DID I KNOW HOW ON-THE-NOSE THIS IDEA TRULY WAS...

Chapter 2

The hidden crown

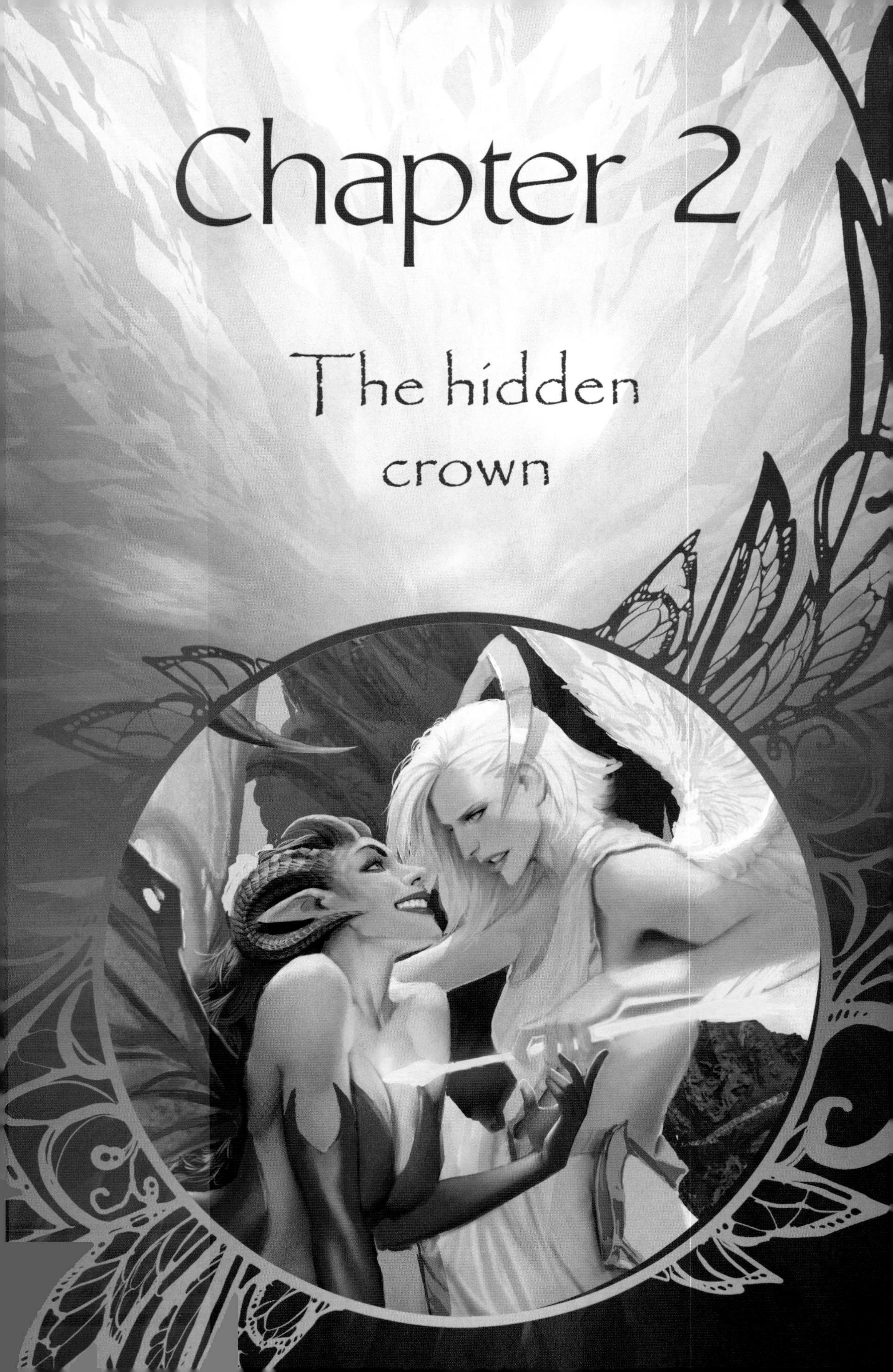

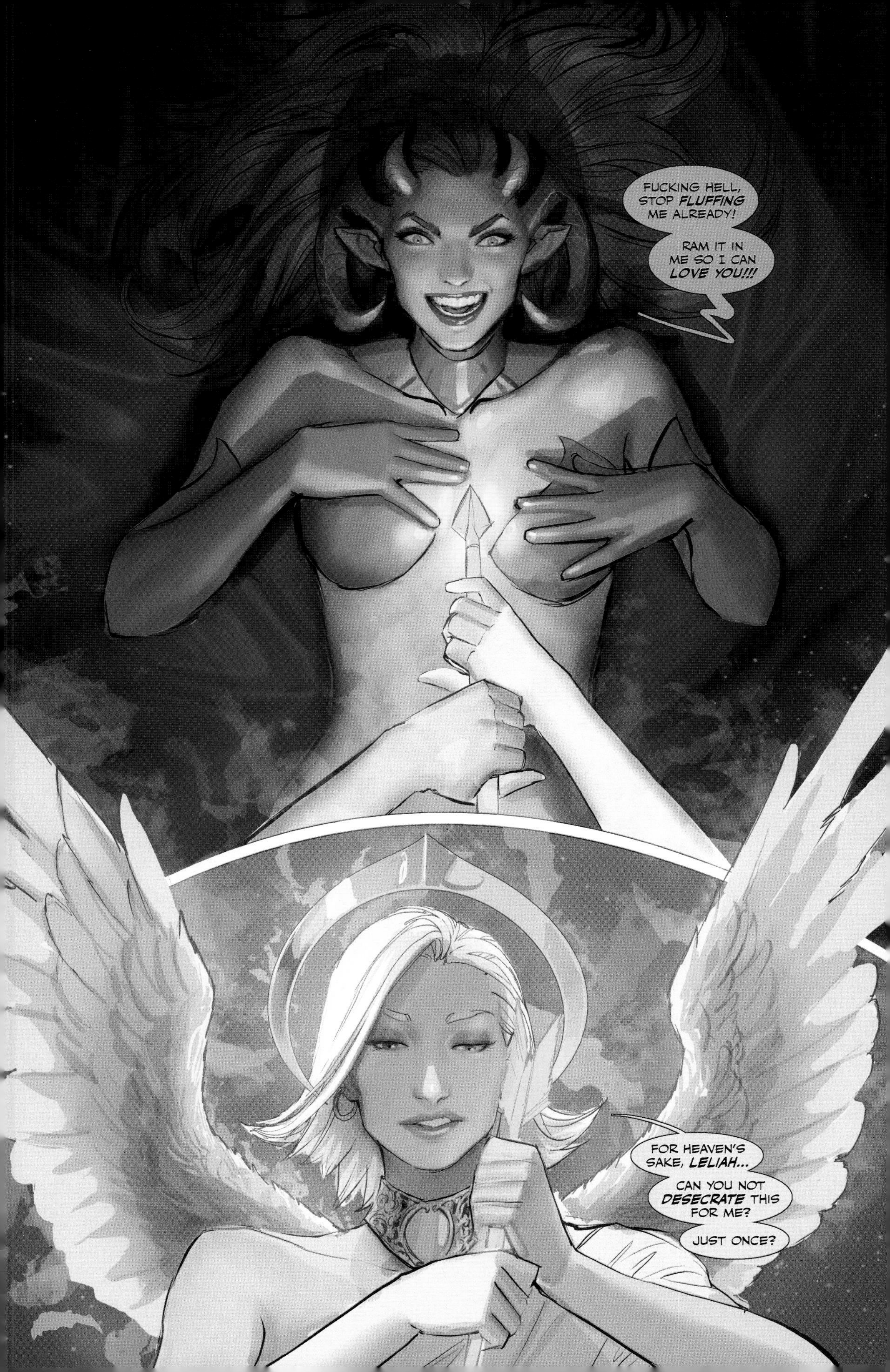
FUCKING HELL, STOP FLUFFING ME ALREADY!
RAM IT IN ME SO I CAN LOVE YOU!!!
FOR HEAVEN'S SAKE, LELIAH...
CAN YOU NOT DESECRATE THIS FOR ME?
JUST ONCE?

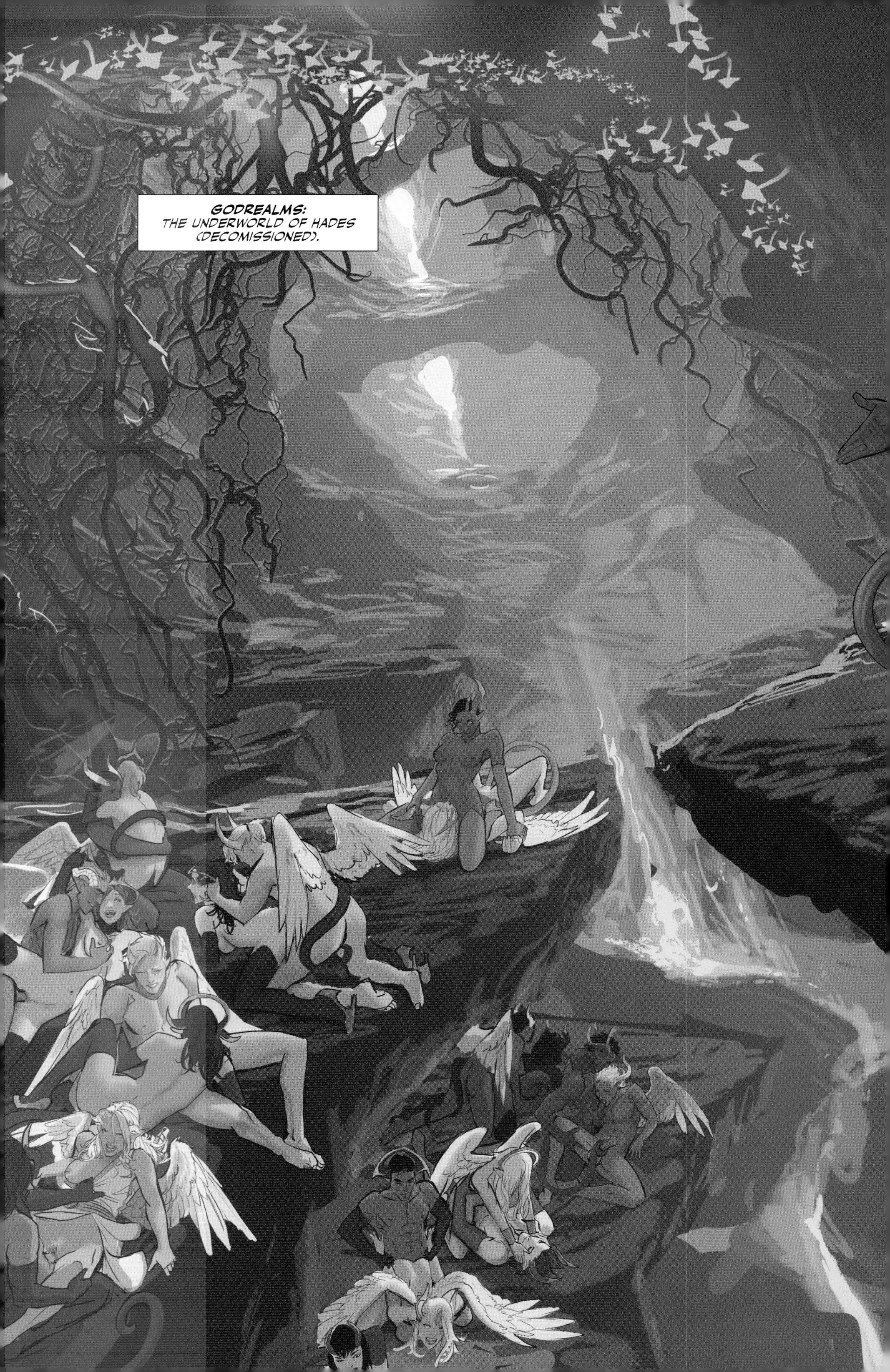
GODREALMS:
THE UNDERWORLD OF HADES
(DECOMISSIONED).

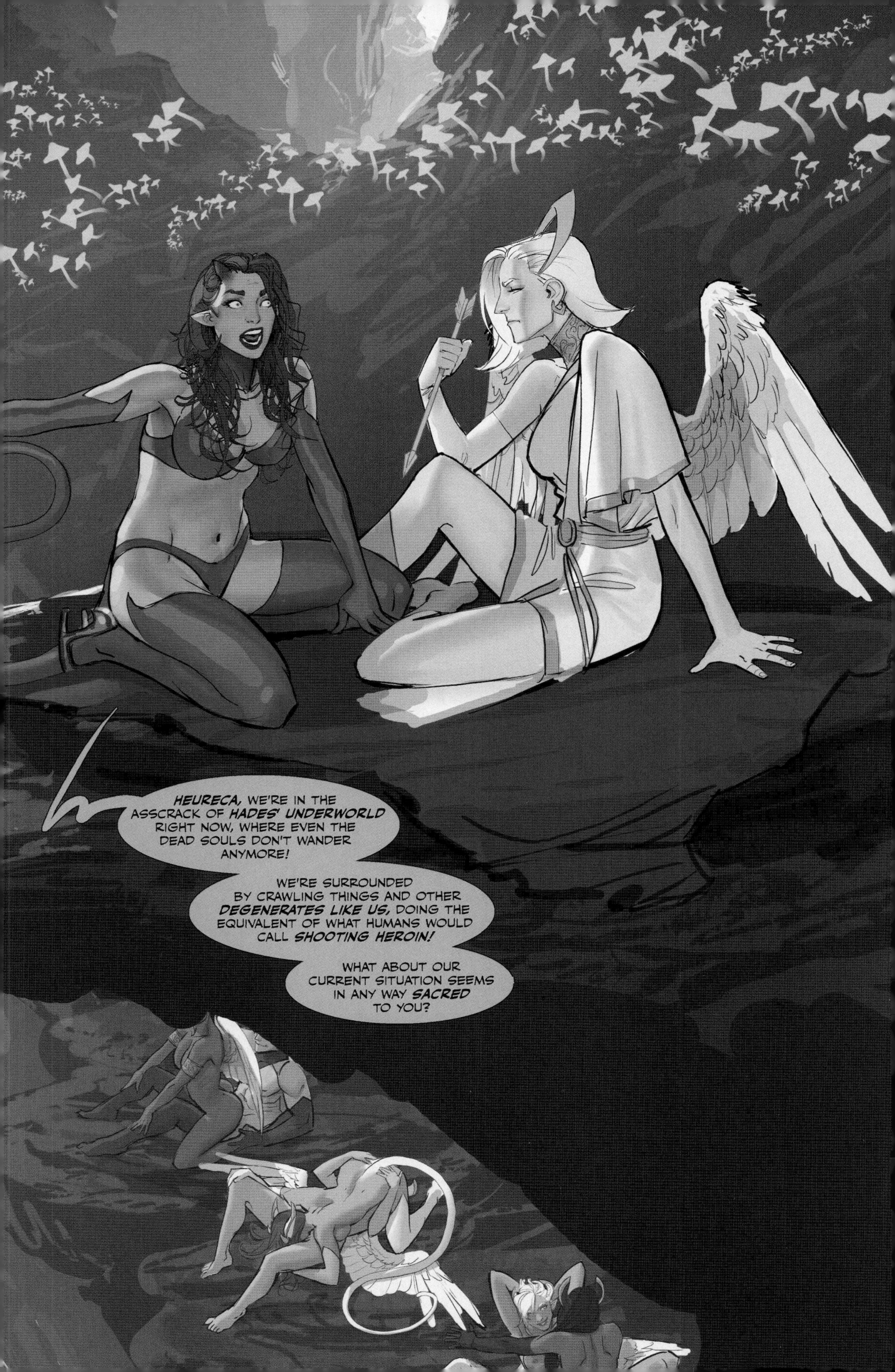
HEURECA, WE'RE IN THE ASSCRACK OF HADES' UNDERWORLD RIGHT NOW, WHERE EVEN THE DEAD SOULS DON'T WANDER ANYMORE!
WE'RE SURROUNDED BY CRAWLING THINGS AND OTHER DEGENERATES LIKE US, DOING THE EQUIVALENT OF WHAT HUMANS WOULD CALL SHOOTING HEROIN!
WHAT ABOUT OUR CURRENT SITUATION SEEMS IN ANY WAY SACRED TO YOU?

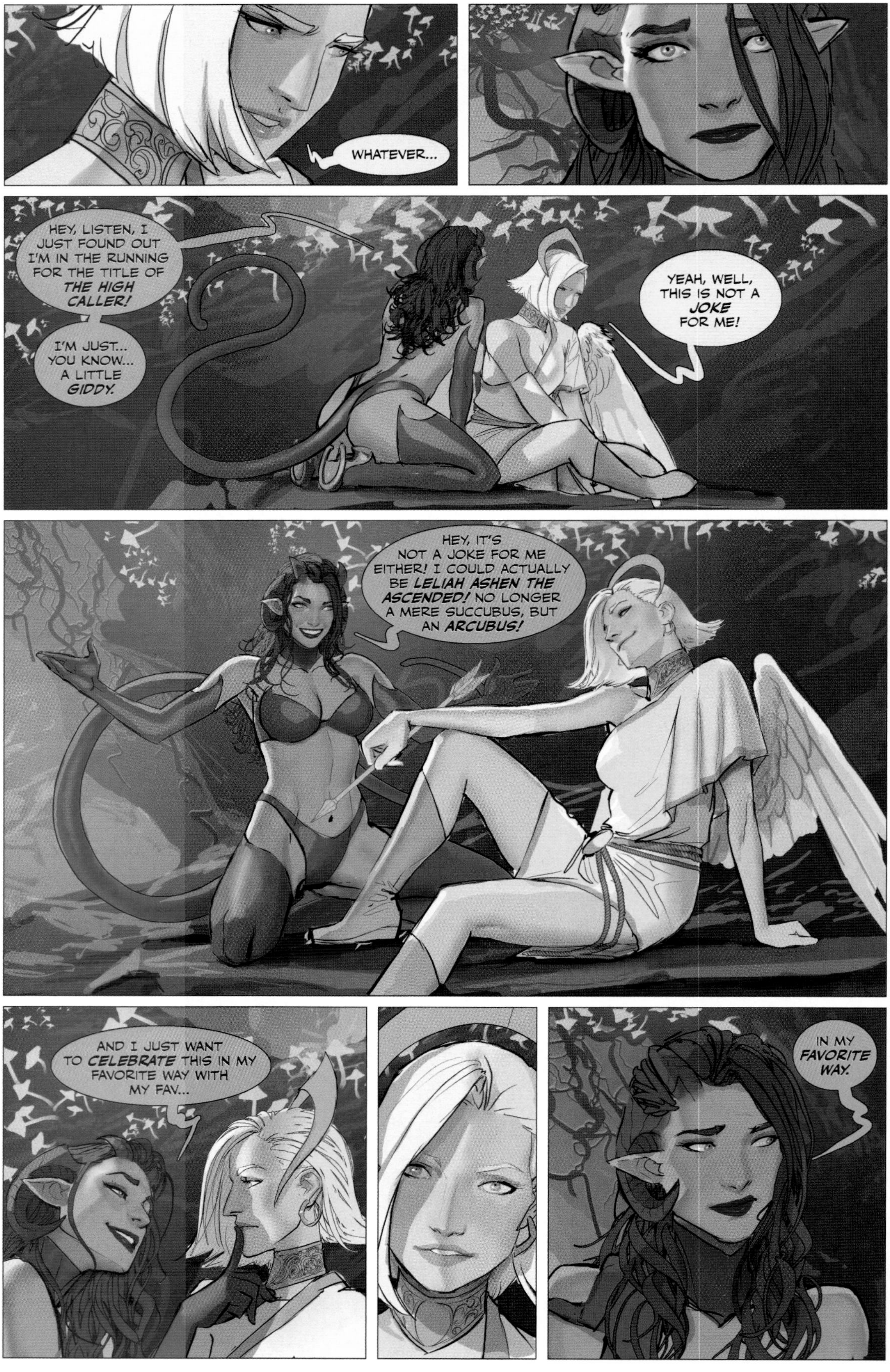
WHATEVER...
HEY, LISTEN, I JUST FOUND OUT I'M IN THE RUNNING FOR THE TITLE OF *THE HIGH CALLER!*
I'M JUST... YOU KNOW... A LITTLE *GIDDY.*
YEAH, WELL, THIS IS NOT A *JOKE* FOR ME!
HEY, IT'S NOT A JOKE FOR ME EITHER! I COULD ACTUALLY BE *LELIAH ASHEN THE ASCENDED!* NO LONGER A MERE SUCCUBUS, BUT AN *ARCUBUS!*
AND I JUST WANT TO *CELEBRATE* THIS IN MY FAVORITE WAY WITH MY FAV...
IN MY *FAVORITE WAY.*

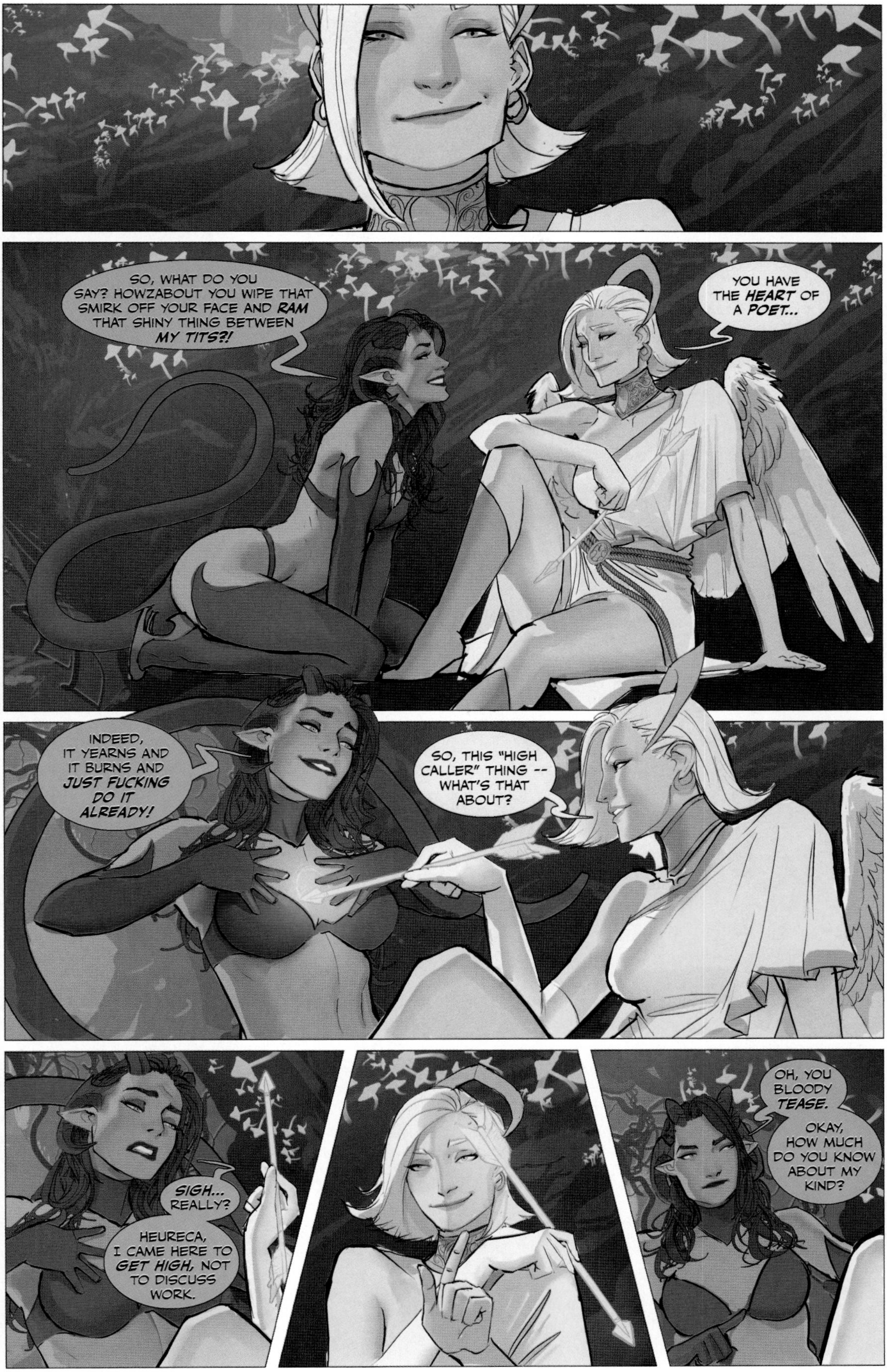

SO, WHAT DO YOU SAY? HOWZABOUT YOU WIPE THAT SMIRK OFF YOUR FACE AND *RAM* THAT SHINY THING BETWEEN *MY TITS?!*
YOU HAVE THE *HEART* OF A *POET...*
INDEED, IT YEARNS AND IT BURNS AND *JUST FUCKING DO IT ALREADY!*
SO, THIS "HIGH CALLER" THING -- WHAT'S THAT ABOUT?
SIGH... REALLY?
HEURECA, I CAME HERE TO *GET HIGH,* NOT TO DISCUSS WORK.
OH, YOU BLOODY *TEASE.*
OKAY, HOW MUCH DO YOU KNOW ABOUT MY KIND?

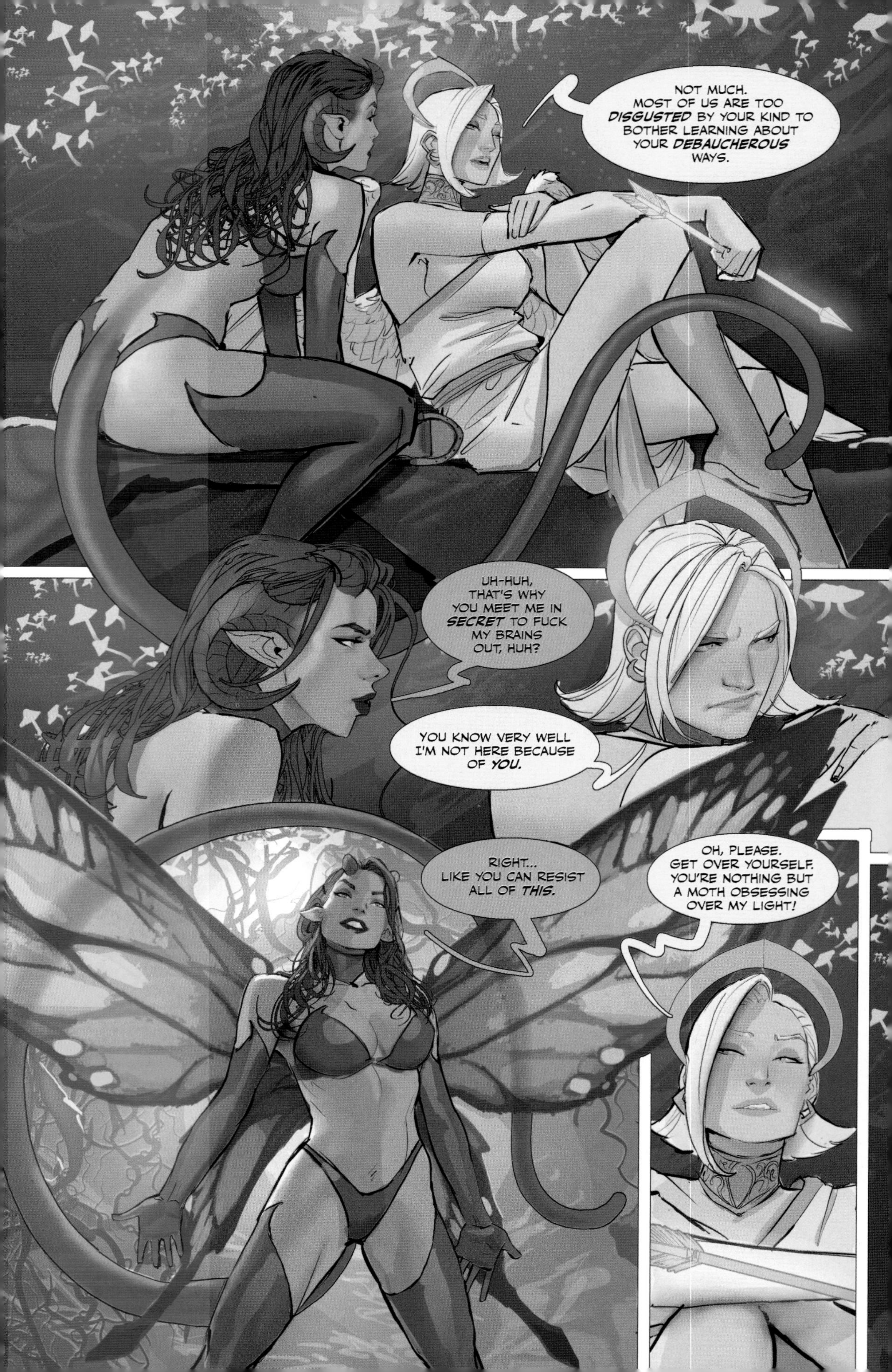
NOT MUCH. MOST OF US ARE TOO DISGUSTED BY YOUR KIND TO BOTHER LEARNING ABOUT YOUR DEBAUCHEROUS WAYS.
UH-HUH, THAT'S WHY YOU MEET ME IN SECRET TO FUCK MY BRAINS OUT, HUH?
YOU KNOW VERY WELL I'M NOT HERE BECAUSE OF YOU.
RIGHT... LIKE YOU CAN RESIST ALL OF THIS.
OH, PLEASE. GET OVER YOURSELF. YOU'RE NOTHING BUT A MOTH OBSESSING OVER MY LIGHT!

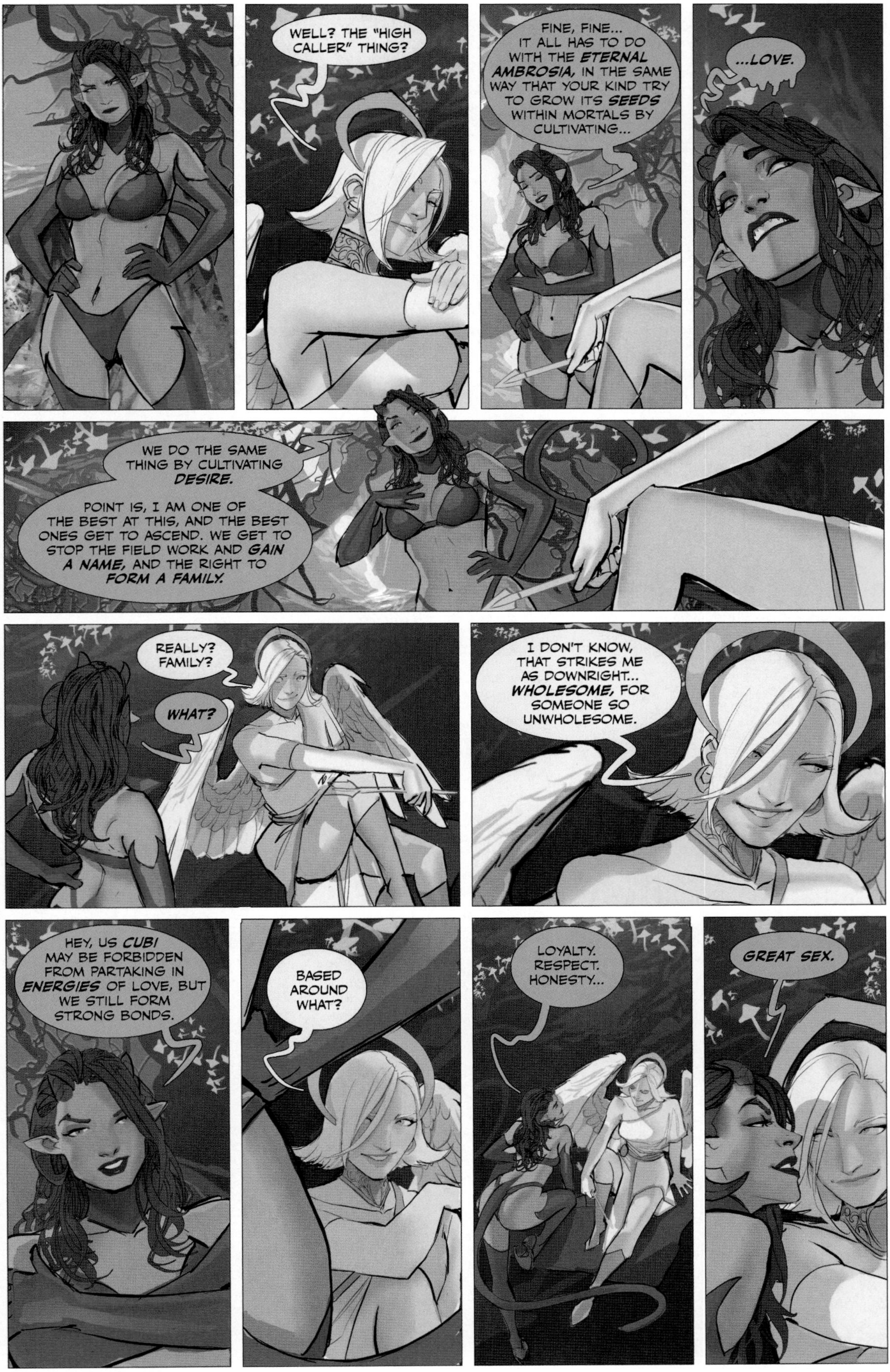
WELL? THE "HIGH CALLER" THING?
FINE, FINE... IT ALL HAS TO DO WITH THE ETERNAL AMBROSIA, IN THE SAME WAY THAT YOUR KIND TRY TO GROW ITS SEEDS WITHIN MORTALS BY CULTIVATING...
...LOVE.
WE DO THE SAME THING BY CULTIVATING DESIRE.
POINT IS, I AM ONE OF THE BEST AT THIS, AND THE BEST ONES GET TO ASCEND. WE GET TO STOP THE FIELD WORK AND GAIN A NAME, AND THE RIGHT TO FORM A FAMILY.
REALLY? FAMILY?
WHAT?
I DON'T KNOW, THAT STRIKES ME AS DOWNRIGHT... WHOLESOME, FOR SOMEONE SO UNWHOLESOME.
HEY, US CUBI MAY BE FORBIDDEN FROM PARTAKING IN ENERGIES OF LOVE, BUT WE STILL FORM STRONG BONDS.
BASED AROUND WHAT?
LOYALTY. RESPECT. HONESTY...
GREAT SEX.

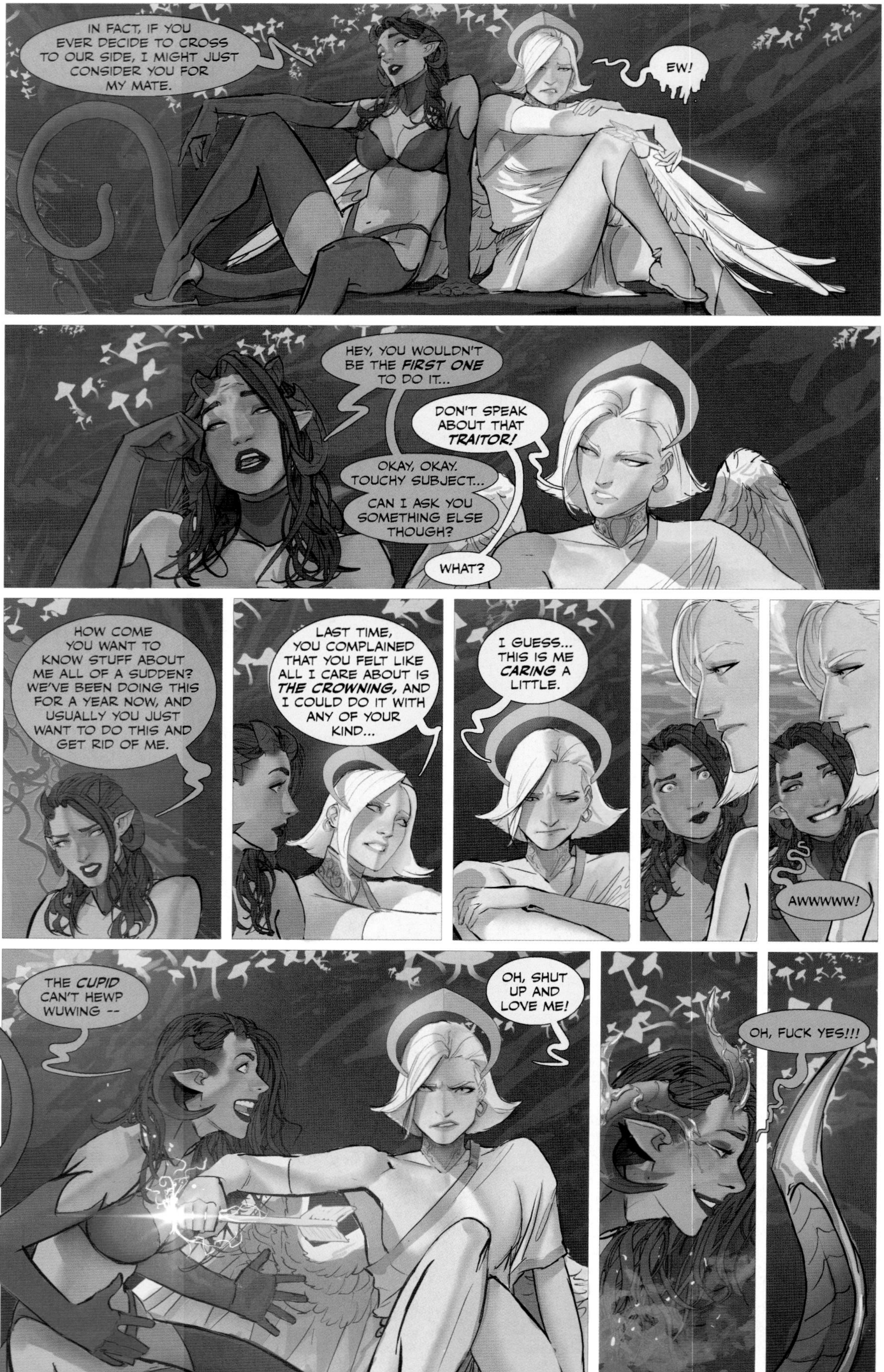
IN FACT, IF YOU EVER DECIDE TO CROSS TO OUR SIDE, I MIGHT JUST CONSIDER YOU FOR MY MATE.
EW!
HEY, YOU WOULDN'T BE THE *FIRST ONE* TO DO IT...
DON'T SPEAK ABOUT THAT *TRAITOR!*
OKAY, OKAY. TOUCHY SUBJECT...
CAN I ASK YOU SOMETHING ELSE THOUGH?
WHAT?
HOW COME YOU WANT TO KNOW STUFF ABOUT ME ALL OF A SUDDEN? WE'VE BEEN DOING THIS FOR A YEAR NOW, AND USUALLY YOU JUST WANT TO DO THIS AND GET RID OF ME.
LAST TIME, YOU COMPLAINED THAT YOU FELT LIKE ALL I CARE ABOUT IS *THE CROWNING,* AND I COULD DO IT WITH ANY OF YOUR KIND...
I GUESS... THIS IS ME *CARING* A LITTLE.
AWWWWW!
THE *CUPID* CAN'T HEWP WUWING --
OH, SHUT UP AND LOVE ME!
OH, FUCK YES!!!

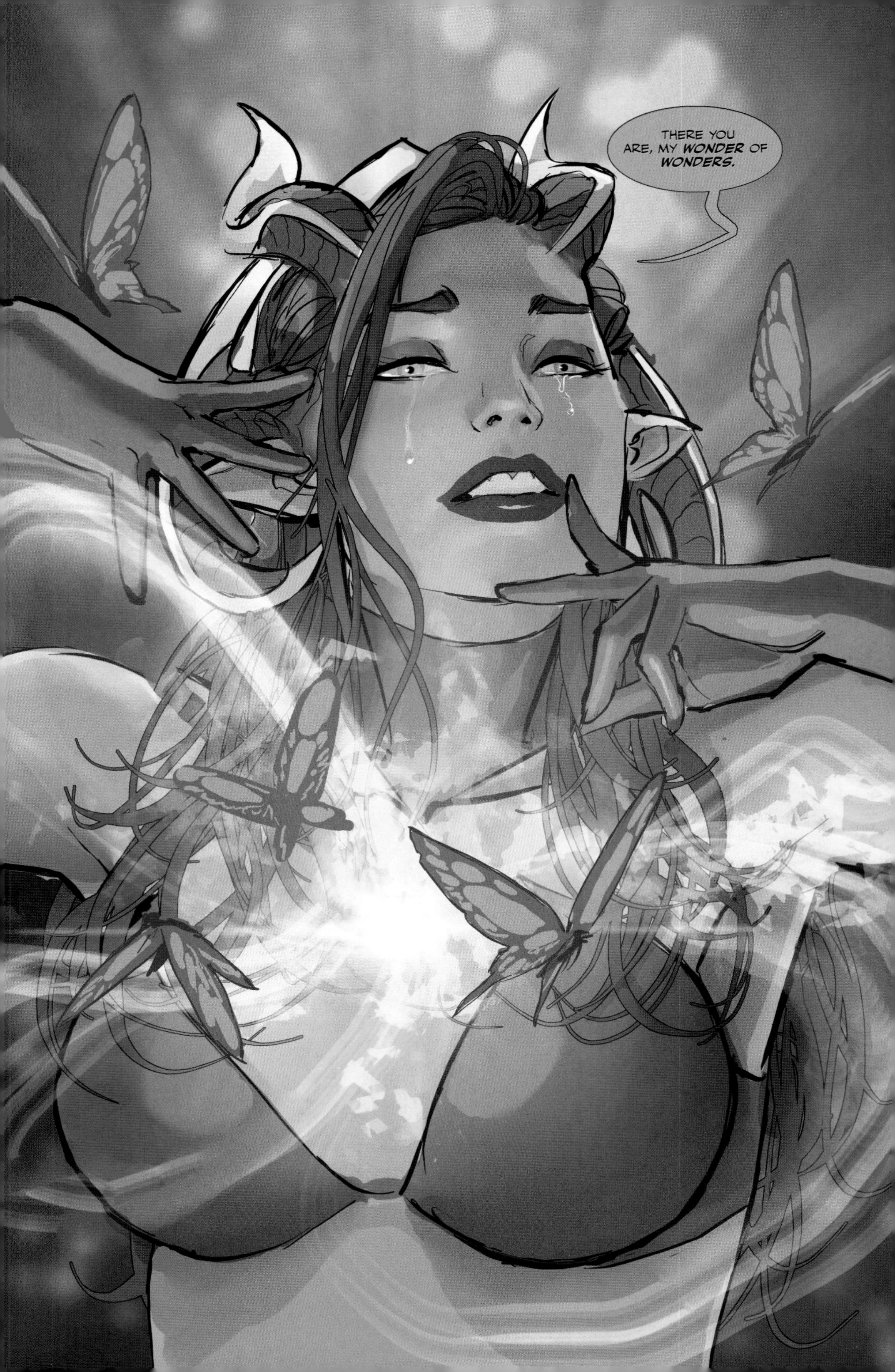
THERE YOU ARE, MY WONDER OF WONDERS.

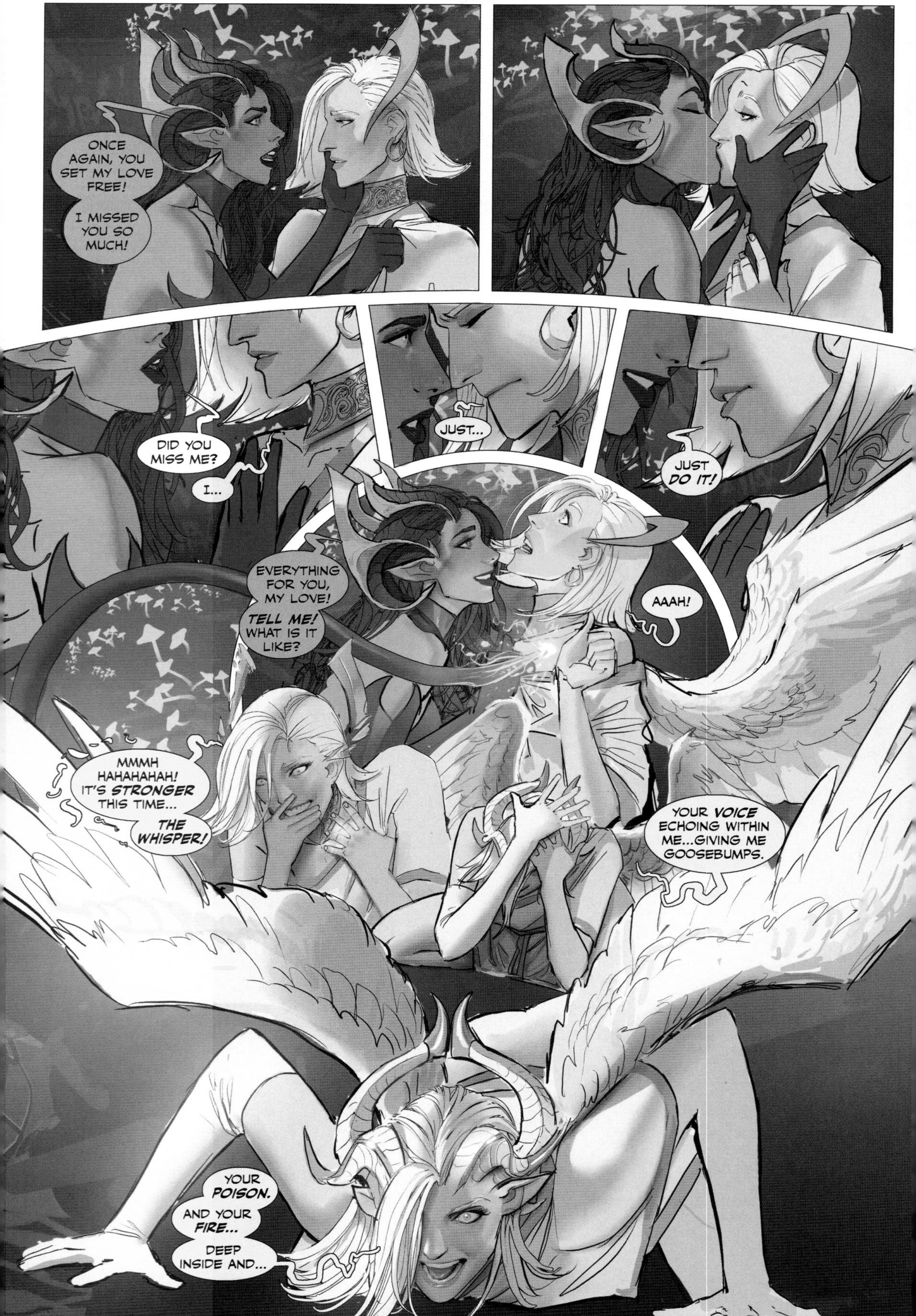
ONCE AGAIN, YOU SET MY LOVE FREE!
I MISSED YOU SO MUCH!
DID YOU MISS ME?
I...
JUST...
JUST DO IT!
EVERYTHING FOR YOU, MY LOVE!
TELL ME! WHAT IS IT LIKE?
AAAH!
MMMH HAHAHAHAH! IT'S STRONGER THIS TIME...
THE WHISPER!
YOUR VOICE ECHOING WITHIN ME...GIVING ME GOOSEBUMPS.
YOUR POISON.
AND YOUR FIRE...
DEEP INSIDE AND...

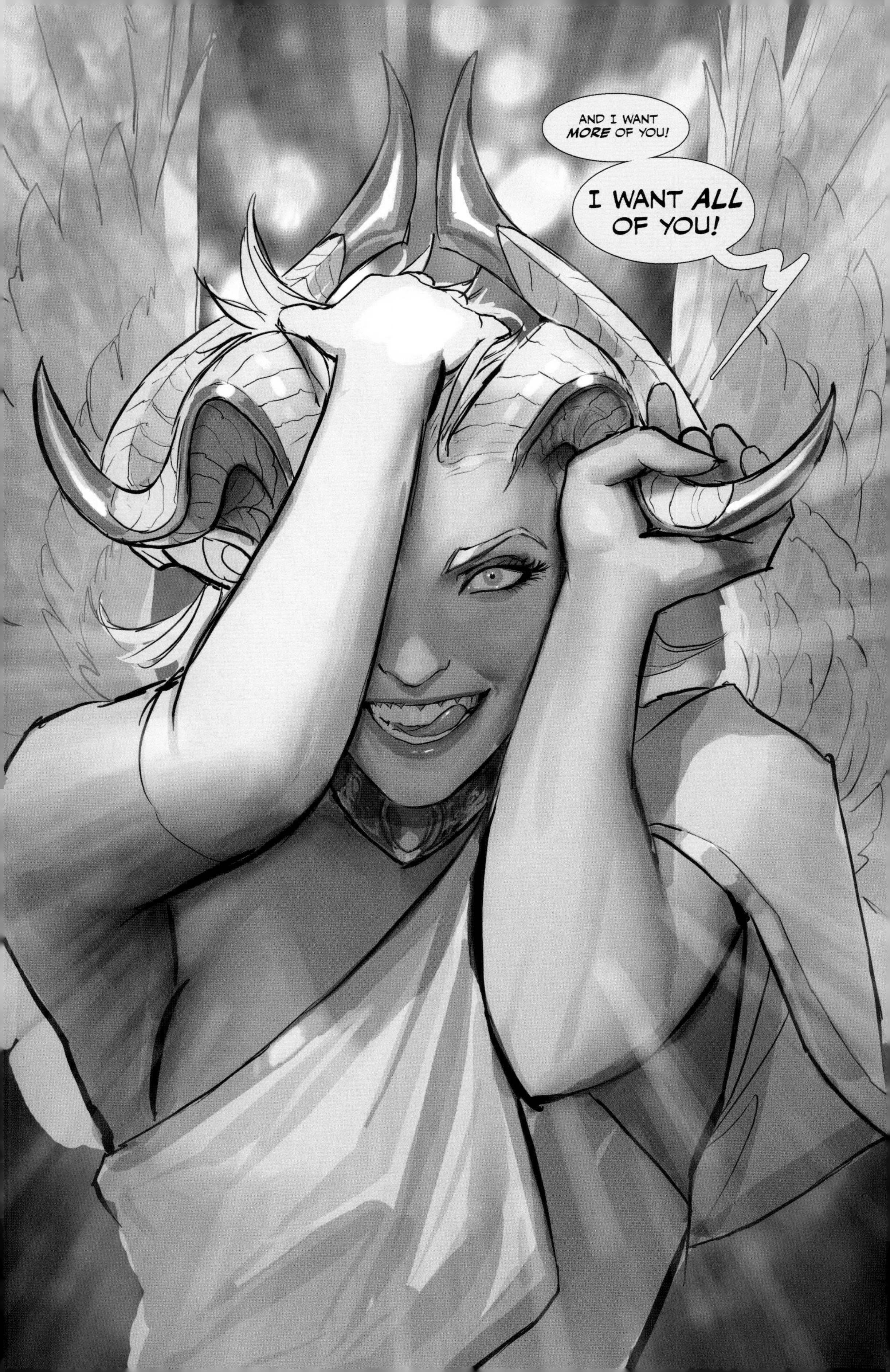
AND I WANT MORE OF YOU!
I WANT ALL OF YOU!

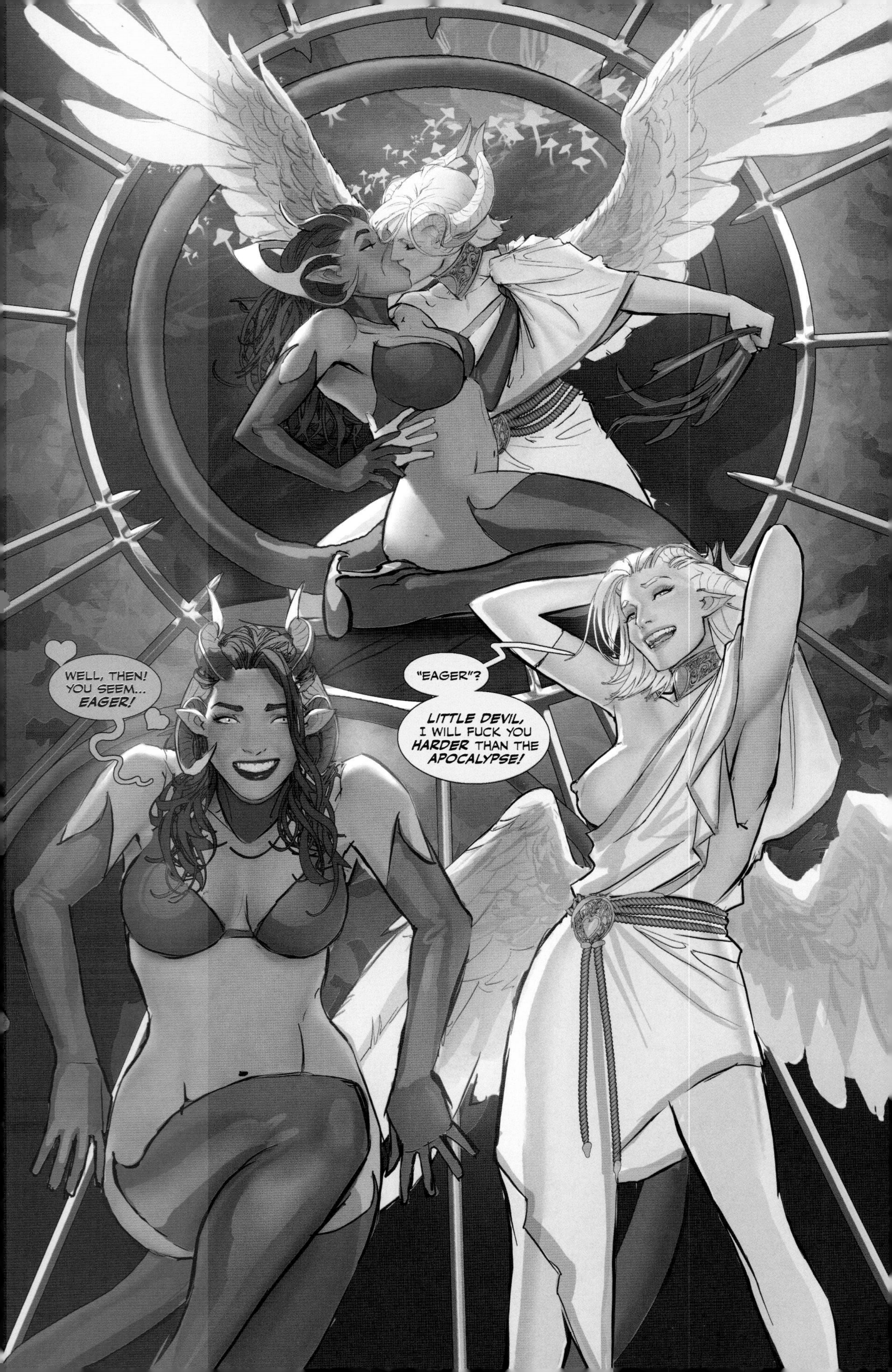
WELL, THEN! YOU SEEM... EAGER!
"EAGER"?
LITTLE DEVIL, I WILL FUCK YOU HARDER THAN THE APOCALYPSE!

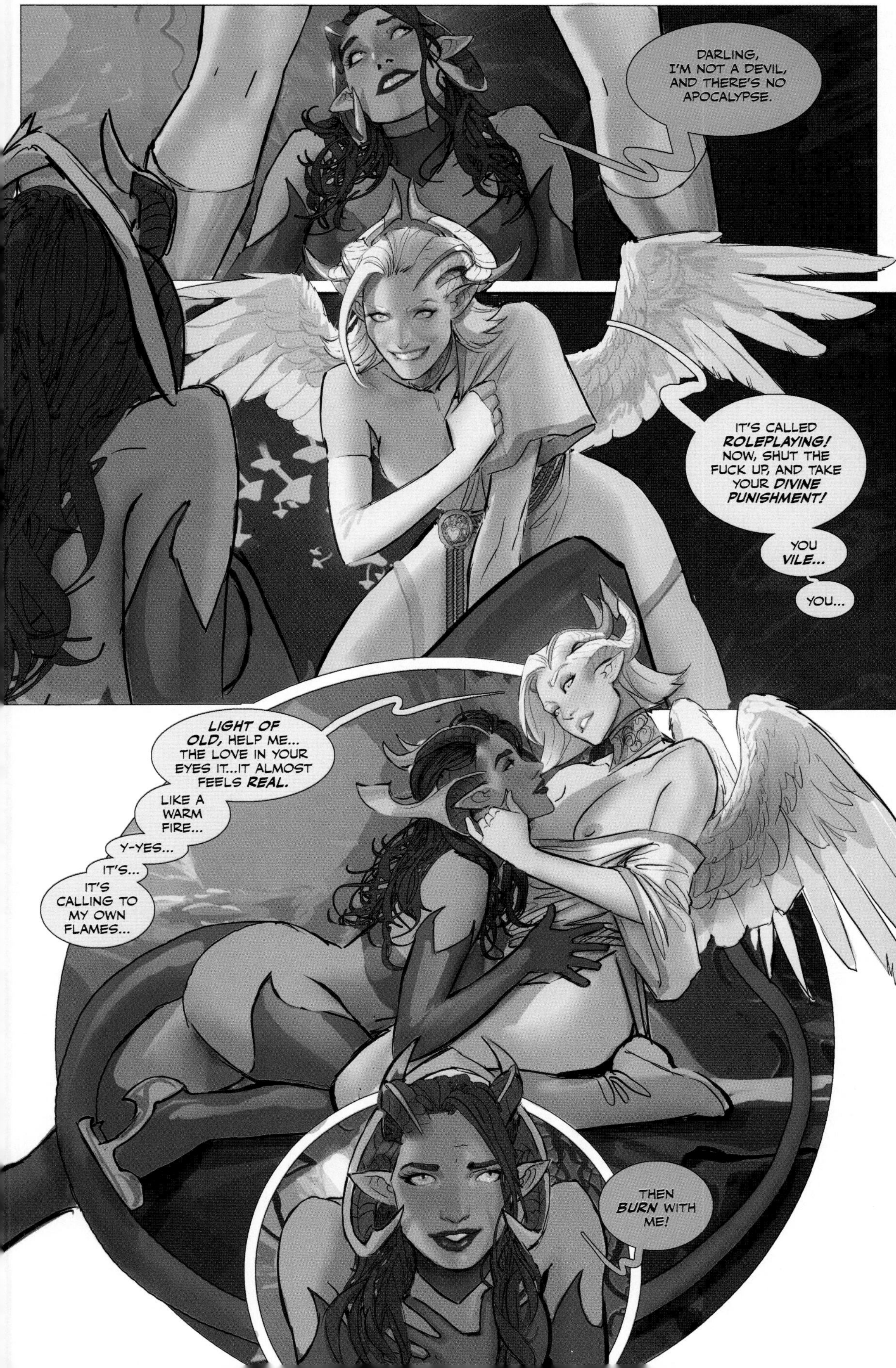
DARLING, I'M NOT A DEVIL, AND THERE'S NO APOCALYPSE.
IT'S CALLED *ROLEPLAYING!* NOW, SHUT THE FUCK UP, AND TAKE YOUR *DIVINE PUNISHMENT!*
YOU *VILE...*
YOU...
LIGHT OF OLD, HELP ME... THE LOVE IN YOUR EYES IT...IT ALMOST FEELS *REAL.*
LIKE A WARM FIRE...
Y-YES...
IT'S...
IT'S CALLING TO MY OWN FLAMES...
THEN *BURN* WITH ME!

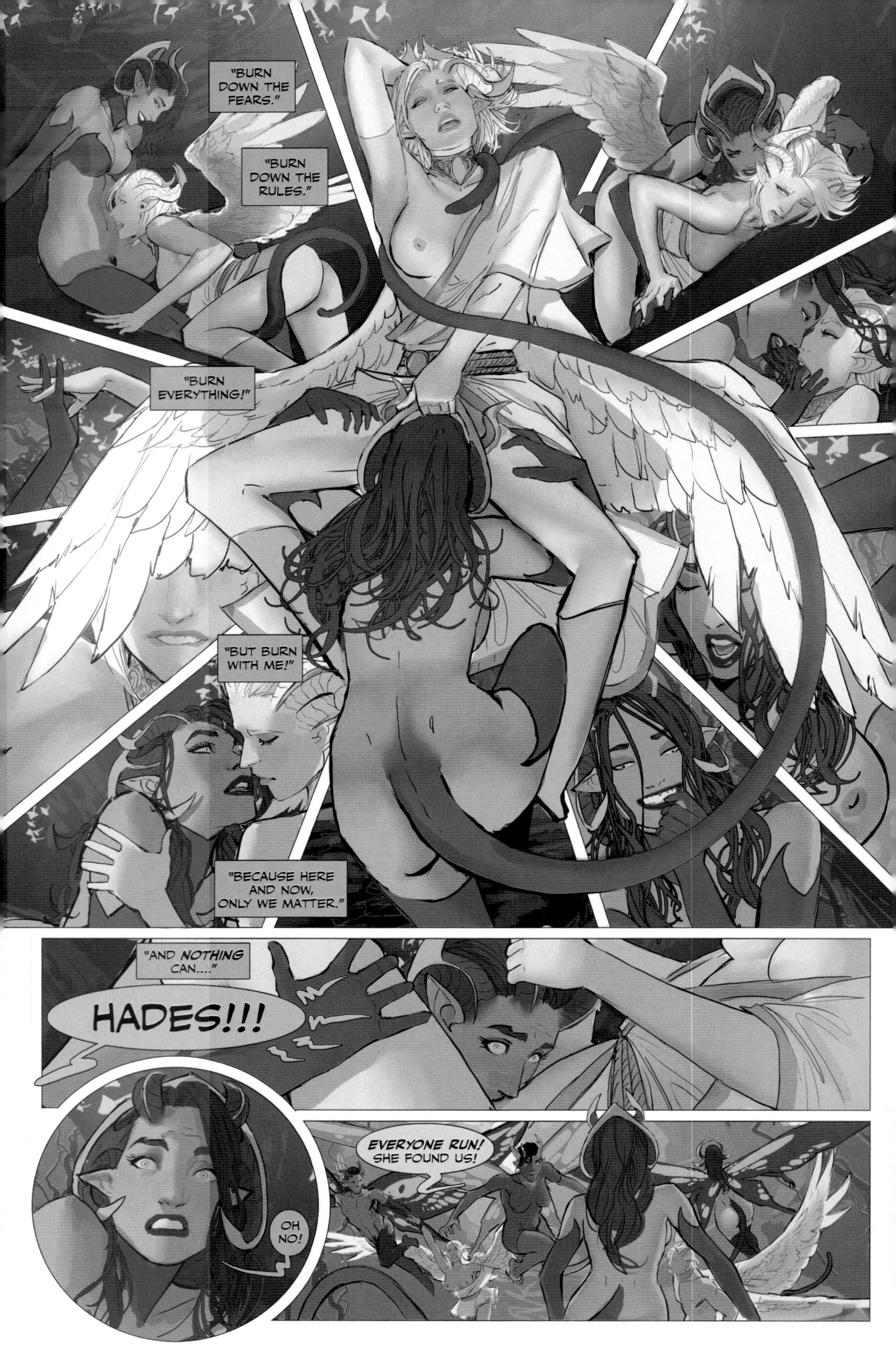
"BURN DOWN THE FEARS."
"BURN DOWN THE RULES."
"BURN EVERYTHING!"
"BUT BURN WITH ME!"
"BECAUSE HERE AND NOW, ONLY WE MATTER."
"AND *NOTHING* CAN...."
HADES!!!
OH NO!
EVERYONE RUN! SHE FOUND US!

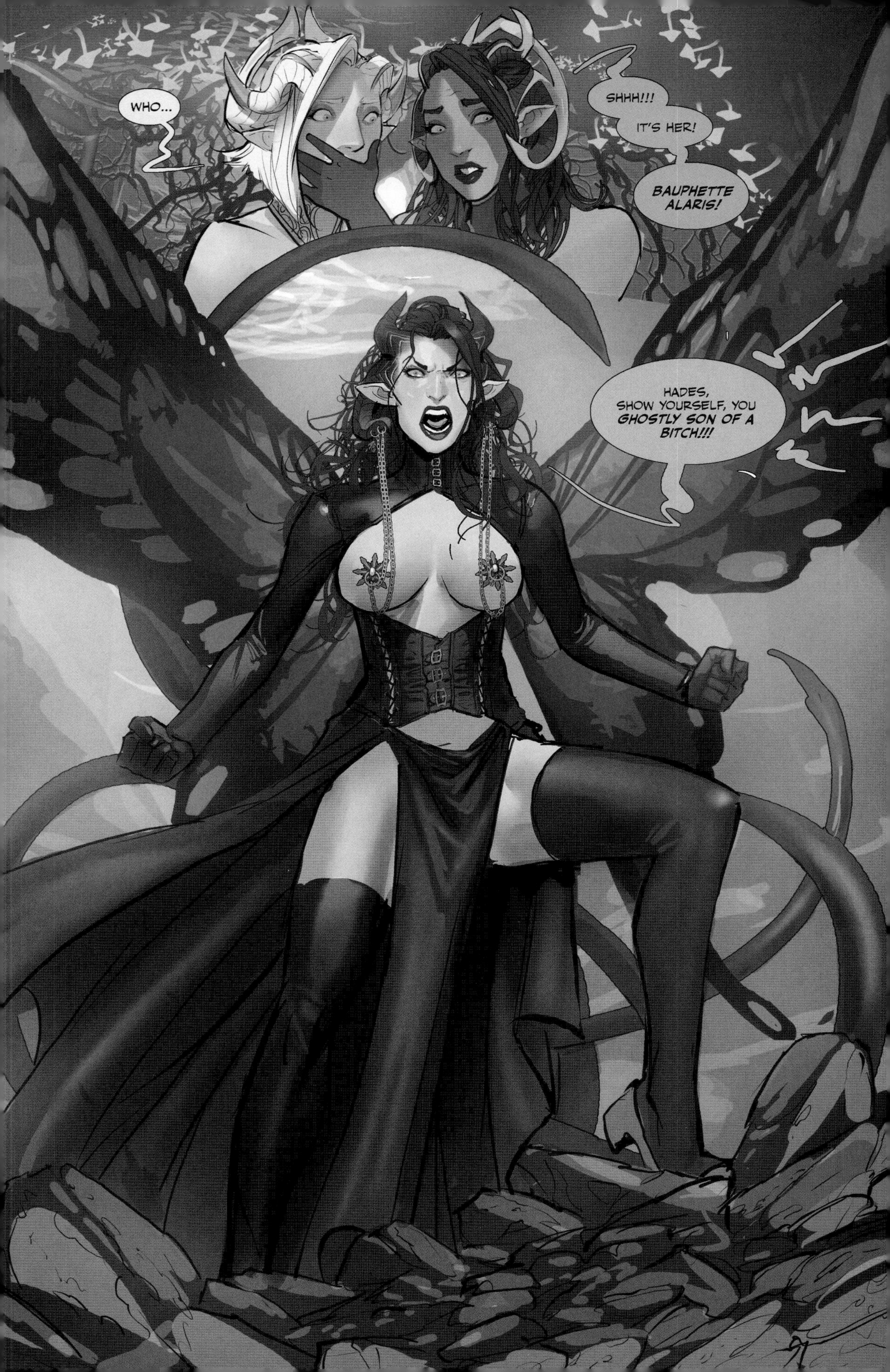
WHO...
SHHH!!!
IT'S HER!
BAUPHETTE ALARIS!
HADES, SHOW YOURSELF, YOU GHOSTLY SON OF A BITCH!!!

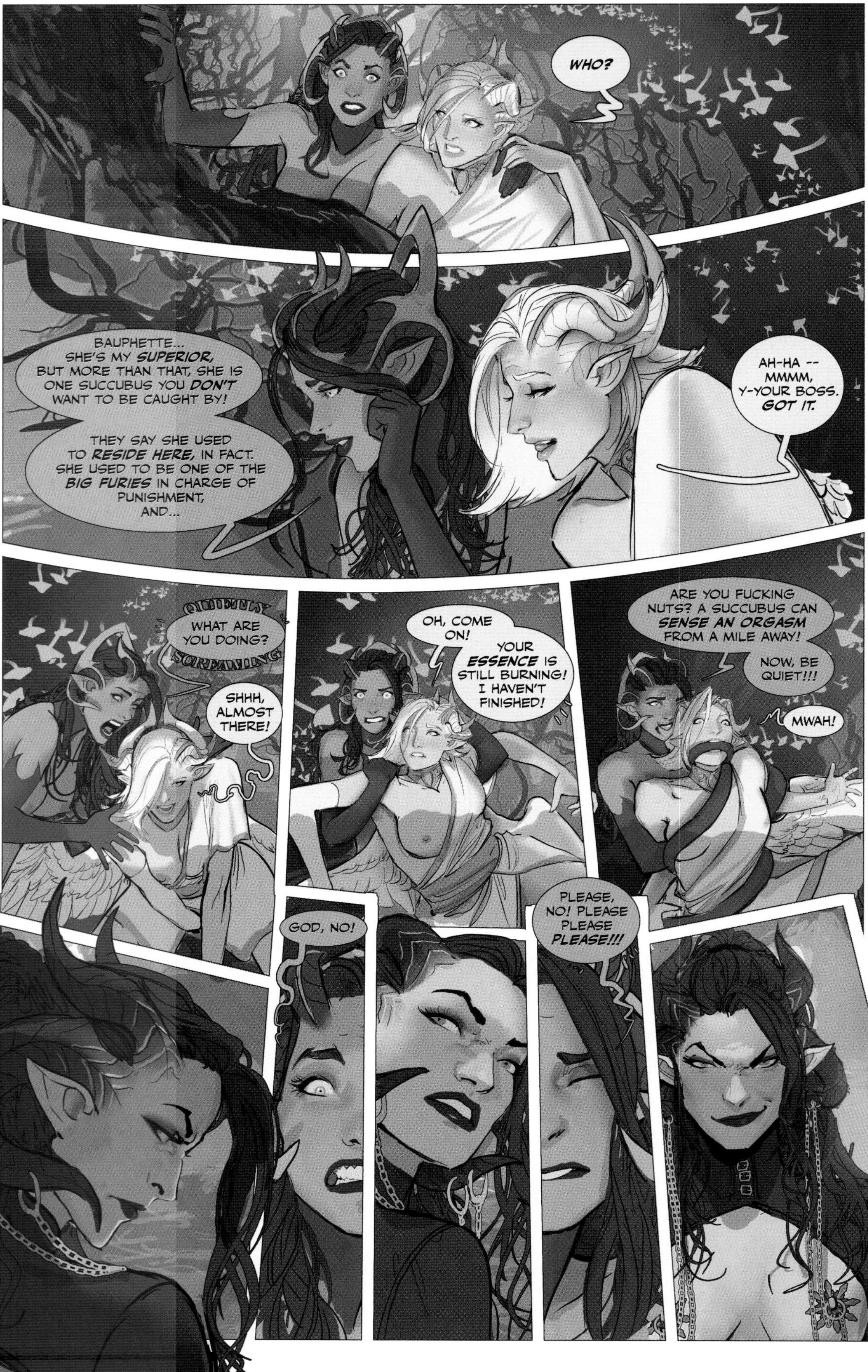
WHO?
BAUPHETTE... SHE'S MY SUPERIOR, BUT MORE THAN THAT, SHE IS ONE SUCCUBUS YOU DON'T WANT TO BE CAUGHT BY!
THEY SAY SHE USED TO RESIDE HERE, IN FACT. SHE USED TO BE ONE OF THE BIG FURIES IN CHARGE OF PUNISHMENT, AND...
AH-HA -- MMMM, Y-YOUR BOSS. GOT IT.
QUIETLY
WHAT ARE YOU DOING?
SCREAMING
SHHH, ALMOST THERE!
OH, COME ON!
YOUR ESSENCE IS STILL BURNING! I HAVEN'T FINISHED!
ARE YOU FUCKING NUTS? A SUCCUBUS CAN SENSE AN ORGASM FROM A MILE AWAY!
NOW, BE QUIET!!!
MWAH!
GOD, NO!
PLEASE, NO! PLEASE PLEASE PLEASE!!!

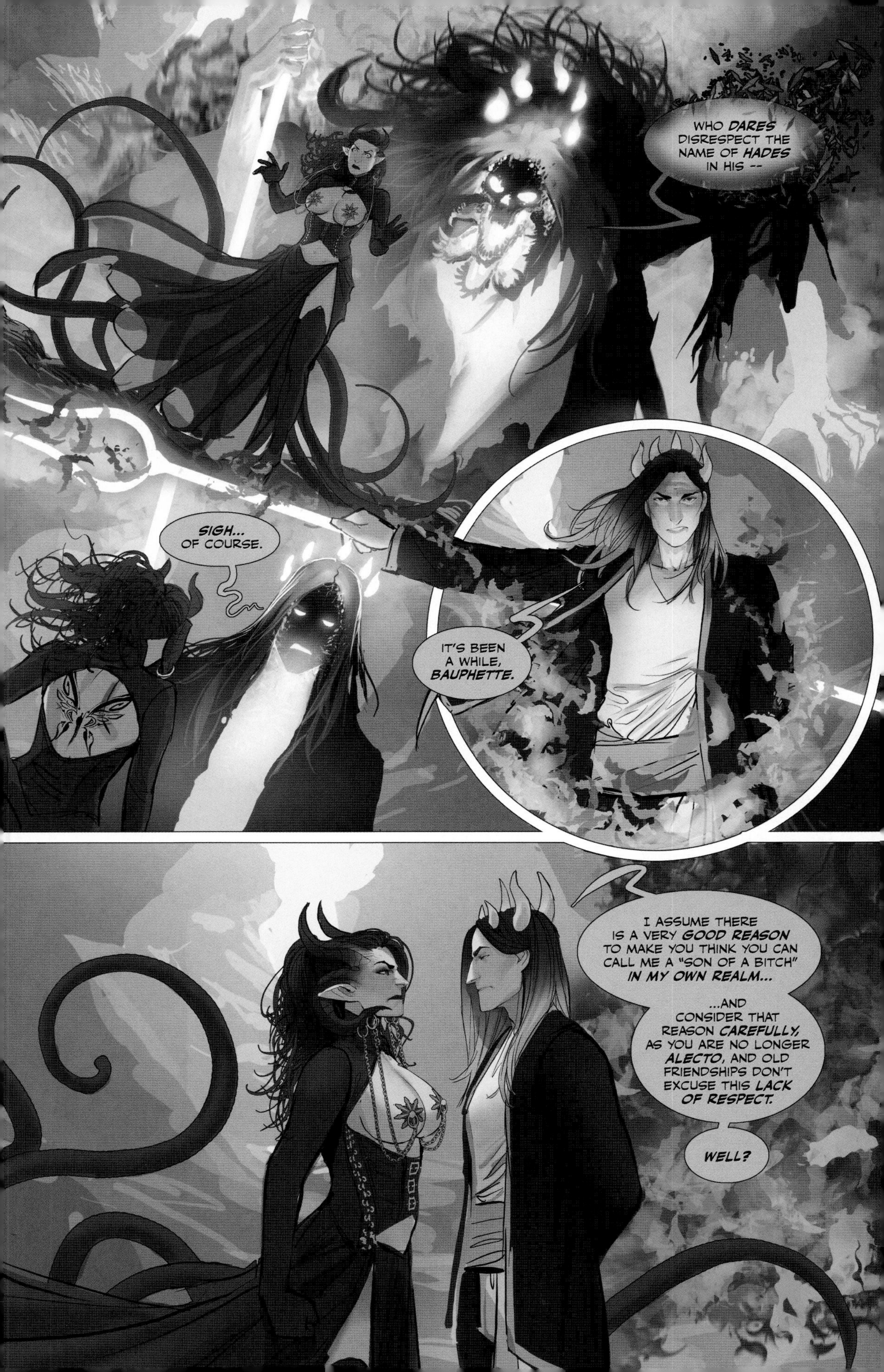
WHO DARES DISRESPECT THE NAME OF HADES IN HIS --
SIGH... OF COURSE.
IT'S BEEN A WHILE, BAUPHETTE.
I ASSUME THERE IS A VERY GOOD REASON TO MAKE YOU THINK YOU CAN CALL ME A "SON OF A BITCH" IN MY OWN REALM...
...AND CONSIDER THAT REASON CAREFULLY, AS YOU ARE NO LONGER ALECTO, AND OLD FRIENDSHIPS DON'T EXCUSE THIS LACK OF RESPECT.
WELL?

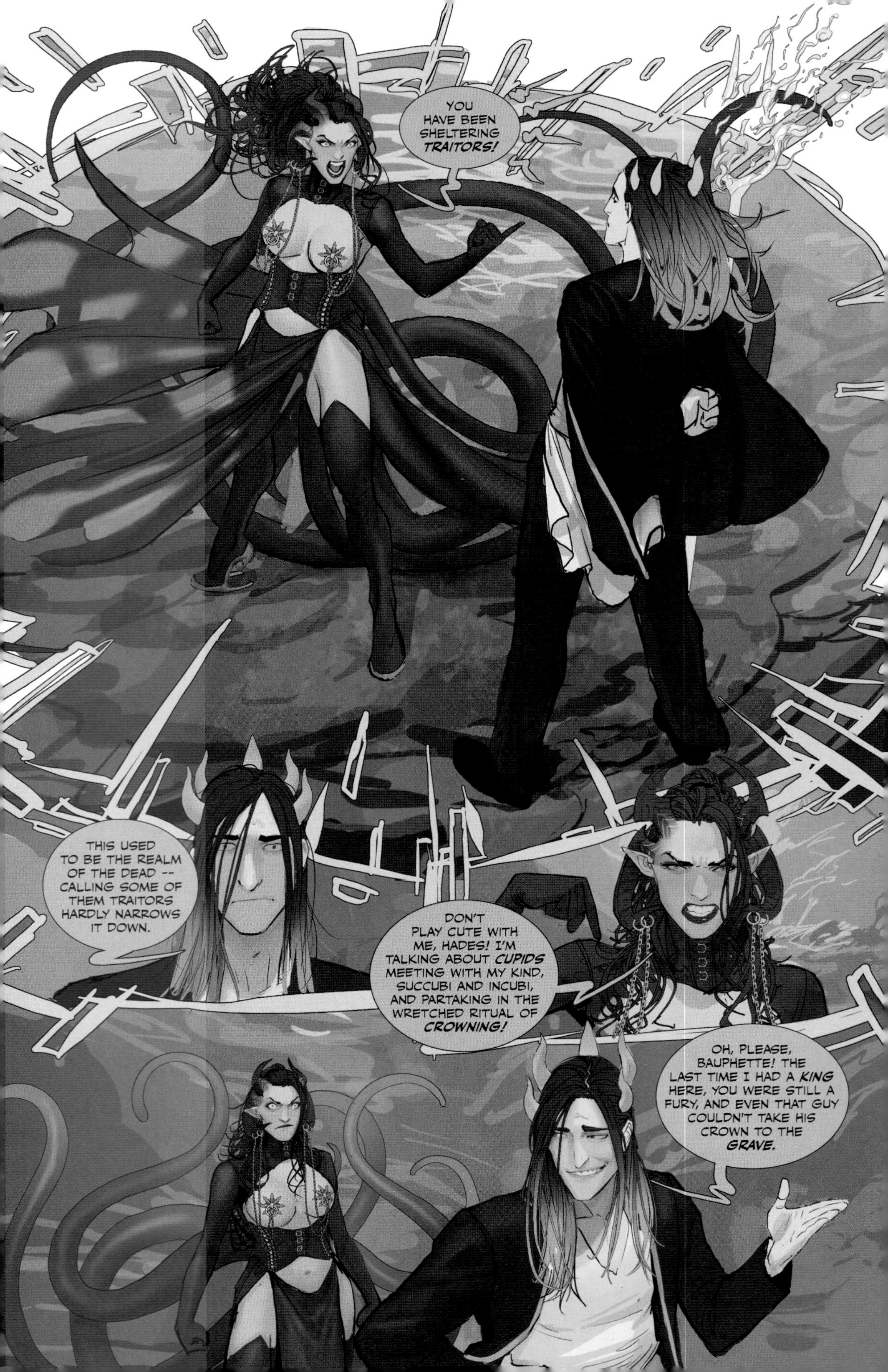
YOU HAVE BEEN SHELTERING *TRAITORS!*
THIS USED TO BE THE REALM OF THE DEAD -- CALLING SOME OF THEM TRAITORS HARDLY NARROWS IT DOWN.
DON'T PLAY CUTE WITH ME, HADES! I'M TALKING ABOUT *CUPIDS* MEETING WITH MY KIND, SUCCUBI AND INCUBI, AND PARTAKING IN THE WRETCHED RITUAL OF *CROWNING!*
OH, PLEASE, BAUPHETTE! THE LAST TIME I HAD A *KING* HERE, YOU WERE STILL A FURY, AND EVEN THAT GUY COULDN'T TAKE HIS CROWN TO THE *GRAVE.*

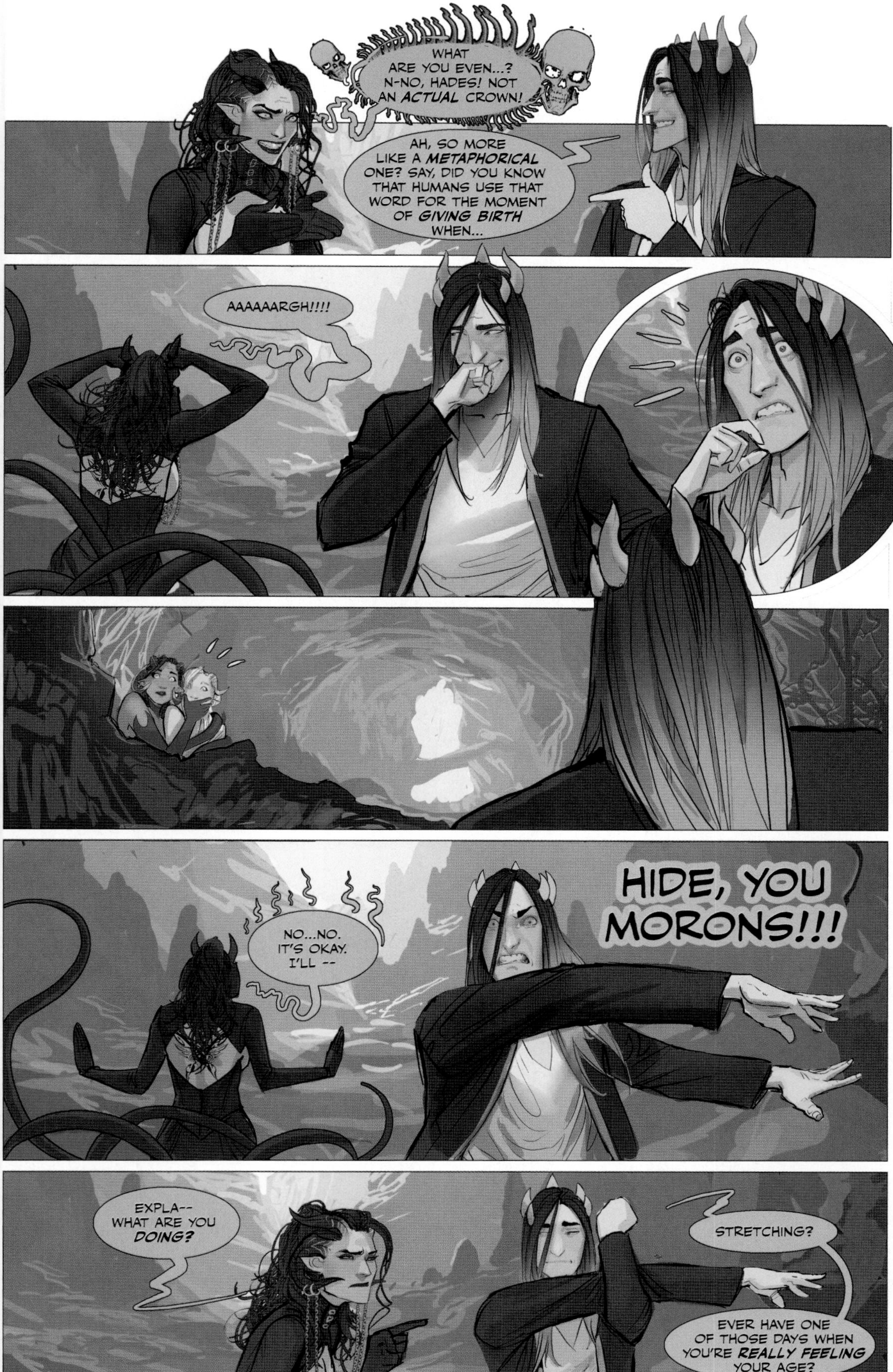
WHAT ARE YOU EVEN...? N-NO, HADES! NOT AN ACTUAL CROWN!
AH, SO MORE LIKE A METAPHORICAL ONE? SAY, DID YOU KNOW THAT HUMANS USE THAT WORD FOR THE MOMENT OF GIVING BIRTH WHEN...
AAAAAARGH!!!!
NO...NO. IT'S OKAY. I'LL --
HIDE, YOU MORONS!!!
EXPLA-- WHAT ARE YOU DOING?
STRETCHING?
EVER HAVE ONE OF THOSE DAYS WHEN YOU'RE REALLY FEELING YOUR AGE?

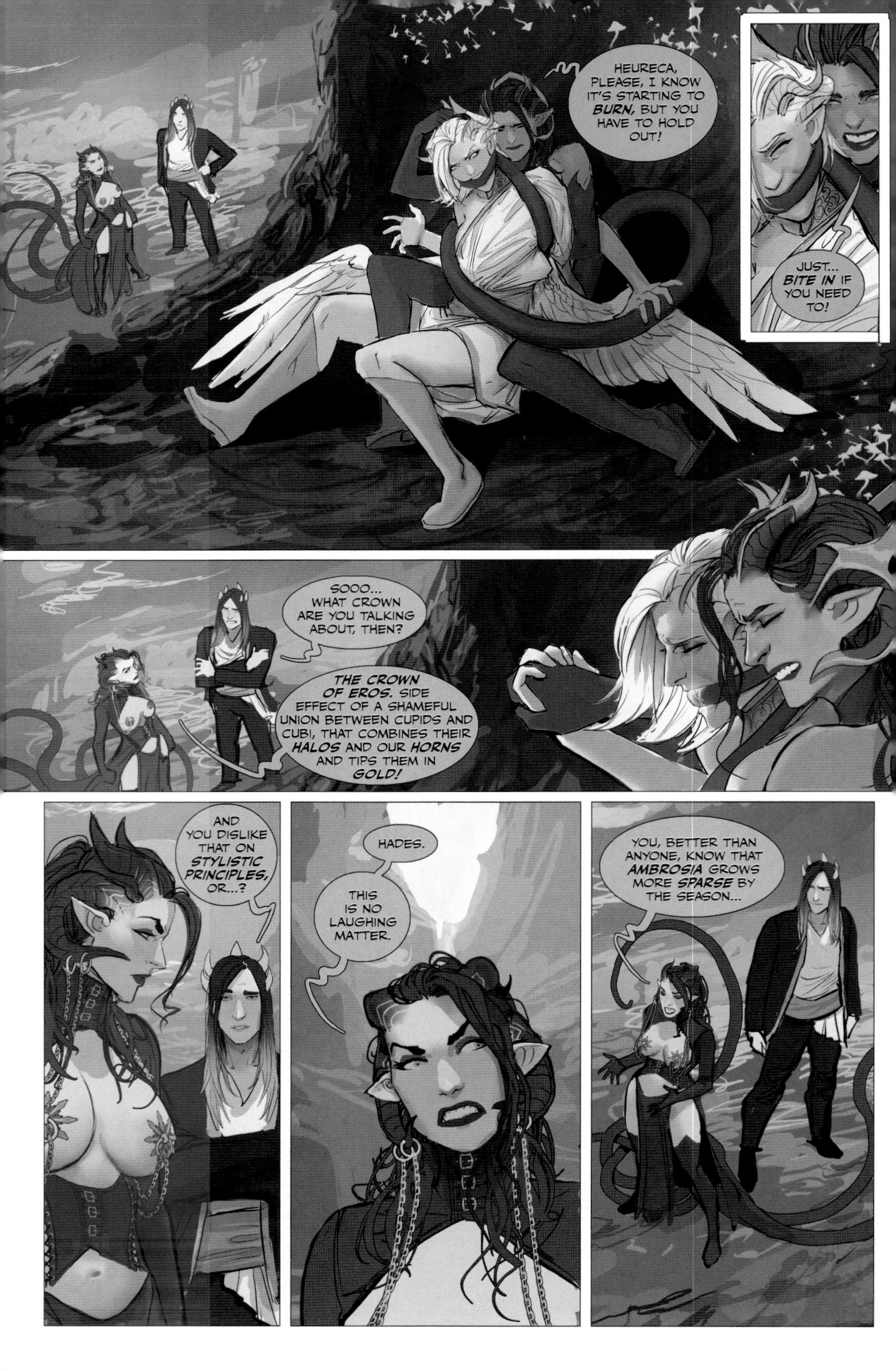
HEURECA, PLEASE, I KNOW IT'S STARTING TO BURN, BUT YOU HAVE TO HOLD OUT!
JUST... BITE IN IF YOU NEED TO!
SOOO... WHAT CROWN ARE YOU TALKING ABOUT, THEN?
THE CROWN OF EROS. SIDE EFFECT OF A SHAMEFUL UNION BETWEEN CUPIDS AND CUBI, THAT COMBINES THEIR HALOS AND OUR HORNS AND TIPS THEM IN GOLD!
AND YOU DISLIKE THAT ON STYLISTIC PRINCIPLES, OR...?
HADES.
THIS IS NO LAUGHING MATTER.
YOU, BETTER THAN ANYONE, KNOW THAT AMBROSIA GROWS MORE SPARSE BY THE SEASON...

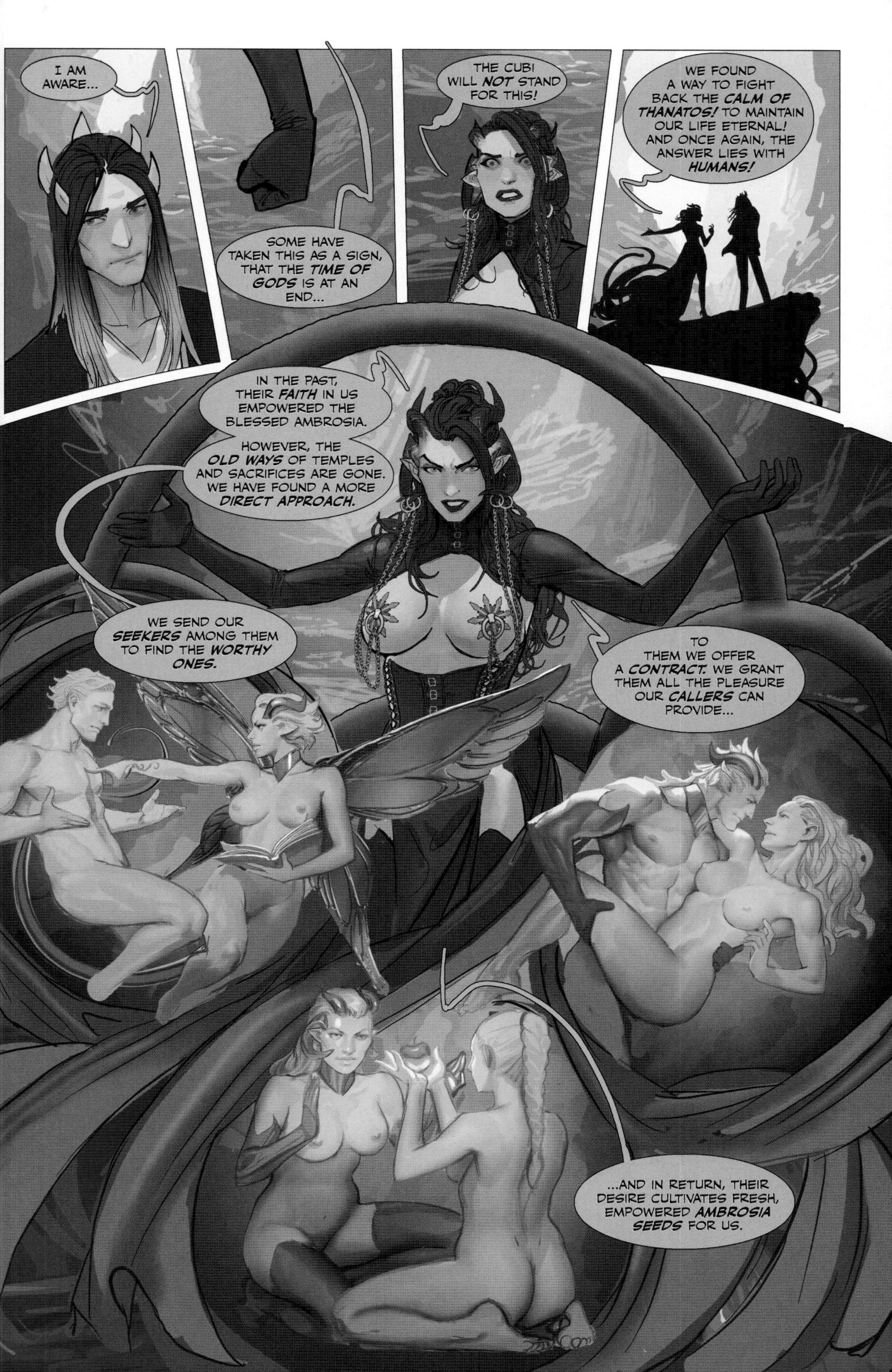
I AM AWARE...
SOME HAVE TAKEN THIS AS A SIGN, THAT THE ***TIME OF GODS*** IS AT AN END...
THE CUBI WILL ***NOT*** STAND FOR THIS!
WE FOUND A WAY TO FIGHT BACK THE ***CALM OF THANATOS!*** TO MAINTAIN OUR LIFE ETERNAL! AND ONCE AGAIN, THE ANSWER LIES WITH ***HUMANS!***
IN THE PAST, THEIR ***FAITH*** IN US EMPOWERED THE BLESSED AMBROSIA.
HOWEVER, THE ***OLD WAYS*** OF TEMPLES AND SACRIFICES ARE GONE. WE HAVE FOUND A MORE ***DIRECT APPROACH.***
WE SEND OUR ***SEEKERS*** AMONG THEM TO FIND THE ***WORTHY ONES.***
TO THEM WE OFFER A ***CONTRACT.*** WE GRANT THEM ALL THE PLEASURE OUR ***CALLERS*** CAN PROVIDE...
...AND IN RETURN, THEIR DESIRE CULTIVATES FRESH, EMPOWERED ***AMBROSIA SEEDS*** FOR US.

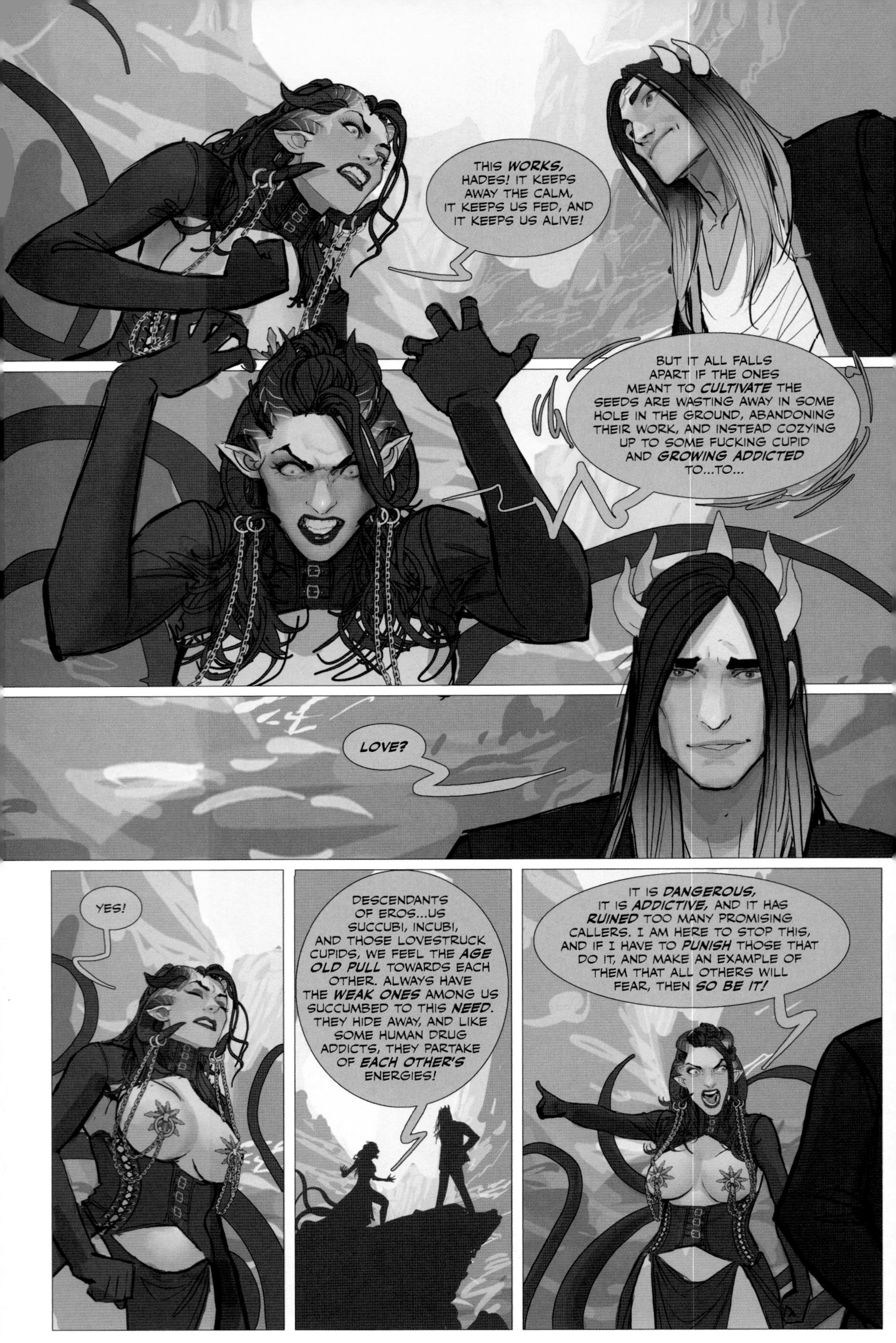
THIS WORKS, HADES! IT KEEPS AWAY THE CALM, IT KEEPS US FED, AND IT KEEPS US ALIVE!
BUT IT ALL FALLS APART IF THE ONES MEANT TO CULTIVATE THE SEEDS ARE WASTING AWAY IN SOME HOLE IN THE GROUND, ABANDONING THEIR WORK, AND INSTEAD COZYING UP TO SOME FUCKING CUPID AND GROWING ADDICTED TO...TO...
LOVE?
YES!
DESCENDANTS OF EROS...US SUCCUBI, INCUBI, AND THOSE LOVESTRUCK CUPIDS, WE FEEL THE AGE OLD PULL TOWARDS EACH OTHER. ALWAYS HAVE THE WEAK ONES AMONG US SUCCUMBED TO THIS NEED. THEY HIDE AWAY, AND LIKE SOME HUMAN DRUG ADDICTS, THEY PARTAKE OF EACH OTHER'S ENERGIES!
IT IS DANGEROUS, IT IS ADDICTIVE, AND IT HAS RUINED TOO MANY PROMISING CALLERS. I AM HERE TO STOP THIS, AND IF I HAVE TO PUNISH THOSE THAT DO IT, AND MAKE AN EXAMPLE OF THEM THAT ALL OTHERS WILL FEAR, THEN SO BE IT!

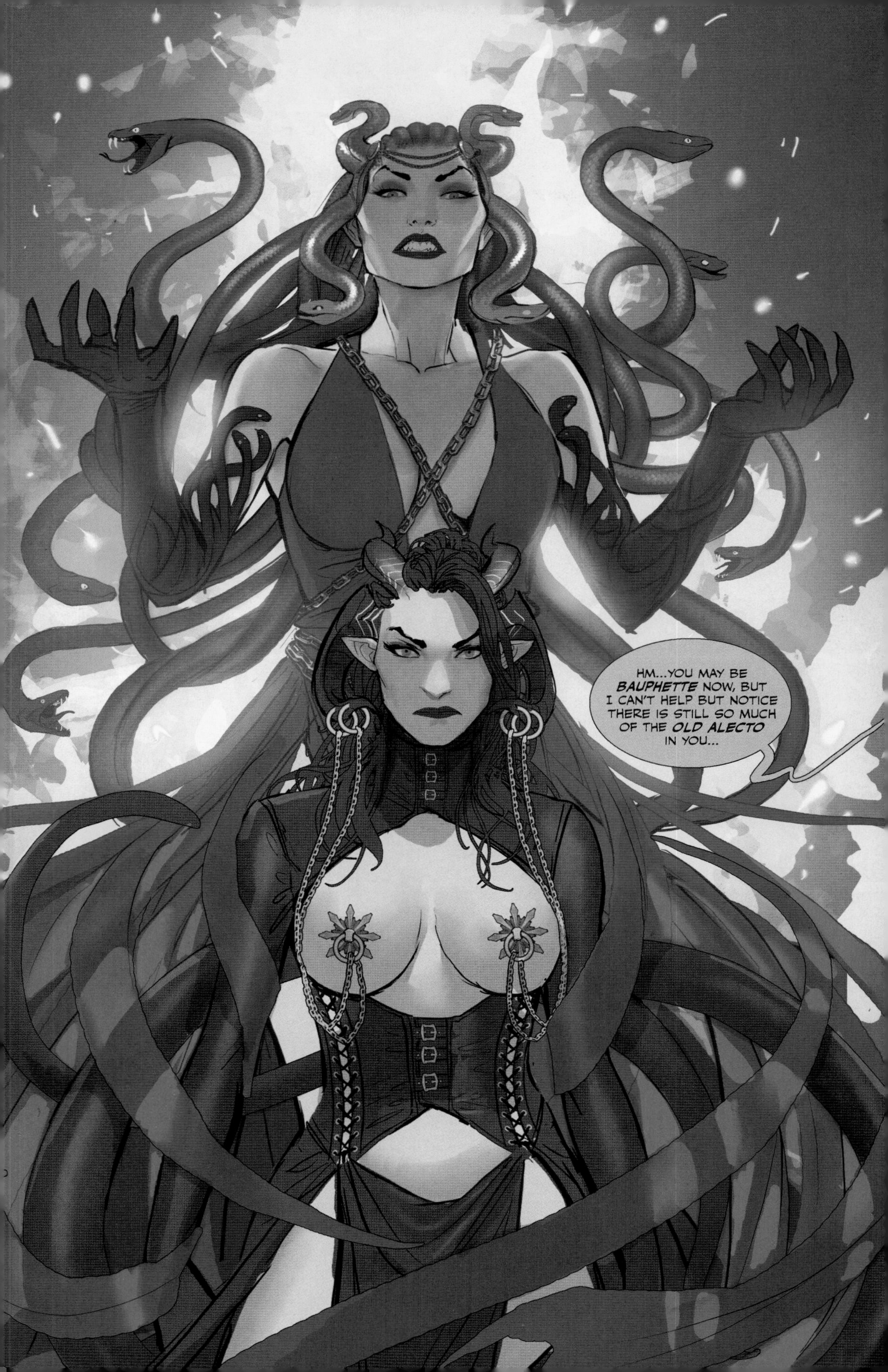
HM...YOU MAY BE ***BAUPHETTE*** NOW, BUT I CAN'T HELP BUT NOTICE THERE IS STILL SO MUCH OF THE ***OLD ALECTO*** IN YOU...

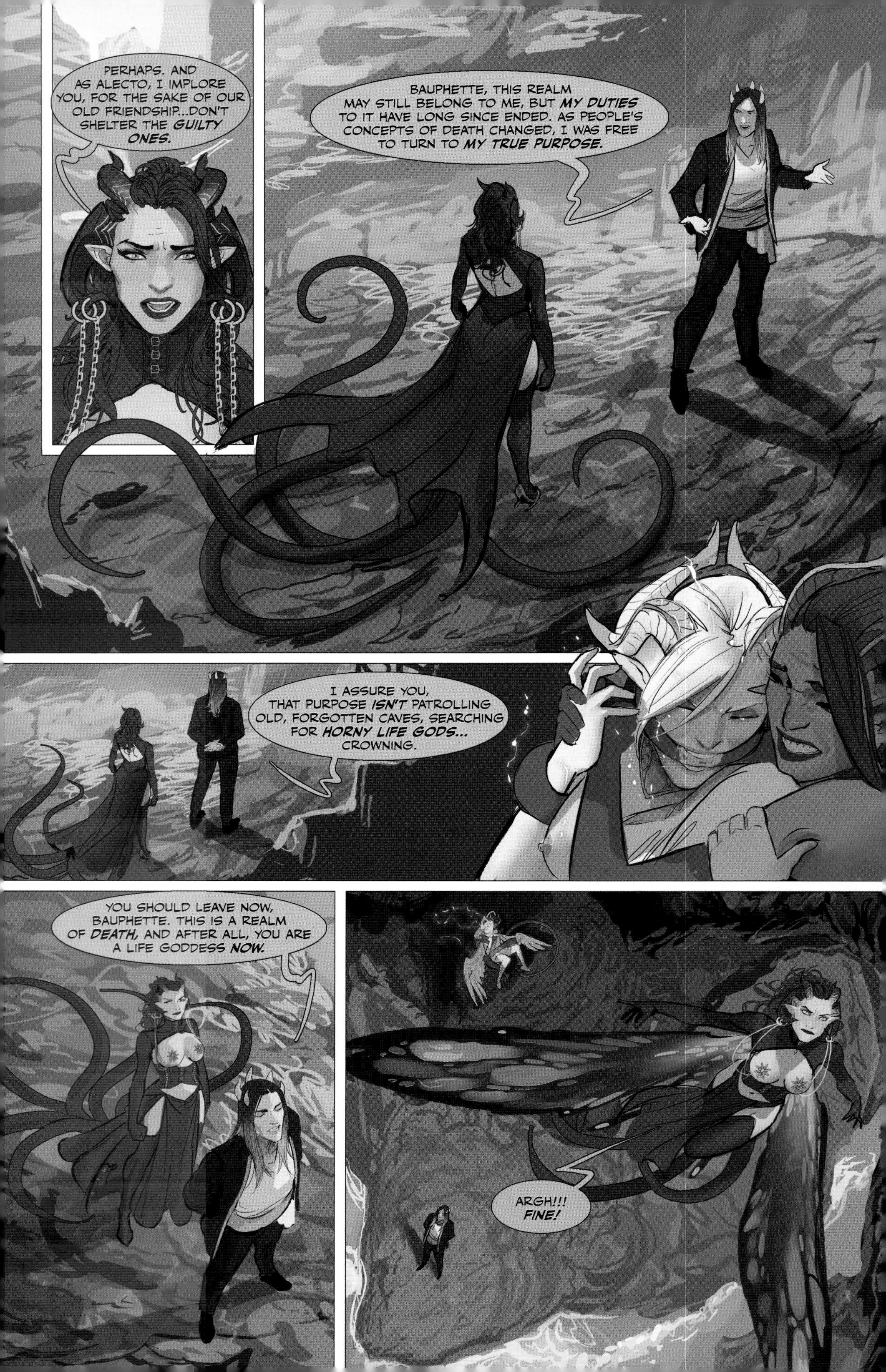
PERHAPS. AND AS ALECTO, I IMPLORE YOU, FOR THE SAKE OF OUR OLD FRIENDSHIP...DON'T SHELTER THE GUILTY ONES.
BAUPHETTE, THIS REALM MAY STILL BELONG TO ME, BUT MY DUTIES TO IT HAVE LONG SINCE ENDED. AS PEOPLE'S CONCEPTS OF DEATH CHANGED, I WAS FREE TO TURN TO MY TRUE PURPOSE.
I ASSURE YOU, THAT PURPOSE ISN'T PATROLLING OLD, FORGOTTEN CAVES, SEARCHING FOR HORNY LIFE GODS... CROWNING.
YOU SHOULD LEAVE NOW, BAUPHETTE. THIS IS A REALM OF DEATH, AND AFTER ALL, YOU ARE A LIFE GODDESS NOW.
ARGH!!! FINE!

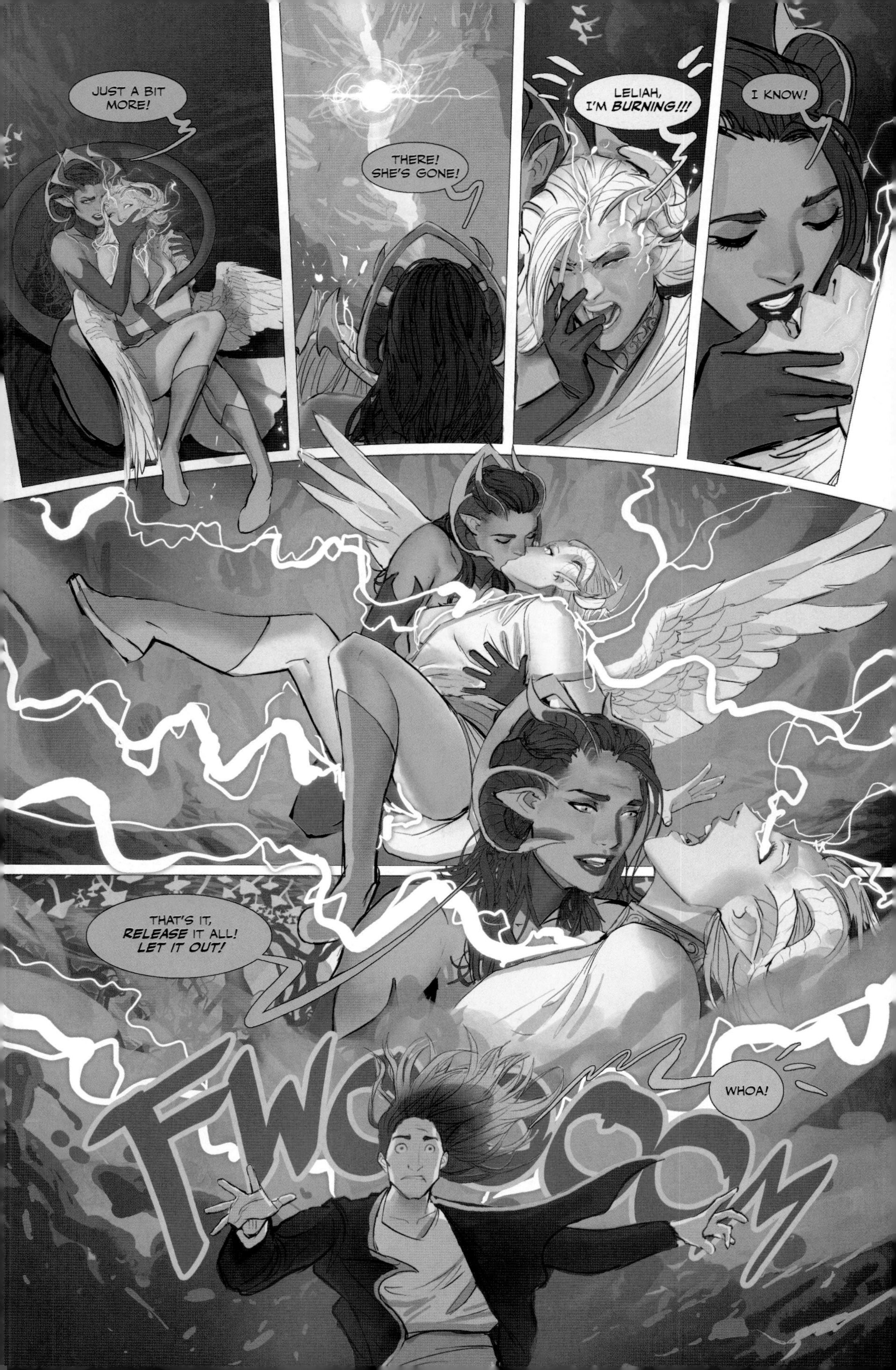
JUST A BIT MORE!
THERE! SHE'S GONE!
LELIAH, I'M **BURNING!!!**
I KNOW!
THAT'S IT, **RELEASE** IT ALL! **LET IT OUT!**
TWOOOOM
WHOA!

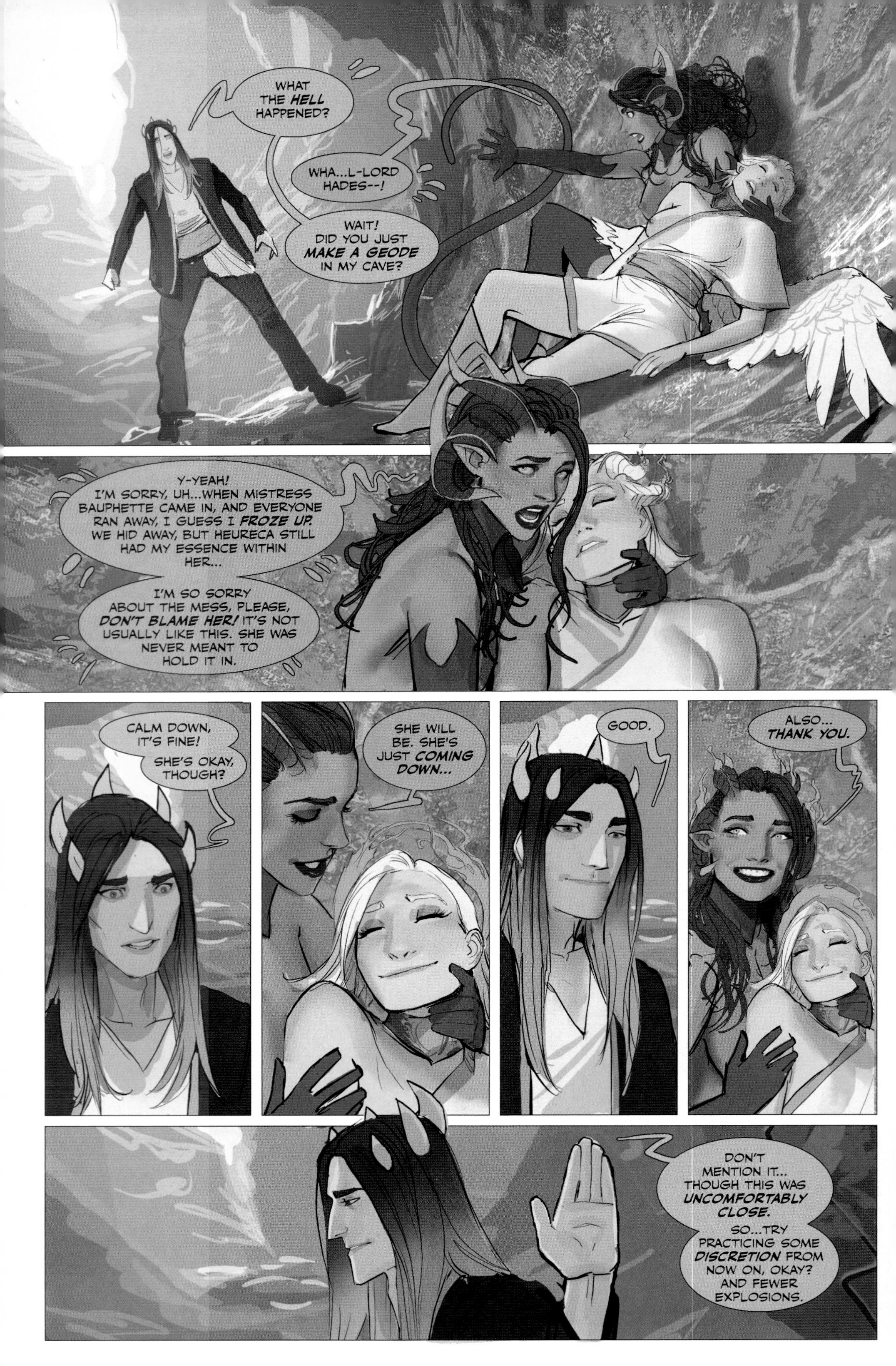
WHAT THE HELL HAPPENED?
WHA...L-LORD HADES--!
WAIT! DID YOU JUST MAKE A GEODE IN MY CAVE?
Y-YEAH! I'M SORRY, UH...WHEN MISTRESS BAUPHETTE CAME IN, AND EVERYONE RAN AWAY, I GUESS I FROZE UP. WE HID AWAY, BUT HEURECA STILL HAD MY ESSENCE WITHIN HER...
I'M SO SORRY ABOUT THE MESS, PLEASE, DON'T BLAME HER! IT'S NOT USUALLY LIKE THIS. SHE WAS NEVER MEANT TO HOLD IT IN.
CALM DOWN, IT'S FINE!
SHE'S OKAY, THOUGH?
SHE WILL BE. SHE'S JUST COMING DOWN...
GOOD.
ALSO... THANK YOU.
DON'T MENTION IT... THOUGH THIS WAS UNCOMFORTABLY CLOSE.
SO...TRY PRACTICING SOME DISCRETION FROM NOW ON, OKAY? AND FEWER EXPLOSIONS.

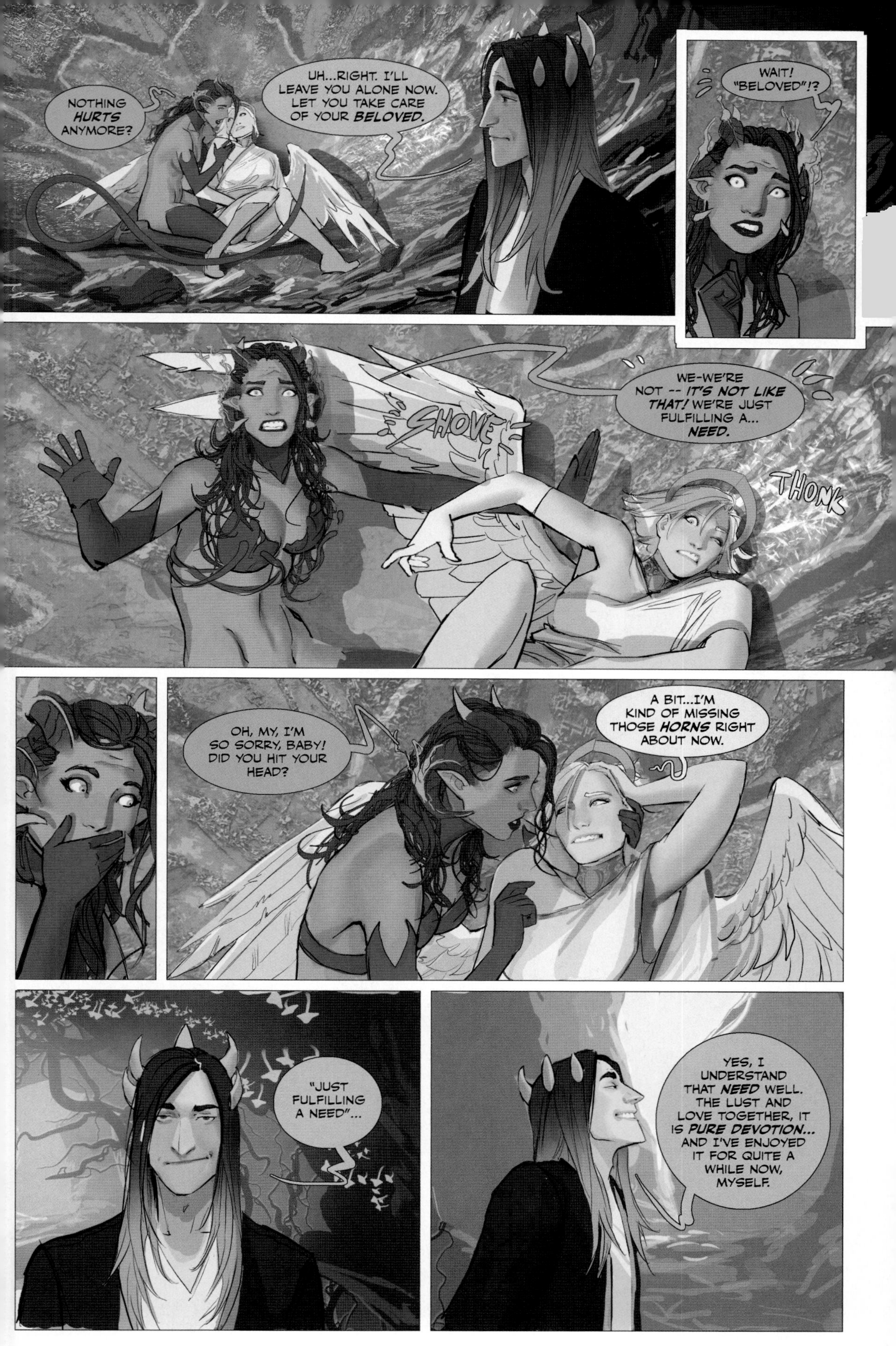
NOTHING HURTS ANYMORE?
UH...RIGHT. I'LL LEAVE YOU ALONE NOW. LET YOU TAKE CARE OF YOUR BELOVED.
WAIT! "BELOVED"!?
SHOVE
WE-WE'RE NOT -- IT'S NOT LIKE THAT! WE'RE JUST FULFILLING A... NEED.
THONK
OH, MY, I'M SO SORRY, BABY! DID YOU HIT YOUR HEAD?
A BIT...I'M KIND OF MISSING THOSE HORNS RIGHT ABOUT NOW.
"JUST FULFILLING A NEED"...
YES, I UNDERSTAND THAT NEED WELL. THE LUST AND LOVE TOGETHER, IT IS PURE DEVOTION... AND I'VE ENJOYED IT FOR QUITE A WHILE NOW, MYSELF.

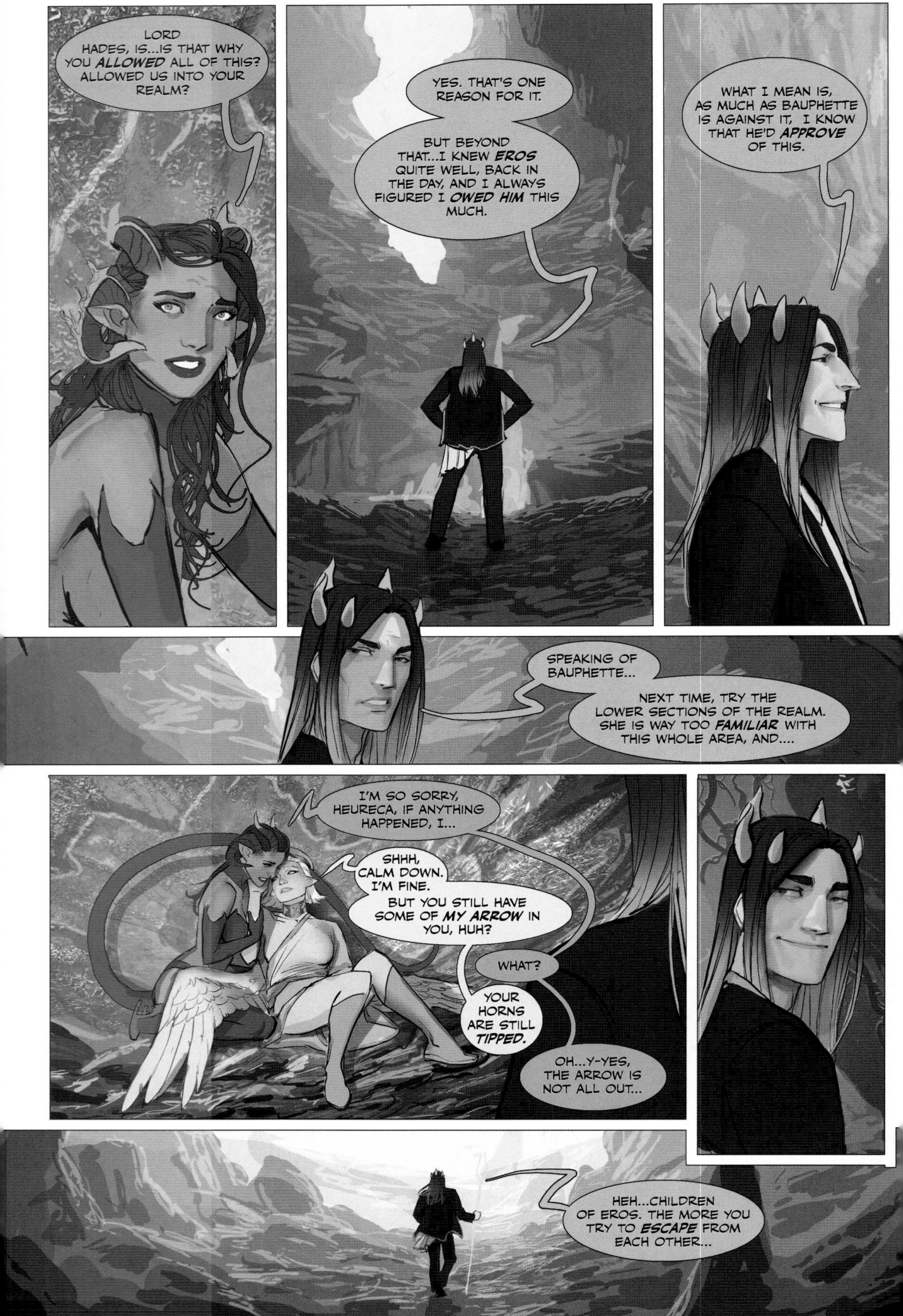
LORD HADES, IS...IS THAT WHY YOU ALLOWED ALL OF THIS? ALLOWED US INTO YOUR REALM?
YES. THAT'S ONE REASON FOR IT.
BUT BEYOND THAT...I KNEW EROS QUITE WELL, BACK IN THE DAY, AND I ALWAYS FIGURED I OWED HIM THIS MUCH.
WHAT I MEAN IS, AS MUCH AS BAUPHETTE IS AGAINST IT, I KNOW THAT HE'D APPROVE OF THIS.
SPEAKING OF BAUPHETTE...
NEXT TIME, TRY THE LOWER SECTIONS OF THE REALM. SHE IS WAY TOO FAMILIAR WITH THIS WHOLE AREA, AND....
I'M SO SORRY, HEURECA, IF ANYTHING HAPPENED, I...
SHHH, CALM DOWN. I'M FINE.
BUT YOU STILL HAVE SOME OF MY ARROW IN YOU, HUH?
WHAT?
YOUR HORNS ARE STILL TIPPED.
OH...Y-YES, THE ARROW IS NOT ALL OUT...
HEH...CHILDREN OF EROS. THE MORE YOU TRY TO ESCAPE FROM EACH OTHER...

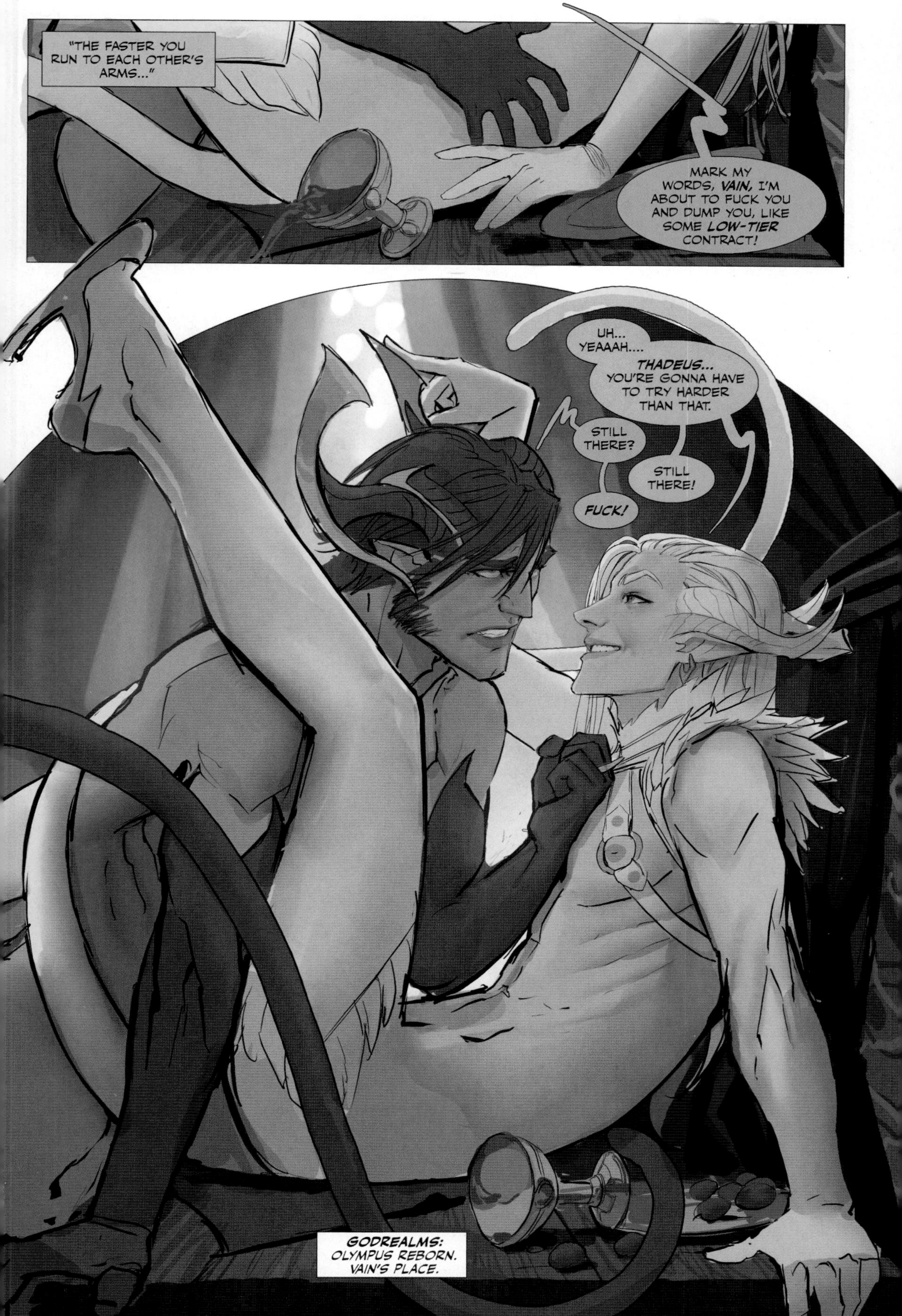
"THE FASTER YOU RUN TO EACH OTHER'S ARMS..."
MARK MY WORDS, **VAIN,** I'M ABOUT TO FUCK YOU AND DUMP YOU, LIKE SOME **LOW-TIER** CONTRACT!
UH... YEAAAH.... ***THADEUS...*** YOU'RE GONNA HAVE TO TRY HARDER THAN THAT.
STILL THERE?
STILL THERE!
FUCK!
GODREALMS: *OLYMPUS REBORN. VAIN'S PLACE.*

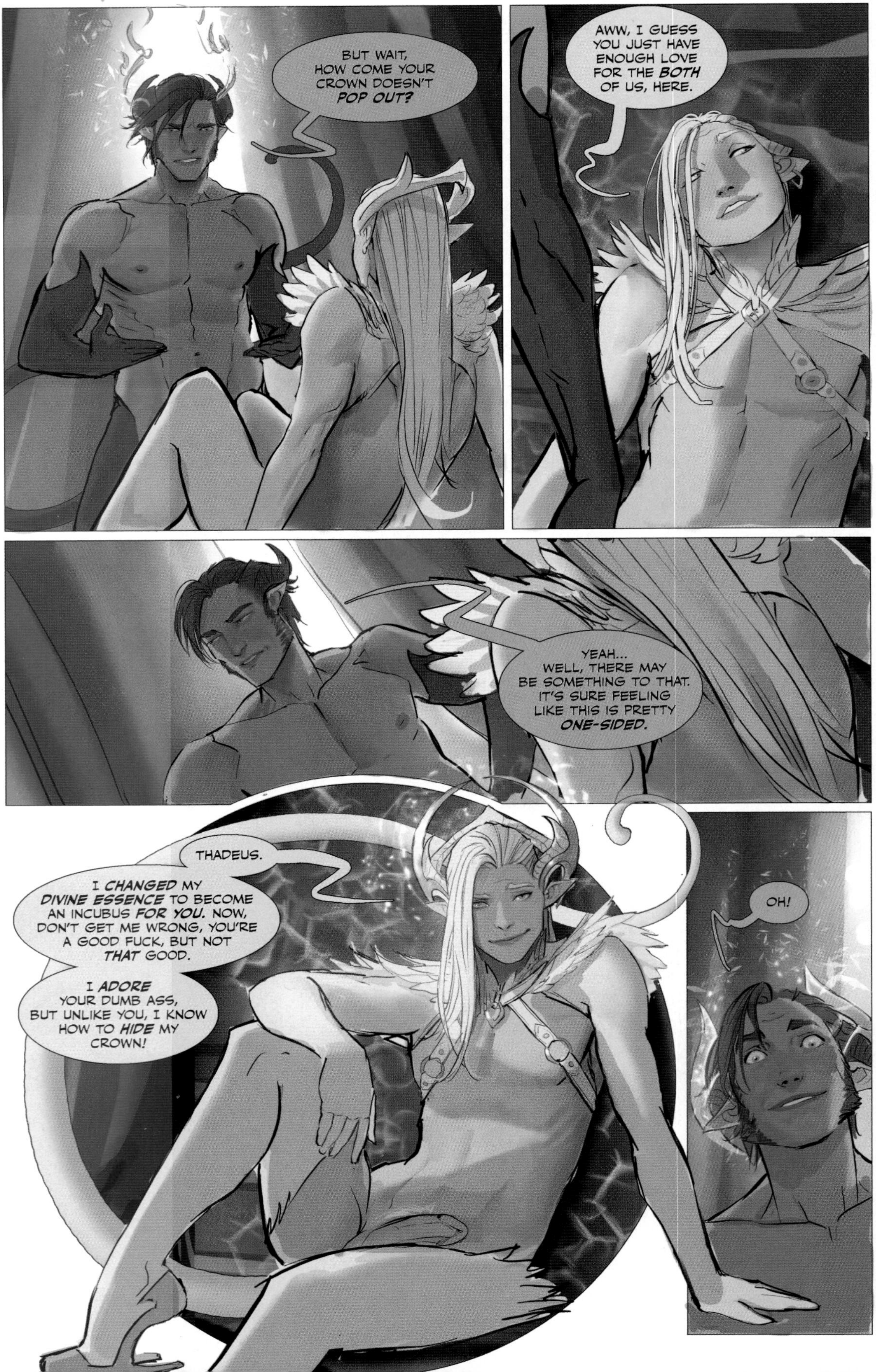
BUT WAIT, HOW COME YOUR CROWN DOESN'T *POP OUT?*
AWW, I GUESS YOU JUST HAVE ENOUGH LOVE FOR THE *BOTH* OF US, HERE.
YEAH... WELL, THERE MAY BE SOMETHING TO THAT. IT'S SURE FEELING LIKE THIS IS PRETTY *ONE-SIDED.*
THADEUS.
I *CHANGED* MY *DIVINE ESSENCE* TO BECOME AN INCUBUS *FOR YOU.* NOW, DON'T GET ME WRONG, YOU'RE A GOOD FUCK, BUT NOT *THAT* GOOD.
I *ADORE* YOUR DUMB ASS, BUT UNLIKE YOU, I KNOW HOW TO *HIDE* MY CROWN!
OH!

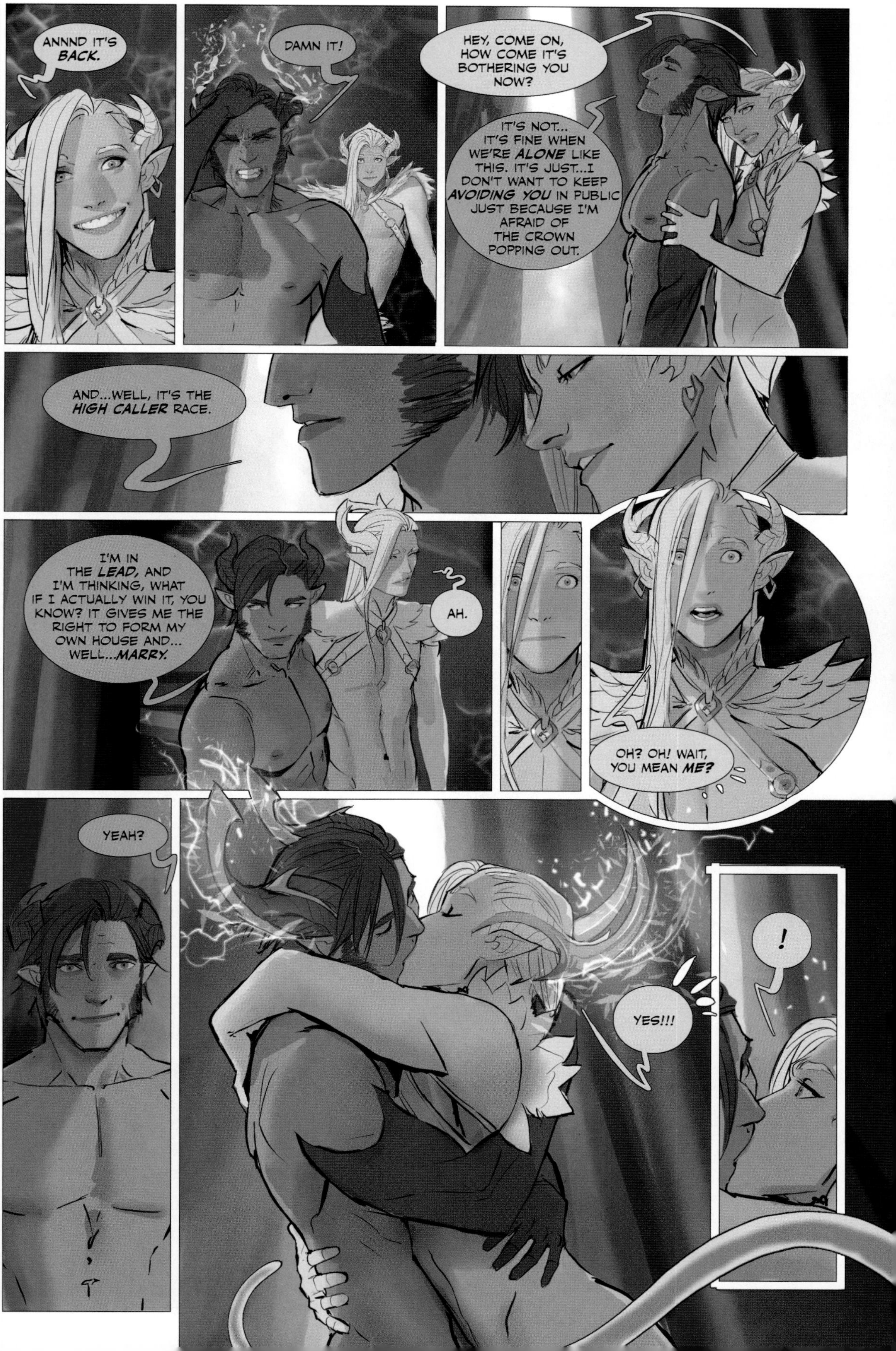
ANNND IT'S BACK.
DAMN IT!
HEY, COME ON, HOW COME IT'S BOTHERING YOU NOW?
IT'S NOT... IT'S FINE WHEN WE'RE ALONE LIKE THIS. IT'S JUST...I DON'T WANT TO KEEP AVOIDING YOU IN PUBLIC JUST BECAUSE I'M AFRAID OF THE CROWN POPPING OUT.
AND...WELL, IT'S THE HIGH CALLER RACE.
I'M IN THE LEAD, AND I'M THINKING, WHAT IF I ACTUALLY WIN IT, YOU KNOW? IT GIVES ME THE RIGHT TO FORM MY OWN HOUSE AND... WELL...MARRY.
AH.
OH? OH! WAIT, YOU MEAN ME?
YEAH?
YES!!!
!

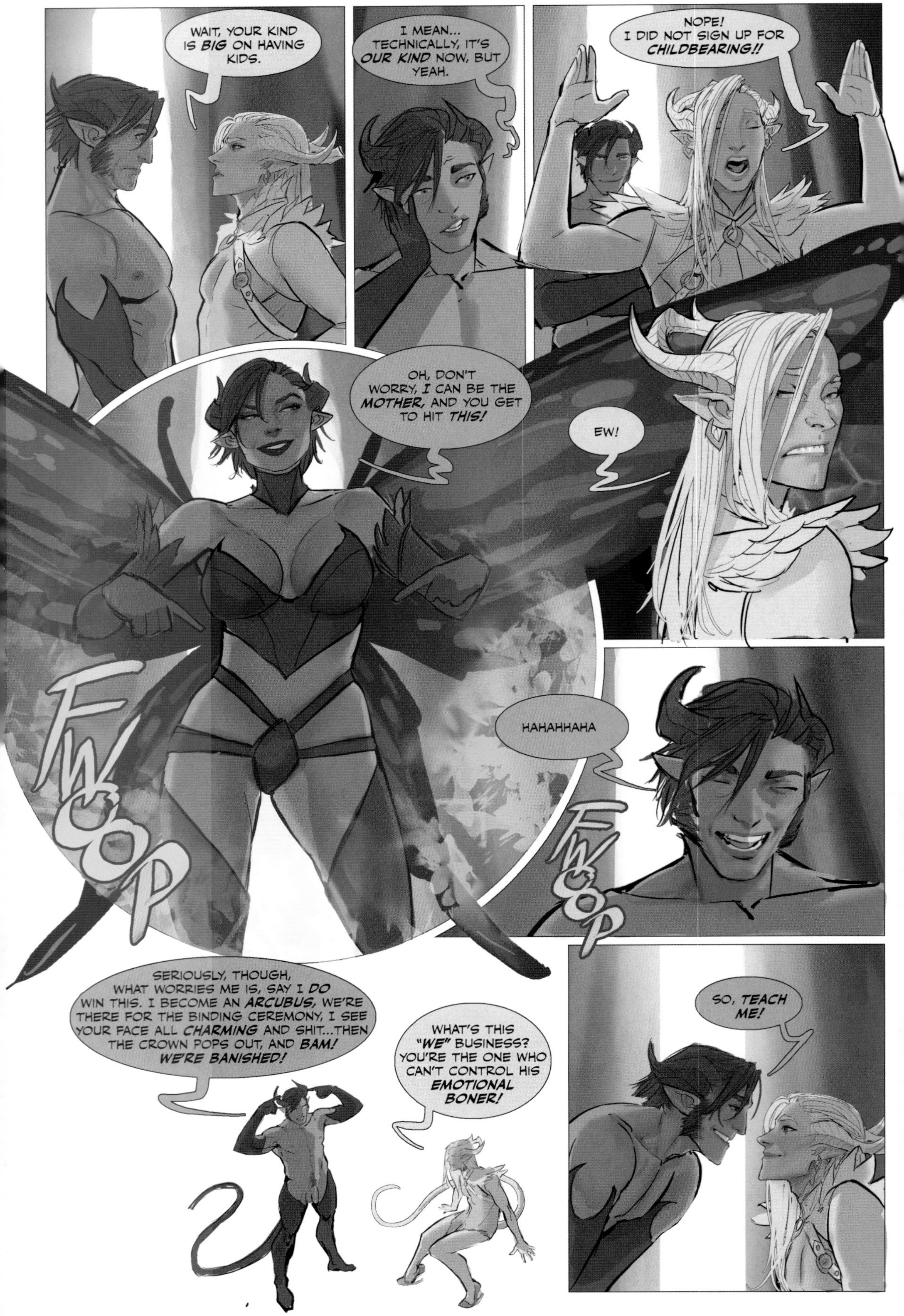
WAIT, YOUR KIND IS BIG ON HAVING KIDS.
I MEAN... TECHNICALLY, IT'S OUR KIND NOW, BUT YEAH.
NOPE! I DID NOT SIGN UP FOR CHILDBEARING!!
OH, DON'T WORRY, I CAN BE THE MOTHER, AND YOU GET TO HIT THIS!
EW!
FWOOP
HAHAHHAHA
FWOOP
SERIOUSLY, THOUGH, WHAT WORRIES ME IS, SAY I DO WIN THIS. I BECOME AN ARCUBUS, WE'RE THERE FOR THE BINDING CEREMONY, I SEE YOUR FACE ALL CHARMING AND SHIT...THEN THE CROWN POPS OUT, AND BAM! WE'RE BANISHED!
WHAT'S THIS "WE" BUSINESS? YOU'RE THE ONE WHO CAN'T CONTROL HIS EMOTIONAL BONER!
SO, TEACH ME!

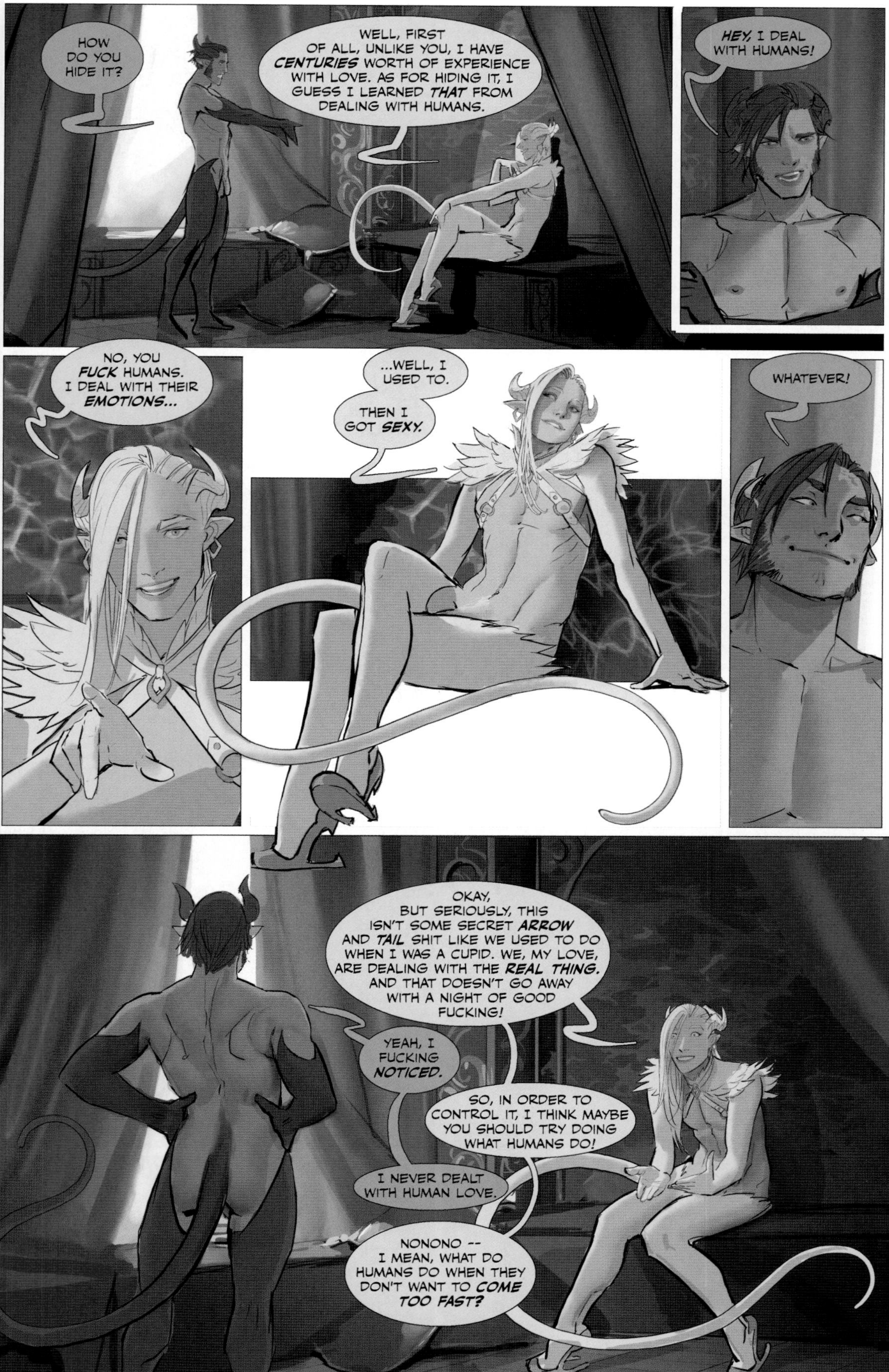
HOW DO YOU HIDE IT?
WELL, FIRST OF ALL, UNLIKE YOU, I HAVE CENTURIES WORTH OF EXPERIENCE WITH LOVE. AS FOR HIDING IT, I GUESS I LEARNED THAT FROM DEALING WITH HUMANS.
HEY, I DEAL WITH HUMANS!
NO, YOU FUCK HUMANS. I DEAL WITH THEIR EMOTIONS...
...WELL, I USED TO.
THEN I GOT SEXY.
WHATEVER!
OKAY, BUT SERIOUSLY, THIS ISN'T SOME SECRET ARROW AND TAIL SHIT LIKE WE USED TO DO WHEN I WAS A CUPID. WE, MY LOVE, ARE DEALING WITH THE REAL THING. AND THAT DOESN'T GO AWAY WITH A NIGHT OF GOOD FUCKING!
YEAH, I FUCKING NOTICED.
SO, IN ORDER TO CONTROL IT, I THINK MAYBE YOU SHOULD TRY DOING WHAT HUMANS DO!
I NEVER DEALT WITH HUMAN LOVE.
NONONO -- I MEAN, WHAT DO HUMANS DO WHEN THEY DON'T WANT TO COME TOO FAST?

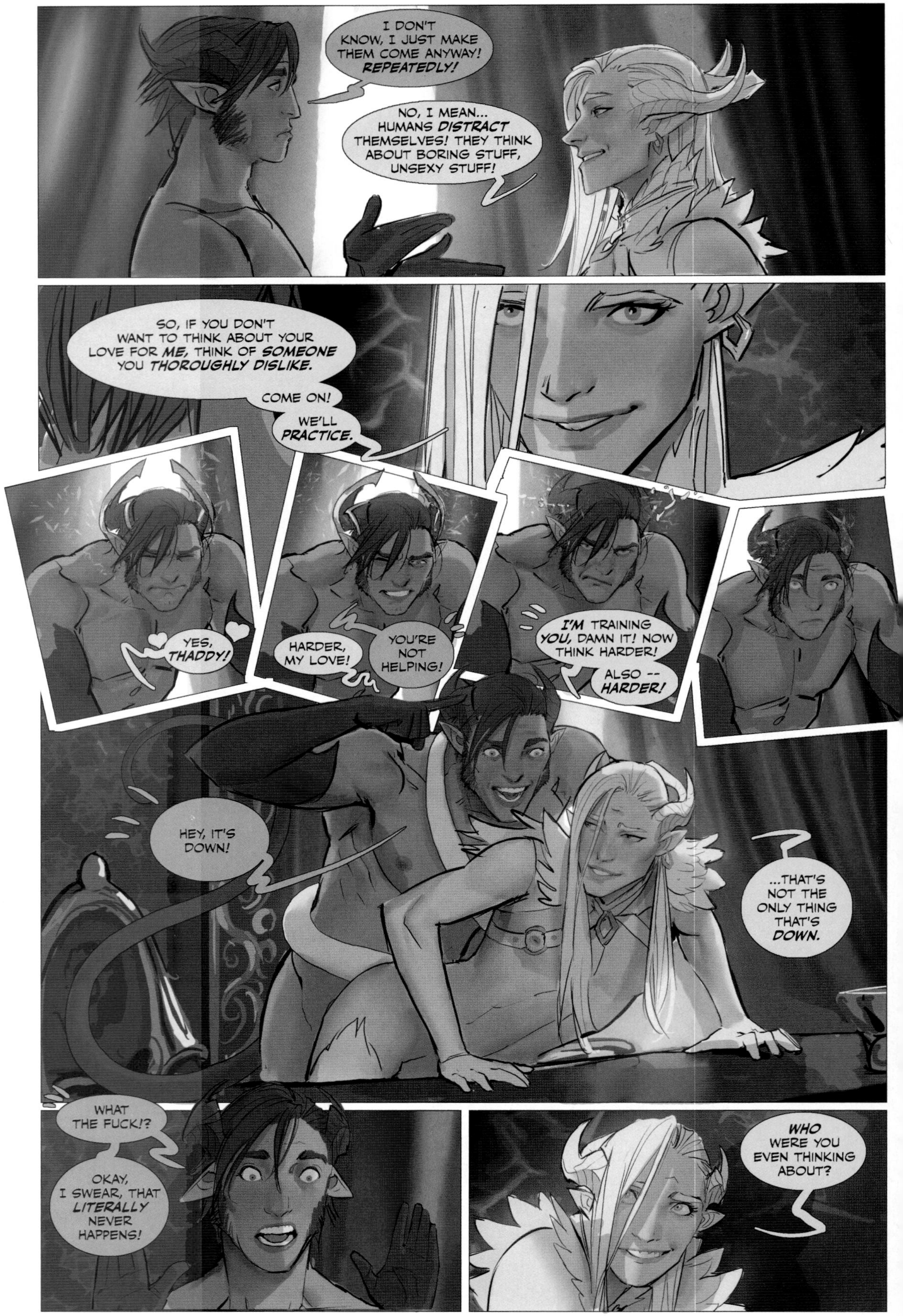
I DON'T KNOW, I JUST MAKE THEM COME ANYWAY! ***REPEATEDLY!***
NO, I MEAN... HUMANS ***DISTRACT*** THEMSELVES! THEY THINK ABOUT BORING STUFF, UNSEXY STUFF!
SO, IF YOU DON'T WANT TO THINK ABOUT YOUR LOVE FOR ***ME,*** THINK OF ***SOMEONE*** YOU ***THOROUGHLY DISLIKE.***
COME ON!
WE'LL ***PRACTICE.***
YES, ***THADDY!***
HARDER, MY LOVE!
YOU'RE NOT HELPING!
I'M TRAINING ***YOU,*** DAMN IT! NOW THINK HARDER!
ALSO -- ***HARDER!***
HEY, IT'S DOWN!
...THAT'S NOT THE ONLY THING THAT'S ***DOWN.***
WHAT THE FUCK!?
OKAY, I SWEAR, THAT ***LITERALLY*** NEVER HAPPENS!
WHO WERE YOU EVEN THINKING ABOUT?

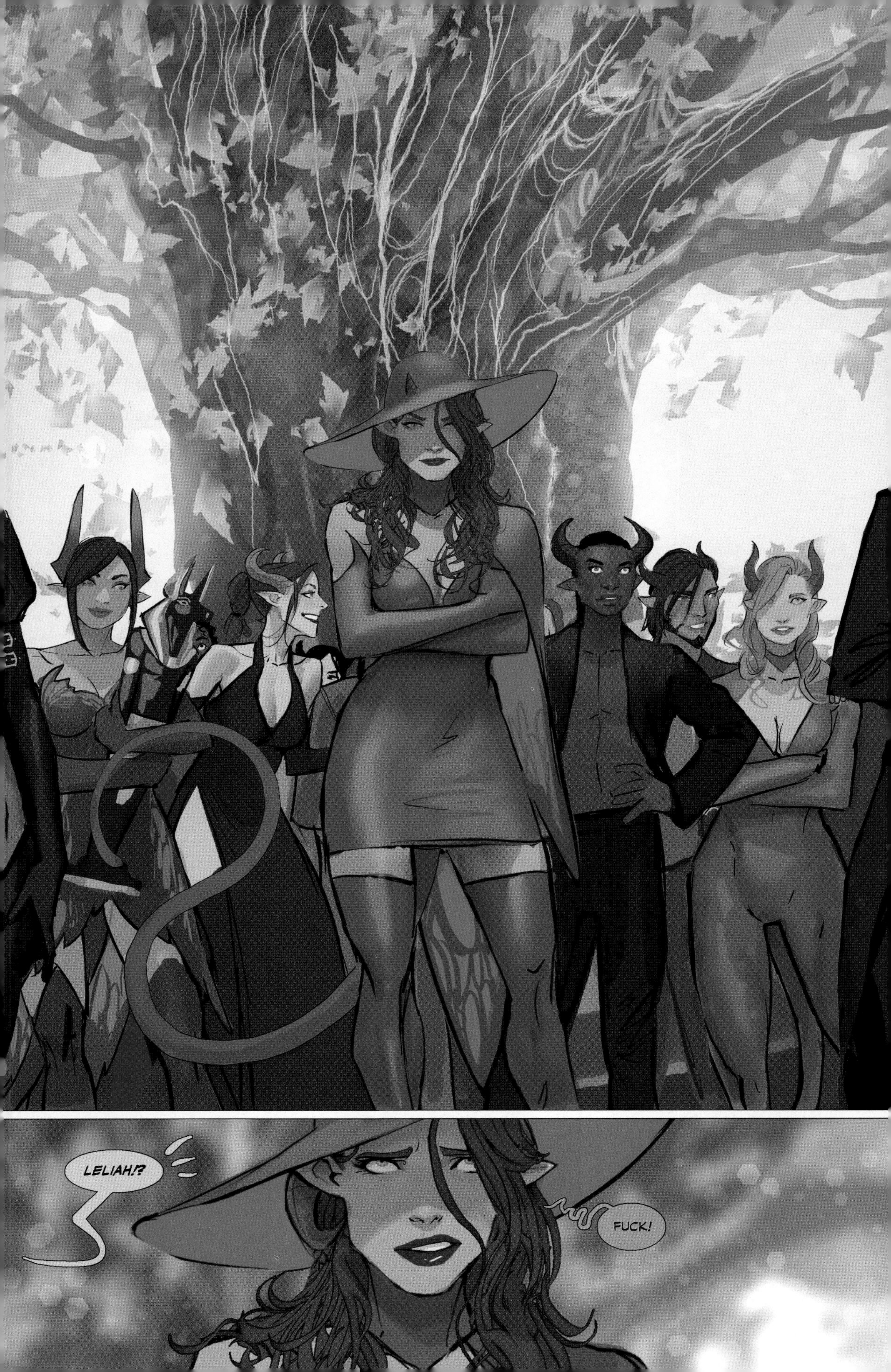
LELIAH!?
FUCK!

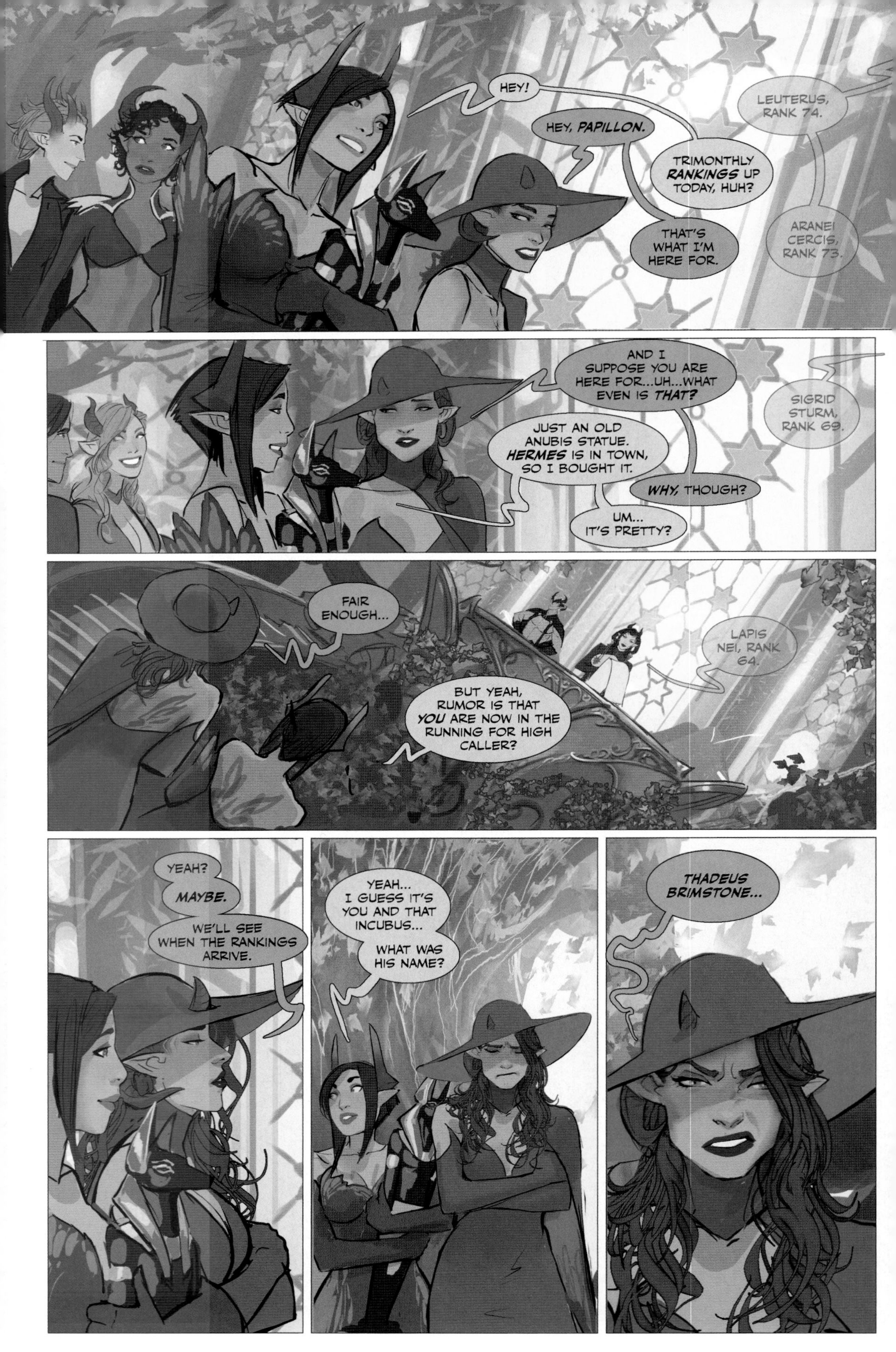
HEY!
HEY, PAPILLON.
TRIMONTHLY RANKINGS UP TODAY, HUH?
THAT'S WHAT I'M HERE FOR.
LEUTERUS, RANK 74.
ARANEI CERCIS, RANK 73.
AND I SUPPOSE YOU ARE HERE FOR...UH...WHAT EVEN IS THAT?
JUST AN OLD ANUBIS STATUE. HERMES IS IN TOWN, SO I BOUGHT IT.
WHY, THOUGH?
UM... IT'S PRETTY?
SIGRID STURM, RANK 69.
FAIR ENOUGH...
BUT YEAH, RUMOR IS THAT YOU ARE NOW IN THE RUNNING FOR HIGH CALLER?
LAPIS NEI, RANK 64.
YEAH?
MAYBE.
WE'LL SEE WHEN THE RANKINGS ARRIVE.
YEAH... I GUESS IT'S YOU AND THAT INCUBUS...
WHAT WAS HIS NAME?
THADEUS BRIMSTONE...

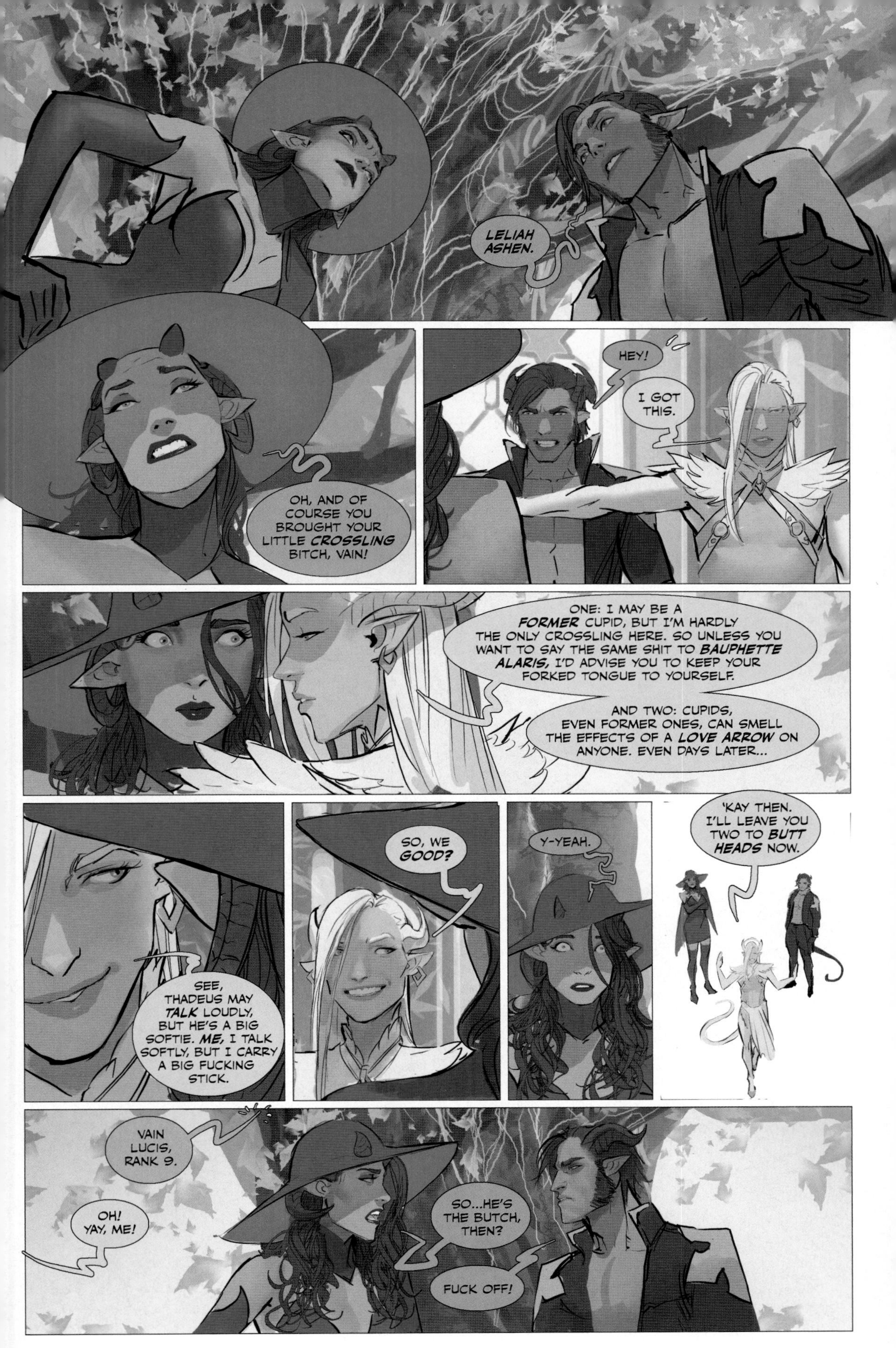
LELIAH ASHEN.
OH, AND OF COURSE YOU BROUGHT YOUR LITTLE CROSSLING BITCH, VAIN!
HEY!
I GOT THIS.
ONE: I MAY BE A FORMER CUPID, BUT I'M HARDLY THE ONLY CROSSLING HERE. SO UNLESS YOU WANT TO SAY THE SAME SHIT TO BAUPHETTE ALARIS, I'D ADVISE YOU TO KEEP YOUR FORKED TONGUE TO YOURSELF.
AND TWO: CUPIDS, EVEN FORMER ONES, CAN SMELL THE EFFECTS OF A LOVE ARROW ON ANYONE. EVEN DAYS LATER...
SEE, THADEUS MAY TALK LOUDLY, BUT HE'S A BIG SOFTIE. ME, I TALK SOFTLY, BUT I CARRY A BIG FUCKING STICK.
SO, WE GOOD?
Y-YEAH.
'KAY THEN. I'LL LEAVE YOU TWO TO BUTT HEADS NOW.
VAIN LUCIS, RANK 9.
OH! YAY, ME!
SO...HE'S THE BUTCH, THEN?
FUCK OFF!

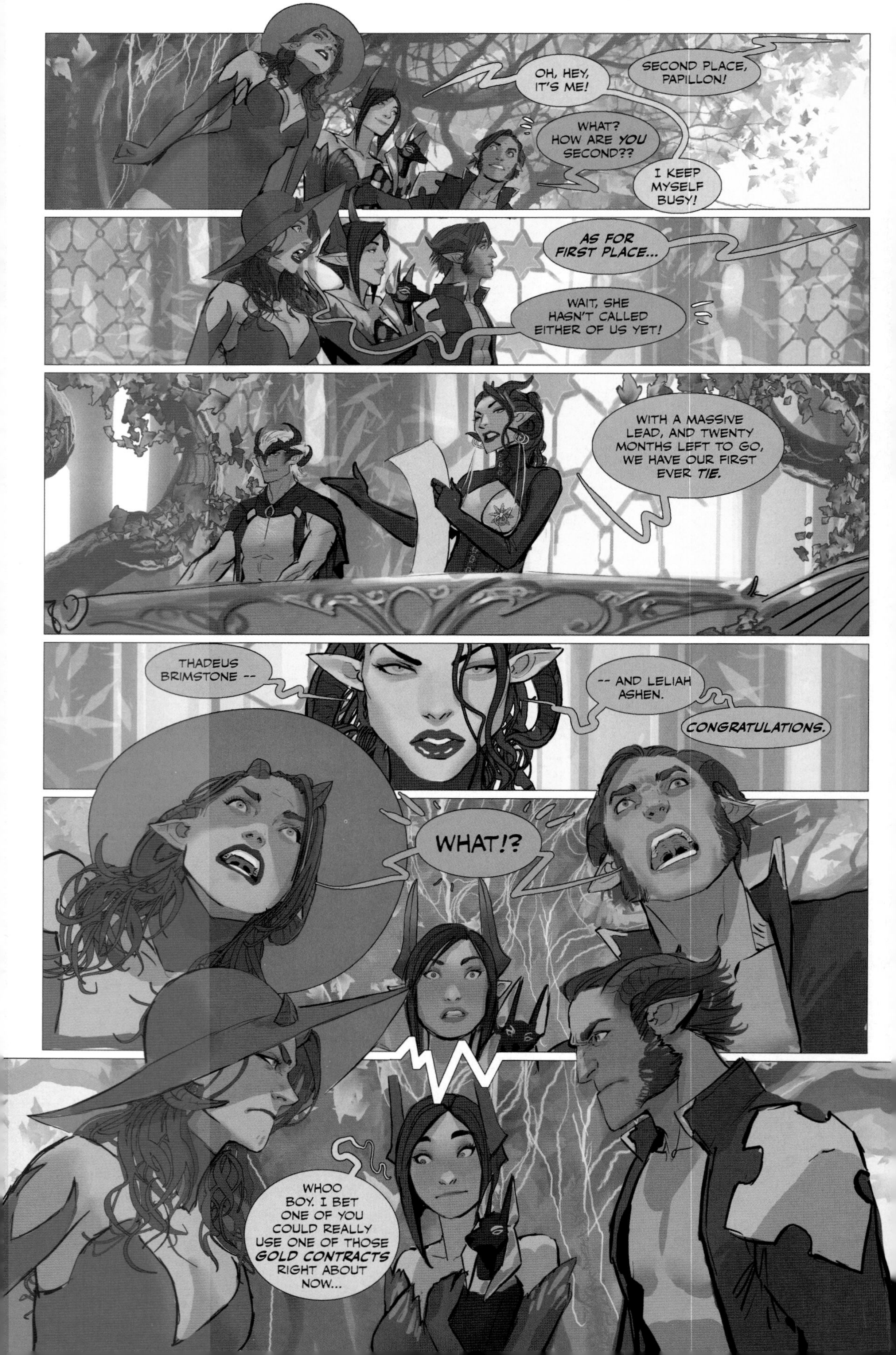
OH, HEY, IT'S ME!
SECOND PLACE, PAPILLON!
WHAT? HOW ARE *YOU* SECOND??
I KEEP MYSELF BUSY!
AS FOR FIRST PLACE...
WAIT, SHE HASN'T CALLED EITHER OF US YET!
WITH A MASSIVE LEAD, AND TWENTY MONTHS LEFT TO GO, WE HAVE OUR FIRST EVER ***TIE.***
THADEUS BRIMSTONE --
-- AND LELIAH ASHEN.
CONGRATULATIONS.
WHAT!?
WHOO BOY. I BET ONE OF YOU COULD REALLY USE ONE OF THOSE ***GOLD CONTRACTS*** RIGHT ABOUT NOW...

Chapter 3

The escapist

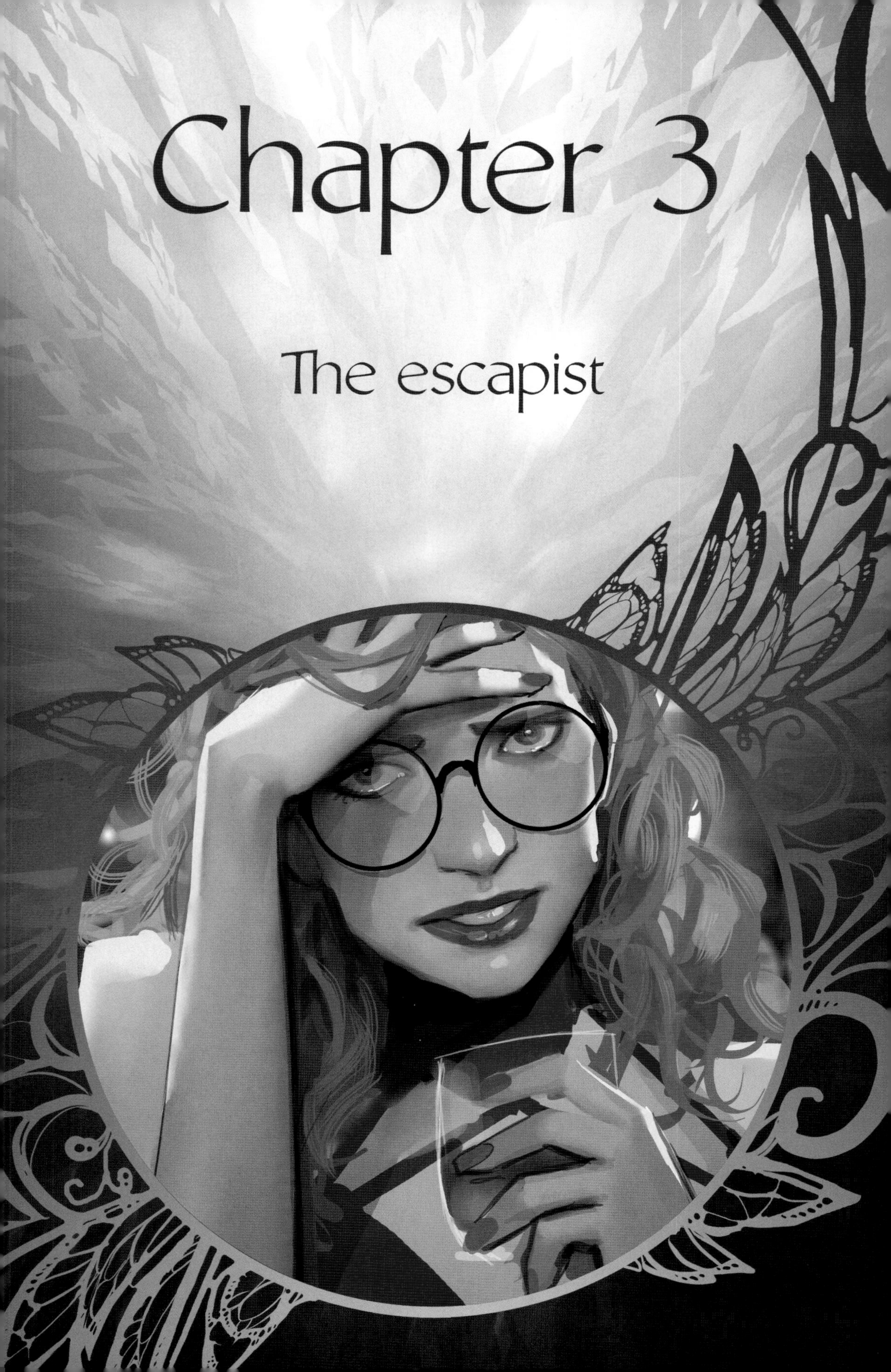

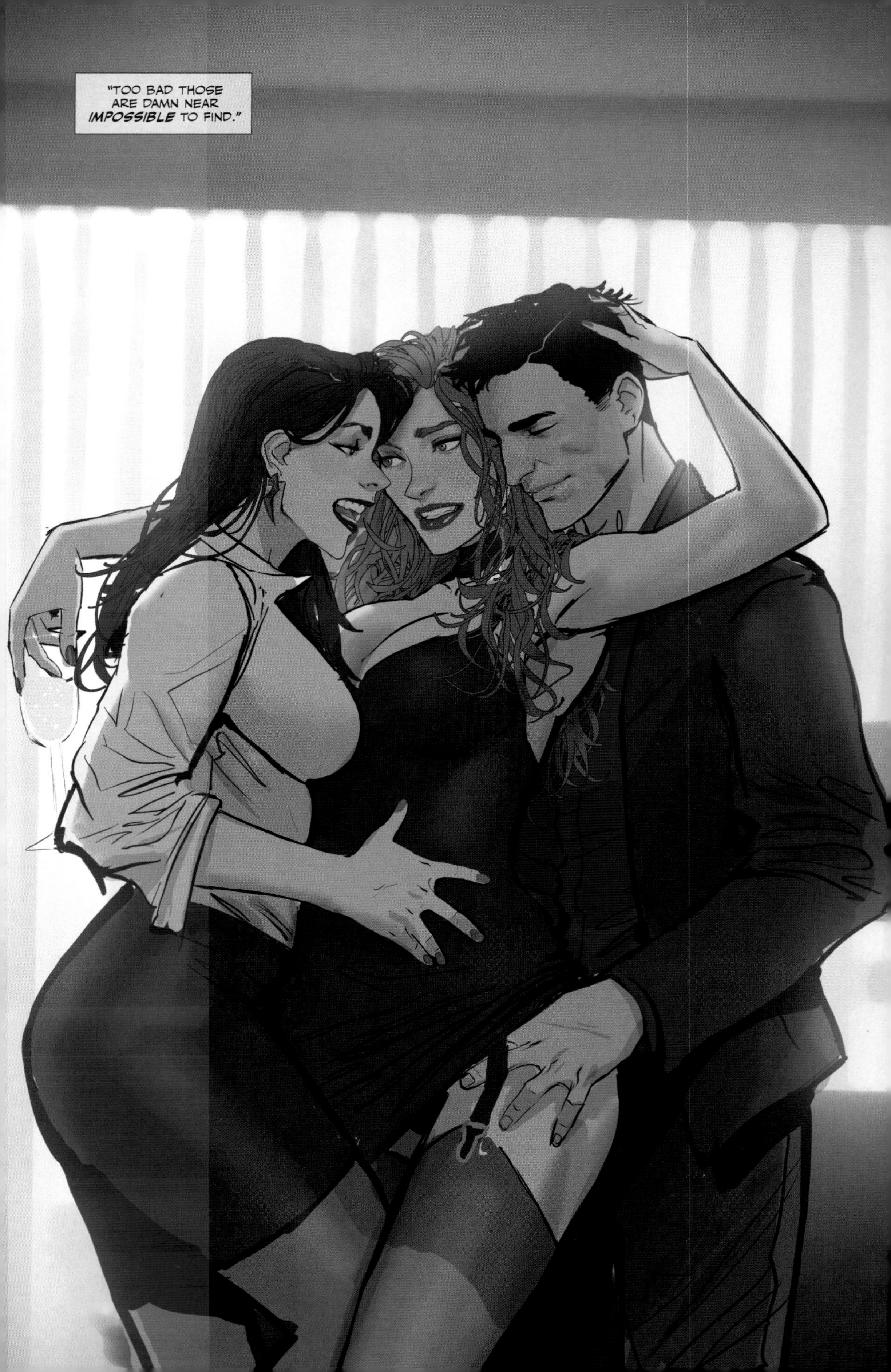
"TOO BAD THOSE ARE DAMN NEAR *IMPOSSIBLE* TO FIND."

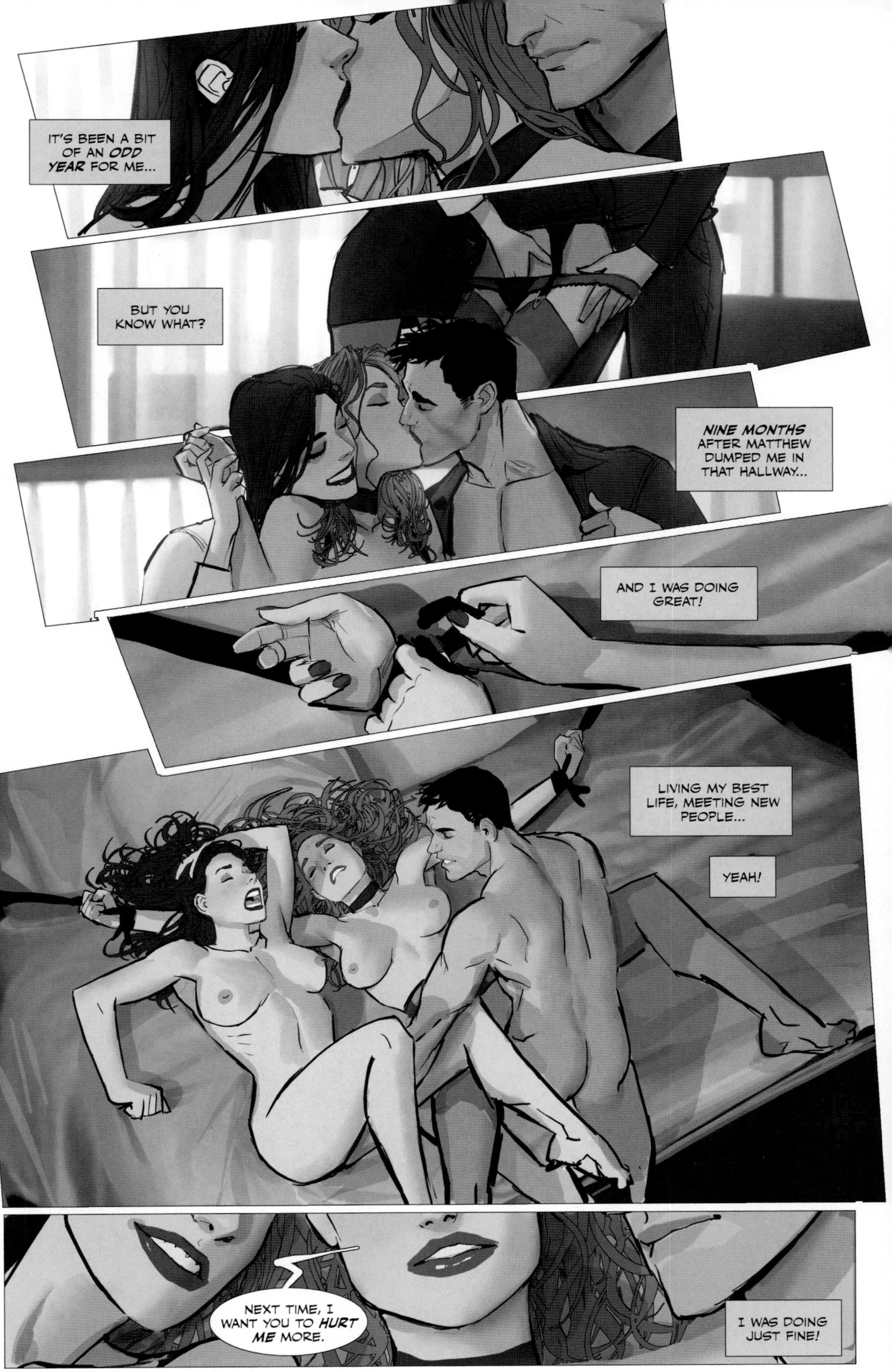
IT'S BEEN A BIT OF AN *ODD YEAR* FOR ME...
BUT YOU KNOW WHAT?
NINE MONTHS AFTER MATTHEW DUMPED ME IN THAT HALLWAY...
AND I WAS DOING GREAT!
LIVING MY BEST LIFE, MEETING NEW PEOPLE...
YEAH!
NEXT TIME, I WANT YOU TO *HURT ME* MORE.
I WAS DOING JUST FINE!

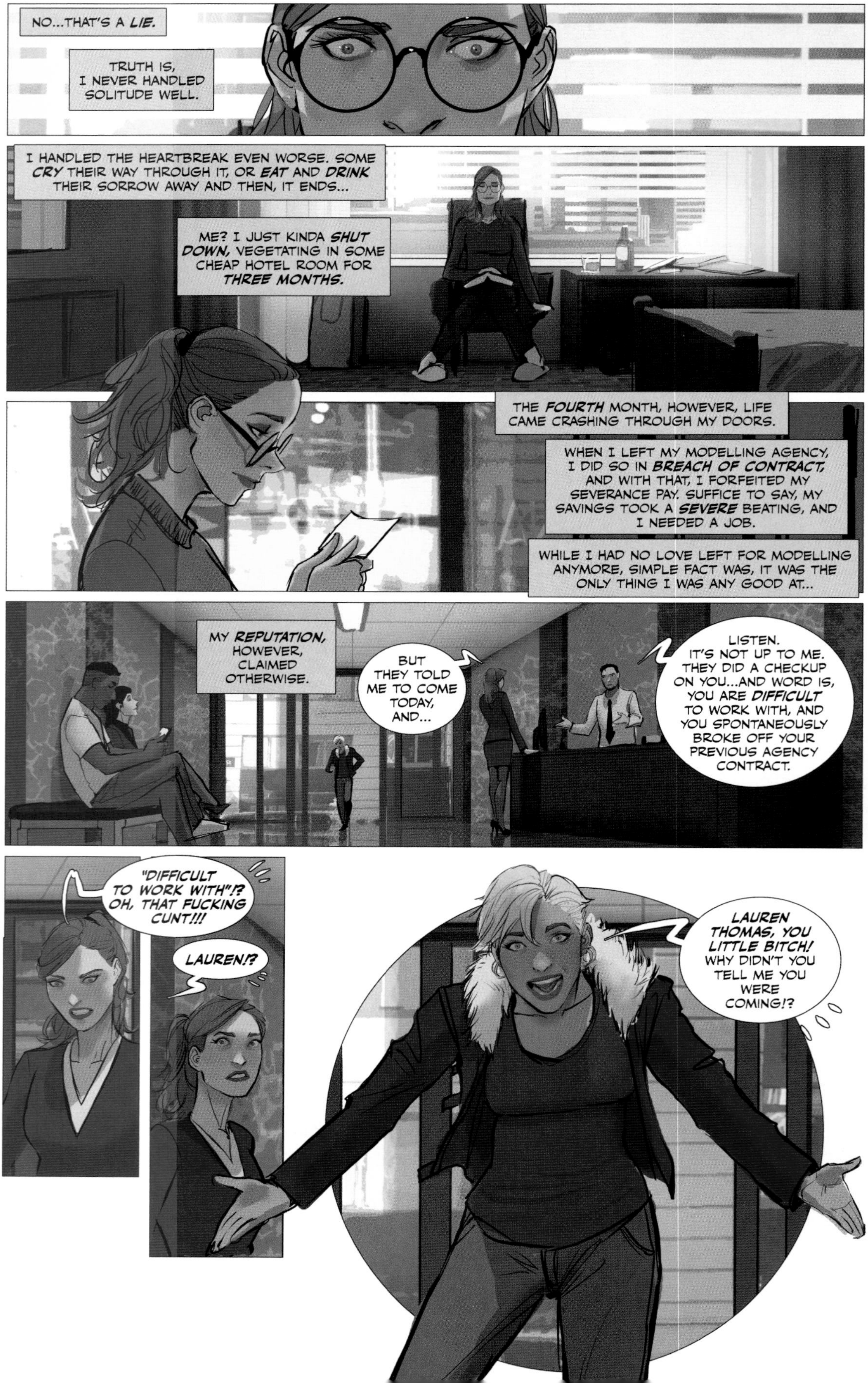
NO...THAT'S A LIE.
TRUTH IS, I NEVER HANDLED SOLITUDE WELL.
I HANDLED THE HEARTBREAK EVEN WORSE. SOME CRY THEIR WAY THROUGH IT, OR EAT AND DRINK THEIR SORROW AWAY AND THEN, IT ENDS...
ME? I JUST KINDA SHUT DOWN, VEGETATING IN SOME CHEAP HOTEL ROOM FOR THREE MONTHS.
THE FOURTH MONTH, HOWEVER, LIFE CAME CRASHING THROUGH MY DOORS.
WHEN I LEFT MY MODELLING AGENCY, I DID SO IN BREACH OF CONTRACT, AND WITH THAT, I FORFEITED MY SEVERANCE PAY. SUFFICE TO SAY, MY SAVINGS TOOK A SEVERE BEATING, AND I NEEDED A JOB.
WHILE I HAD NO LOVE LEFT FOR MODELLING ANYMORE, SIMPLE FACT WAS, IT WAS THE ONLY THING I WAS ANY GOOD AT...
MY REPUTATION, HOWEVER, CLAIMED OTHERWISE.
BUT THEY TOLD ME TO COME TODAY, AND...
LISTEN. IT'S NOT UP TO ME. THEY DID A CHECKUP ON YOU...AND WORD IS, YOU ARE DIFFICULT TO WORK WITH, AND YOU SPONTANEOUSLY BROKE OFF YOUR PREVIOUS AGENCY CONTRACT.
"DIFFICULT TO WORK WITH"!? OH, THAT FUCKING CUNT!!!
LAUREN!?
LAUREN THOMAS, YOU LITTLE BITCH! WHY DIDN'T YOU TELL ME YOU WERE COMING!?

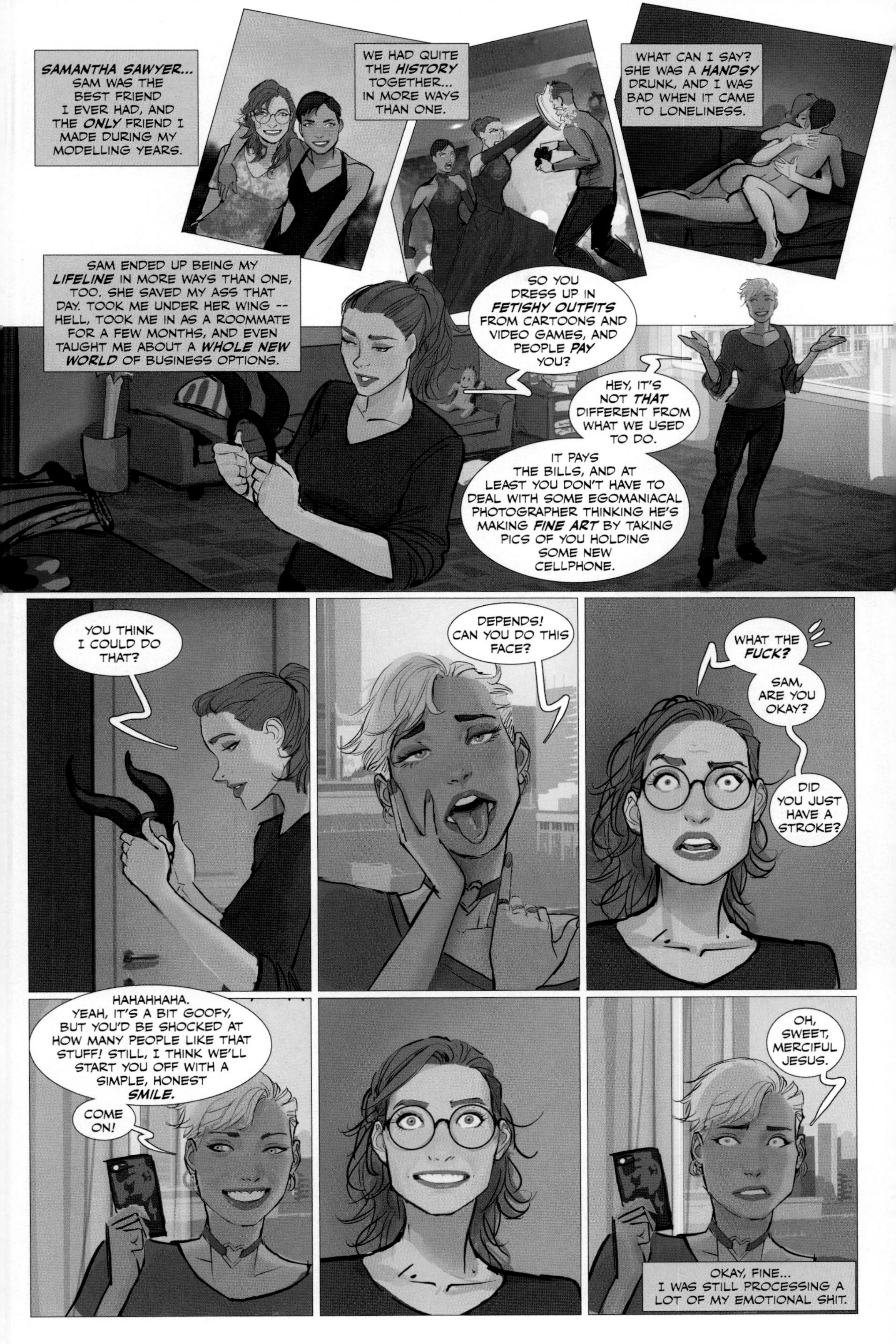
SAMANTHA SAWYER... SAM WAS THE BEST FRIEND I EVER HAD, AND THE ONLY FRIEND I MADE DURING MY MODELLING YEARS.
WE HAD QUITE THE HISTORY TOGETHER... IN MORE WAYS THAN ONE.
WHAT CAN I SAY? SHE WAS A HANDSY DRUNK, AND I WAS BAD WHEN IT CAME TO LONELINESS.
SAM ENDED UP BEING MY LIFELINE IN MORE WAYS THAN ONE, TOO. SHE SAVED MY ASS THAT DAY. TOOK ME UNDER HER WING -- HELL, TOOK ME IN AS A ROOMMATE FOR A FEW MONTHS, AND EVEN TAUGHT ME ABOUT A WHOLE NEW WORLD OF BUSINESS OPTIONS.
SO YOU DRESS UP IN FETISHY OUTFITS FROM CARTOONS AND VIDEO GAMES, AND PEOPLE PAY YOU?
HEY, IT'S NOT THAT DIFFERENT FROM WHAT WE USED TO DO.
IT PAYS THE BILLS, AND AT LEAST YOU DON'T HAVE TO DEAL WITH SOME EGOMANIACAL PHOTOGRAPHER THINKING HE'S MAKING FINE ART BY TAKING PICS OF YOU HOLDING SOME NEW CELLPHONE.
YOU THINK I COULD DO THAT?
DEPENDS! CAN YOU DO THIS FACE?
WHAT THE FUCK?
SAM, ARE YOU OKAY?
DID YOU JUST HAVE A STROKE?
HAHAHHAHA. YEAH, IT'S A BIT GOOFY, BUT YOU'D BE SHOCKED AT HOW MANY PEOPLE LIKE THAT STUFF! STILL, I THINK WE'LL START YOU OFF WITH A SIMPLE, HONEST SMILE.
COME ON!
OH, SWEET, MERCIFUL JESUS.
OKAY, FINE... I WAS STILL PROCESSING A LOT OF MY EMOTIONAL SHIT.

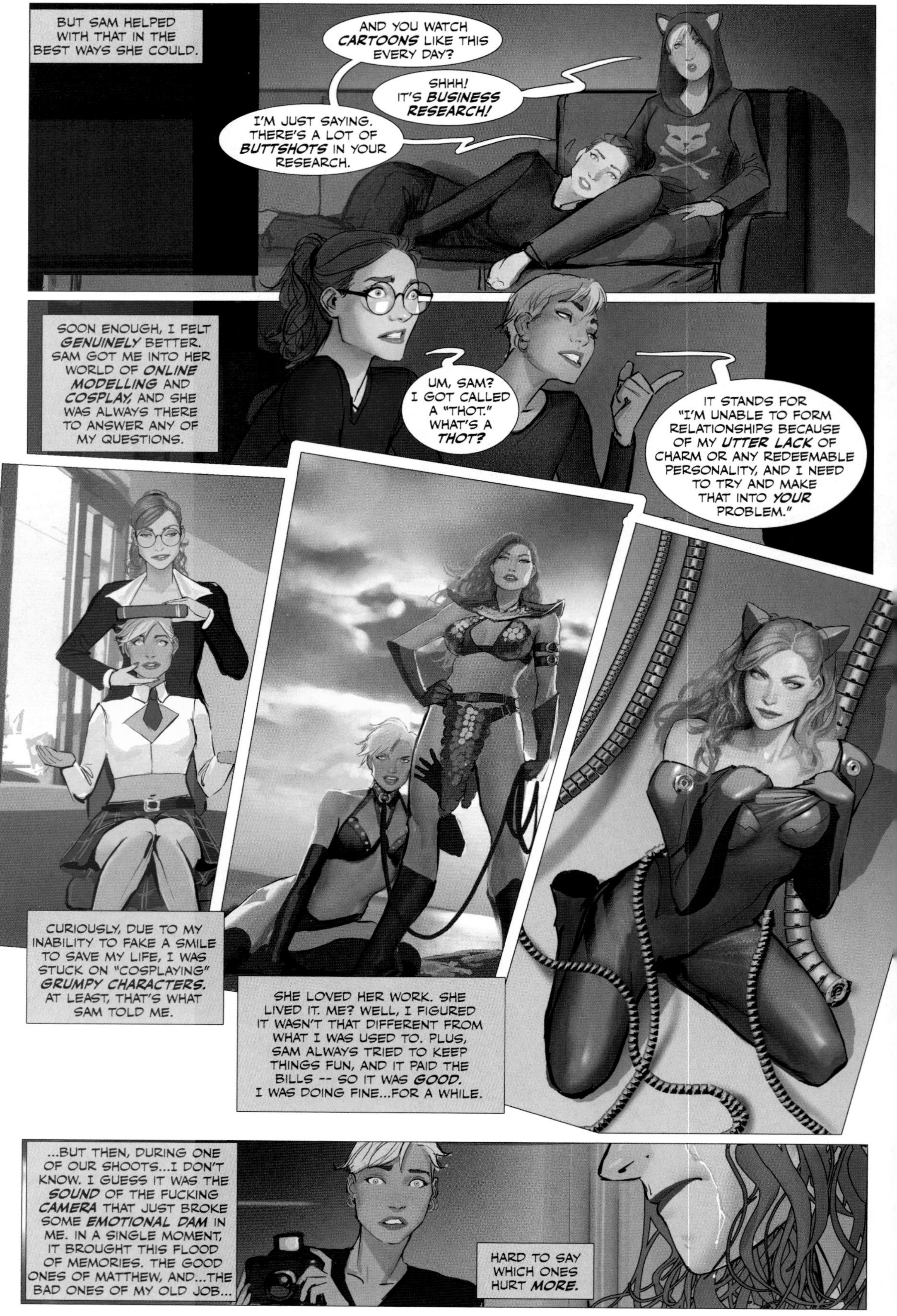

BUT SAM HELPED WITH THAT IN THE BEST WAYS SHE COULD.
AND YOU WATCH *CARTOONS* LIKE THIS EVERY DAY?
SHHH! IT'S *BUSINESS RESEARCH!*
I'M JUST SAYING. THERE'S A LOT OF *BUTTSHOTS* IN YOUR RESEARCH.
SOON ENOUGH, I FELT *GENUINELY* BETTER. SAM GOT ME INTO HER WORLD OF *ONLINE MODELLING* AND *COSPLAY,* AND SHE WAS ALWAYS THERE TO ANSWER ANY OF MY QUESTIONS.
UM, SAM? I GOT CALLED A "THOT." WHAT'S A *THOT?*
IT STANDS FOR "I'M UNABLE TO FORM RELATIONSHIPS BECAUSE OF MY *UTTER LACK* OF CHARM OR ANY REDEEMABLE PERSONALITY, AND I NEED TO TRY AND MAKE THAT INTO *YOUR* PROBLEM."
CURIOUSLY, DUE TO MY INABILITY TO FAKE A SMILE TO SAVE MY LIFE, I WAS STUCK ON "COSPLAYING" *GRUMPY CHARACTERS.* AT LEAST, THAT'S WHAT SAM TOLD ME.
SHE LOVED HER WORK. SHE LIVED IT. ME? WELL, I FIGURED IT WASN'T THAT DIFFERENT FROM WHAT I WAS USED TO. PLUS, SAM ALWAYS TRIED TO KEEP THINGS FUN, AND IT PAID THE BILLS -- SO IT WAS *GOOD.* I WAS DOING FINE...FOR A WHILE.
...BUT THEN, DURING ONE OF OUR SHOOTS...I DON'T KNOW. I GUESS IT WAS THE *SOUND* OF THE FUCKING *CAMERA* THAT JUST BROKE SOME *EMOTIONAL DAM* IN ME. IN A SINGLE MOMENT, IT BROUGHT THIS FLOOD OF MEMORIES. THE GOOD ONES OF MATTHEW, AND...THE BAD ONES OF MY OLD JOB...
HARD TO SAY WHICH ONES HURT *MORE.*

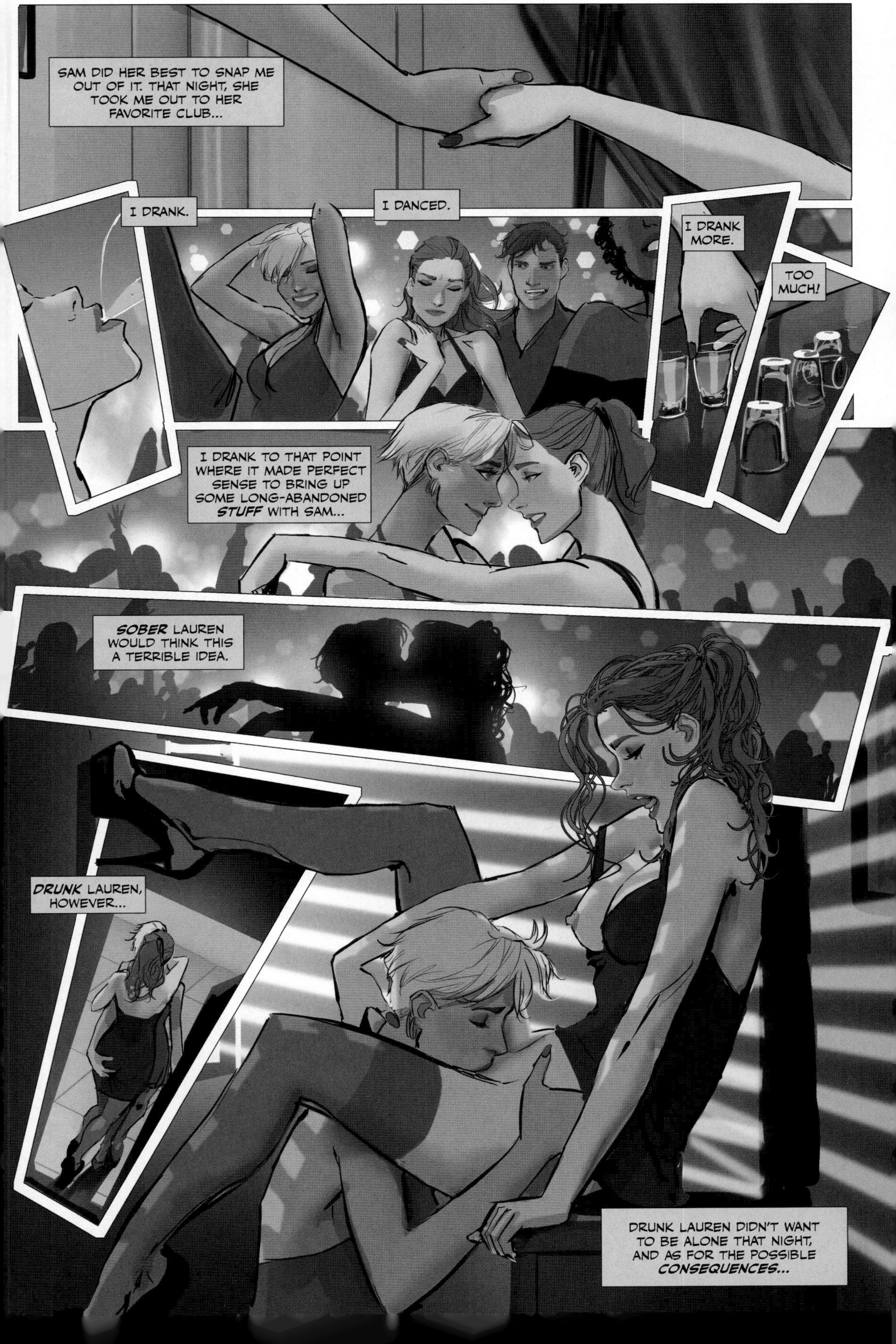
SAM DID HER BEST TO SNAP ME OUT OF IT. THAT NIGHT, SHE TOOK ME OUT TO HER FAVORITE CLUB...
I DRANK.
I DANCED.
I DRANK MORE.
TOO MUCH!
I DRANK TO THAT POINT WHERE IT MADE PERFECT SENSE TO BRING UP SOME LONG-ABANDONED *STUFF* WITH SAM...
SOBER LAUREN WOULD THINK THIS A TERRIBLE IDEA.
DRUNK LAUREN, HOWEVER...
DRUNK LAUREN DIDN'T WANT TO BE ALONE THAT NIGHT, AND AS FOR THE POSSIBLE *CONSEQUENCES*...

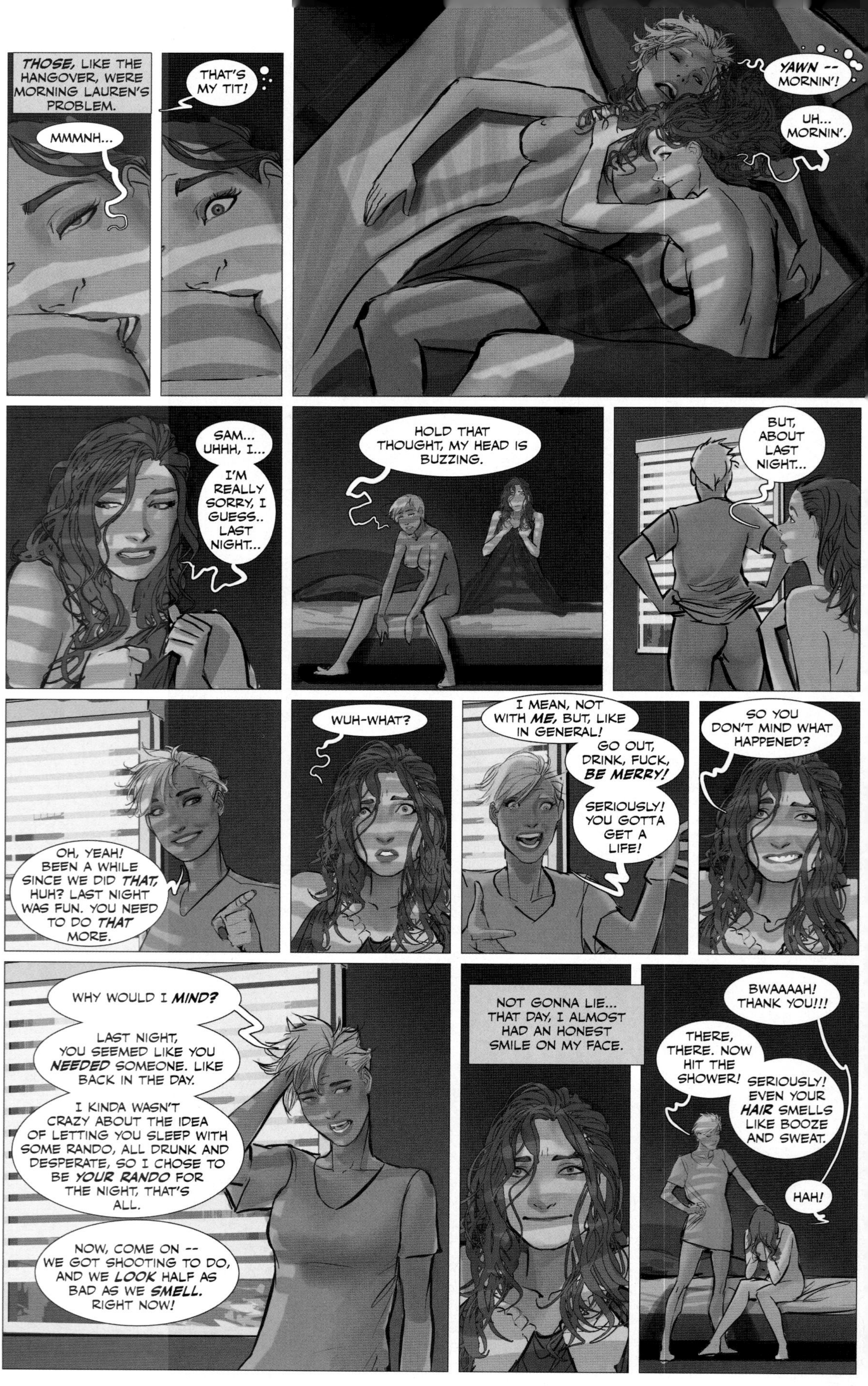
THOSE, LIKE THE HANGOVER, WERE MORNING LAUREN'S PROBLEM.
MMMNH...
THAT'S MY TIT!
YAWN -- MORNIN'!
UH... MORNIN'.
SAM... UHHH, I...
I'M REALLY SORRY, I GUESS.. LAST NIGHT...
HOLD THAT THOUGHT, MY HEAD IS BUZZING.
BUT, ABOUT LAST NIGHT...
OH, YEAH! BEEN A WHILE SINCE WE DID THAT, HUH? LAST NIGHT WAS FUN. YOU NEED TO DO THAT MORE.
WUH-WHAT?
I MEAN, NOT WITH ME, BUT, LIKE IN GENERAL!
GO OUT, DRINK, FUCK, BE MERRY!
SERIOUSLY! YOU GOTTA GET A LIFE!
SO YOU DON'T MIND WHAT HAPPENED?
WHY WOULD I MIND?
LAST NIGHT, YOU SEEMED LIKE YOU NEEDED SOMEONE. LIKE BACK IN THE DAY.
I KINDA WASN'T CRAZY ABOUT THE IDEA OF LETTING YOU SLEEP WITH SOME RANDO, ALL DRUNK AND DESPERATE, SO I CHOSE TO BE YOUR RANDO FOR THE NIGHT, THAT'S ALL.
NOW, COME ON -- WE GOT SHOOTING TO DO, AND WE LOOK HALF AS BAD AS WE SMELL. RIGHT NOW!
NOT GONNA LIE... THAT DAY, I ALMOST HAD AN HONEST SMILE ON MY FACE.
BWAAAAH! THANK YOU!!!
THERE, THERE. NOW HIT THE SHOWER!
SERIOUSLY! EVEN YOUR HAIR SMELLS LIKE BOOZE AND SWEAT.
HAH!

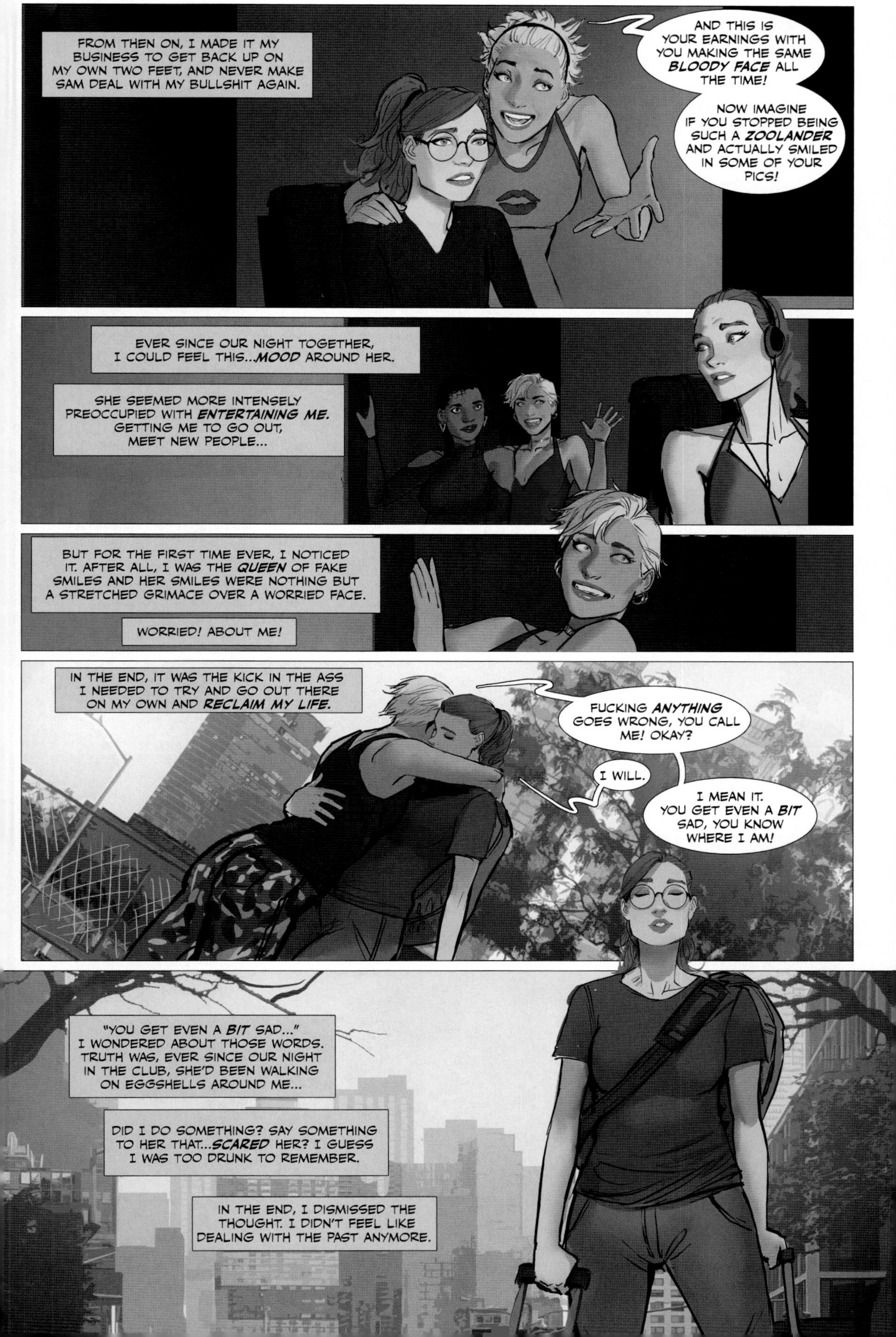
FROM THEN ON, I MADE IT MY BUSINESS TO GET BACK UP ON MY OWN TWO FEET, AND NEVER MAKE SAM DEAL WITH MY BULLSHIT AGAIN.
AND THIS IS YOUR EARNINGS WITH YOU MAKING THE SAME BLOODY FACE ALL THE TIME!
NOW IMAGINE IF YOU STOPPED BEING SUCH A ZOOLANDER AND ACTUALLY SMILED IN SOME OF YOUR PICS!
EVER SINCE OUR NIGHT TOGETHER, I COULD FEEL THIS...MOOD AROUND HER.
SHE SEEMED MORE INTENSELY PREOCCUPIED WITH ENTERTAINING ME. GETTING ME TO GO OUT, MEET NEW PEOPLE...
BUT FOR THE FIRST TIME EVER, I NOTICED IT. AFTER ALL, I WAS THE QUEEN OF FAKE SMILES AND HER SMILES WERE NOTHING BUT A STRETCHED GRIMACE OVER A WORRIED FACE.
WORRIED! ABOUT ME!
IN THE END, IT WAS THE KICK IN THE ASS I NEEDED TO TRY AND GO OUT THERE ON MY OWN AND RECLAIM MY LIFE.
FUCKING ANYTHING GOES WRONG, YOU CALL ME! OKAY?
I WILL.
I MEAN IT. YOU GET EVEN A BIT SAD, YOU KNOW WHERE I AM!
"YOU GET EVEN A BIT SAD..." I WONDERED ABOUT THOSE WORDS. TRUTH WAS, EVER SINCE OUR NIGHT IN THE CLUB, SHE'D BEEN WALKING ON EGGSHELLS AROUND ME...
DID I DO SOMETHING? SAY SOMETHING TO HER THAT...SCARED HER? I GUESS I WAS TOO DRUNK TO REMEMBER.
IN THE END, I DISMISSED THE THOUGHT. I DIDN'T FEEL LIKE DEALING WITH THE PAST ANYMORE.

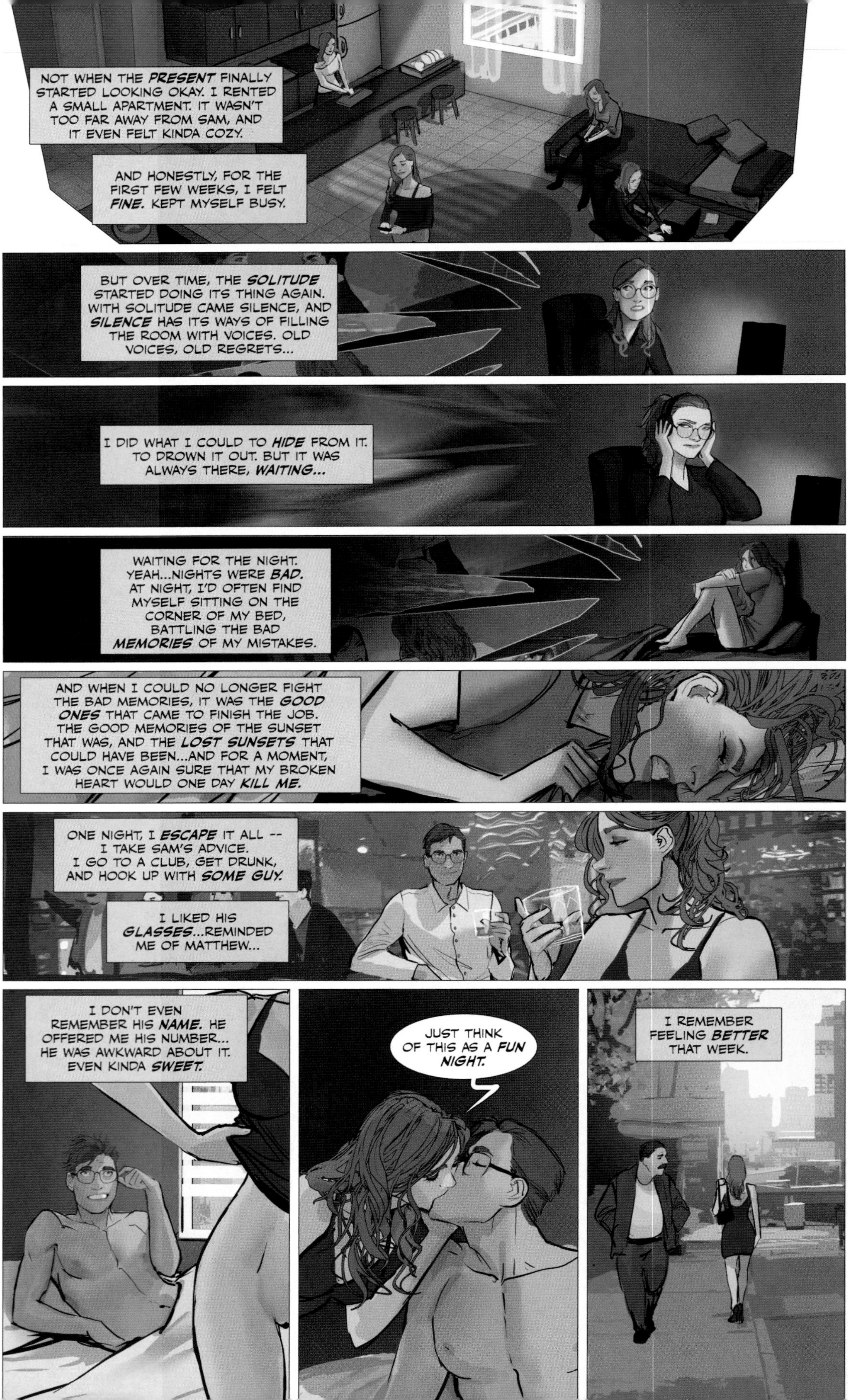
NOT WHEN THE PRESENT FINALLY STARTED LOOKING OKAY. I RENTED A SMALL APARTMENT. IT WASN'T TOO FAR AWAY FROM SAM, AND IT EVEN FELT KINDA COZY.
AND HONESTLY, FOR THE FIRST FEW WEEKS, I FELT FINE. KEPT MYSELF BUSY.
BUT OVER TIME, THE SOLITUDE STARTED DOING ITS THING AGAIN. WITH SOLITUDE CAME SILENCE, AND SILENCE HAS ITS WAYS OF FILLING THE ROOM WITH VOICES. OLD VOICES, OLD REGRETS...
I DID WHAT I COULD TO HIDE FROM IT. TO DROWN IT OUT. BUT IT WAS ALWAYS THERE, WAITING...
WAITING FOR THE NIGHT. YEAH...NIGHTS WERE BAD. AT NIGHT, I'D OFTEN FIND MYSELF SITTING ON THE CORNER OF MY BED, BATTLING THE BAD MEMORIES OF MY MISTAKES.
AND WHEN I COULD NO LONGER FIGHT THE BAD MEMORIES, IT WAS THE GOOD ONES THAT CAME TO FINISH THE JOB. THE GOOD MEMORIES OF THE SUNSET THAT WAS, AND THE LOST SUNSETS THAT COULD HAVE BEEN...AND FOR A MOMENT, I WAS ONCE AGAIN SURE THAT MY BROKEN HEART WOULD ONE DAY KILL ME.
ONE NIGHT, I ESCAPE IT ALL -- I TAKE SAM'S ADVICE. I GO TO A CLUB, GET DRUNK, AND HOOK UP WITH SOME GUY.
I LIKED HIS GLASSES...REMINDED ME OF MATTHEW...
I DON'T EVEN REMEMBER HIS NAME. HE OFFERED ME HIS NUMBER... HE WAS AWKWARD ABOUT IT. EVEN KINDA SWEET.
JUST THINK OF THIS AS A FUN NIGHT.
I REMEMBER FEELING BETTER THAT WEEK.

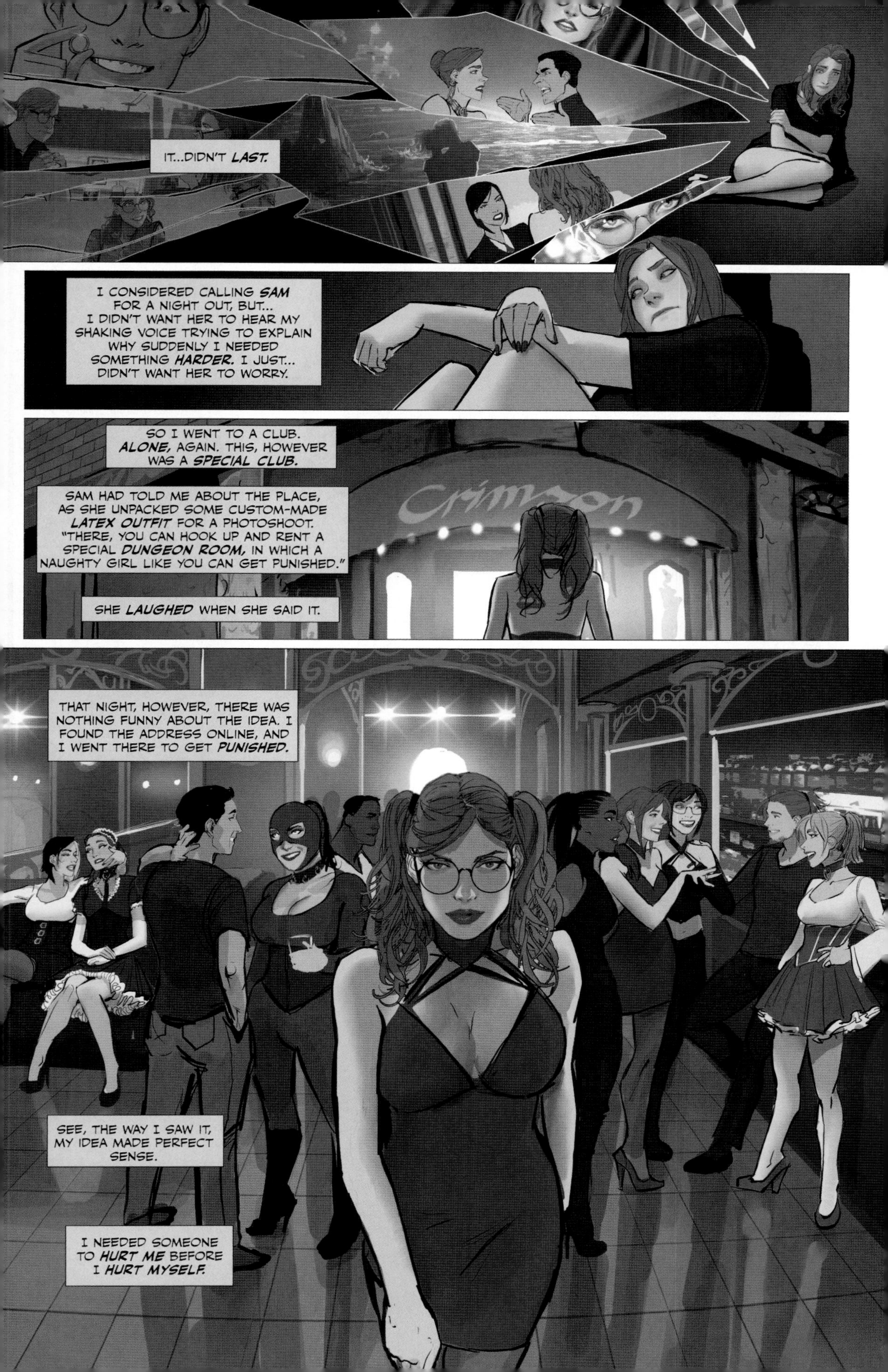
IT...DIDN'T LAST.
I CONSIDERED CALLING SAM FOR A NIGHT OUT, BUT... I DIDN'T WANT HER TO HEAR MY SHAKING VOICE TRYING TO EXPLAIN WHY SUDDENLY I NEEDED SOMETHING HARDER. I JUST... DIDN'T WANT HER TO WORRY.
SO I WENT TO A CLUB. ALONE, AGAIN. THIS, HOWEVER WAS A SPECIAL CLUB.
Crimson
SAM HAD TOLD ME ABOUT THE PLACE, AS SHE UNPACKED SOME CUSTOM-MADE LATEX OUTFIT FOR A PHOTOSHOOT. "THERE, YOU CAN HOOK UP AND RENT A SPECIAL DUNGEON ROOM, IN WHICH A NAUGHTY GIRL LIKE YOU CAN GET PUNISHED."
SHE LAUGHED WHEN SHE SAID IT.
THAT NIGHT, HOWEVER, THERE WAS NOTHING FUNNY ABOUT THE IDEA. I FOUND THE ADDRESS ONLINE, AND I WENT THERE TO GET PUNISHED.
SEE, THE WAY I SAW IT, MY IDEA MADE PERFECT SENSE.
I NEEDED SOMEONE TO HURT ME BEFORE I HURT MYSELF.

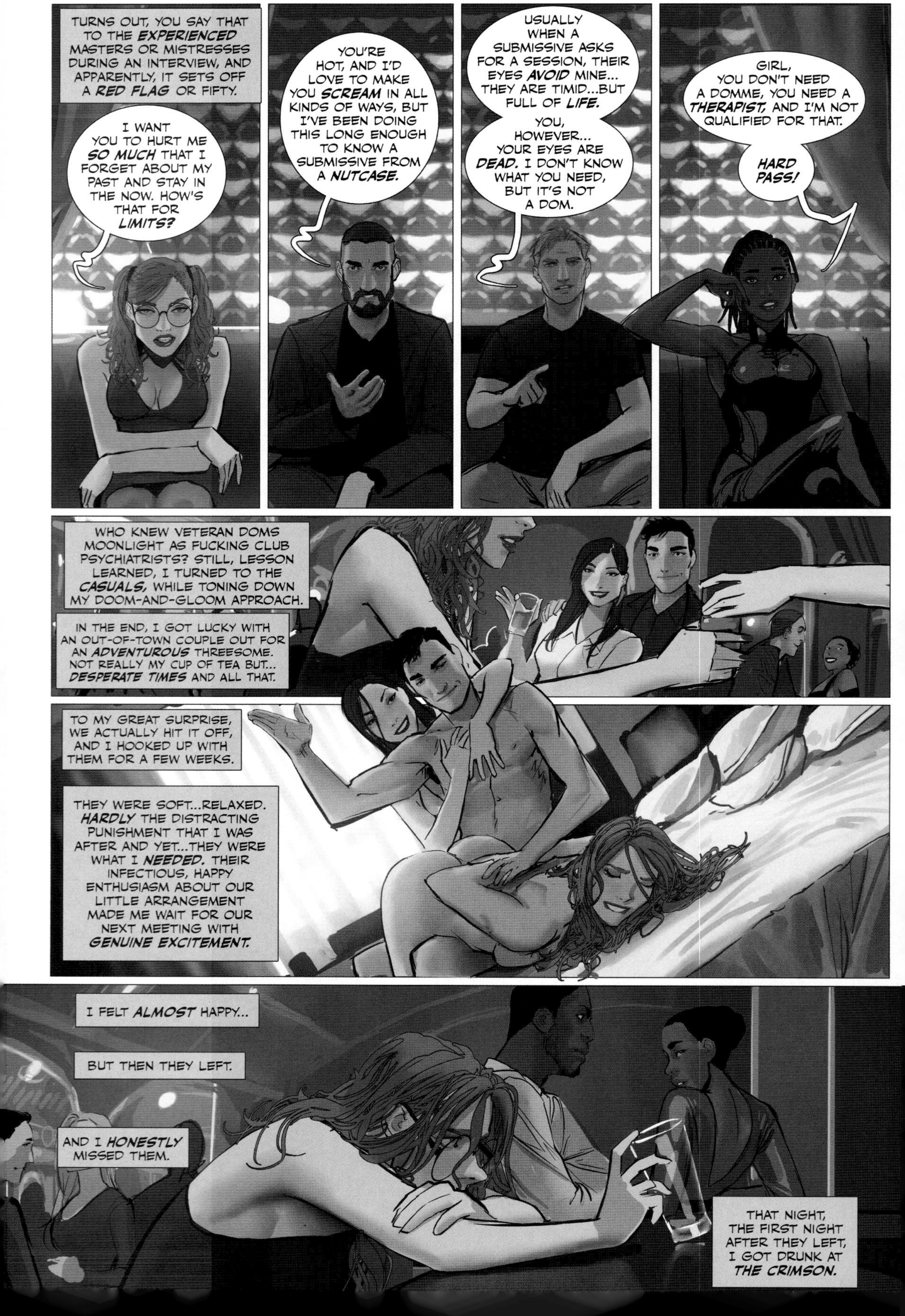

TURNS OUT, YOU SAY THAT TO THE EXPERIENCED MASTERS OR MISTRESSES DURING AN INTERVIEW, AND APPARENTLY, IT SETS OFF A RED FLAG OR FIFTY.
I WANT YOU TO HURT ME SO MUCH THAT I FORGET ABOUT MY PAST AND STAY IN THE NOW. HOW'S THAT FOR LIMITS?
YOU'RE HOT, AND I'D LOVE TO MAKE YOU SCREAM IN ALL KINDS OF WAYS, BUT I'VE BEEN DOING THIS LONG ENOUGH TO KNOW A SUBMISSIVE FROM A NUTCASE.
USUALLY WHEN A SUBMISSIVE ASKS FOR A SESSION, THEIR EYES AVOID MINE... THEY ARE TIMID...BUT FULL OF LIFE.
YOU, HOWEVER... YOUR EYES ARE DEAD. I DON'T KNOW WHAT YOU NEED, BUT IT'S NOT A DOM.
GIRL, YOU DON'T NEED A DOMME, YOU NEED A THERAPIST, AND I'M NOT QUALIFIED FOR THAT.
HARD PASS!
WHO KNEW VETERAN DOMS MOONLIGHT AS FUCKING CLUB PSYCHIATRISTS? STILL, LESSON LEARNED, I TURNED TO THE CASUALS, WHILE TONING DOWN MY DOOM-AND-GLOOM APPROACH.
IN THE END, I GOT LUCKY WITH AN OUT-OF-TOWN COUPLE OUT FOR AN ADVENTUROUS THREESOME. NOT REALLY MY CUP OF TEA BUT... DESPERATE TIMES AND ALL THAT.
TO MY GREAT SURPRISE, WE ACTUALLY HIT IT OFF, AND I HOOKED UP WITH THEM FOR A FEW WEEKS.
THEY WERE SOFT...RELAXED. HARDLY THE DISTRACTING PUNISHMENT THAT I WAS AFTER AND YET...THEY WERE WHAT I NEEDED. THEIR INFECTIOUS, HAPPY ENTHUSIASM ABOUT OUR LITTLE ARRANGEMENT MADE ME WAIT FOR OUR NEXT MEETING WITH GENUINE EXCITEMENT.
I FELT ALMOST HAPPY...
BUT THEN THEY LEFT.
AND I HONESTLY MISSED THEM.
THAT NIGHT, THE FIRST NIGHT AFTER THEY LEFT, I GOT DRUNK AT THE CRIMSON.

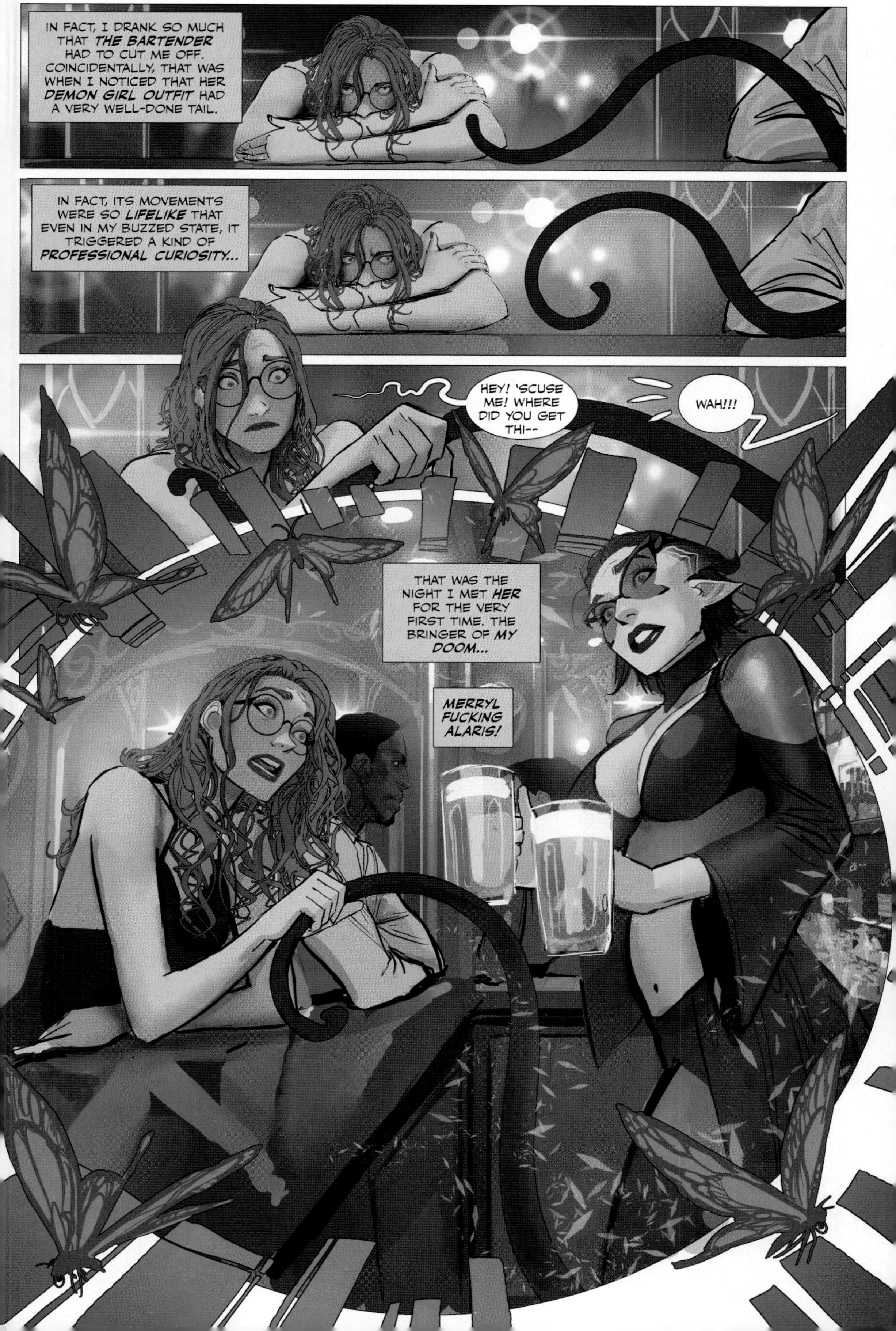
IN FACT, I DRANK SO MUCH THAT THE BARTENDER HAD TO CUT ME OFF. COINCIDENTALLY, THAT WAS WHEN I NOTICED THAT HER DEMON GIRL OUTFIT HAD A VERY WELL-DONE TAIL.
IN FACT, ITS MOVEMENTS WERE SO LIFELIKE THAT EVEN IN MY BUZZED STATE, IT TRIGGERED A KIND OF PROFESSIONAL CURIOSITY...
HEY! 'SCUSE ME! WHERE DID YOU GET THI--
WAH!!!
THAT WAS THE NIGHT I MET HER FOR THE VERY FIRST TIME. THE BRINGER OF MY DOOM...
MERRYL FUCKING ALARIS!

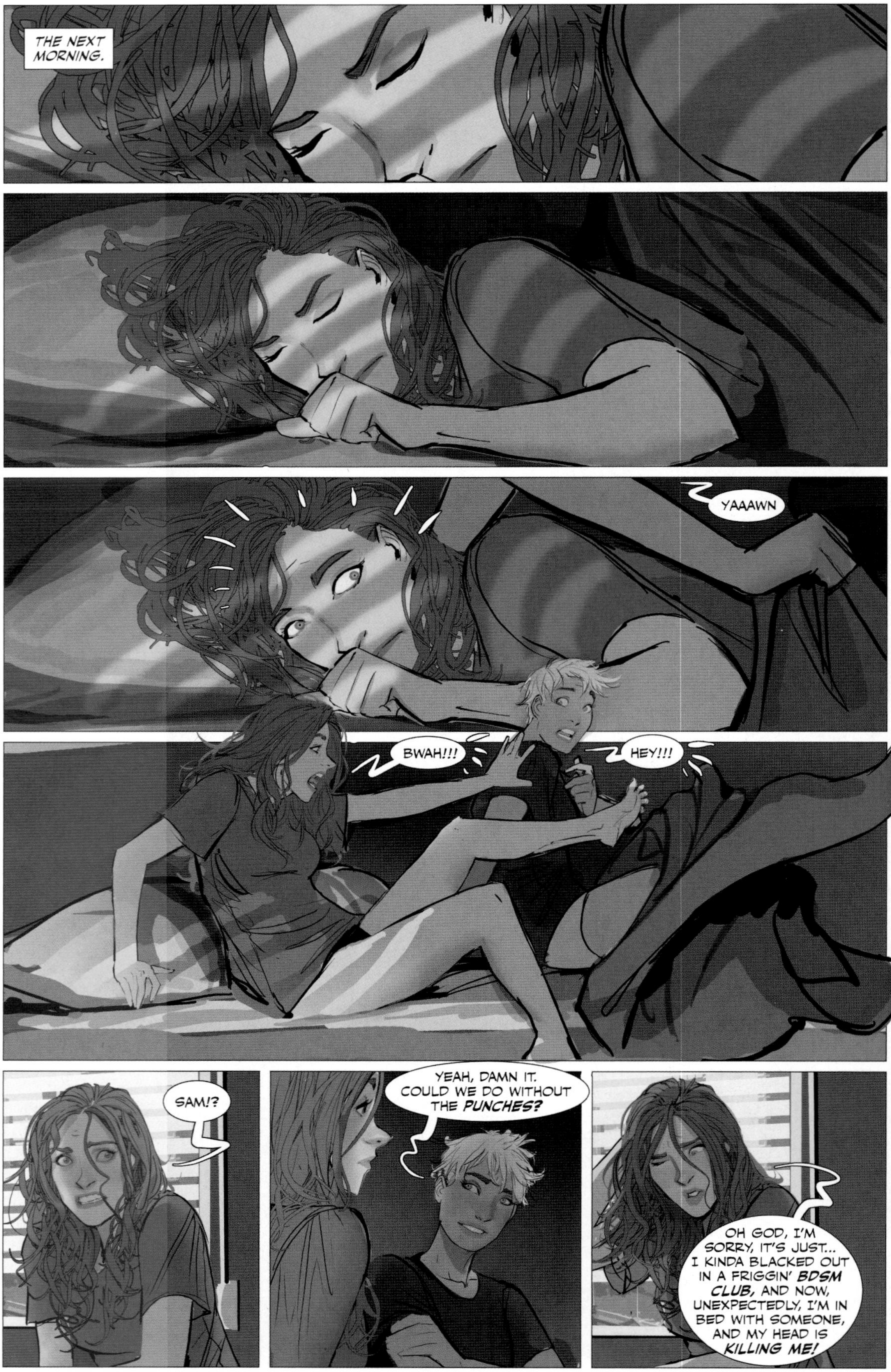
THE NEXT MORNING.
YAAAWN
BWAH!!!
HEY!!!
SAM!?
YEAH, DAMN IT. COULD WE DO WITHOUT THE PUNCHES?
OH GOD, I'M SORRY, IT'S JUST... I KINDA BLACKED OUT IN A FRIGGIN' BDSM CLUB, AND NOW, UNEXPECTEDLY, I'M IN BED WITH SOMEONE, AND MY HEAD IS KILLING ME!

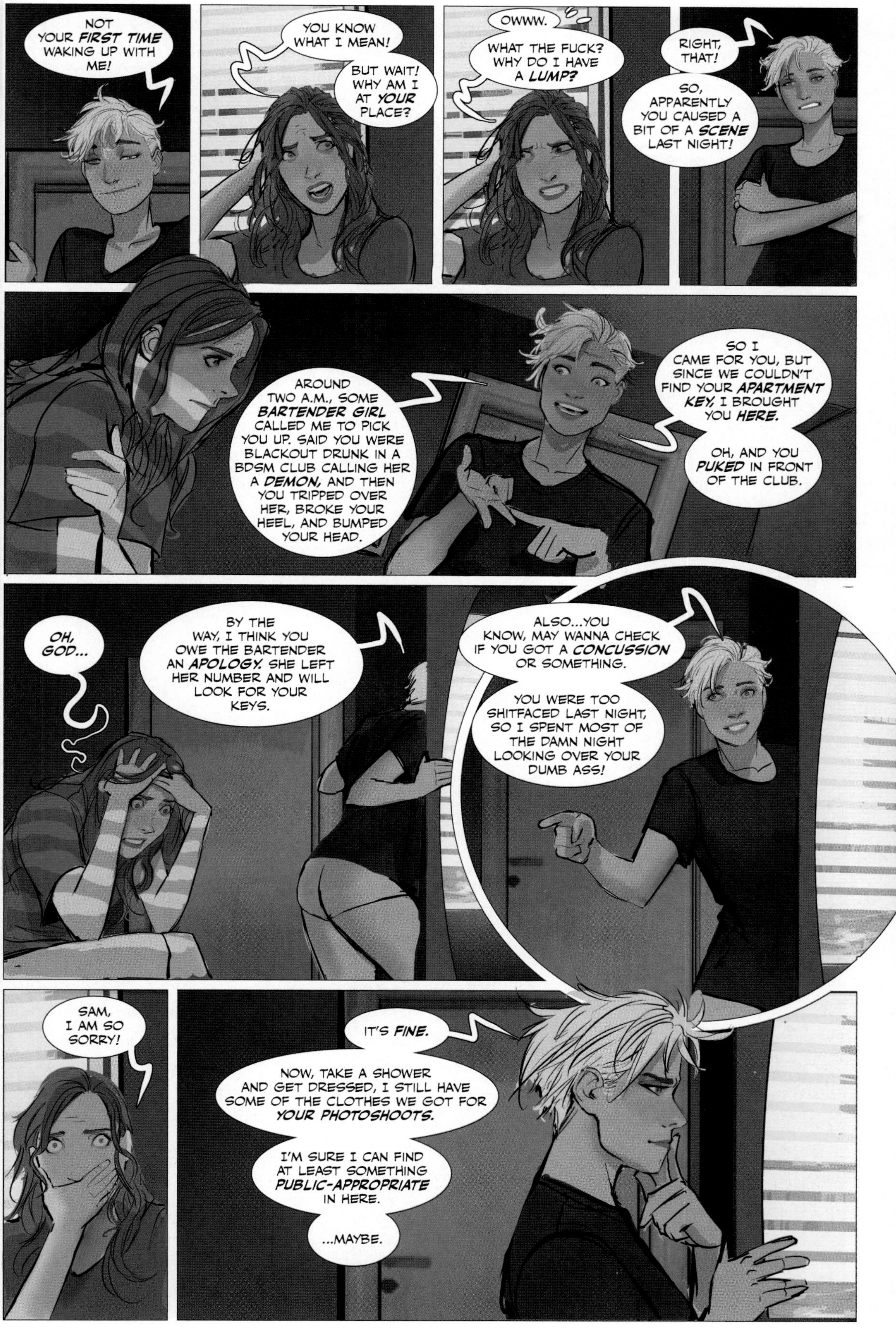
NOT YOUR FIRST TIME WAKING UP WITH ME!
YOU KNOW WHAT I MEAN!
BUT WAIT! WHY AM I AT YOUR PLACE?
OWWW.
WHAT THE FUCK? WHY DO I HAVE A LUMP?
RIGHT, THAT!
SO, APPARENTLY YOU CAUSED A BIT OF A SCENE LAST NIGHT!
AROUND TWO A.M., SOME BARTENDER GIRL CALLED ME TO PICK YOU UP. SAID YOU WERE BLACKOUT DRUNK IN A BDSM CLUB CALLING HER A DEMON, AND THEN YOU TRIPPED OVER HER, BROKE YOUR HEEL, AND BUMPED YOUR HEAD.
SO I CAME FOR YOU, BUT SINCE WE COULDN'T FIND YOUR APARTMENT KEY, I BROUGHT YOU HERE.
OH, AND YOU PUKED IN FRONT OF THE CLUB.
OH, GOD...
BY THE WAY, I THINK YOU OWE THE BARTENDER AN APOLOGY. SHE LEFT HER NUMBER AND WILL LOOK FOR YOUR KEYS.
ALSO...YOU KNOW, MAY WANNA CHECK IF YOU GOT A CONCUSSION OR SOMETHING.
YOU WERE TOO SHITFACED LAST NIGHT, SO I SPENT MOST OF THE DAMN NIGHT LOOKING OVER YOUR DUMB ASS!
SAM, I AM SO SORRY!
IT'S FINE.
NOW, TAKE A SHOWER AND GET DRESSED, I STILL HAVE SOME OF THE CLOTHES WE GOT FOR YOUR PHOTOSHOOTS.
I'M SURE I CAN FIND AT LEAST SOMETHING PUBLIC-APPROPRIATE IN HERE.
...MAYBE.

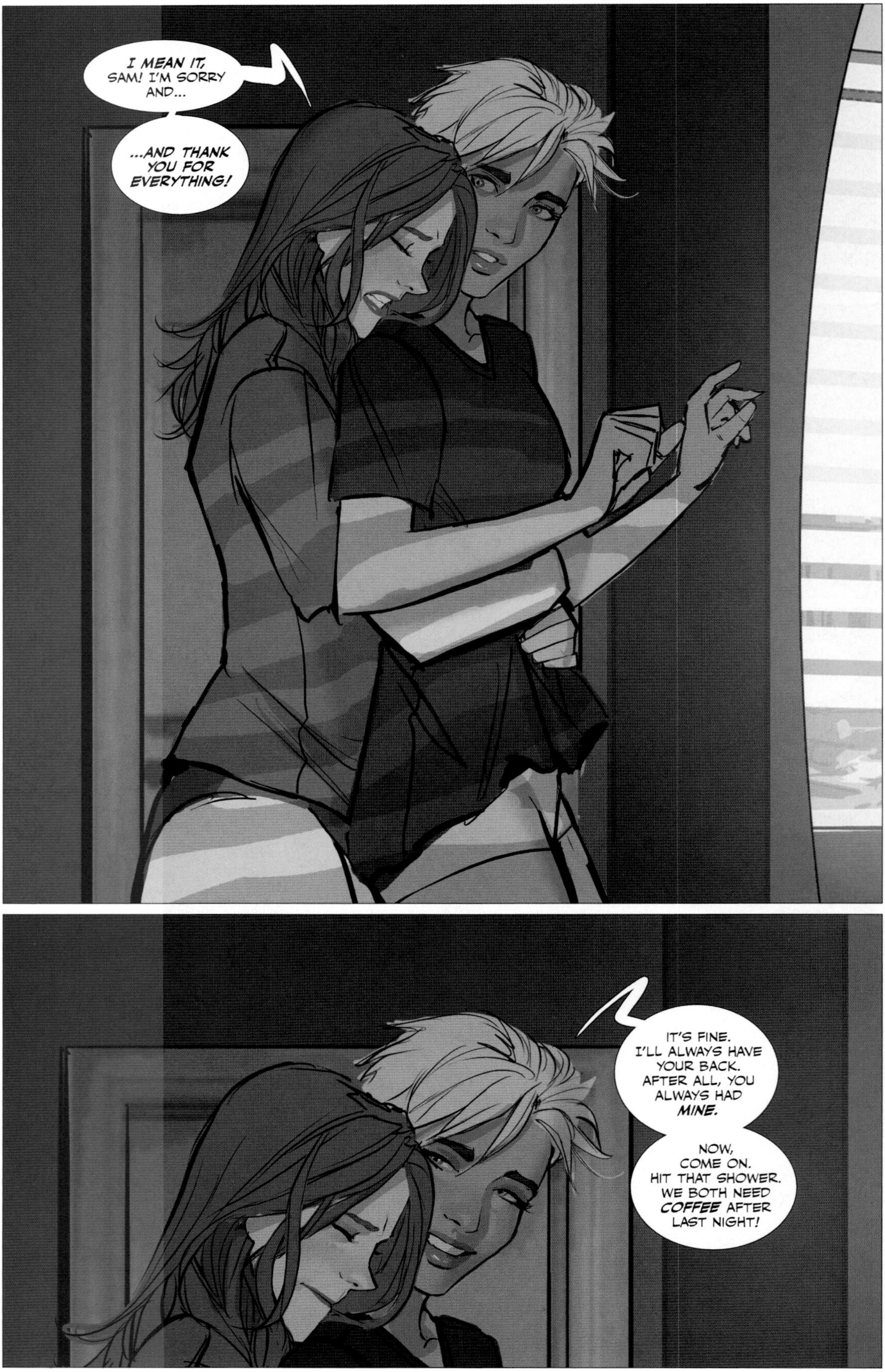
I MEAN IT, SAM! I'M SORRY AND...
...AND THANK YOU FOR EVERYTHING!
IT'S FINE. I'LL ALWAYS HAVE YOUR BACK. AFTER ALL, YOU ALWAYS HAD MINE.
NOW, COME ON. HIT THAT SHOWER. WE BOTH NEED COFFEE AFTER LAST NIGHT!

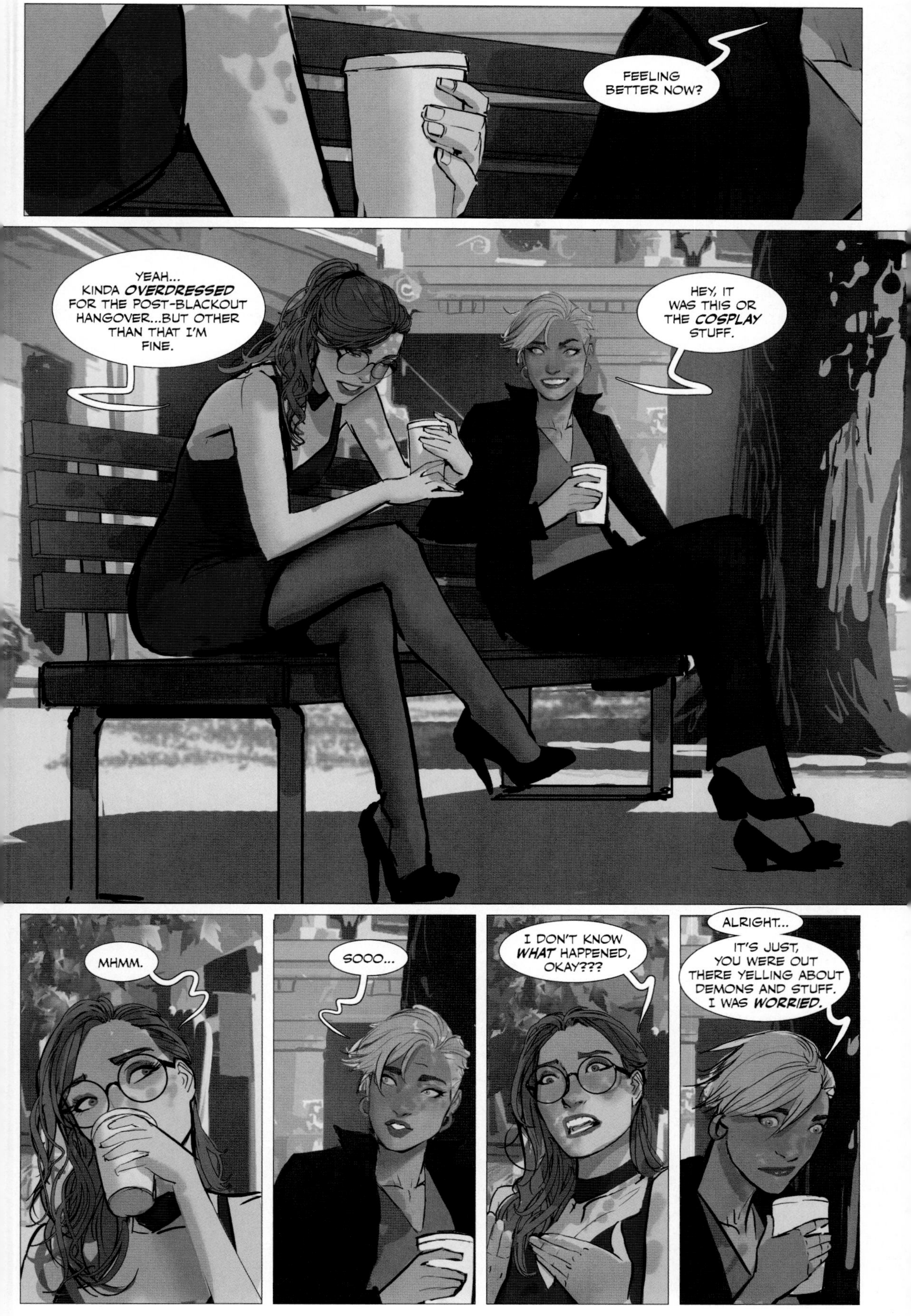
FEELING BETTER NOW?
YEAH... KINDA **OVERDRESSED** FOR THE POST-BLACKOUT HANGOVER...BUT OTHER THAN THAT I'M FINE.
HEY, IT WAS THIS OR THE **COSPLAY** STUFF.
MHMM.
SOOO...
I DON'T KNOW **WHAT** HAPPENED, OKAY???
ALRIGHT...
IT'S JUST, YOU WERE OUT THERE YELLING ABOUT DEMONS AND STUFF. I WAS **WORRIED.**

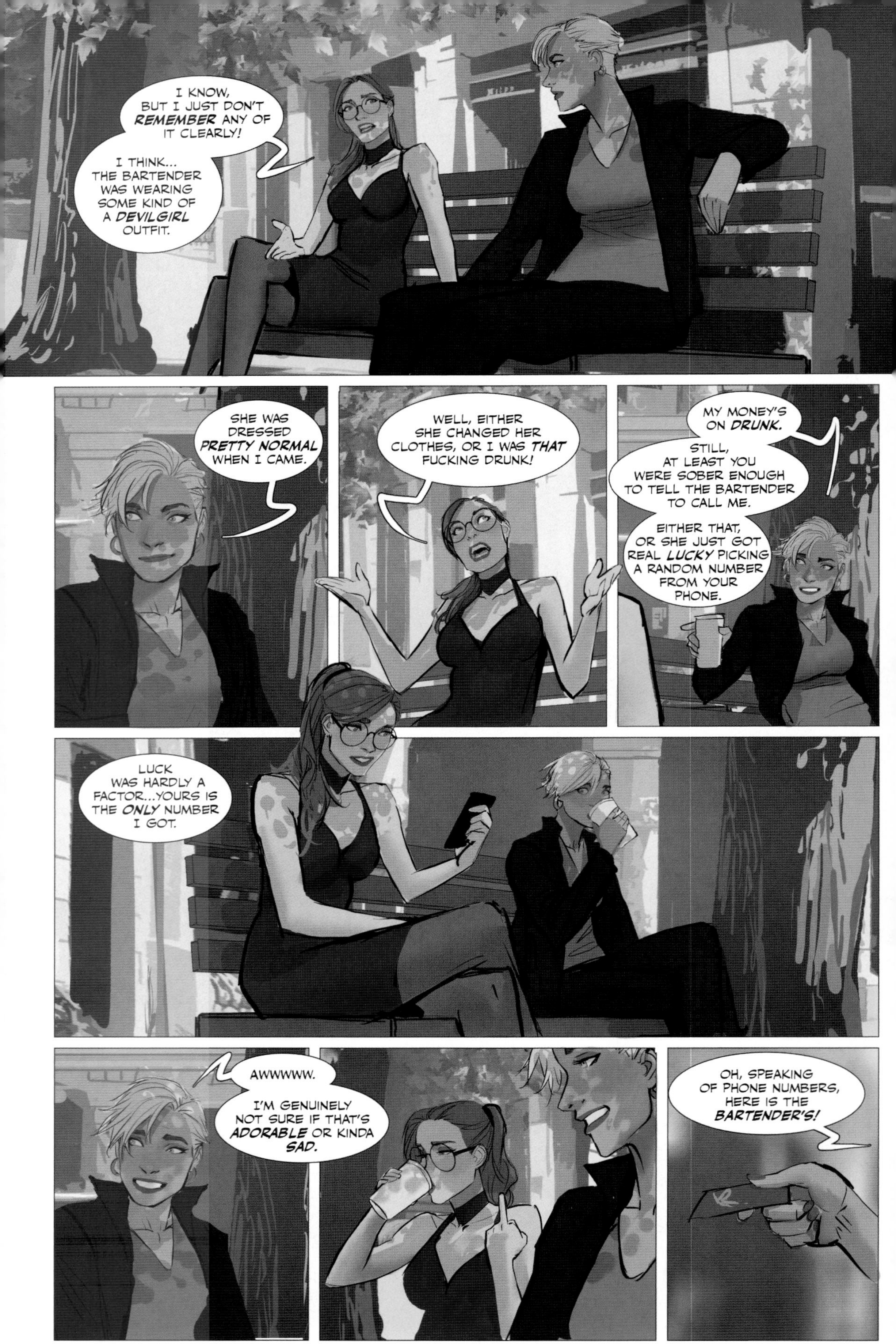
I KNOW, BUT I JUST DON'T *REMEMBER* ANY OF IT CLEARLY!
I THINK... THE BARTENDER WAS WEARING SOME KIND OF A *DEVILGIRL* OUTFIT.
SHE WAS DRESSED *PRETTY NORMAL* WHEN I CAME.
WELL, EITHER SHE CHANGED HER CLOTHES, OR I WAS *THAT* FUCKING DRUNK!
MY MONEY'S ON *DRUNK.*
STILL, AT LEAST YOU WERE SOBER ENOUGH TO TELL THE BARTENDER TO CALL ME.
EITHER THAT, OR SHE JUST GOT REAL *LUCKY* PICKING A RANDOM NUMBER FROM YOUR PHONE.
LUCK WAS HARDLY A FACTOR...YOURS IS THE *ONLY* NUMBER I GOT.
AWWWWW.
I'M GENUINELY NOT SURE IF THAT'S *ADORABLE* OR KINDA *SAD.*
OH, SPEAKING OF PHONE NUMBERS, HERE IS THE *BARTENDER'S!*

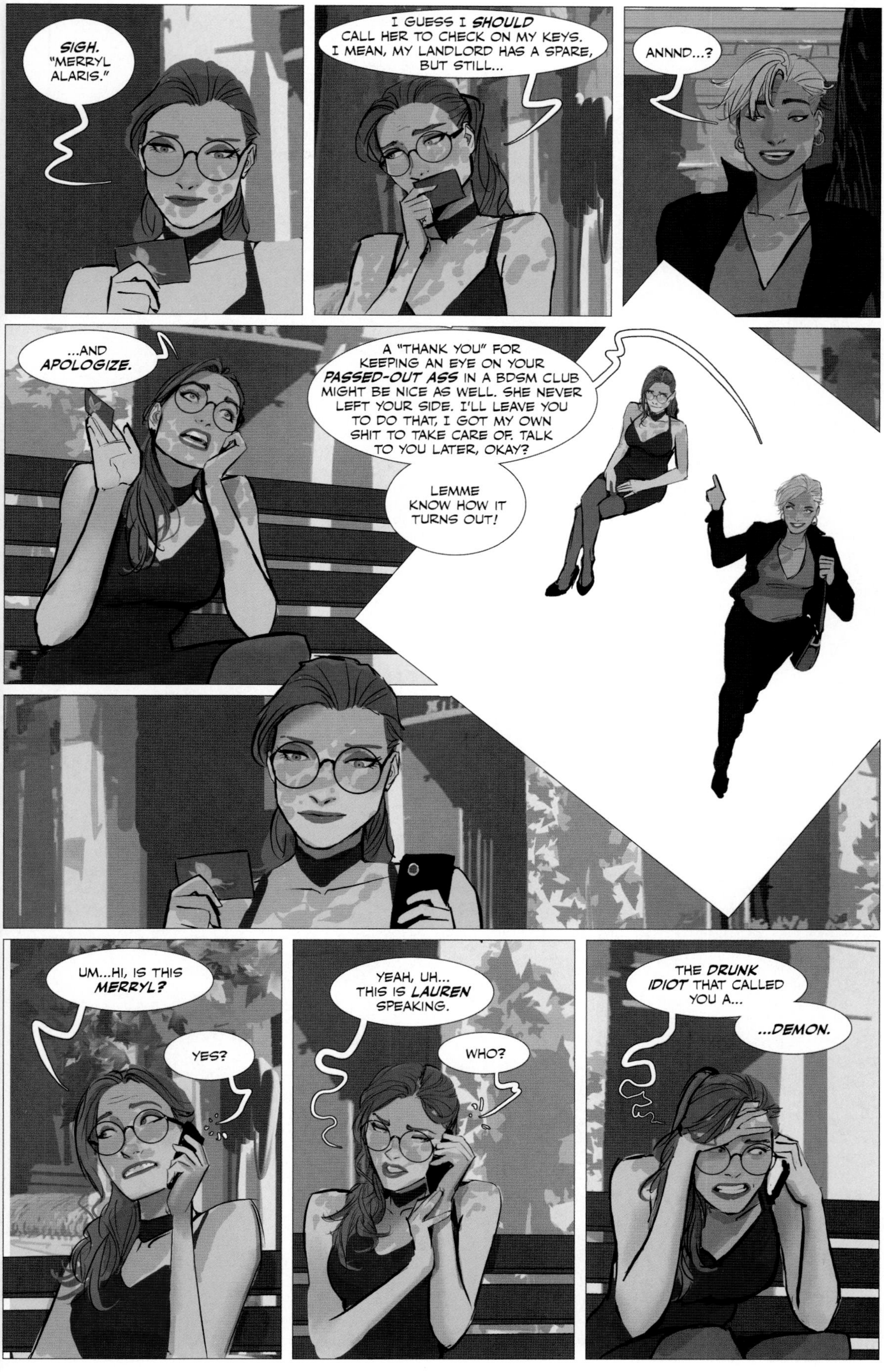
SIGH. "MERRYL ALARIS."
I GUESS I SHOULD CALL HER TO CHECK ON MY KEYS. I MEAN, MY LANDLORD HAS A SPARE, BUT STILL...
ANNND...?
...AND APOLOGIZE.
A "THANK YOU" FOR KEEPING AN EYE ON YOUR PASSED-OUT ASS IN A BDSM CLUB MIGHT BE NICE AS WELL. SHE NEVER LEFT YOUR SIDE. I'LL LEAVE YOU TO DO THAT, I GOT MY OWN SHIT TO TAKE CARE OF. TALK TO YOU LATER, OKAY?
LEMME KNOW HOW IT TURNS OUT!
UM...HI, IS THIS MERRYL?
YES?
YEAH, UH... THIS IS LAUREN SPEAKING.
WHO?
THE DRUNK IDIOT THAT CALLED YOU A...
...DEMON.

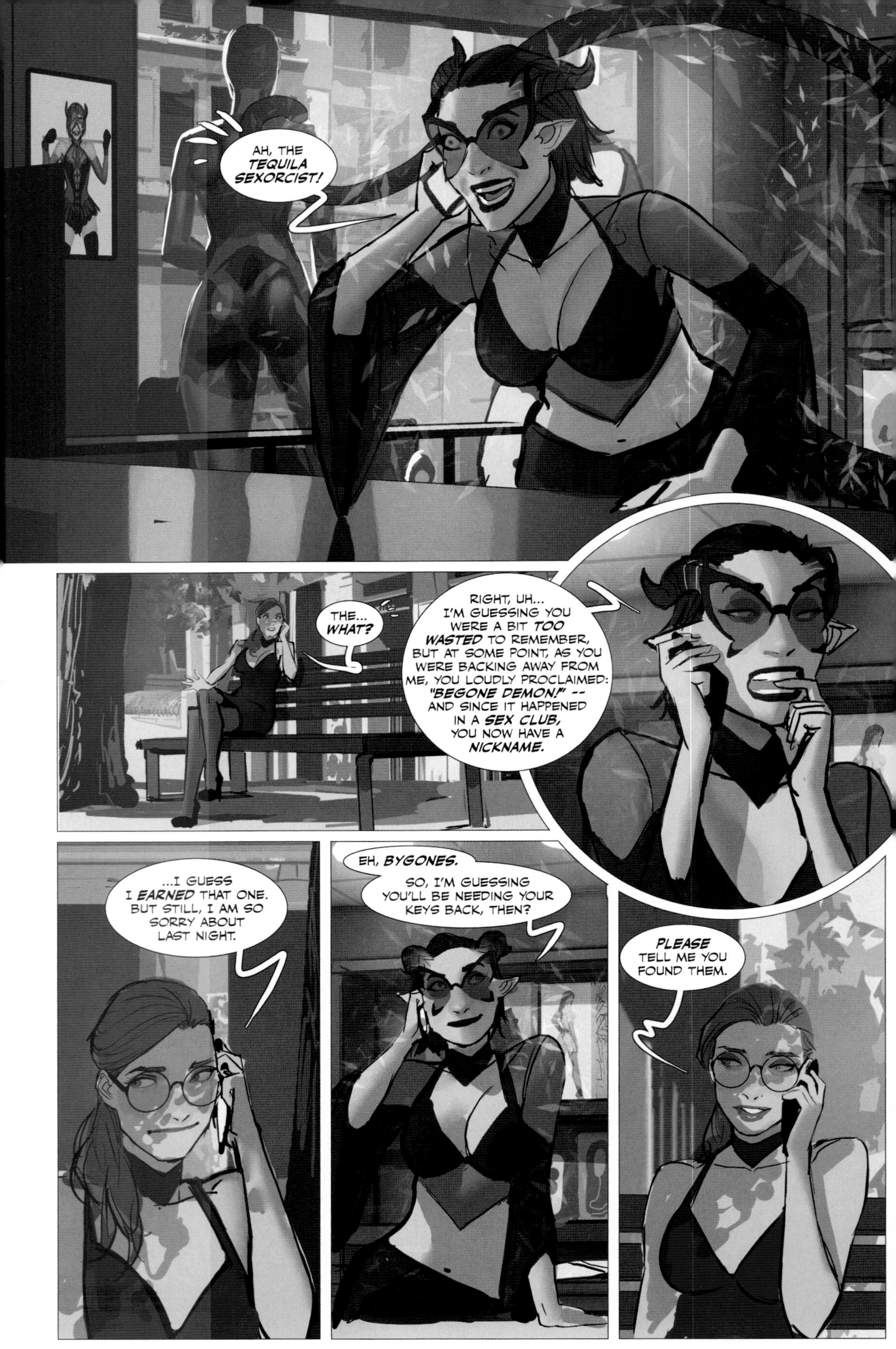
AH, THE TEQUILA SEXORCIST!
THE... WHAT?
RIGHT, UH... I'M GUESSING YOU WERE A BIT TOO WASTED TO REMEMBER, BUT AT SOME POINT, AS YOU WERE BACKING AWAY FROM ME, YOU LOUDLY PROCLAIMED: "BEGONE DEMON!" -- AND SINCE IT HAPPENED IN A SEX CLUB, YOU NOW HAVE A NICKNAME.
...I GUESS I EARNED THAT ONE. BUT STILL, I AM SO SORRY ABOUT LAST NIGHT.
EH, BYGONES.
SO, I'M GUESSING YOU'LL BE NEEDING YOUR KEYS BACK, THEN?
PLEASE TELL ME YOU FOUND THEM.

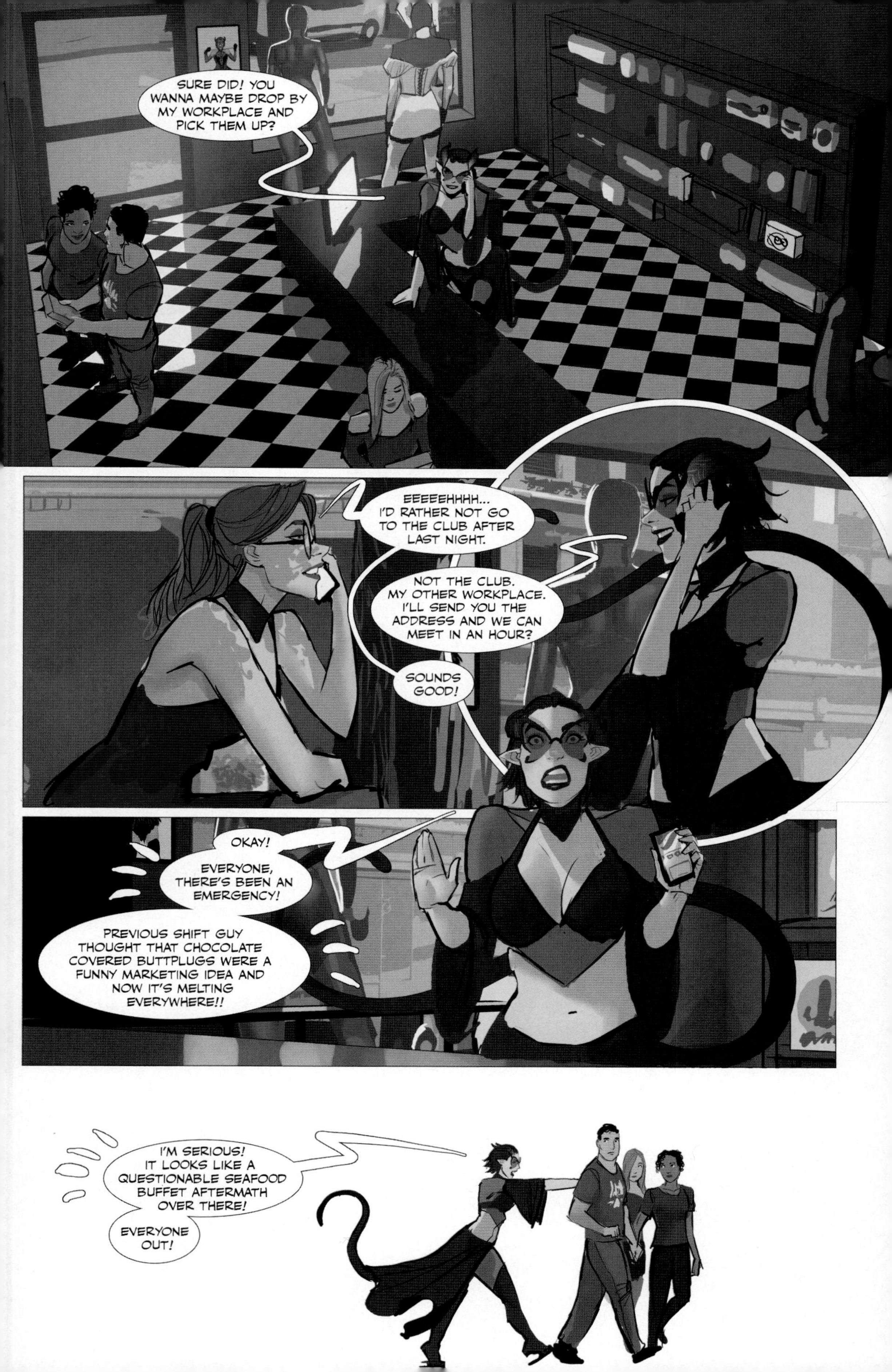
SURE DID! YOU WANNA MAYBE DROP BY MY WORKPLACE AND PICK THEM UP?
EEEEEHHHH... I'D RATHER NOT GO TO THE CLUB AFTER LAST NIGHT.
NOT THE CLUB. MY OTHER WORKPLACE. I'LL SEND YOU THE ADDRESS AND WE CAN MEET IN AN HOUR?
SOUNDS GOOD!
OKAY!
EVERYONE, THERE'S BEEN AN EMERGENCY!
PREVIOUS SHIFT GUY THOUGHT THAT CHOCOLATE COVERED BUTTPLUGS WERE A FUNNY MARKETING IDEA AND NOW IT'S MELTING EVERYWHERE!!
I'M SERIOUS! IT LOOKS LIKE A QUESTIONABLE SEAFOOD BUFFET AFTERMATH OVER THERE!
EVERYONE OUT!

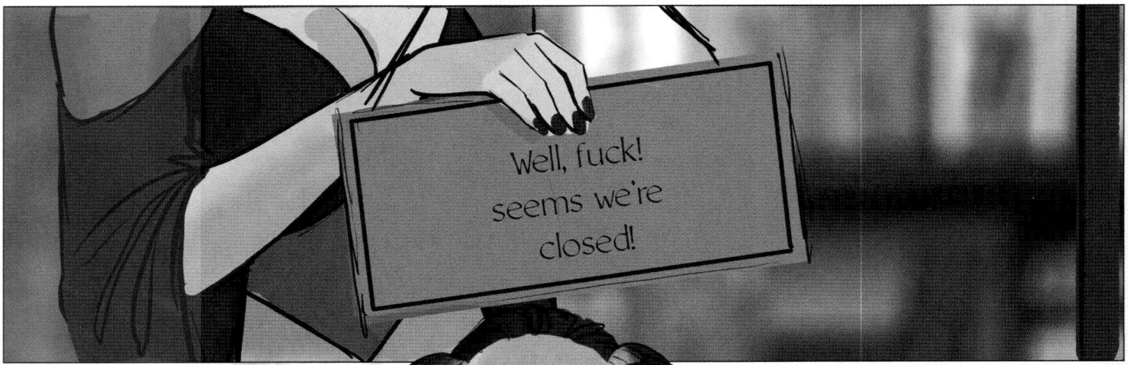
Well, fuck!
seems we're
closed!

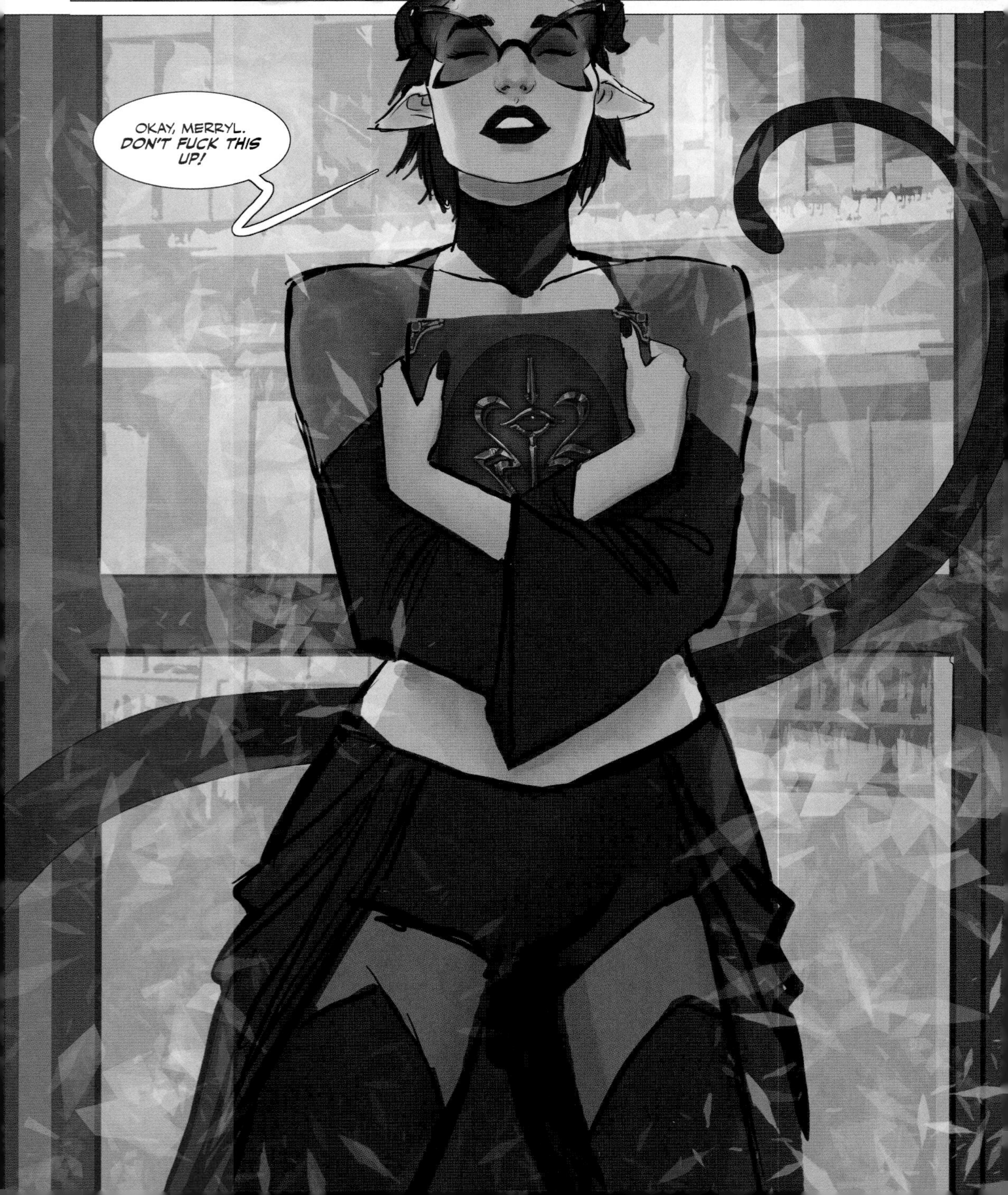
OKAY, MERRYL. ***DON'T FUCK THIS UP!***

Chapter 4

The Fine print

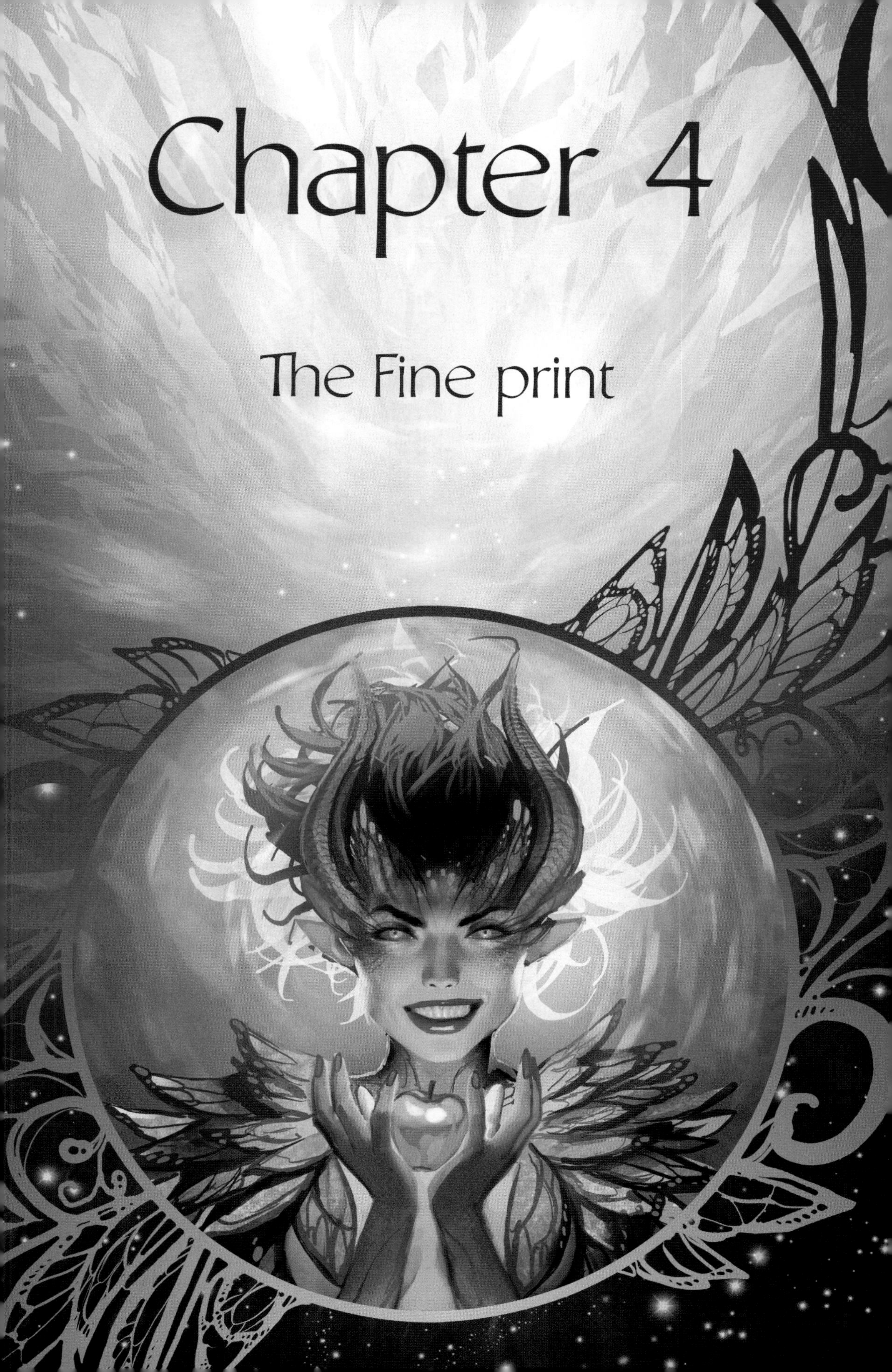

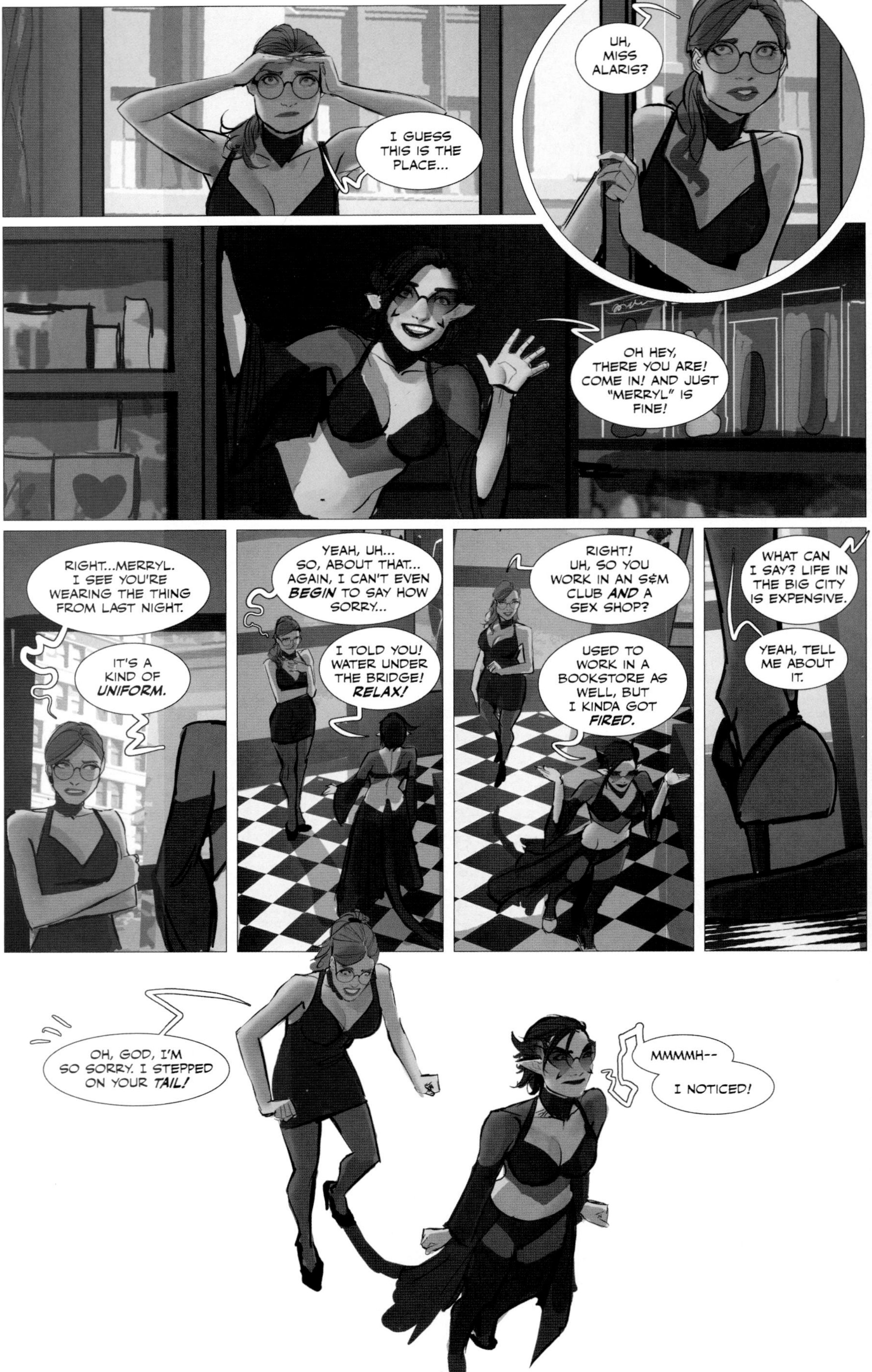
I GUESS THIS IS THE PLACE...
UH, MISS ALARIS?
OH HEY, THERE YOU ARE! COME IN! AND JUST "MERRYL" IS FINE!
RIGHT...MERRYL. I SEE YOU'RE WEARING THE THING FROM LAST NIGHT.
IT'S A KIND OF *UNIFORM.*
YEAH, UH... SO, ABOUT THAT... AGAIN, I CAN'T EVEN *BEGIN* TO SAY HOW SORRY...
I TOLD YOU! WATER UNDER THE BRIDGE! *RELAX!*
RIGHT! UH, SO YOU WORK IN AN S&M CLUB *AND* A SEX SHOP?
USED TO WORK IN A BOOKSTORE AS WELL, BUT I KINDA GOT *FIRED.*
WHAT CAN I SAY? LIFE IN THE BIG CITY IS EXPENSIVE.
YEAH, TELL ME ABOUT IT.
OH, GOD, I'M SO SORRY. I STEPPED ON YOUR *TAIL!*
MMMMH--
I NOTICED!

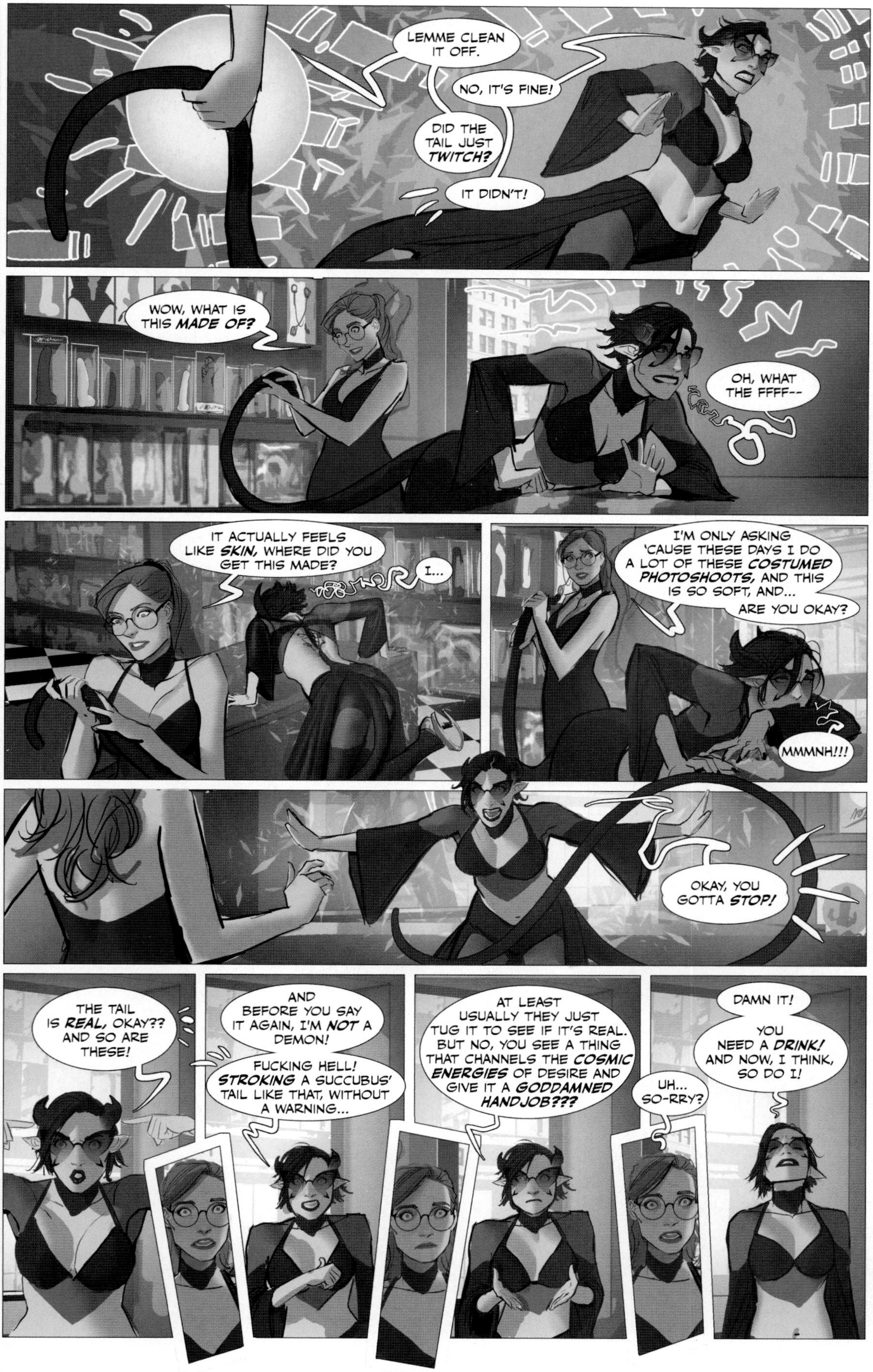
LEMME CLEAN IT OFF.
NO, IT'S FINE!
DID THE TAIL JUST TWITCH?
IT DIDN'T!
WOW, WHAT IS THIS MADE OF?
OH, WHAT THE FFFF--
IT ACTUALLY FEELS LIKE SKIN, WHERE DID YOU GET THIS MADE?
I...
I'M ONLY ASKING 'CAUSE THESE DAYS I DO A LOT OF THESE COSTUMED PHOTOSHOOTS, AND THIS IS SO SOFT, AND...
ARE YOU OKAY?
MMMNH!!!
OKAY, YOU GOTTA STOP!
THE TAIL IS REAL, OKAY?? AND SO ARE THESE!
AND BEFORE YOU SAY IT AGAIN, I'M NOT A DEMON!
FUCKING HELL! STROKING A SUCCUBUS' TAIL LIKE THAT, WITHOUT A WARNING...
AT LEAST USUALLY THEY JUST TUG IT TO SEE IF IT'S REAL. BUT NO, YOU SEE A THING THAT CHANNELS THE COSMIC ENERGIES OF DESIRE AND GIVE IT A GODDAMNED HANDJOB???
UH... SO-RRY?
DAMN IT!
YOU NEED A DRINK! AND NOW, I THINK, SO DO I!

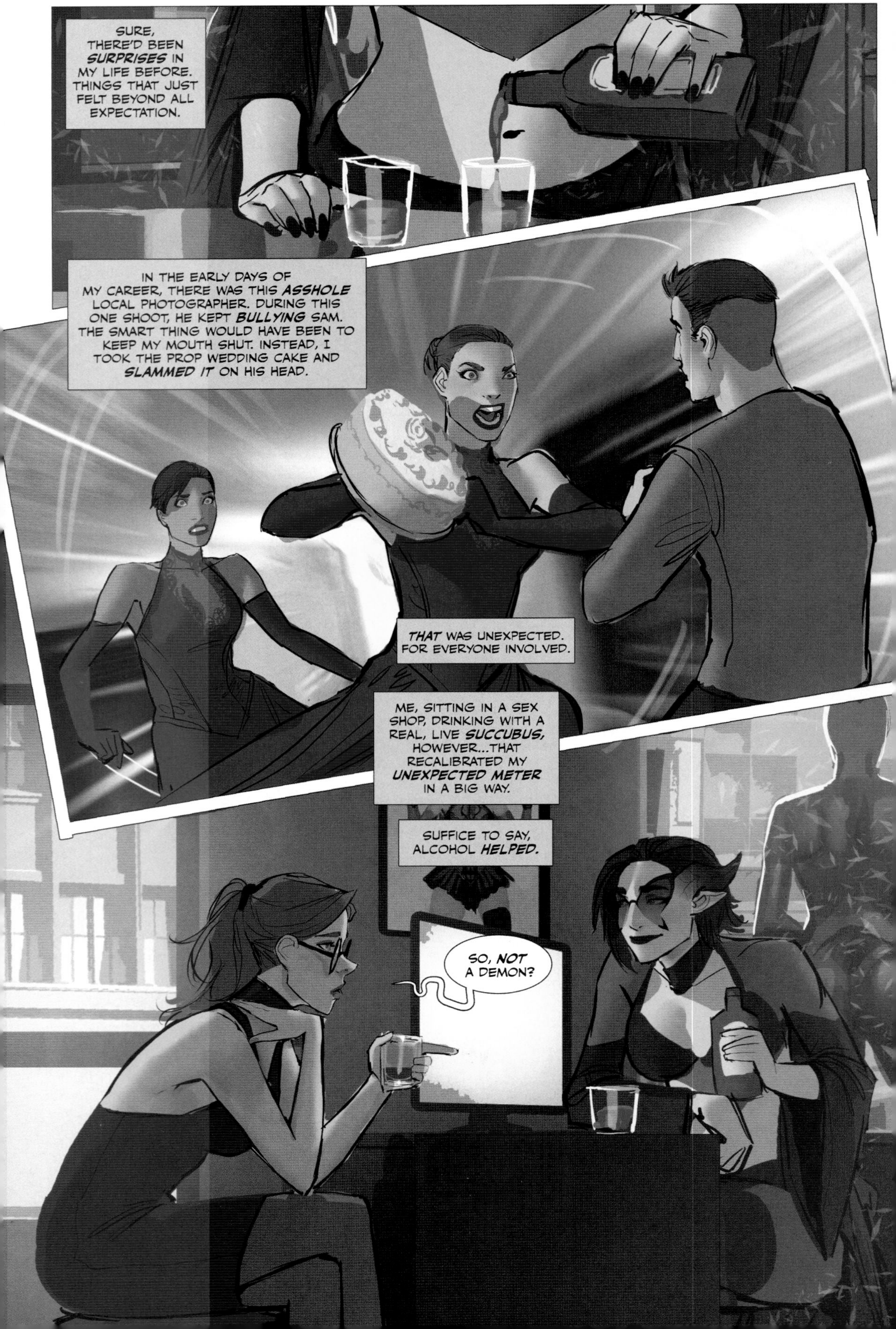
SURE, THERE'D BEEN *SURPRISES* IN MY LIFE BEFORE. THINGS THAT JUST FELT BEYOND ALL EXPECTATION.
IN THE EARLY DAYS OF MY CAREER, THERE WAS THIS *ASSHOLE* LOCAL PHOTOGRAPHER. DURING THIS ONE SHOOT, HE KEPT *BULLYING* SAM. THE SMART THING WOULD HAVE BEEN TO KEEP MY MOUTH SHUT. INSTEAD, I TOOK THE PROP WEDDING CAKE AND *SLAMMED IT* ON HIS HEAD.
THAT WAS UNEXPECTED. FOR EVERYONE INVOLVED.
ME, SITTING IN A SEX SHOP, DRINKING WITH A REAL, LIVE *SUCCUBUS,* HOWEVER...THAT RECALIBRATED MY *UNEXPECTED METER* IN A BIG WAY.
SUFFICE TO SAY, ALCOHOL *HELPED.*
SO, *NOT* A DEMON?

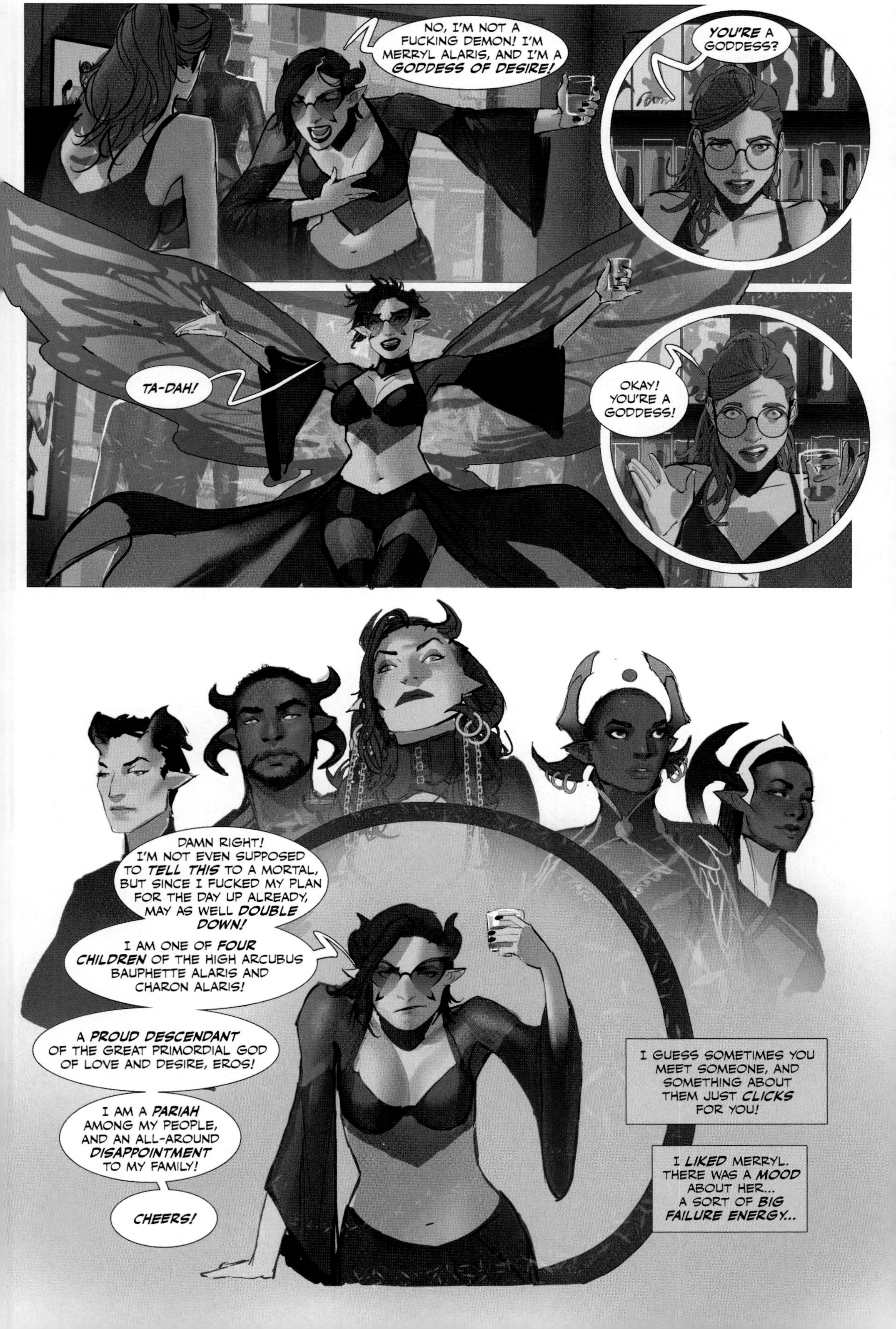
NO, I'M NOT A FUCKING DEMON! I'M MERRYL ALARIS, AND I'M A GODDESS OF DESIRE!
YOU'RE A GODDESS?
TA-DAH!
OKAY! YOU'RE A GODDESS!
DAMN RIGHT! I'M NOT EVEN SUPPOSED TO TELL THIS TO A MORTAL, BUT SINCE I FUCKED MY PLAN FOR THE DAY UP ALREADY, MAY AS WELL DOUBLE DOWN!
I AM ONE OF FOUR CHILDREN OF THE HIGH ARCUBUS BAUPHETTE ALARIS AND CHARON ALARIS!
A PROUD DESCENDANT OF THE GREAT PRIMORDIAL GOD OF LOVE AND DESIRE, EROS!
I AM A PARIAH AMONG MY PEOPLE, AND AN ALL-AROUND DISAPPOINTMENT TO MY FAMILY!
CHEERS!
I GUESS SOMETIMES YOU MEET SOMEONE, AND SOMETHING ABOUT THEM JUST CLICKS FOR YOU!
I LIKED MERRYL. THERE WAS A MOOD ABOUT HER... A SORT OF BIG FAILURE ENERGY...

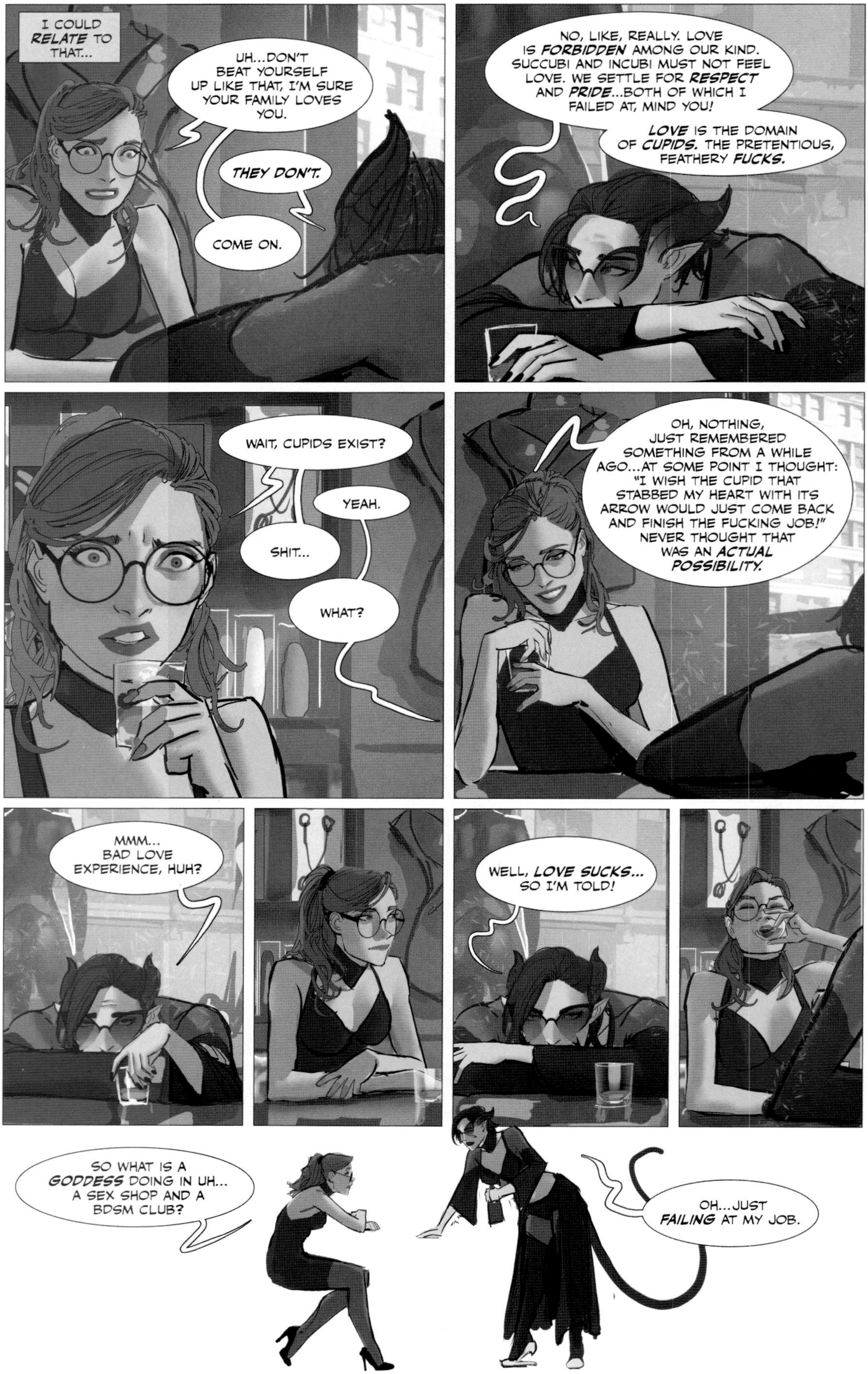
I COULD RELATE TO THAT...
UH...DON'T BEAT YOURSELF UP LIKE THAT, I'M SURE YOUR FAMILY LOVES YOU.
THEY DON'T.
COME ON.
NO, LIKE, REALLY. LOVE IS FORBIDDEN AMONG OUR KIND. SUCCUBI AND INCUBI MUST NOT FEEL LOVE. WE SETTLE FOR RESPECT AND PRIDE...BOTH OF WHICH I FAILED AT, MIND YOU!
LOVE IS THE DOMAIN OF CUPIDS. THE PRETENTIOUS, FEATHERY FUCKS.
WAIT, CUPIDS EXIST?
YEAH.
SHIT...
WHAT?
OH, NOTHING, JUST REMEMBERED SOMETHING FROM A WHILE AGO...AT SOME POINT I THOUGHT: "I WISH THE CUPID THAT STABBED MY HEART WITH ITS ARROW WOULD JUST COME BACK AND FINISH THE FUCKING JOB!" NEVER THOUGHT THAT WAS AN ACTUAL POSSIBILITY.
MMM... BAD LOVE EXPERIENCE, HUH?
WELL, LOVE SUCKS... SO I'M TOLD!
SO WHAT IS A GODDESS DOING IN UH... A SEX SHOP AND A BDSM CLUB?
OH...JUST FAILING AT MY JOB.

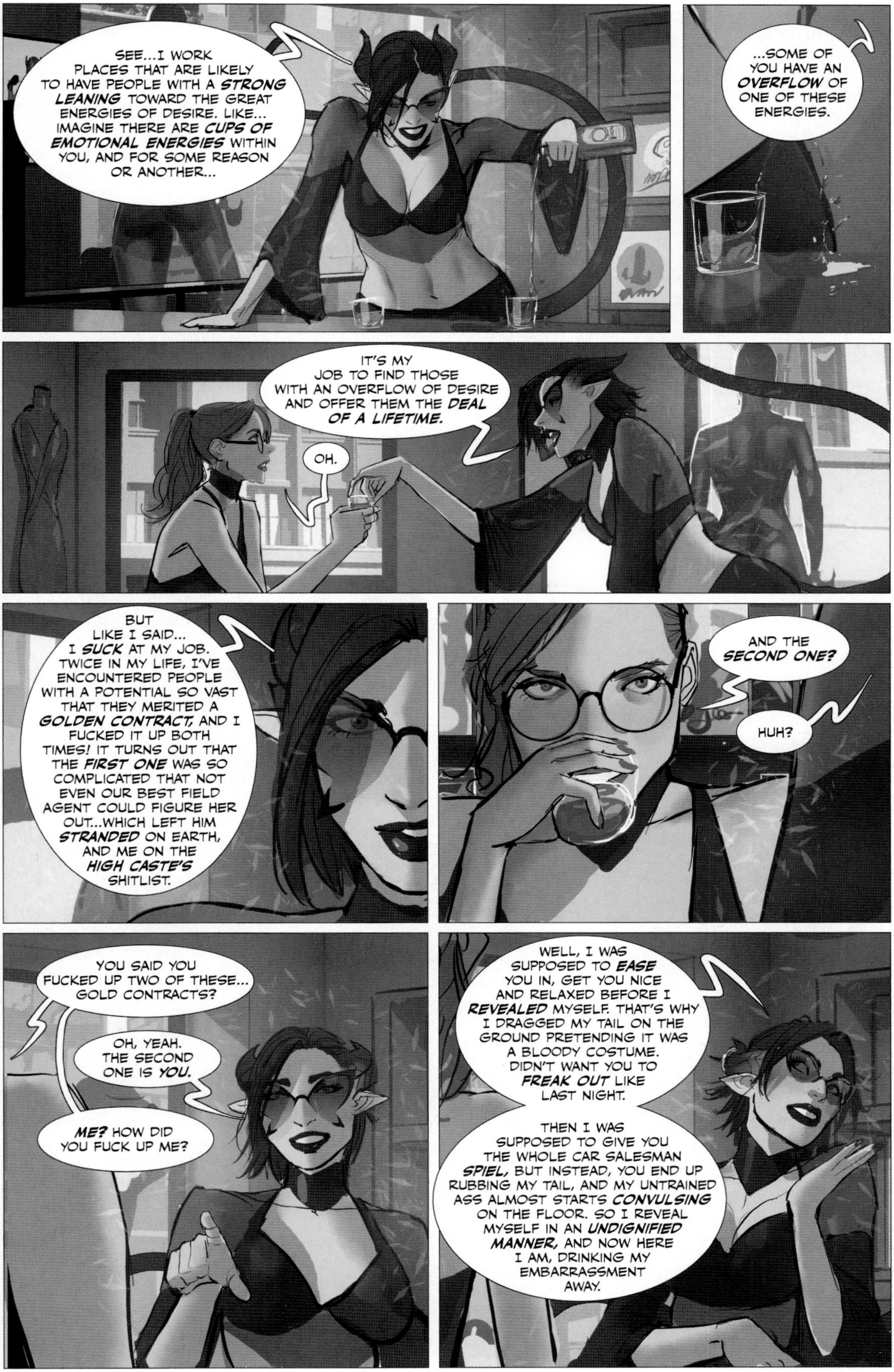
SEE...I WORK PLACES THAT ARE LIKELY TO HAVE PEOPLE WITH A STRONG LEANING TOWARD THE GREAT ENERGIES OF DESIRE. LIKE... IMAGINE THERE ARE CUPS OF EMOTIONAL ENERGIES WITHIN YOU, AND FOR SOME REASON OR ANOTHER...
...SOME OF YOU HAVE AN OVERFLOW OF ONE OF THESE ENERGIES.
IT'S MY JOB TO FIND THOSE WITH AN OVERFLOW OF DESIRE AND OFFER THEM THE DEAL OF A LIFETIME.
OH.
BUT LIKE I SAID... I SUCK AT MY JOB. TWICE IN MY LIFE, I'VE ENCOUNTERED PEOPLE WITH A POTENTIAL SO VAST THAT THEY MERITED A GOLDEN CONTRACT, AND I FUCKED IT UP BOTH TIMES! IT TURNS OUT THAT THE FIRST ONE WAS SO COMPLICATED THAT NOT EVEN OUR BEST FIELD AGENT COULD FIGURE HER OUT...WHICH LEFT HIM STRANDED ON EARTH, AND ME ON THE HIGH CASTE'S SHITLIST.
AND THE SECOND ONE?
HUH?
YOU SAID YOU FUCKED UP TWO OF THESE... GOLD CONTRACTS?
OH, YEAH. THE SECOND ONE IS YOU.
ME? HOW DID YOU FUCK UP ME?
WELL, I WAS SUPPOSED TO EASE YOU IN, GET YOU NICE AND RELAXED BEFORE I REVEALED MYSELF. THAT'S WHY I DRAGGED MY TAIL ON THE GROUND PRETENDING IT WAS A BLOODY COSTUME. DIDN'T WANT YOU TO FREAK OUT LIKE LAST NIGHT.
THEN I WAS SUPPOSED TO GIVE YOU THE WHOLE CAR SALESMAN SPIEL, BUT INSTEAD, YOU END UP RUBBING MY TAIL, AND MY UNTRAINED ASS ALMOST STARTS CONVULSING ON THE FLOOR. SO I REVEAL MYSELF IN AN UNDIGNIFIED MANNER, AND NOW HERE I AM, DRINKING MY EMBARRASSMENT AWAY.

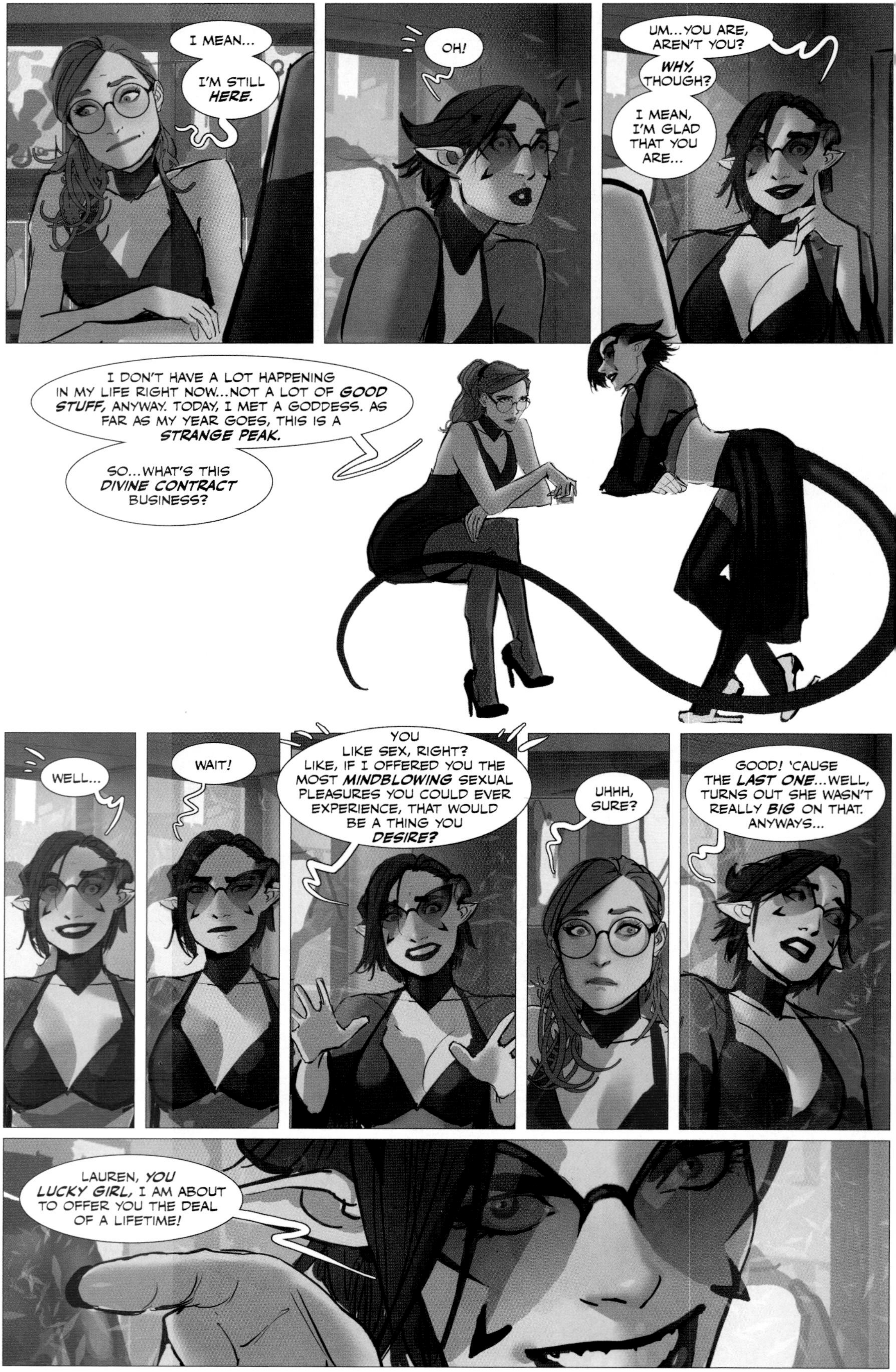
I MEAN...
I'M STILL HERE.
OH!
UM...YOU ARE, AREN'T YOU?
WHY, THOUGH?
I MEAN, I'M GLAD THAT YOU ARE...
I DON'T HAVE A LOT HAPPENING IN MY LIFE RIGHT NOW...NOT A LOT OF GOOD STUFF, ANYWAY. TODAY, I MET A GODDESS. AS FAR AS MY YEAR GOES, THIS IS A STRANGE PEAK.
SO...WHAT'S THIS DIVINE CONTRACT BUSINESS?
WELL...
WAIT!
YOU LIKE SEX, RIGHT? LIKE, IF I OFFERED YOU THE MOST MINDBLOWING SEXUAL PLEASURES YOU COULD EVER EXPERIENCE, THAT WOULD BE A THING YOU DESIRE?
UHHH, SURE?
GOOD! 'CAUSE THE LAST ONE...WELL, TURNS OUT SHE WASN'T REALLY BIG ON THAT. ANYWAYS...
LAUREN, YOU LUCKY GIRL, I AM ABOUT TO OFFER YOU THE DEAL OF A LIFETIME!

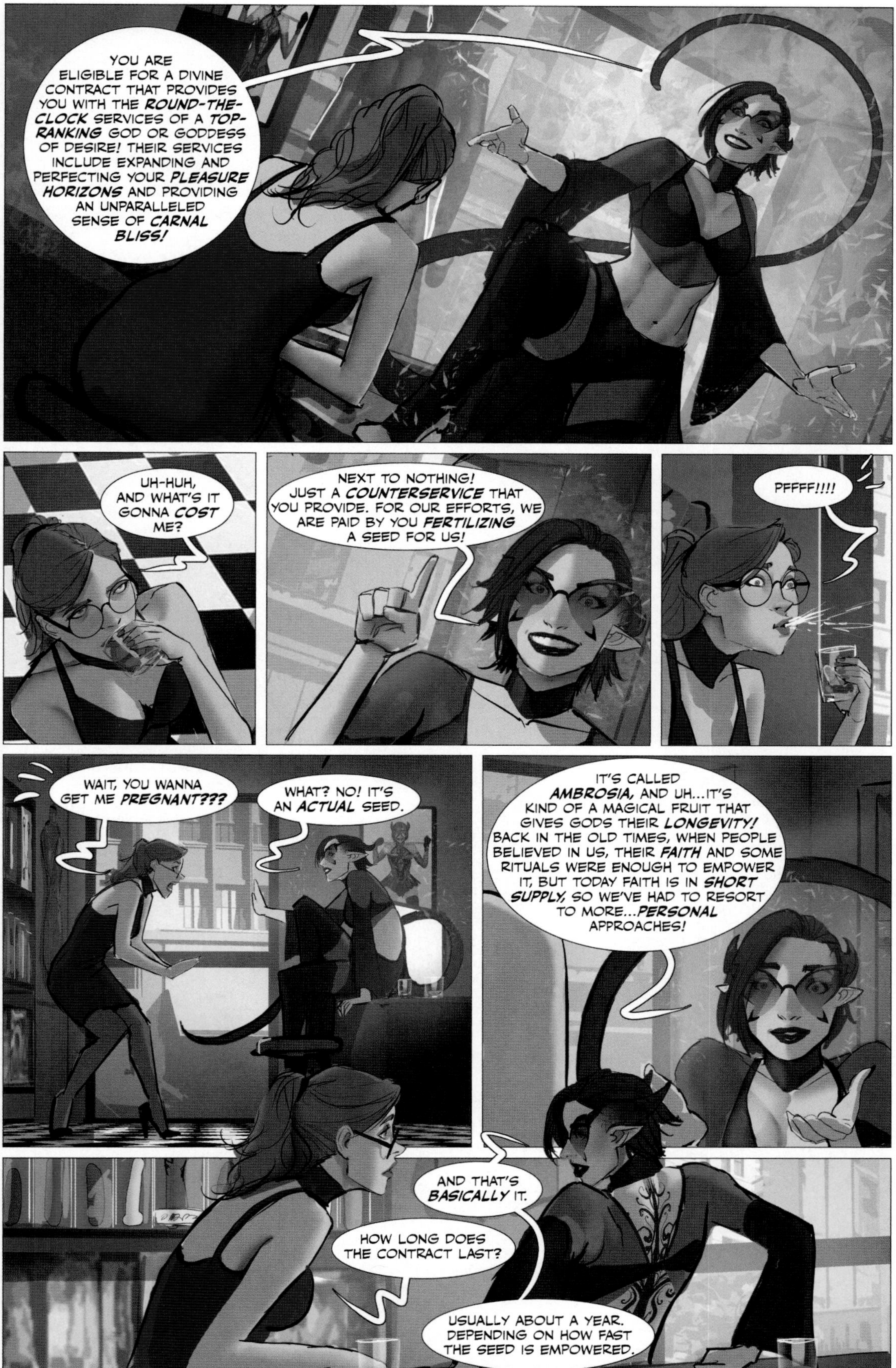
YOU ARE ELIGIBLE FOR A DIVINE CONTRACT THAT PROVIDES YOU WITH THE ROUND-THE-CLOCK SERVICES OF A TOP-RANKING GOD OR GODDESS OF DESIRE! THEIR SERVICES INCLUDE EXPANDING AND PERFECTING YOUR PLEASURE HORIZONS AND PROVIDING AN UNPARALLELED SENSE OF CARNAL BLISS!
UH-HUH, AND WHAT'S IT GONNA COST ME?
NEXT TO NOTHING! JUST A COUNTERSERVICE THAT YOU PROVIDE. FOR OUR EFFORTS, WE ARE PAID BY YOU FERTILIZING A SEED FOR US!
PFFFF!!!!
WAIT, YOU WANNA GET ME PREGNANT???
WHAT? NO! IT'S AN ACTUAL SEED.
IT'S CALLED AMBROSIA, AND UH...IT'S KIND OF A MAGICAL FRUIT THAT GIVES GODS THEIR LONGEVITY! BACK IN THE OLD TIMES, WHEN PEOPLE BELIEVED IN US, THEIR FAITH AND SOME RITUALS WERE ENOUGH TO EMPOWER IT, BUT TODAY FAITH IS IN SHORT SUPPLY, SO WE'VE HAD TO RESORT TO MORE...PERSONAL APPROACHES!
AND THAT'S BASICALLY IT.
HOW LONG DOES THE CONTRACT LAST?
USUALLY ABOUT A YEAR. DEPENDING ON HOW FAST THE SEED IS EMPOWERED.

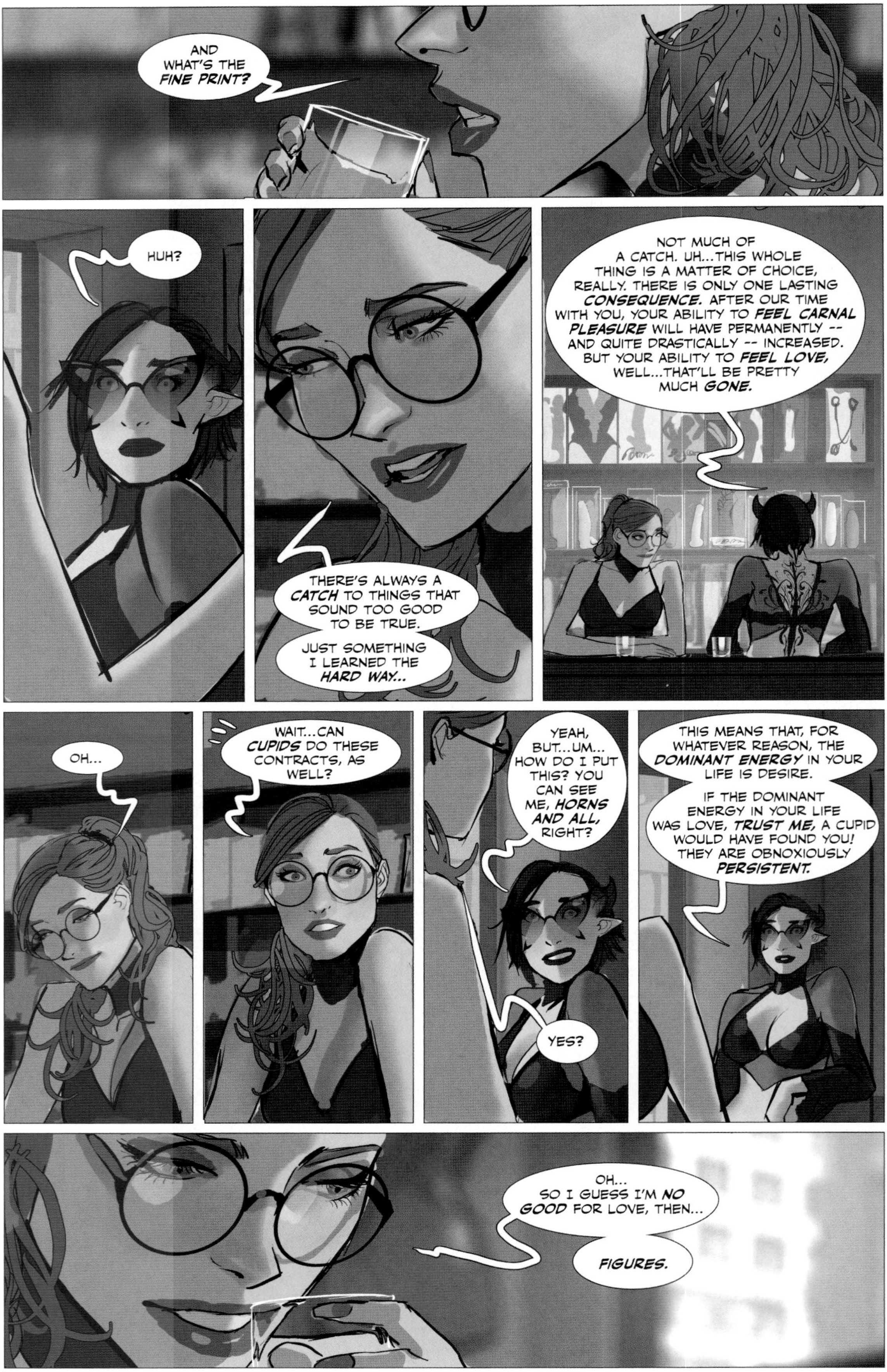
AND WHAT'S THE *FINE PRINT?*
HUH?
THERE'S ALWAYS A *CATCH* TO THINGS THAT SOUND TOO GOOD TO BE TRUE.
JUST SOMETHING I LEARNED THE *HARD WAY...*
NOT MUCH OF A CATCH. UH...THIS WHOLE THING IS A MATTER OF CHOICE, REALLY. THERE IS ONLY ONE LASTING *CONSEQUENCE.* AFTER OUR TIME WITH YOU, YOUR ABILITY TO *FEEL CARNAL PLEASURE* WILL HAVE PERMANENTLY -- AND QUITE DRASTICALLY -- INCREASED. BUT YOUR ABILITY TO *FEEL LOVE,* WELL...THAT'LL BE PRETTY MUCH *GONE.*
OH...
WAIT...CAN *CUPIDS* DO THESE CONTRACTS, AS WELL?
YEAH, BUT...UM... HOW DO I PUT THIS? YOU CAN SEE ME, *HORNS AND ALL,* RIGHT?
YES?
THIS MEANS THAT, FOR WHATEVER REASON, THE *DOMINANT ENERGY* IN YOUR LIFE IS DESIRE.
IF THE DOMINANT ENERGY IN YOUR LIFE WAS LOVE, *TRUST ME,* A CUPID WOULD HAVE FOUND YOU! THEY ARE OBNOXIOUSLY *PERSISTENT.*
OH... SO I GUESS I'M *NO GOOD* FOR LOVE, THEN...
FIGURES.

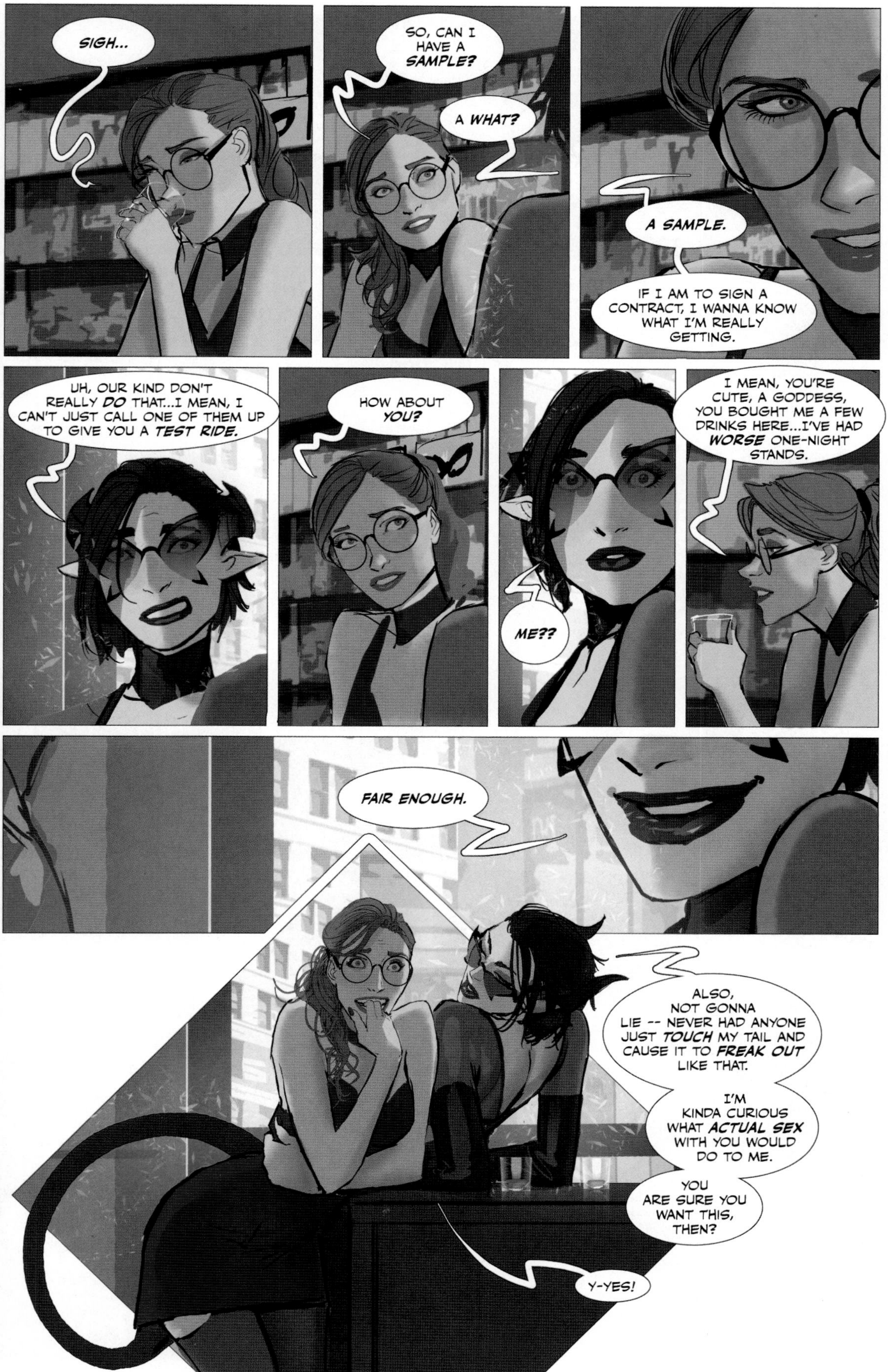
SIGH...
SO, CAN I HAVE A SAMPLE?
A WHAT?
A SAMPLE.
IF I AM TO SIGN A CONTRACT, I WANNA KNOW WHAT I'M REALLY GETTING.
UH, OUR KIND DON'T REALLY DO THAT...I MEAN, I CAN'T JUST CALL ONE OF THEM UP TO GIVE YOU A TEST RIDE.
HOW ABOUT YOU?
ME??
I MEAN, YOU'RE CUTE, A GODDESS, YOU BOUGHT ME A FEW DRINKS HERE...I'VE HAD WORSE ONE-NIGHT STANDS.
FAIR ENOUGH.
ALSO, NOT GONNA LIE -- NEVER HAD ANYONE JUST TOUCH MY TAIL AND CAUSE IT TO FREAK OUT LIKE THAT.
I'M KINDA CURIOUS WHAT ACTUAL SEX WITH YOU WOULD DO TO ME.
YOU ARE SURE YOU WANT THIS, THEN?
Y-YES!

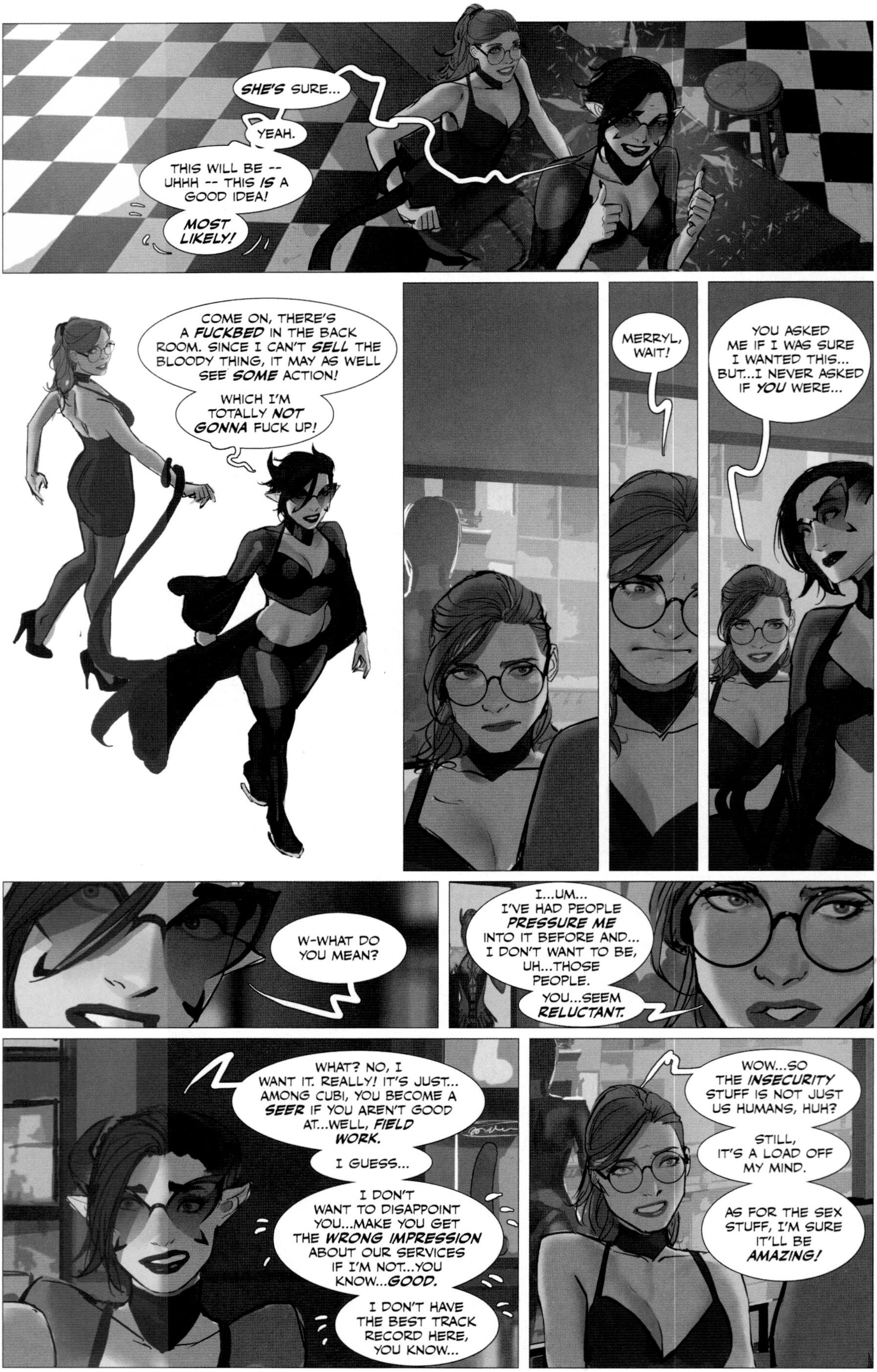
SHE'S SURE...
YEAH.
THIS WILL BE -- UHHH -- THIS IS A GOOD IDEA!
MOST LIKELY!
COME ON, THERE'S A FUCKBED IN THE BACK ROOM. SINCE I CAN'T SELL THE BLOODY THING, IT MAY AS WELL SEE SOME ACTION!
WHICH I'M TOTALLY NOT GONNA FUCK UP!
MERRYL, WAIT!
YOU ASKED ME IF I WAS SURE I WANTED THIS... BUT...I NEVER ASKED IF YOU WERE...
W-WHAT DO YOU MEAN?
I...UM... I'VE HAD PEOPLE PRESSURE ME INTO IT BEFORE AND... I DON'T WANT TO BE, UH...THOSE PEOPLE.
YOU...SEEM RELUCTANT.
WHAT? NO, I WANT IT. REALLY! IT'S JUST... AMONG CUBI, YOU BECOME A SEER IF YOU AREN'T GOOD AT...WELL, FIELD WORK.
I GUESS...
I DON'T WANT TO DISAPPOINT YOU...MAKE YOU GET THE WRONG IMPRESSION ABOUT OUR SERVICES IF I'M NOT...YOU KNOW...GOOD.
I DON'T HAVE THE BEST TRACK RECORD HERE, YOU KNOW...
WOW...SO THE INSECURITY STUFF IS NOT JUST US HUMANS, HUH?
STILL, IT'S A LOAD OFF MY MIND.
AS FOR THE SEX STUFF, I'M SURE IT'LL BE AMAZING!

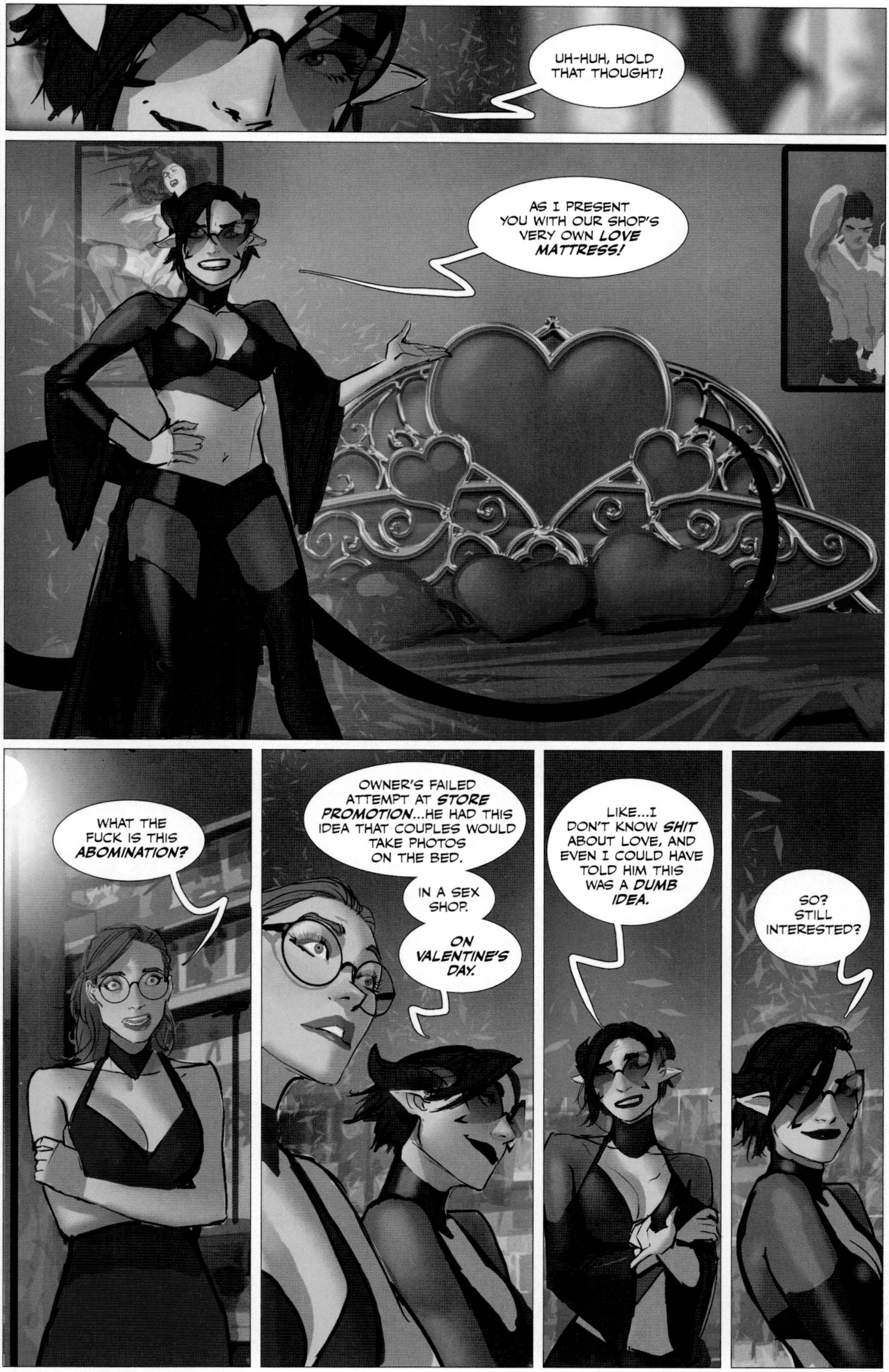
UH-HUH, HOLD THAT THOUGHT!
AS I PRESENT YOU WITH OUR SHOP'S VERY OWN LOVE MATTRESS!
WHAT THE FUCK IS THIS ABOMINATION?
OWNER'S FAILED ATTEMPT AT STORE PROMOTION...HE HAD THIS IDEA THAT COUPLES WOULD TAKE PHOTOS ON THE BED.
IN A SEX SHOP.
ON VALENTINE'S DAY.
LIKE...I DON'T KNOW SHIT ABOUT LOVE, AND EVEN I COULD HAVE TOLD HIM THIS WAS A DUMB IDEA.
SO? STILL INTERESTED?

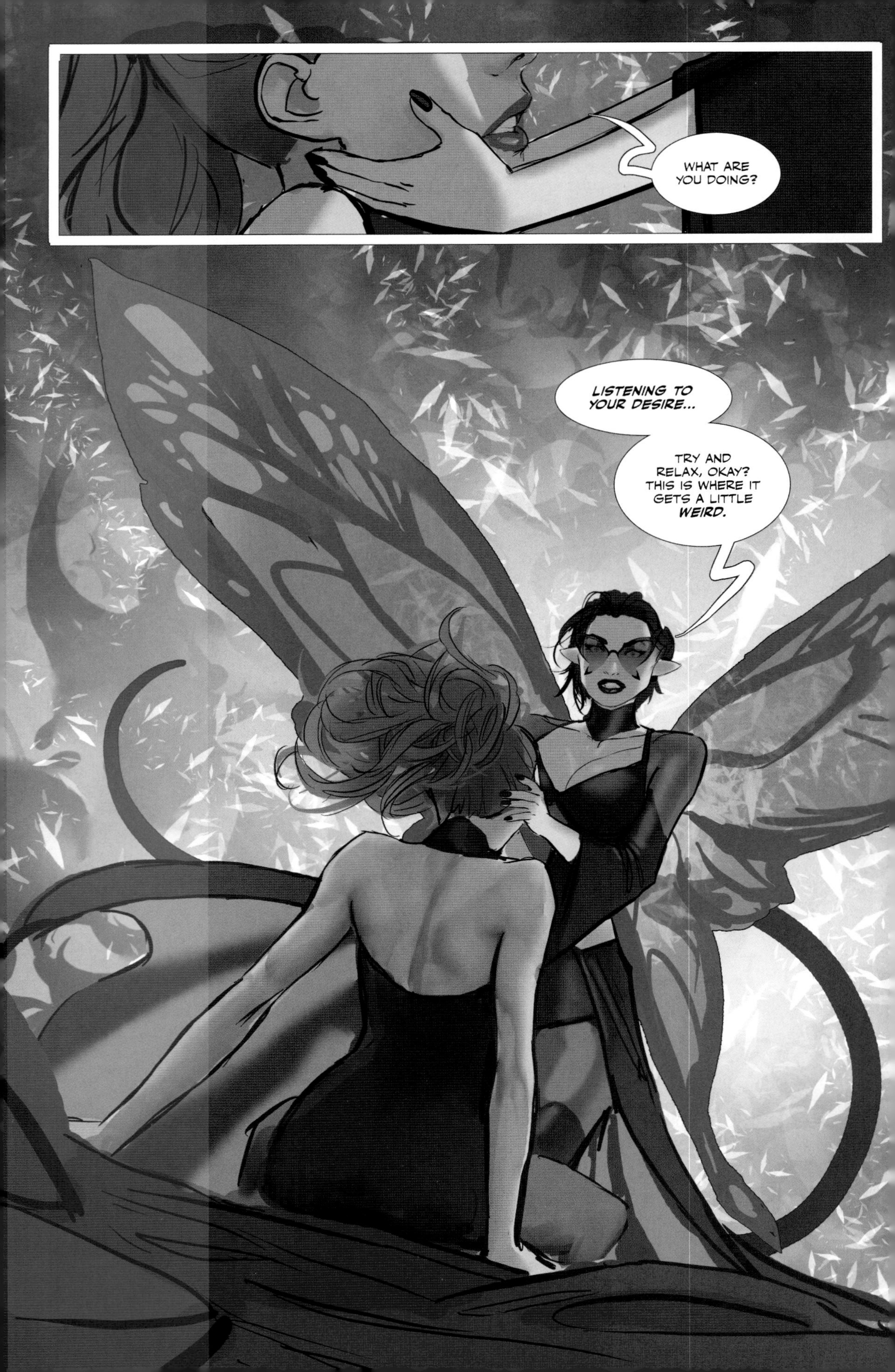
WHAT ARE YOU DOING?
LISTENING TO YOUR DESIRE...
TRY AND RELAX, OKAY? THIS IS WHERE IT GETS A LITTLE WEIRD.

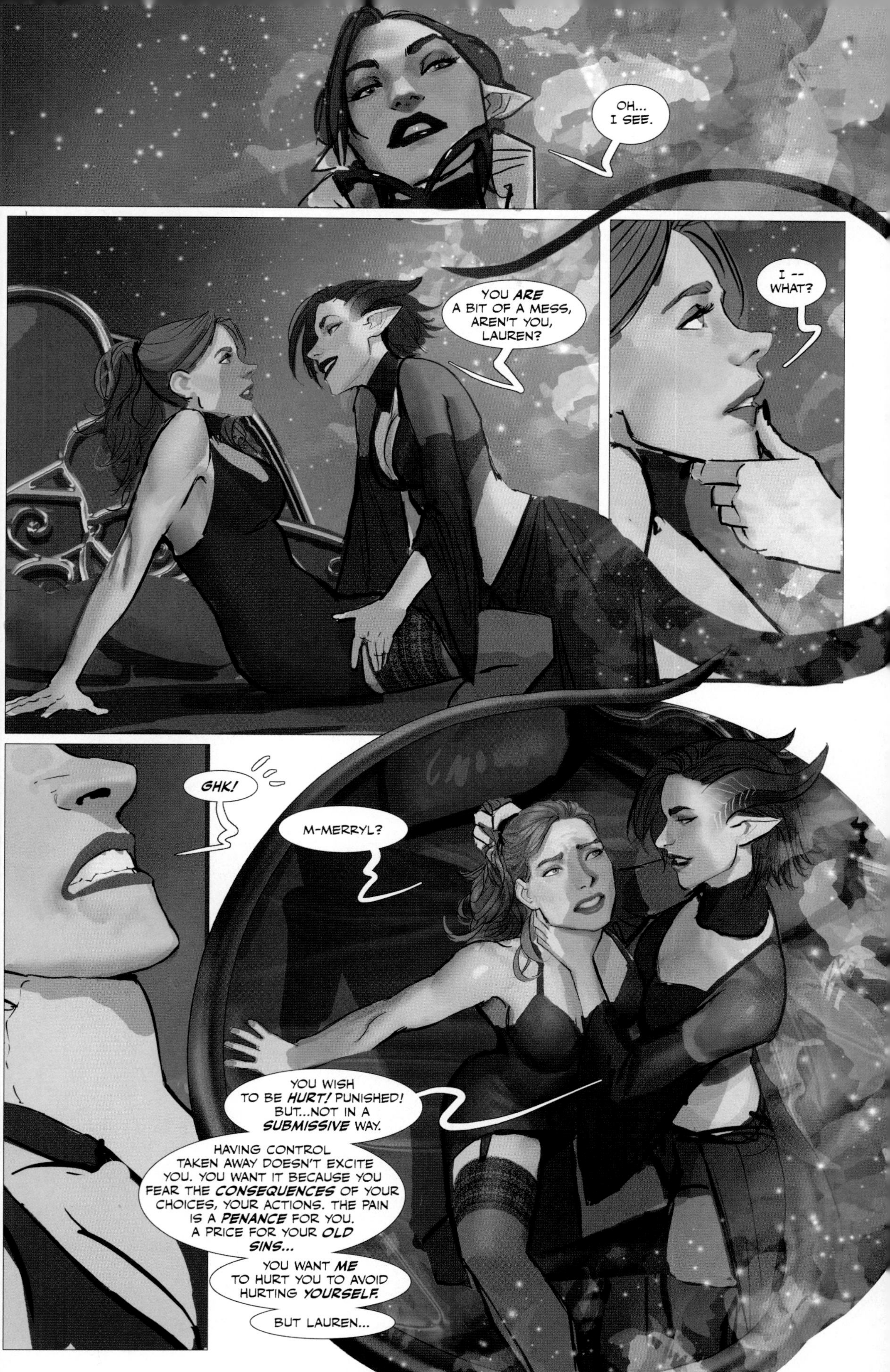
OH... I SEE.
YOU *ARE* A BIT OF A MESS, AREN'T YOU, LAUREN?
I -- WHAT?
GHK!
M-MERRYL?
YOU WISH TO BE *HURT!* PUNISHED! BUT...NOT IN A *SUBMISSIVE* WAY.
HAVING CONTROL TAKEN AWAY DOESN'T EXCITE YOU. YOU WANT IT BECAUSE YOU FEAR THE *CONSEQUENCES* OF YOUR CHOICES, YOUR ACTIONS. THE PAIN IS A *PENANCE* FOR YOU. A PRICE FOR YOUR *OLD SINS...*
YOU WANT *ME* TO HURT YOU TO AVOID HURTING *YOURSELF.*
BUT LAUREN...

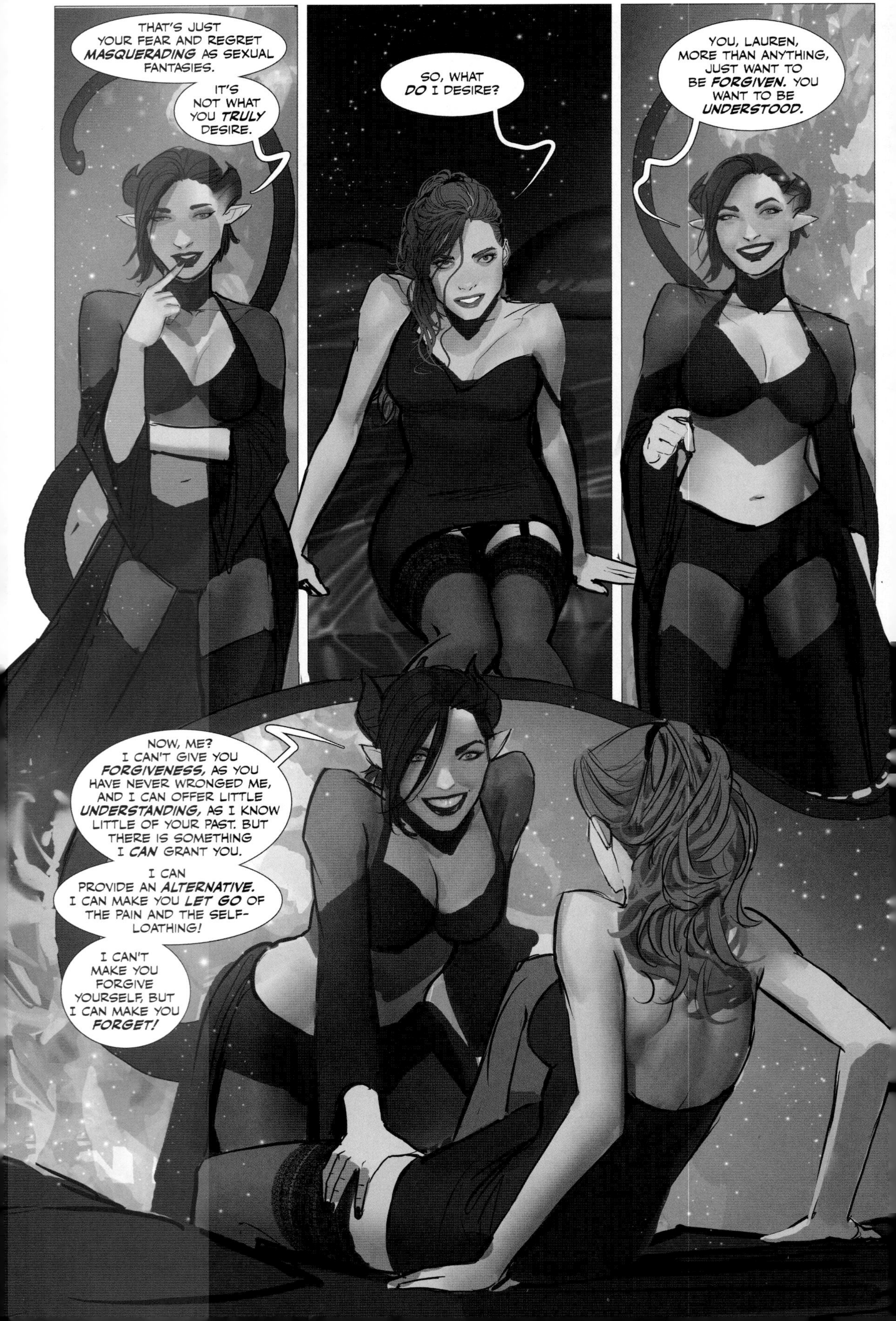
THAT'S JUST YOUR FEAR AND REGRET MASQUERADING AS SEXUAL FANTASIES.
IT'S NOT WHAT YOU TRULY DESIRE.
SO, WHAT DO I DESIRE?
YOU, LAUREN, MORE THAN ANYTHING, JUST WANT TO BE FORGIVEN. YOU WANT TO BE UNDERSTOOD.
NOW, ME? I CAN'T GIVE YOU FORGIVENESS, AS YOU HAVE NEVER WRONGED ME, AND I CAN OFFER LITTLE UNDERSTANDING, AS I KNOW LITTLE OF YOUR PAST. BUT THERE IS SOMETHING I CAN GRANT YOU.
I CAN PROVIDE AN ALTERNATIVE. I CAN MAKE YOU LET GO OF THE PAIN AND THE SELF-LOATHING!
I CAN'T MAKE YOU FORGIVE YOURSELF, BUT I CAN MAKE YOU FORGET!

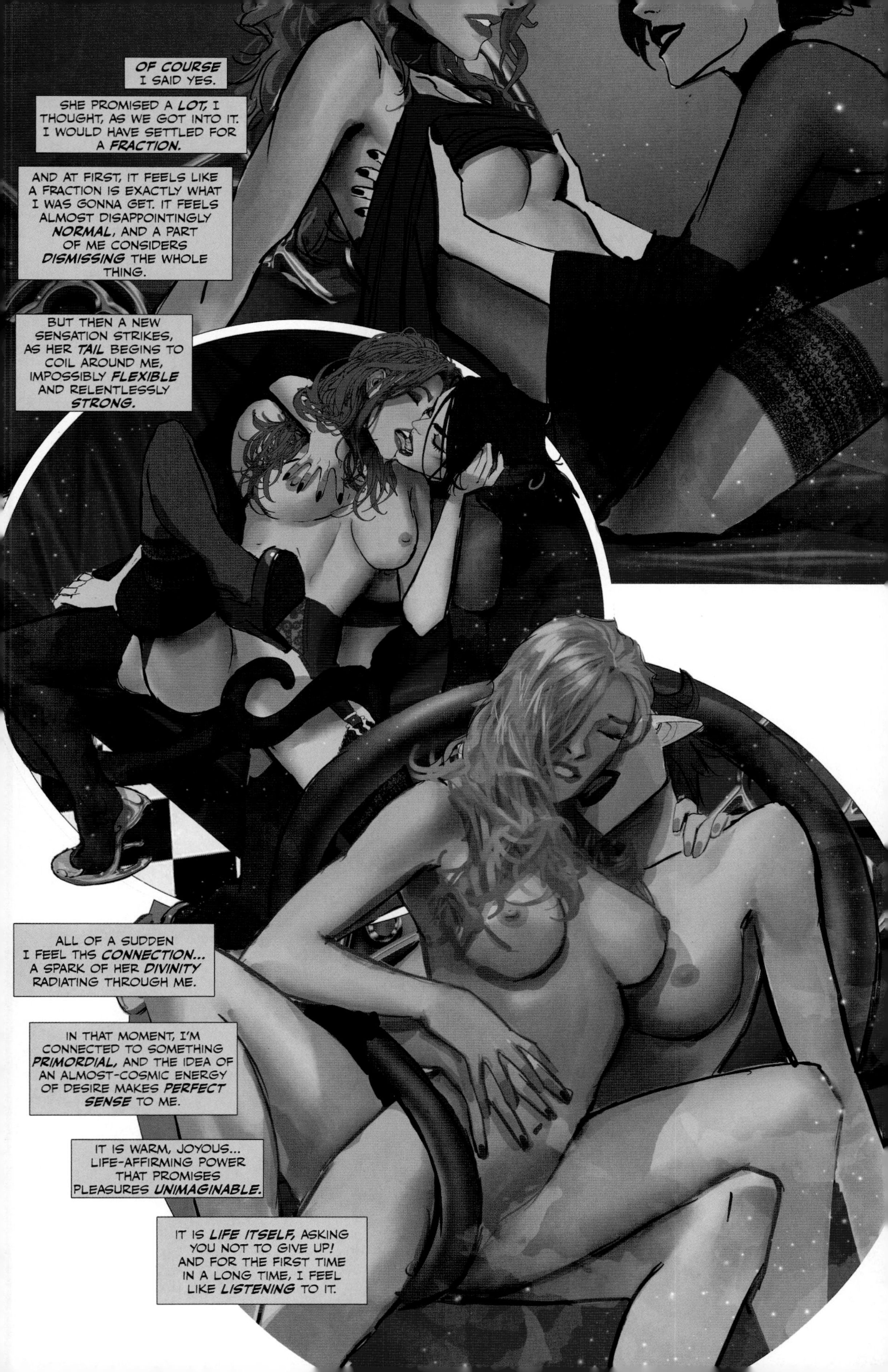
OF COURSE I SAID YES.
SHE PROMISED A LOT, I THOUGHT, AS WE GOT INTO IT. I WOULD HAVE SETTLED FOR A FRACTION.
AND AT FIRST, IT FEELS LIKE A FRACTION IS EXACTLY WHAT I WAS GONNA GET. IT FEELS ALMOST DISAPPOINTINGLY NORMAL, AND A PART OF ME CONSIDERS DISMISSING THE WHOLE THING.
BUT THEN A NEW SENSATION STRIKES, AS HER TAIL BEGINS TO COIL AROUND ME, IMPOSSIBLY FLEXIBLE AND RELENTLESSLY STRONG.
ALL OF A SUDDEN I FEEL THS CONNECTION... A SPARK OF HER DIVINITY RADIATING THROUGH ME.
IN THAT MOMENT, I'M CONNECTED TO SOMETHING PRIMORDIAL, AND THE IDEA OF AN ALMOST-COSMIC ENERGY OF DESIRE MAKES PERFECT SENSE TO ME.
IT IS WARM, JOYOUS... LIFE-AFFIRMING POWER THAT PROMISES PLEASURES UNIMAGINABLE.
IT IS LIFE ITSELF, ASKING YOU NOT TO GIVE UP! AND FOR THE FIRST TIME IN A LONG TIME, I FEEL LIKE LISTENING TO IT.

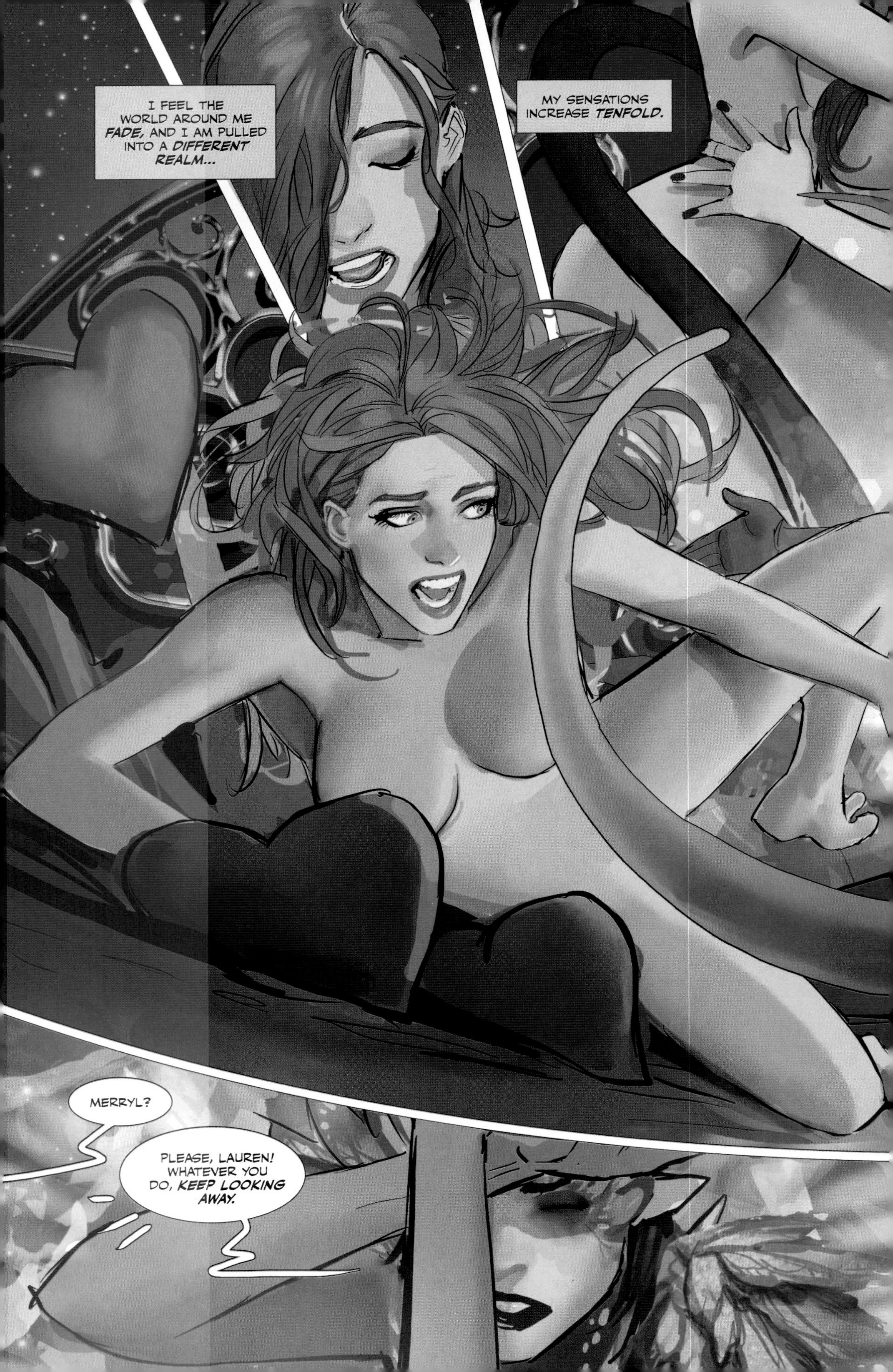
I FEEL THE WORLD AROUND ME *FADE,* AND I AM PULLED INTO A *DIFFERENT REALM...*
MY SENSATIONS INCREASE *TENFOLD.*
MERRYL?
PLEASE, LAUREN! WHATEVER YOU DO, *KEEP LOOKING AWAY.*

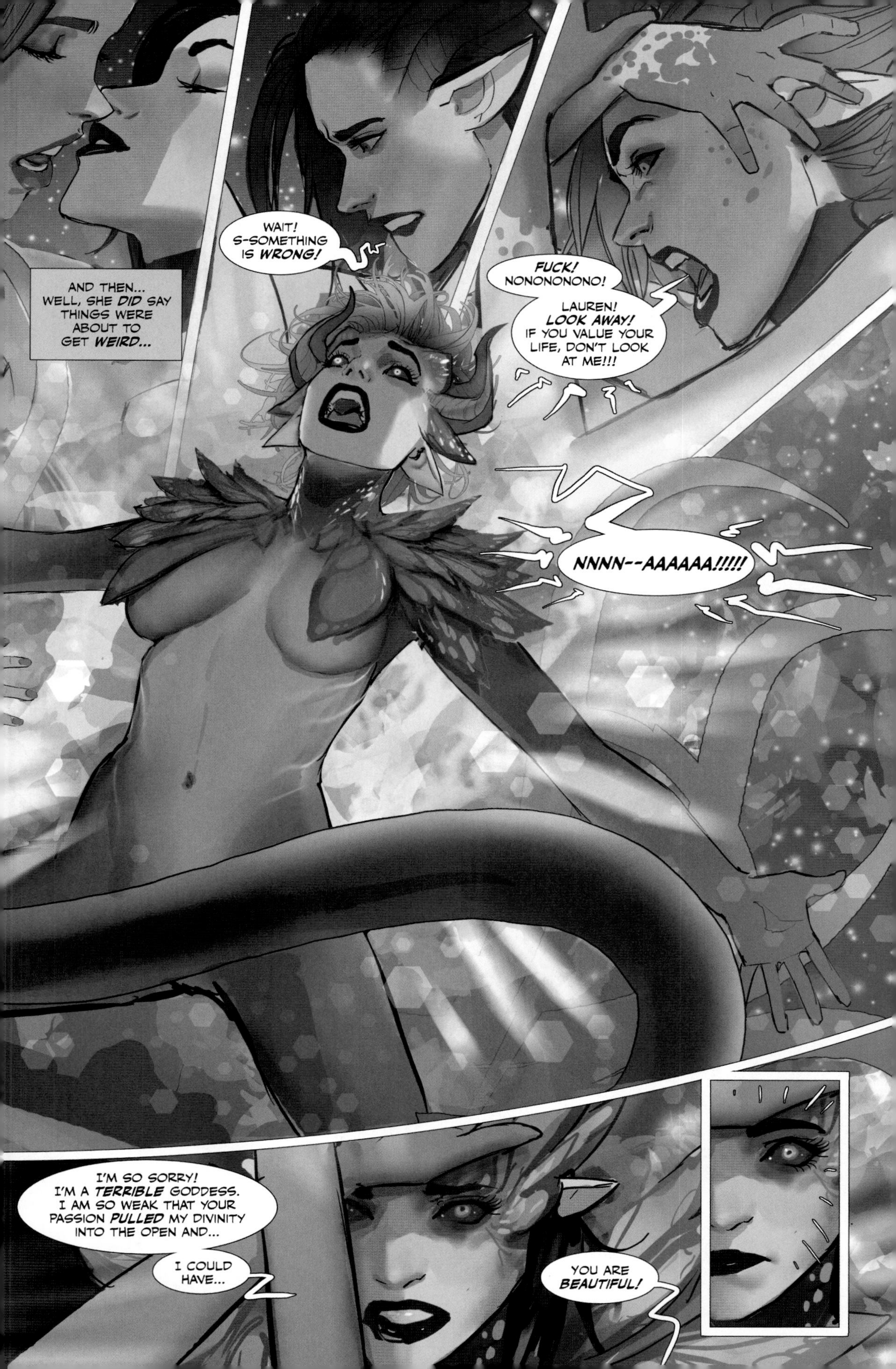
AND THEN... WELL, SHE DID SAY THINGS WERE ABOUT TO GET WEIRD...
WAIT! S-SOMETHING IS WRONG!
FUCK! NONONONONO!
LAUREN! LOOK AWAY! IF YOU VALUE YOUR LIFE, DON'T LOOK AT ME!!!
NNNN--AAAAAA!!!!!
I'M SO SORRY! I'M A TERRIBLE GODDESS. I AM SO WEAK THAT YOUR PASSION PULLED MY DIVINITY INTO THE OPEN AND...
I COULD HAVE...
YOU ARE BEAUTIFUL!

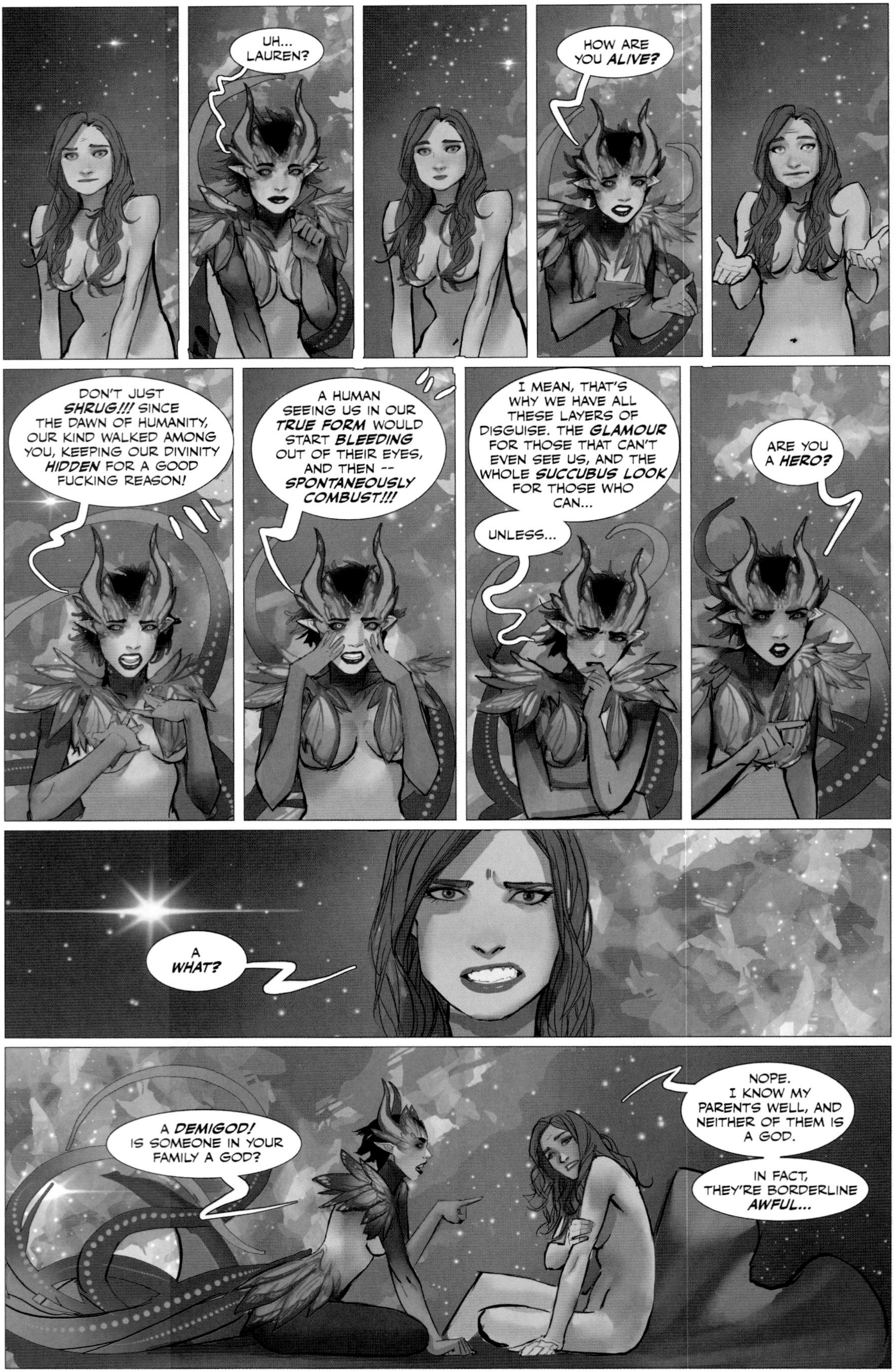
UH... LAUREN?
HOW ARE YOU ALIVE?
DON'T JUST SHRUG!!! SINCE THE DAWN OF HUMANITY, OUR KIND WALKED AMONG YOU, KEEPING OUR DIVINITY HIDDEN FOR A GOOD FUCKING REASON!
A HUMAN SEEING US IN OUR TRUE FORM WOULD START BLEEDING OUT OF THEIR EYES, AND THEN -- SPONTANEOUSLY COMBUST!!!
I MEAN, THAT'S WHY WE HAVE ALL THESE LAYERS OF DISGUISE. THE GLAMOUR FOR THOSE THAT CAN'T EVEN SEE US, AND THE WHOLE SUCCUBUS LOOK FOR THOSE WHO CAN...
UNLESS...
ARE YOU A HERO?
A WHAT?
A DEMIGOD! IS SOMEONE IN YOUR FAMILY A GOD?
NOPE. I KNOW MY PARENTS WELL, AND NEITHER OF THEM IS A GOD.
IN FACT, THEY'RE BORDERLINE AWFUL...

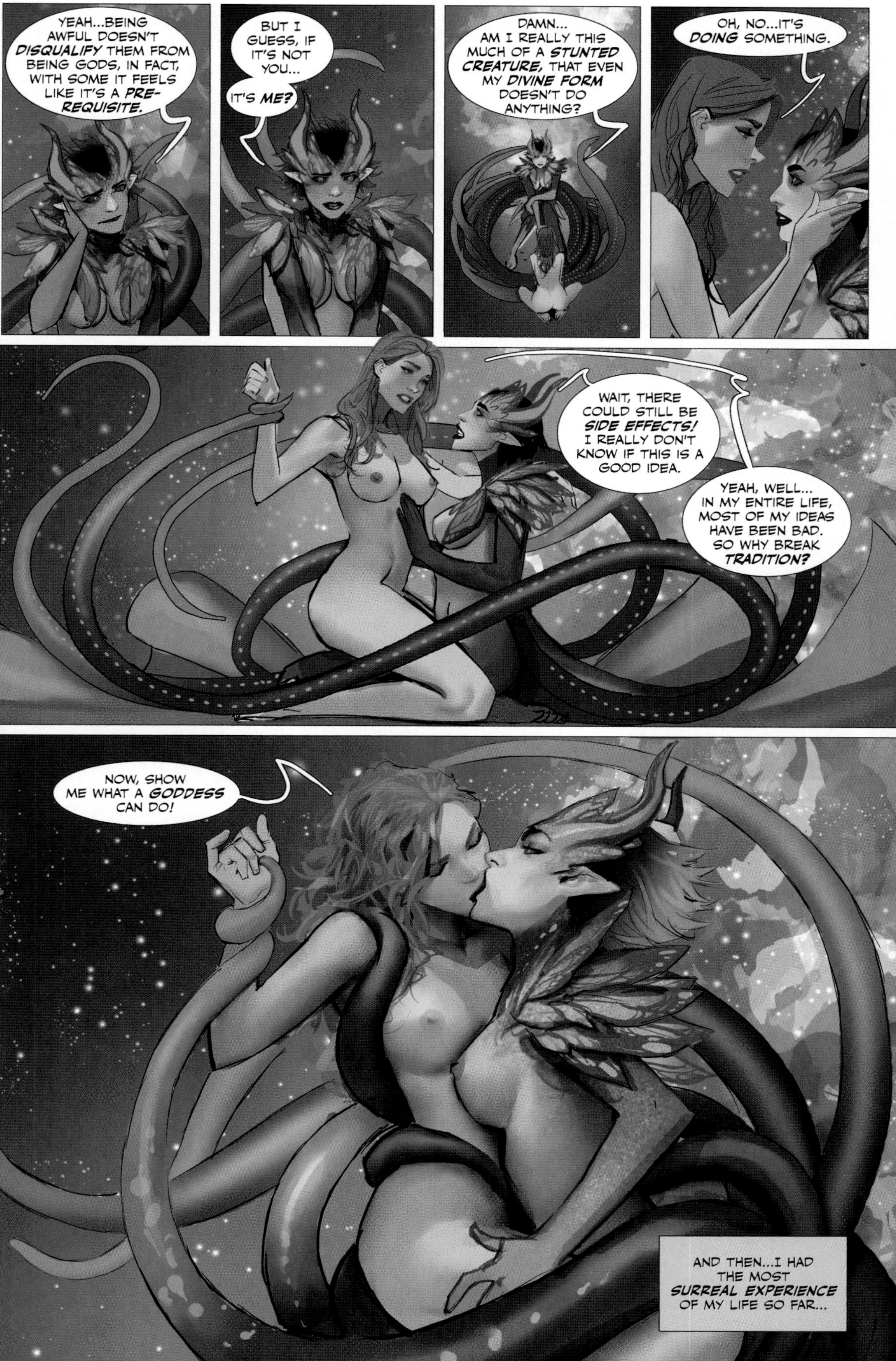
YEAH...BEING AWFUL DOESN'T *DISQUALIFY* THEM FROM BEING GODS, IN FACT, WITH SOME IT FEELS LIKE IT'S A *PRE-REQUISITE.*
BUT I GUESS, IF IT'S NOT YOU...
IT'S *ME?*
DAMN... AM I REALLY THIS MUCH OF A *STUNTED CREATURE,* THAT EVEN MY *DIVINE FORM* DOESN'T DO ANYTHING?
OH, NO...IT'S *DOING* SOMETHING.
WAIT, THERE COULD STILL BE *SIDE EFFECTS!* I REALLY DON'T KNOW IF THIS IS A GOOD IDEA.
YEAH, WELL... IN MY ENTIRE LIFE, MOST OF MY IDEAS HAVE BEEN BAD. SO WHY BREAK *TRADITION?*
NOW, SHOW ME WHAT A *GODDESS* CAN DO!
AND THEN...I HAD THE MOST *SURREAL EXPERIENCE* OF MY LIFE SO FAR...

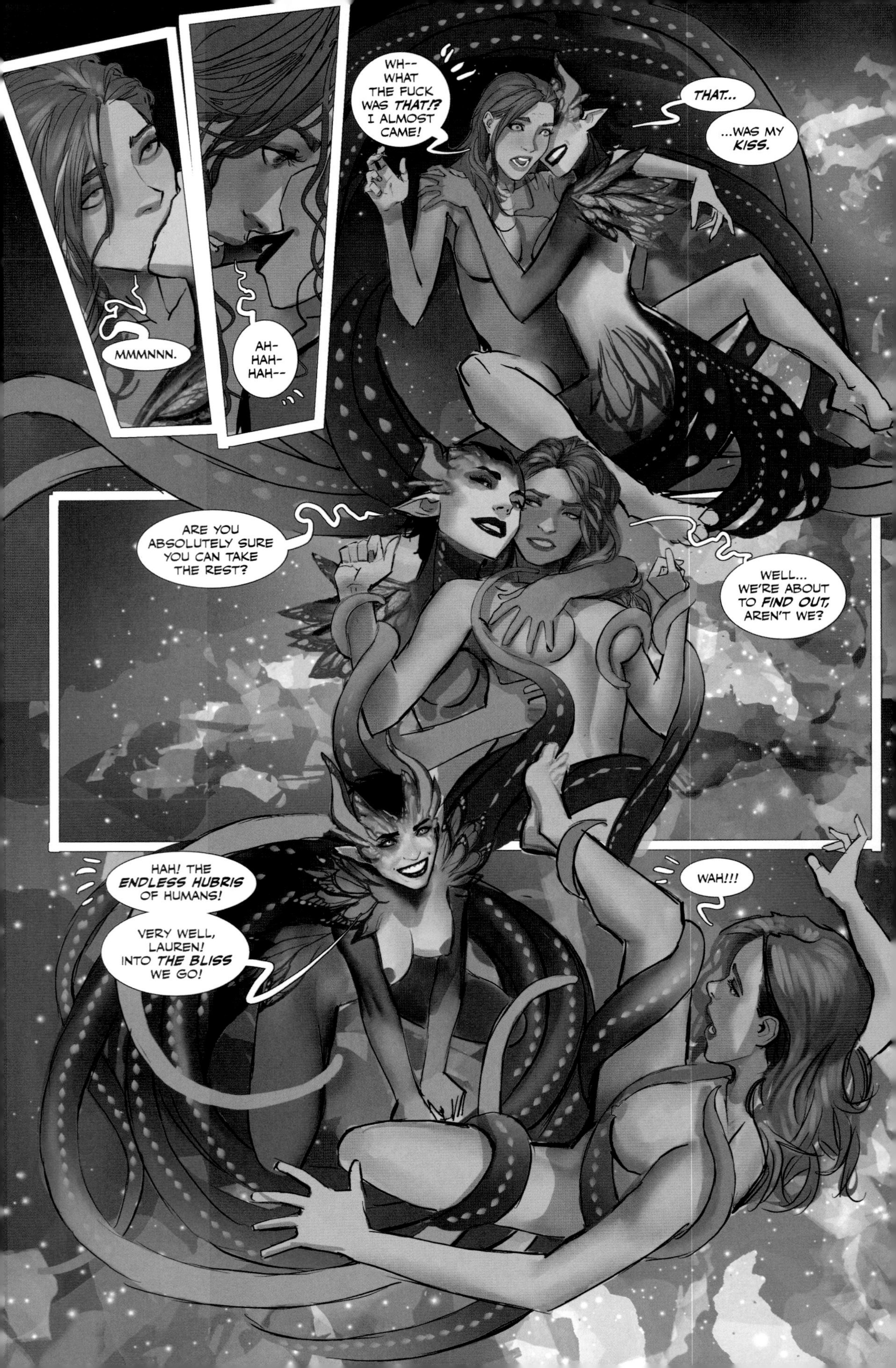
MMMNNN.
AH-HAH-HAH--
WH--WHAT THE FUCK WAS THAT!? I ALMOST CAME!
THAT...
...WAS MY KISS.
ARE YOU ABSOLUTELY SURE YOU CAN TAKE THE REST?
WELL... WE'RE ABOUT TO FIND OUT, AREN'T WE?
HAH! THE ENDLESS HUBRIS OF HUMANS!
VERY WELL, LAUREN! INTO THE BLISS WE GO!
WAH!!!

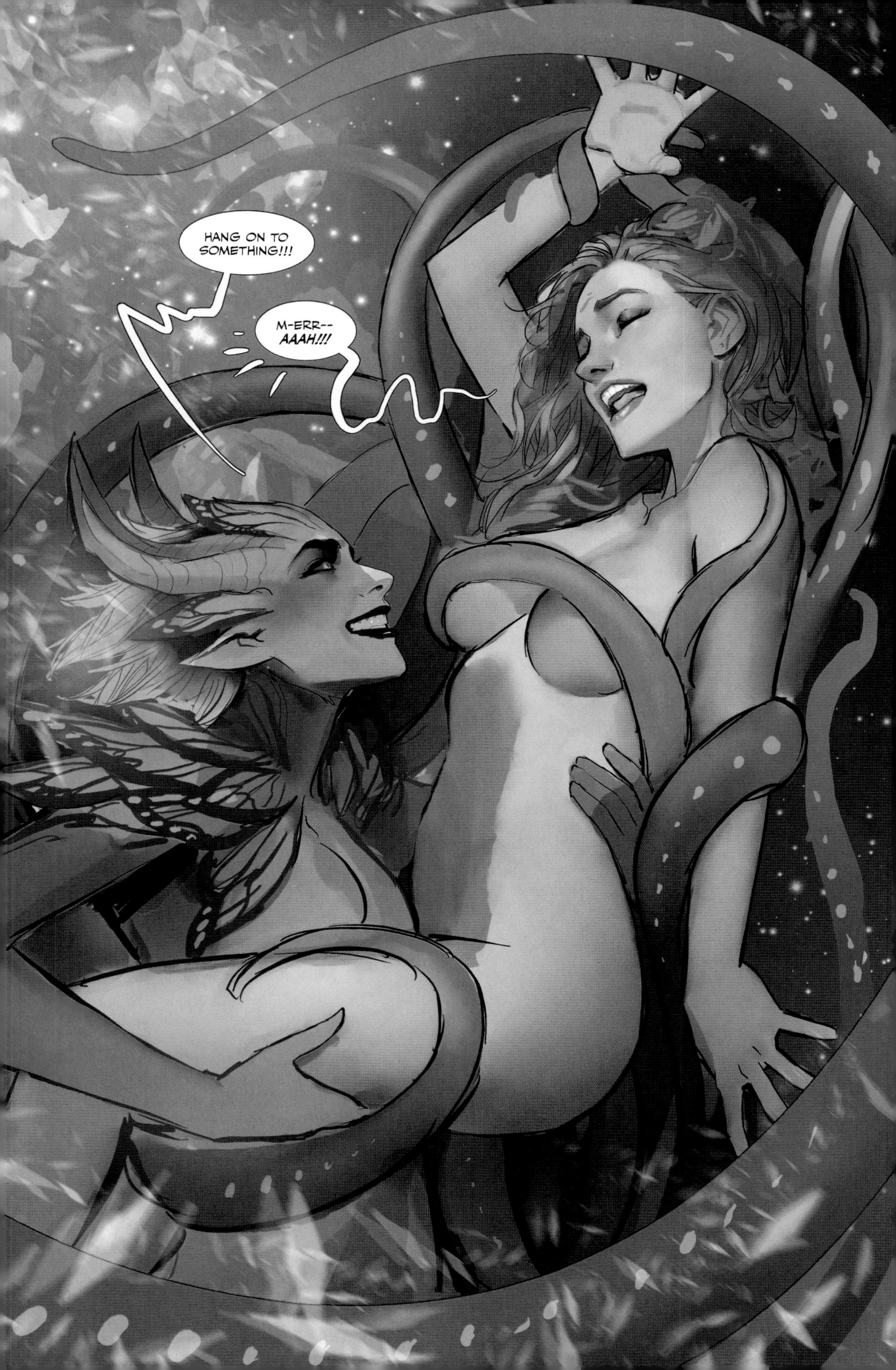
HANG ON TO SOMETHING!!!
M-ERR-- AAAH!!!

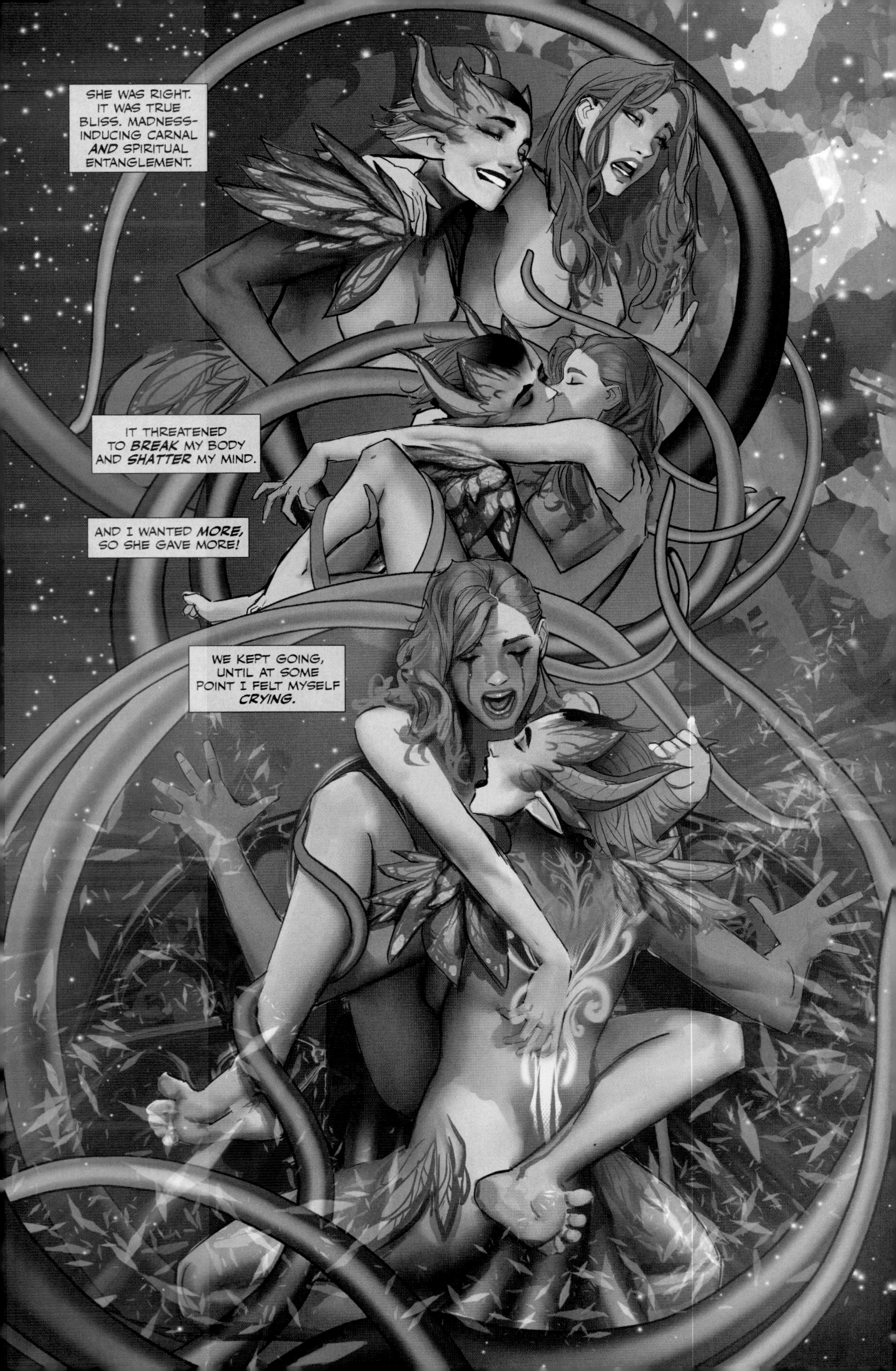
SHE WAS RIGHT. IT WAS TRUE BLISS. MADNESS-INDUCING CARNAL AND SPIRITUAL ENTANGLEMENT.
IT THREATENED TO BREAK MY BODY AND SHATTER MY MIND.
AND I WANTED MORE, SO SHE GAVE MORE!
WE KEPT GOING, UNTIL AT SOME POINT I FELT MYSELF CRYING.

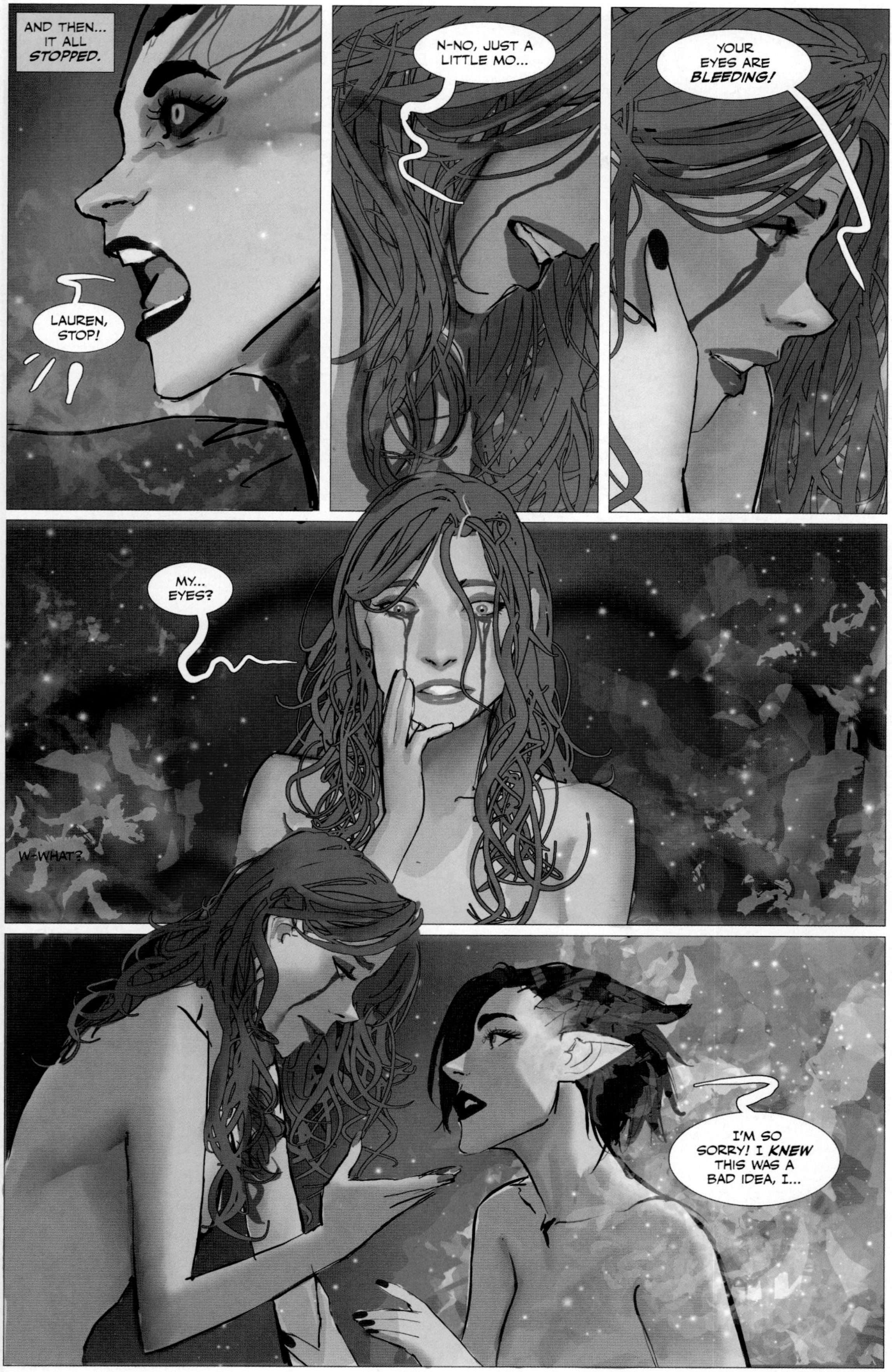
AND THEN... IT ALL STOPPED.
LAUREN, STOP!
N-NO, JUST A LITTLE MO...
YOUR EYES ARE BLEEDING!
MY... EYES?
W-WHAT?
I'M SO SORRY! I KNEW THIS WAS A BAD IDEA, I...

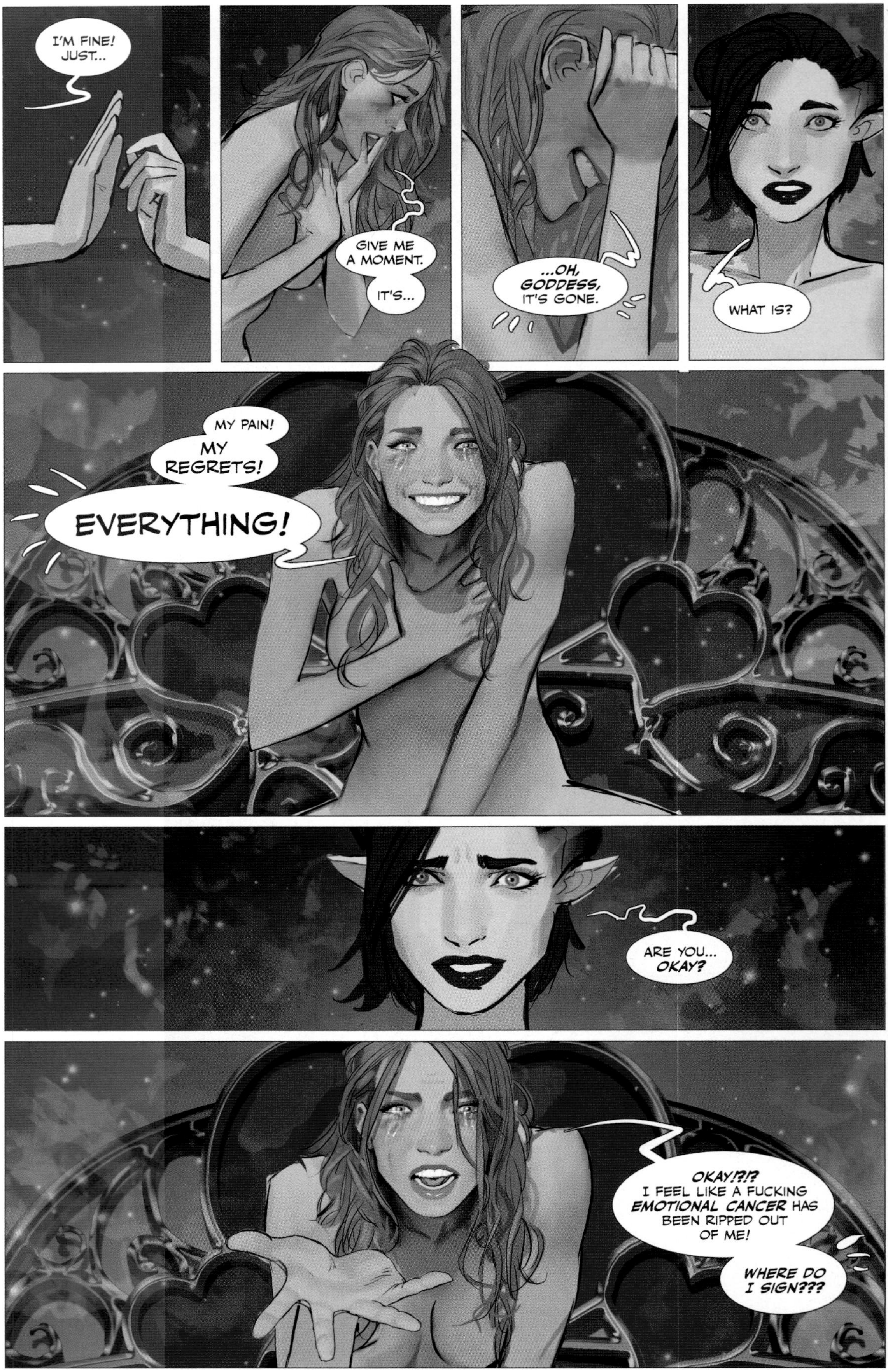
I'M FINE! JUST...
GIVE ME A MOMENT.
IT'S...
...OH, GODDESS, IT'S GONE.
WHAT IS?
MY PAIN!
MY REGRETS!
EVERYTHING!
ARE YOU... OKAY?
OKAY!?!? I FEEL LIKE A FUCKING EMOTIONAL CANCER HAS BEEN RIPPED OUT OF ME!
WHERE DO I SIGN???

Chapter 5

The crossroads

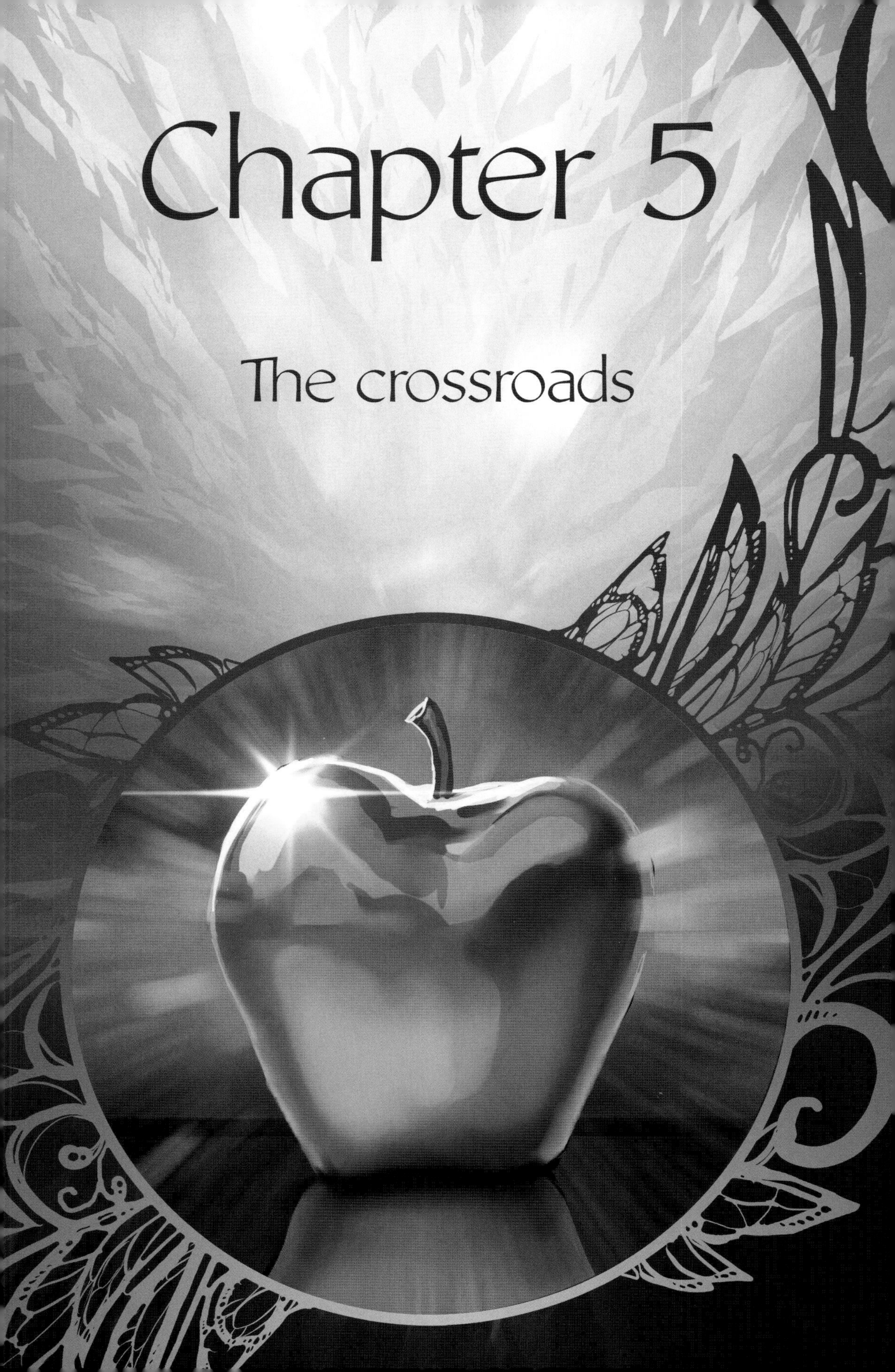

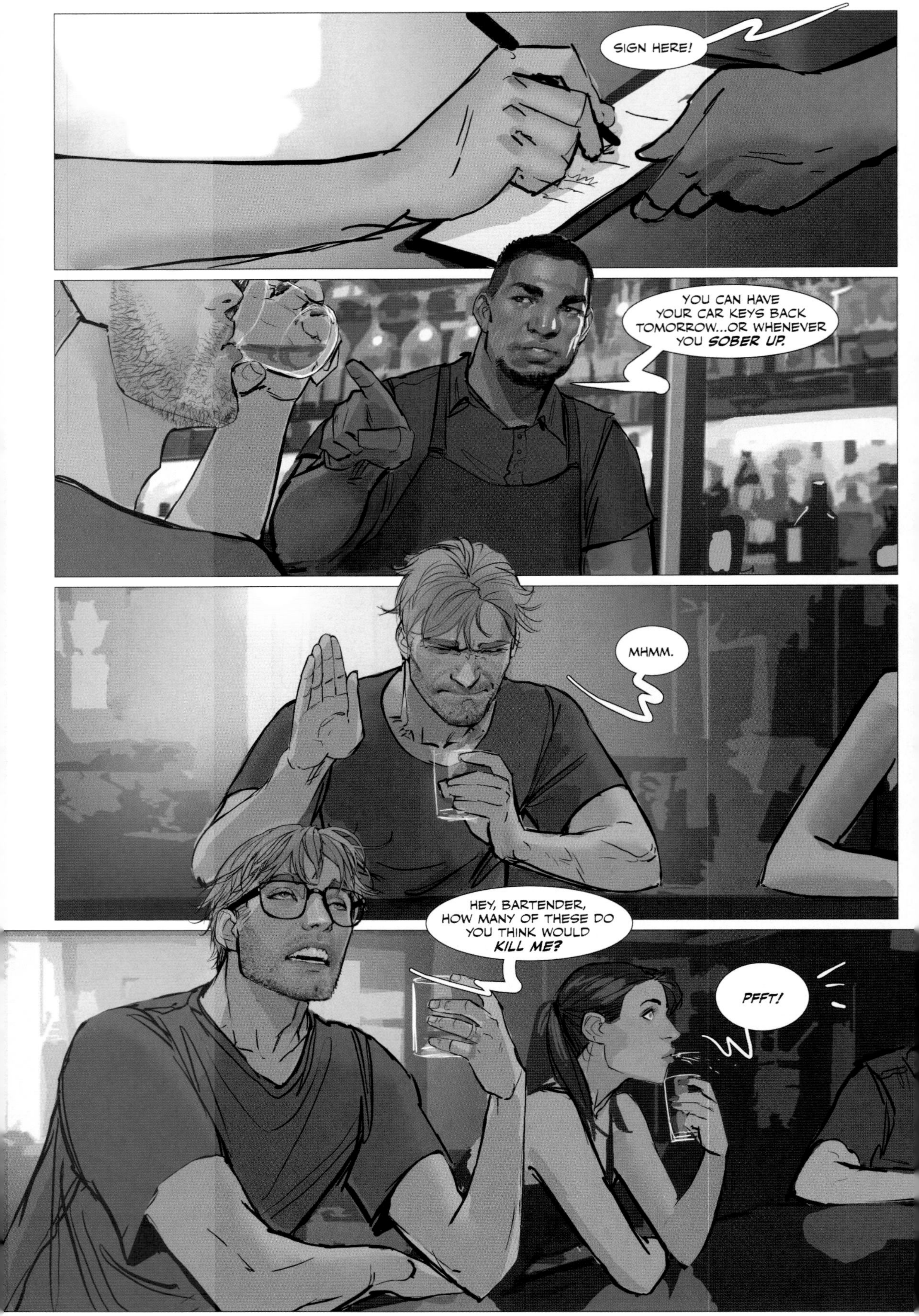
SIGN HERE!
YOU CAN HAVE YOUR CAR KEYS BACK TOMORROW...OR WHENEVER YOU **SOBER UP.**
MHMM.
HEY, BARTENDER, HOW MANY OF THESE DO YOU THINK WOULD **KILL ME?**
PFFT!

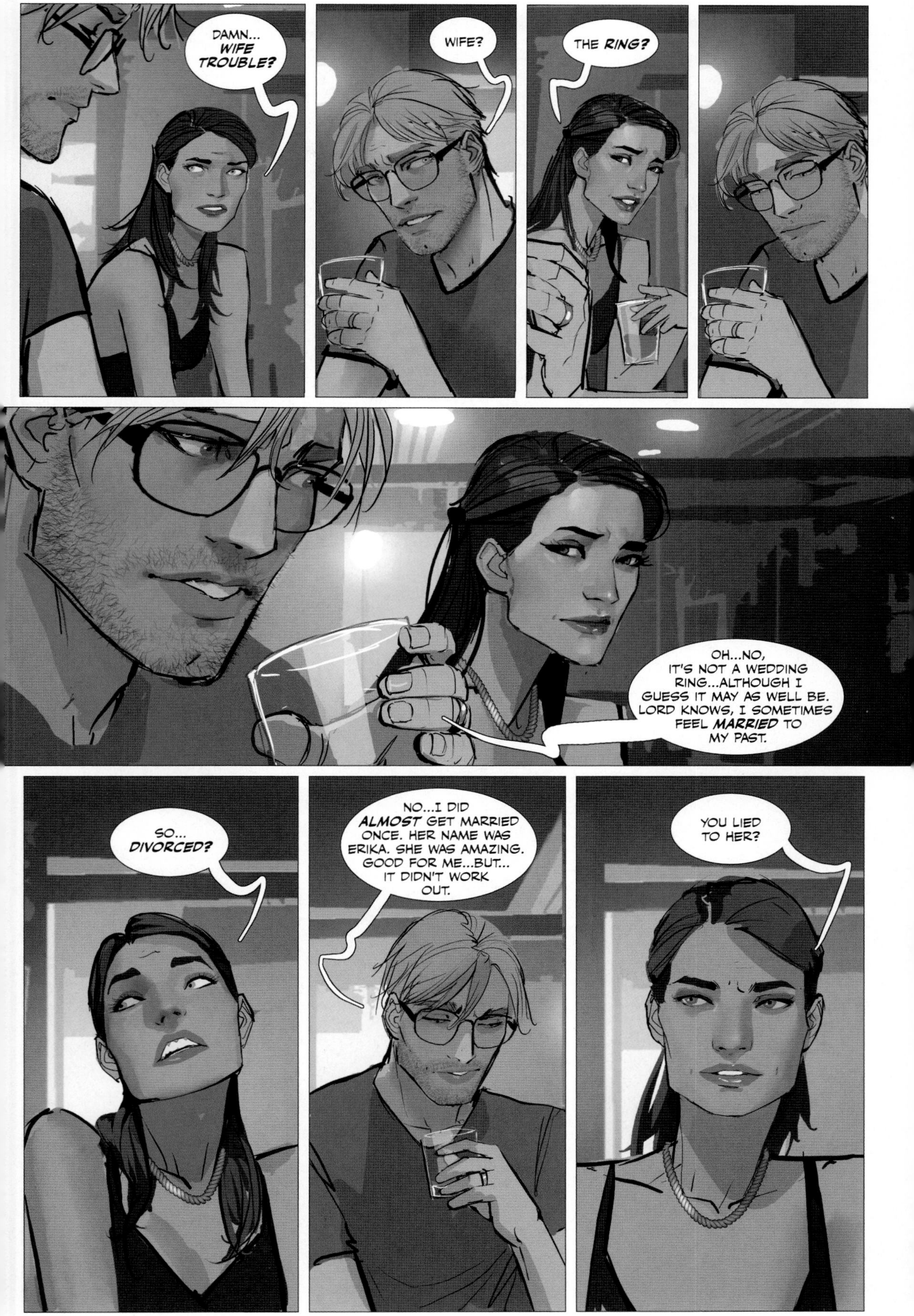
DAMN... WIFE TROUBLE?
WIFE?
THE RING?
OH...NO, IT'S NOT A WEDDING RING...ALTHOUGH I GUESS IT MAY AS WELL BE. LORD KNOWS, I SOMETIMES FEEL MARRIED TO MY PAST.
SO... DIVORCED?
NO...I DID ALMOST GET MARRIED ONCE. HER NAME WAS ERIKA. SHE WAS AMAZING. GOOD FOR ME...BUT... IT DIDN'T WORK OUT.
YOU LIED TO HER?

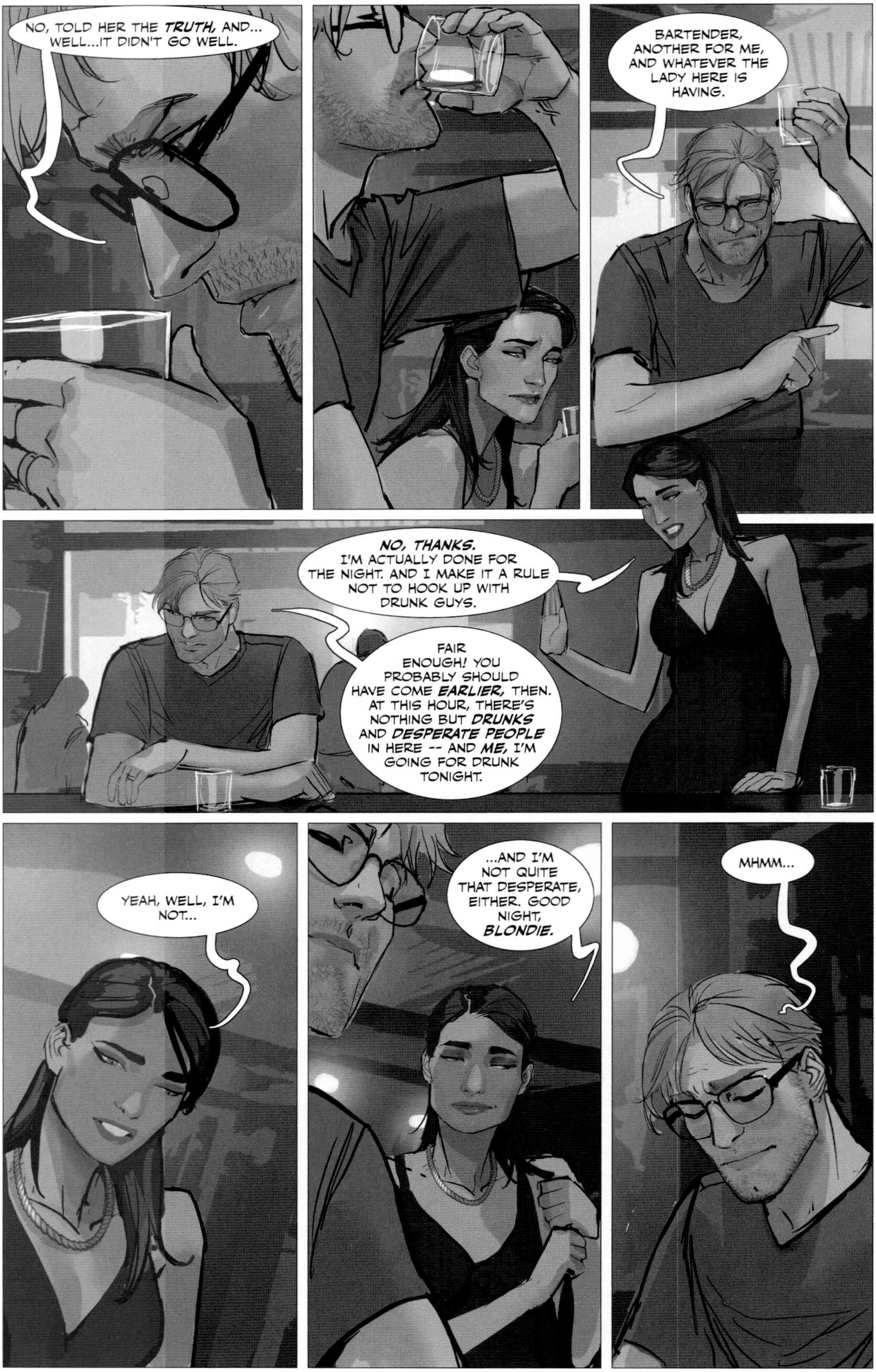
NO, TOLD HER THE ***TRUTH,*** AND... WELL...IT DIDN'T GO WELL.
BARTENDER, ANOTHER FOR ME, AND WHATEVER THE LADY HERE IS HAVING.
NO, THANKS. I'M ACTUALLY DONE FOR THE NIGHT. AND I MAKE IT A RULE NOT TO HOOK UP WITH DRUNK GUYS.
FAIR ENOUGH! YOU PROBABLY SHOULD HAVE COME ***EARLIER,*** THEN. AT THIS HOUR, THERE'S NOTHING BUT ***DRUNKS*** AND ***DESPERATE PEOPLE*** IN HERE -- AND ***ME,*** I'M GOING FOR DRUNK TONIGHT.
YEAH, WELL, I'M NOT...
...AND I'M NOT QUITE THAT DESPERATE, EITHER. GOOD NIGHT, ***BLONDIE.***
MHMM...

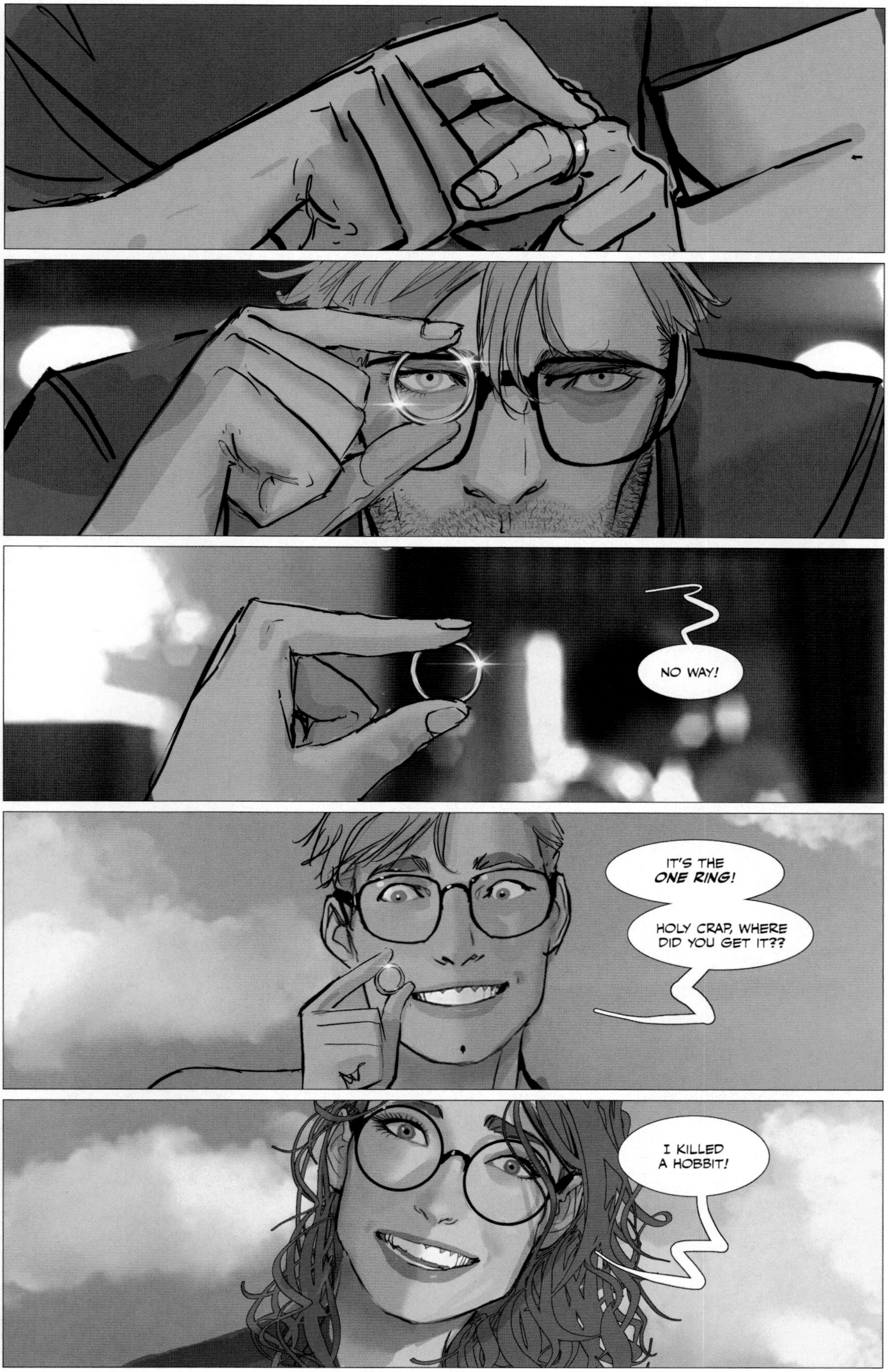
NO WAY!
IT'S THE *ONE RING!*
HOLY CRAP, WHERE DID YOU GET IT??
I KILLED A HOBBIT!

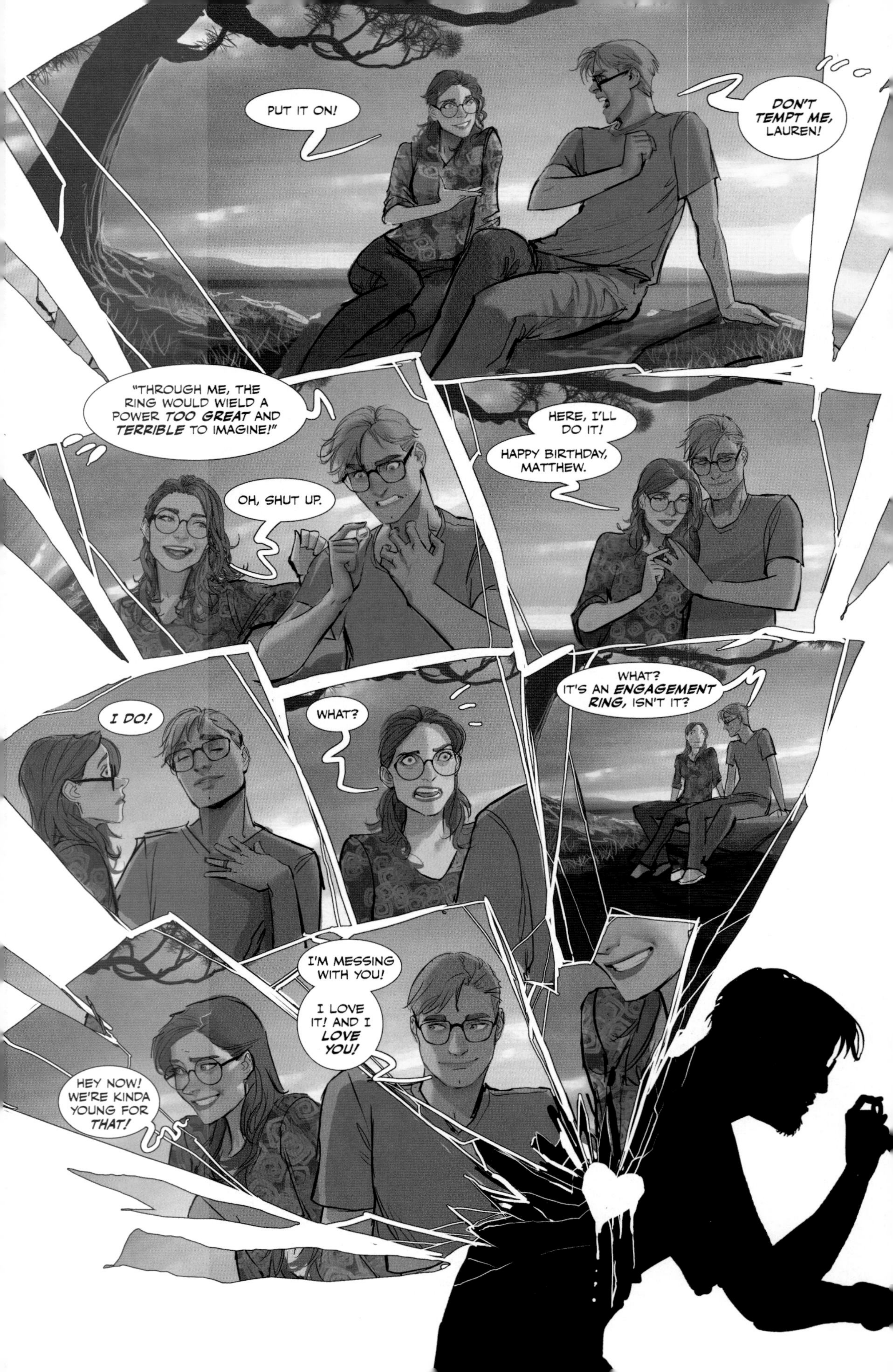
PUT IT ON!
DON'T TEMPT ME, LAUREN!
"THROUGH ME, THE RING WOULD WIELD A POWER TOO GREAT AND TERRIBLE TO IMAGINE!"
OH, SHUT UP.
HERE, I'LL DO IT!
HAPPY BIRTHDAY, MATTHEW.
I DO!
WHAT?
WHAT? IT'S AN ENGAGEMENT RING, ISN'T IT?
HEY NOW! WE'RE KINDA YOUNG FOR THAT!
I'M MESSING WITH YOU!
I LOVE IT! AND I LOVE YOU!

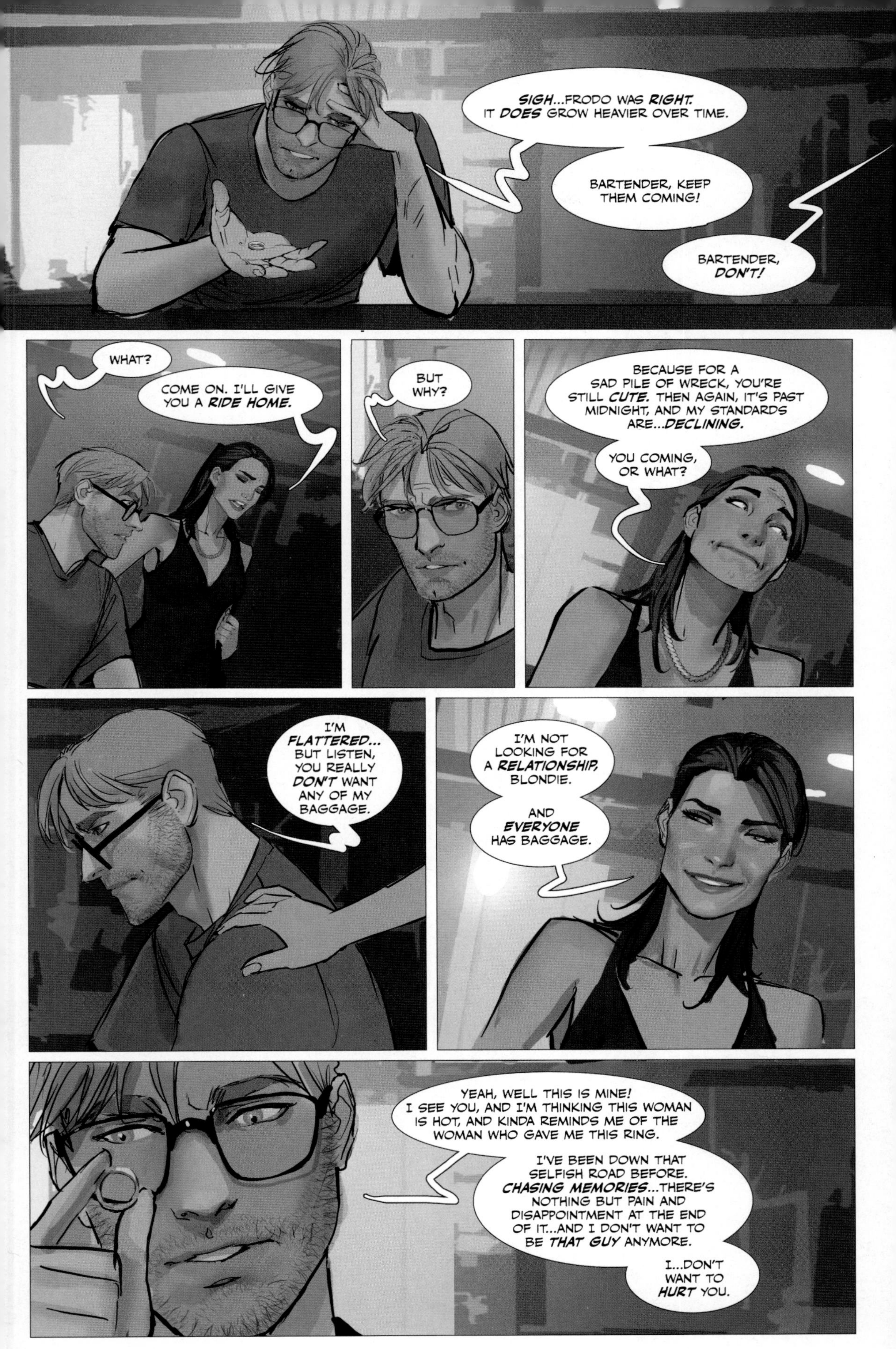
SIGH...FRODO WAS RIGHT. IT DOES GROW HEAVIER OVER TIME.
BARTENDER, KEEP THEM COMING!
BARTENDER, DON'T!
WHAT?
COME ON. I'LL GIVE YOU A RIDE HOME.
BUT WHY?
BECAUSE FOR A SAD PILE OF WRECK, YOU'RE STILL CUTE. THEN AGAIN, IT'S PAST MIDNIGHT, AND MY STANDARDS ARE...DECLINING.
YOU COMING, OR WHAT?
I'M FLATTERED... BUT LISTEN, YOU REALLY DON'T WANT ANY OF MY BAGGAGE.
I'M NOT LOOKING FOR A RELATIONSHIP, BLONDIE.
AND EVERYONE HAS BAGGAGE.
YEAH, WELL THIS IS MINE! I SEE YOU, AND I'M THINKING THIS WOMAN IS HOT, AND KINDA REMINDS ME OF THE WOMAN WHO GAVE ME THIS RING.
I'VE BEEN DOWN THAT SELFISH ROAD BEFORE. CHASING MEMORIES...THERE'S NOTHING BUT PAIN AND DISAPPOINTMENT AT THE END OF IT...AND I DON'T WANT TO BE THAT GUY ANYMORE.
I...DON'T WANT TO HURT YOU.

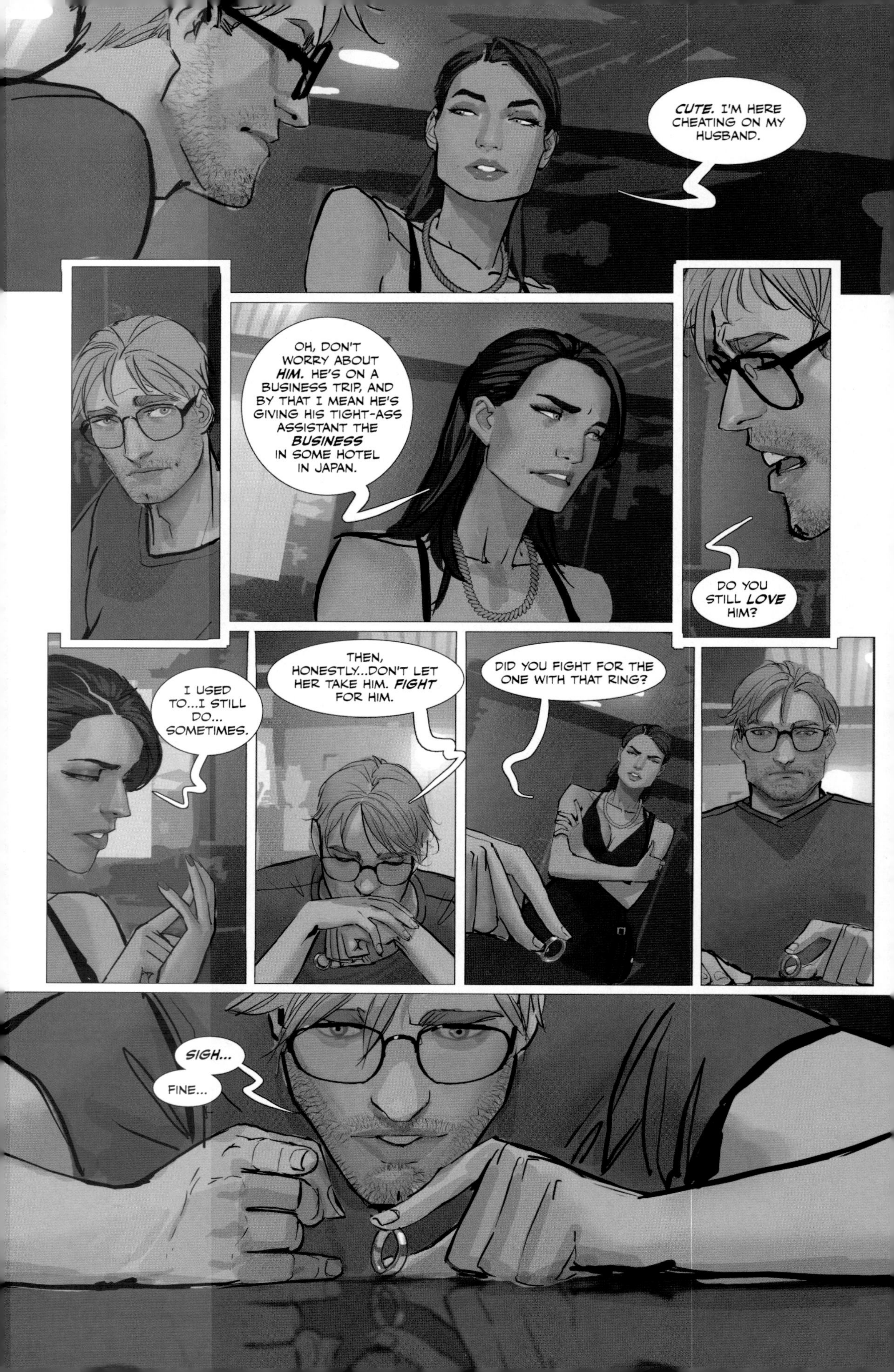
CUTE. I'M HERE CHEATING ON MY HUSBAND.
OH, DON'T WORRY ABOUT HIM. HE'S ON A BUSINESS TRIP, AND BY THAT I MEAN HE'S GIVING HIS TIGHT-ASS ASSISTANT THE BUSINESS IN SOME HOTEL IN JAPAN.
DO YOU STILL LOVE HIM?
I USED TO...I STILL DO... SOMETIMES.
THEN, HONESTLY...DON'T LET HER TAKE HIM. FIGHT FOR HIM.
DID YOU FIGHT FOR THE ONE WITH THAT RING?
SIGH...
FINE...

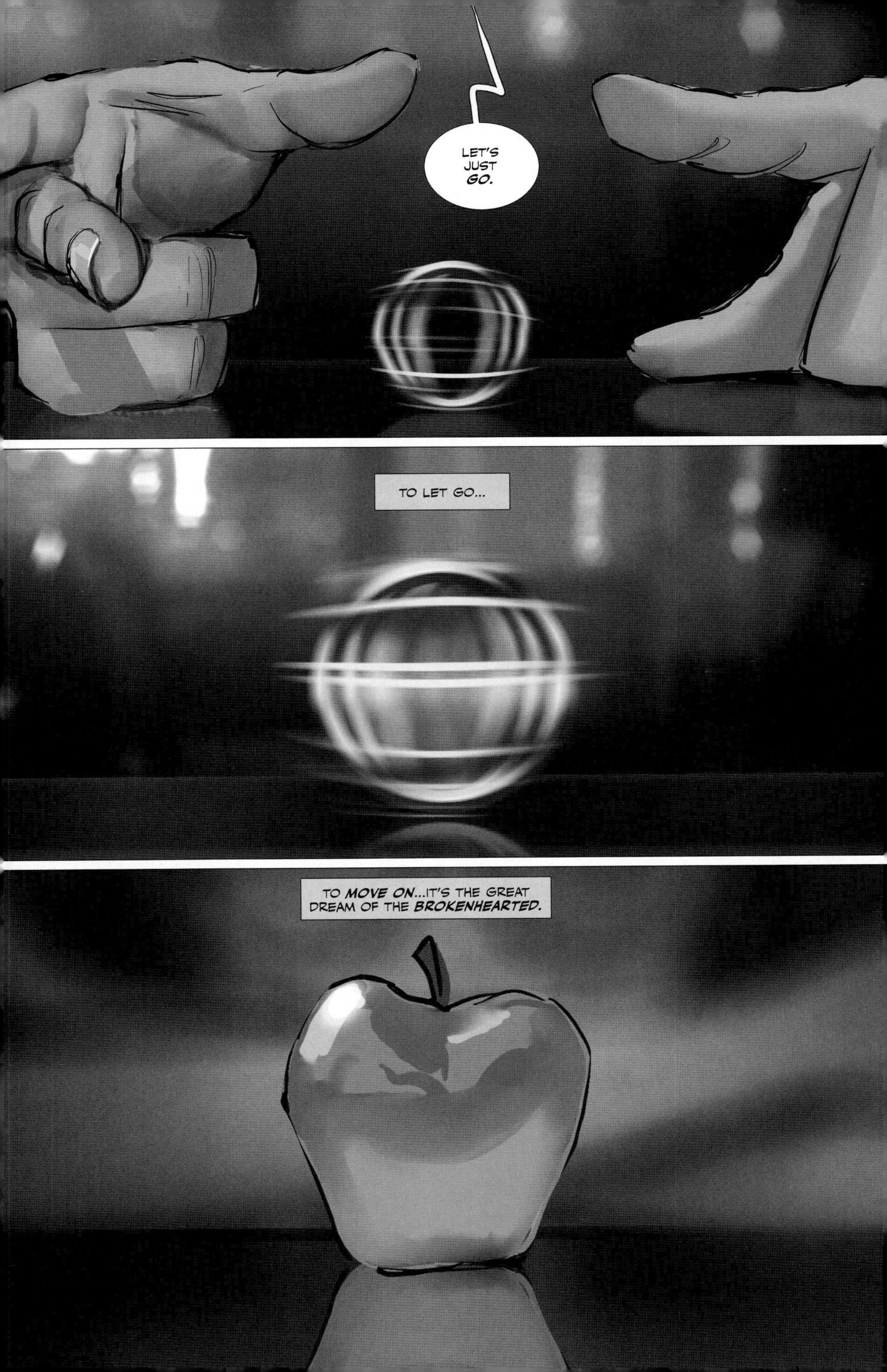
LET'S JUST GO.
TO LET GO...
TO MOVE ON...IT'S THE GREAT DREAM OF THE BROKENHEARTED.

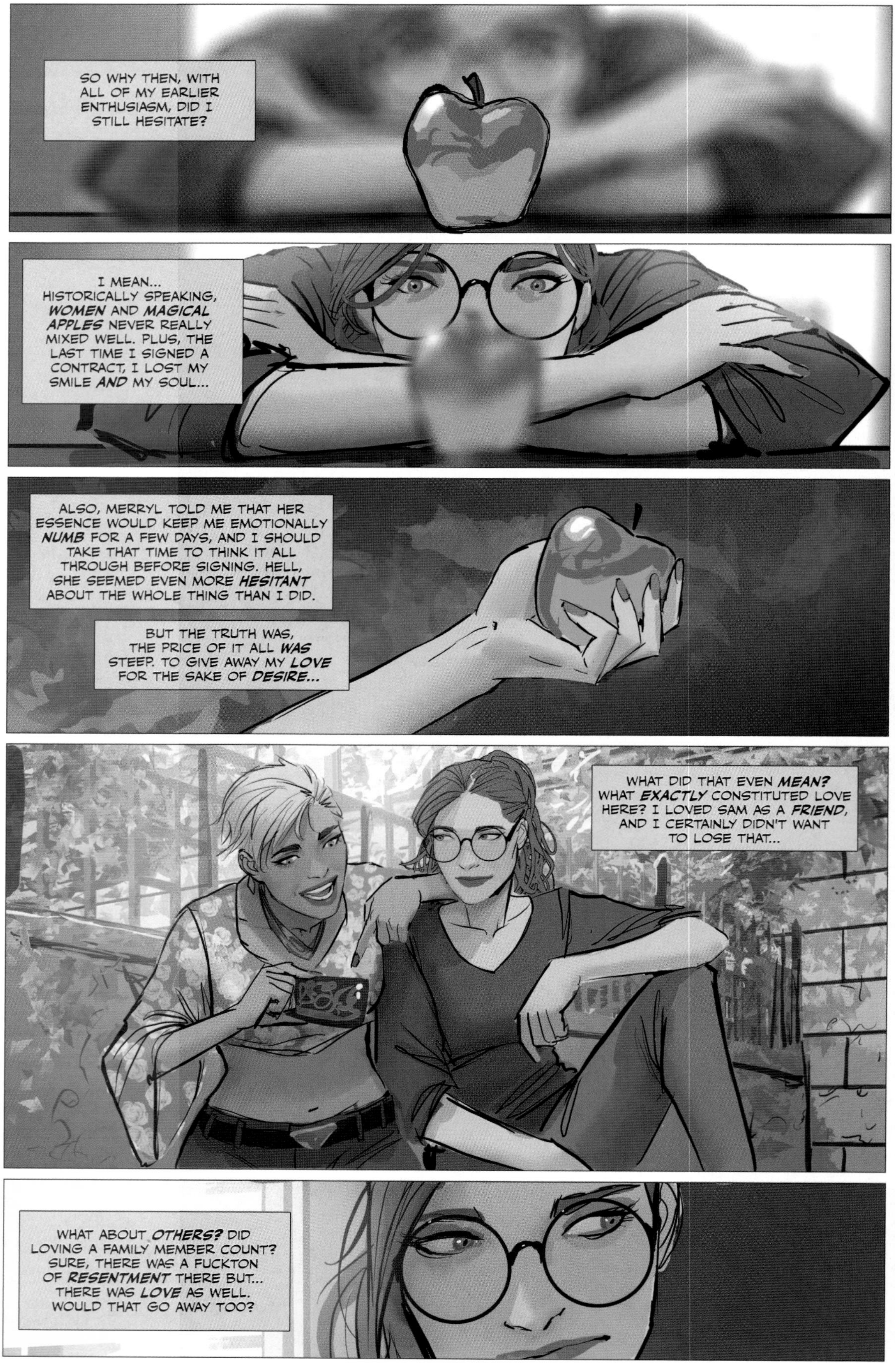
SO WHY THEN, WITH ALL OF MY EARLIER ENTHUSIASM, DID I STILL HESITATE?
I MEAN... HISTORICALLY SPEAKING, WOMEN AND MAGICAL APPLES NEVER REALLY MIXED WELL. PLUS, THE LAST TIME I SIGNED A CONTRACT, I LOST MY SMILE AND MY SOUL...
ALSO, MERRYL TOLD ME THAT HER ESSENCE WOULD KEEP ME EMOTIONALLY NUMB FOR A FEW DAYS, AND I SHOULD TAKE THAT TIME TO THINK IT ALL THROUGH BEFORE SIGNING. HELL, SHE SEEMED EVEN MORE HESITANT ABOUT THE WHOLE THING THAN I DID.
BUT THE TRUTH WAS, THE PRICE OF IT ALL WAS STEEP. TO GIVE AWAY MY LOVE FOR THE SAKE OF DESIRE...
WHAT DID THAT EVEN MEAN? WHAT EXACTLY CONSTITUTED LOVE HERE? I LOVED SAM AS A FRIEND, AND I CERTAINLY DIDN'T WANT TO LOSE THAT...
WHAT ABOUT OTHERS? DID LOVING A FAMILY MEMBER COUNT? SURE, THERE WAS A FUCKTON OF RESENTMENT THERE BUT... THERE WAS LOVE AS WELL. WOULD THAT GO AWAY TOO?

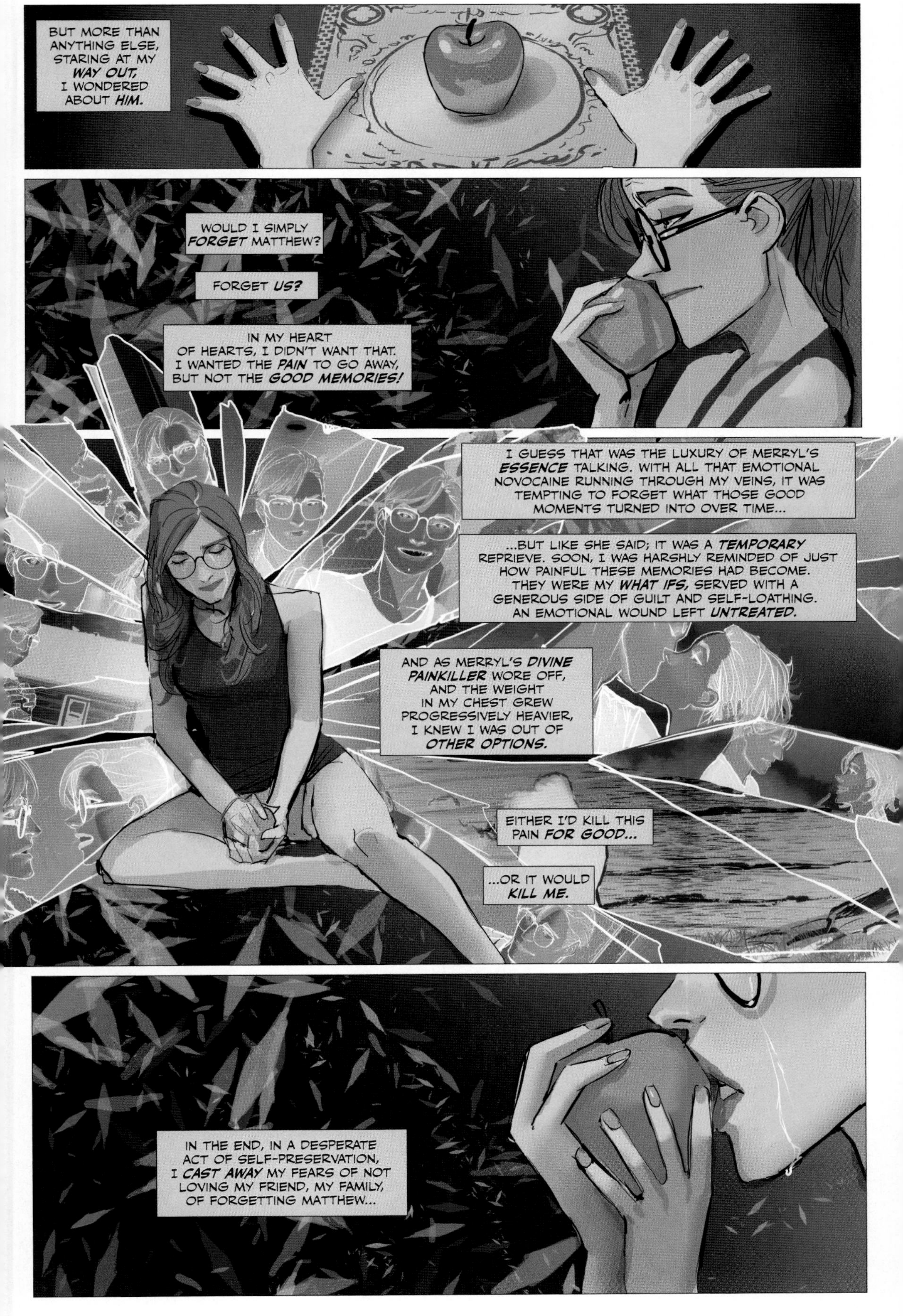
BUT MORE THAN ANYTHING ELSE, STARING AT MY WAY OUT, I WONDERED ABOUT HIM.
WOULD I SIMPLY FORGET MATTHEW?
FORGET US?
IN MY HEART OF HEARTS, I DIDN'T WANT THAT. I WANTED THE PAIN TO GO AWAY, BUT NOT THE GOOD MEMORIES!
I GUESS THAT WAS THE LUXURY OF MERRYL'S ESSENCE TALKING. WITH ALL THAT EMOTIONAL NOVOCAINE RUNNING THROUGH MY VEINS, IT WAS TEMPTING TO FORGET WHAT THOSE GOOD MOMENTS TURNED INTO OVER TIME...
...BUT LIKE SHE SAID; IT WAS A TEMPORARY REPRIEVE. SOON, I WAS HARSHLY REMINDED OF JUST HOW PAINFUL THESE MEMORIES HAD BECOME. THEY WERE MY WHAT IFS, SERVED WITH A GENEROUS SIDE OF GUILT AND SELF-LOATHING. AN EMOTIONAL WOUND LEFT UNTREATED.
AND AS MERRYL'S DIVINE PAINKILLER WORE OFF, AND THE WEIGHT IN MY CHEST GREW PROGRESSIVELY HEAVIER, I KNEW I WAS OUT OF OTHER OPTIONS.
EITHER I'D KILL THIS PAIN FOR GOOD...
...OR IT WOULD KILL ME.
IN THE END, IN A DESPERATE ACT OF SELF-PRESERVATION, I CAST AWAY MY FEARS OF NOT LOVING MY FRIEND, MY FAMILY, OF FORGETTING MATTHEW...

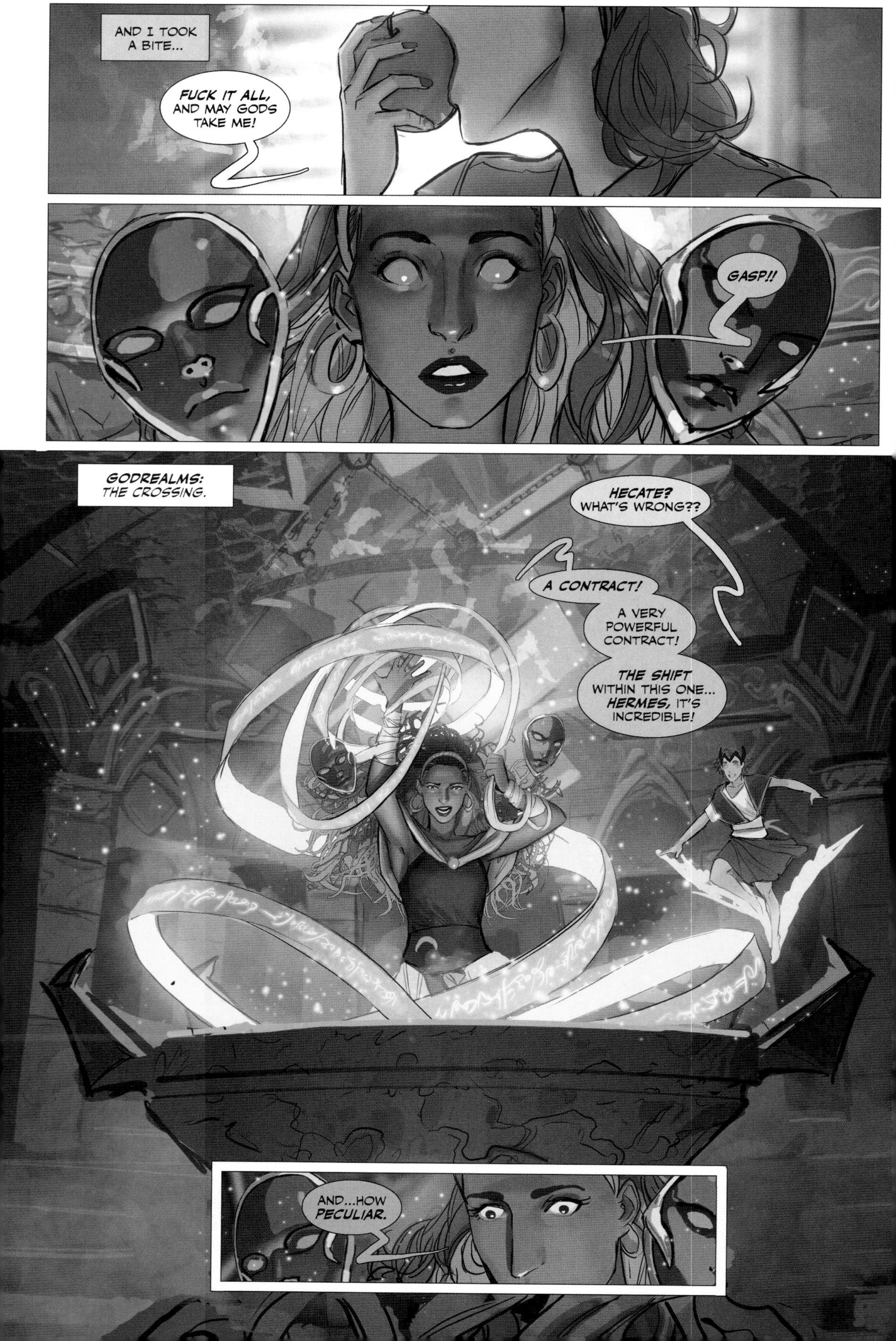
AND I TOOK A BITE...
FUCK IT ALL, AND MAY GODS TAKE ME!
GASP!!
GODREALMS: THE CROSSING.
HECATE? WHAT'S WRONG??
A CONTRACT!
A VERY POWERFUL CONTRACT!
THE SHIFT WITHIN THIS ONE... HERMES, IT'S INCREDIBLE!
AND...HOW PECULIAR.

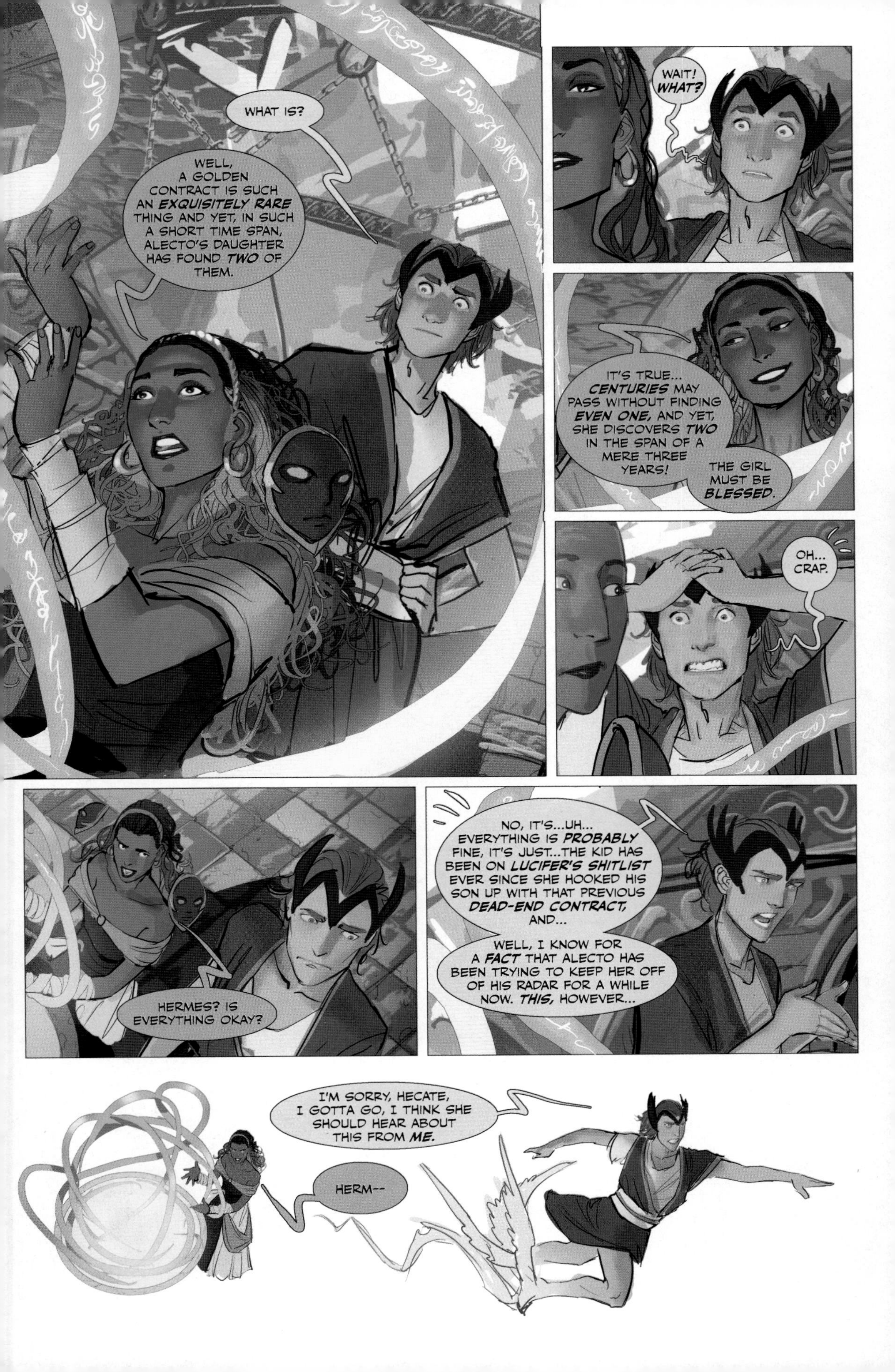
WHAT IS?
WELL, A GOLDEN CONTRACT IS SUCH AN EXQUISITELY RARE THING AND YET, IN SUCH A SHORT TIME SPAN, ALECTO'S DAUGHTER HAS FOUND TWO OF THEM.
WAIT! WHAT?
IT'S TRUE... CENTURIES MAY PASS WITHOUT FINDING EVEN ONE, AND YET, SHE DISCOVERS TWO IN THE SPAN OF A MERE THREE YEARS!
THE GIRL MUST BE BLESSED.
OH... CRAP.
HERMES? IS EVERYTHING OKAY?
NO, IT'S...UH... EVERYTHING IS PROBABLY FINE, IT'S JUST...THE KID HAS BEEN ON LUCIFER'S SHITLIST EVER SINCE SHE HOOKED HIS SON UP WITH THAT PREVIOUS DEAD-END CONTRACT, AND...
WELL, I KNOW FOR A FACT THAT ALECTO HAS BEEN TRYING TO KEEP HER OFF OF HIS RADAR FOR A WHILE NOW. THIS, HOWEVER...
I'M SORRY, HECATE, I GOTTA GO, I THINK SHE SHOULD HEAR ABOUT THIS FROM ME.
HERM--

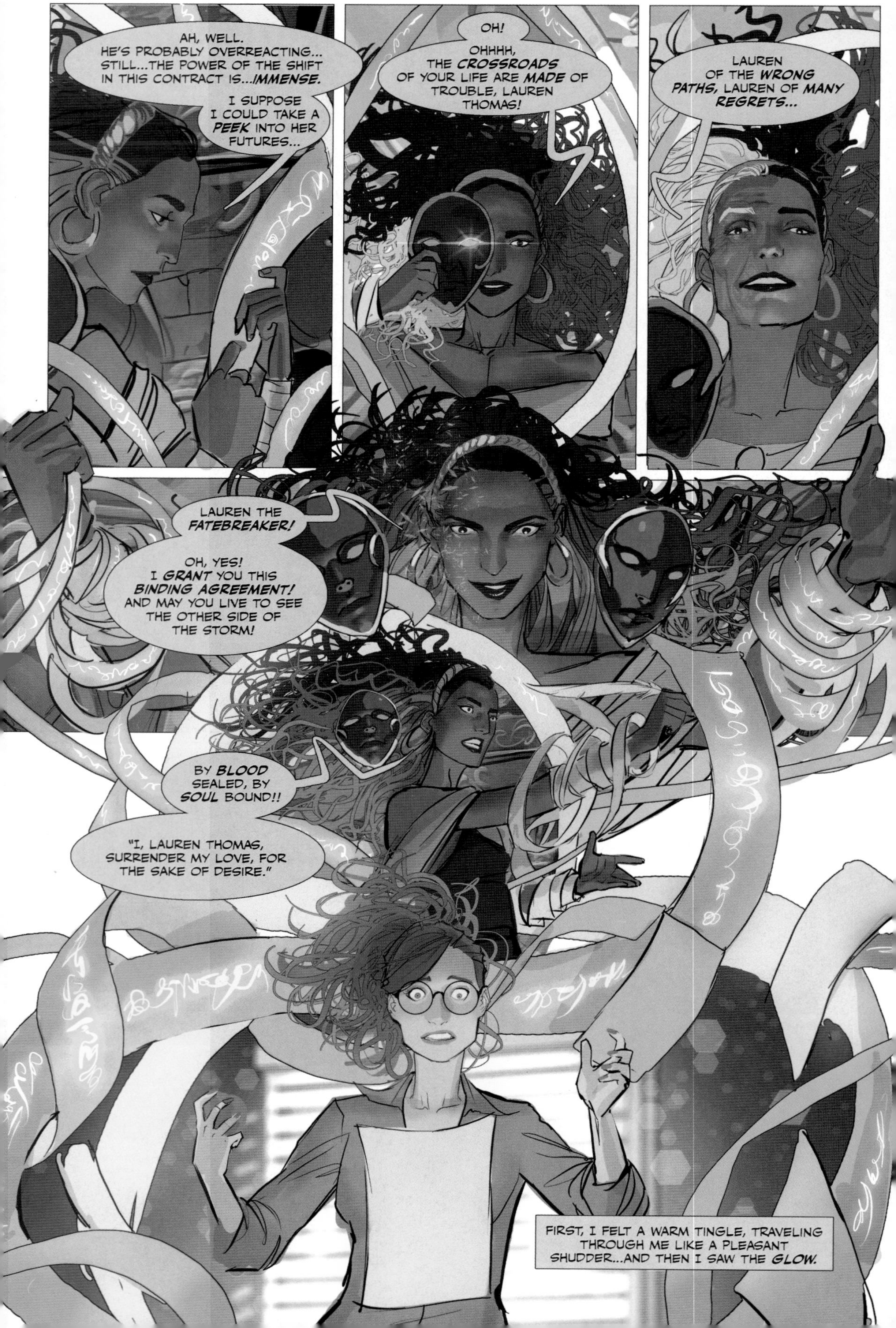
AH, WELL. HE'S PROBABLY OVERREACTING... STILL...THE POWER OF THE SHIFT IN THIS CONTRACT IS...IMMENSE.
I SUPPOSE I COULD TAKE A PEEK INTO HER FUTURES...
OH!
OHHHH, THE CROSSROADS OF YOUR LIFE ARE MADE OF TROUBLE, LAUREN THOMAS!
LAUREN OF THE WRONG PATHS, LAUREN OF MANY REGRETS...
LAUREN THE FATEBREAKER!
OH, YES! I GRANT YOU THIS BINDING AGREEMENT! AND MAY YOU LIVE TO SEE THE OTHER SIDE OF THE STORM!
BY BLOOD SEALED, BY SOUL BOUND!!
"I, LAUREN THOMAS, SURRENDER MY LOVE, FOR THE SAKE OF DESIRE."
FIRST, I FELT A WARM TINGLE, TRAVELING THROUGH ME LIKE A PLEASANT SHUDDER...AND THEN I SAW THE GLOW.

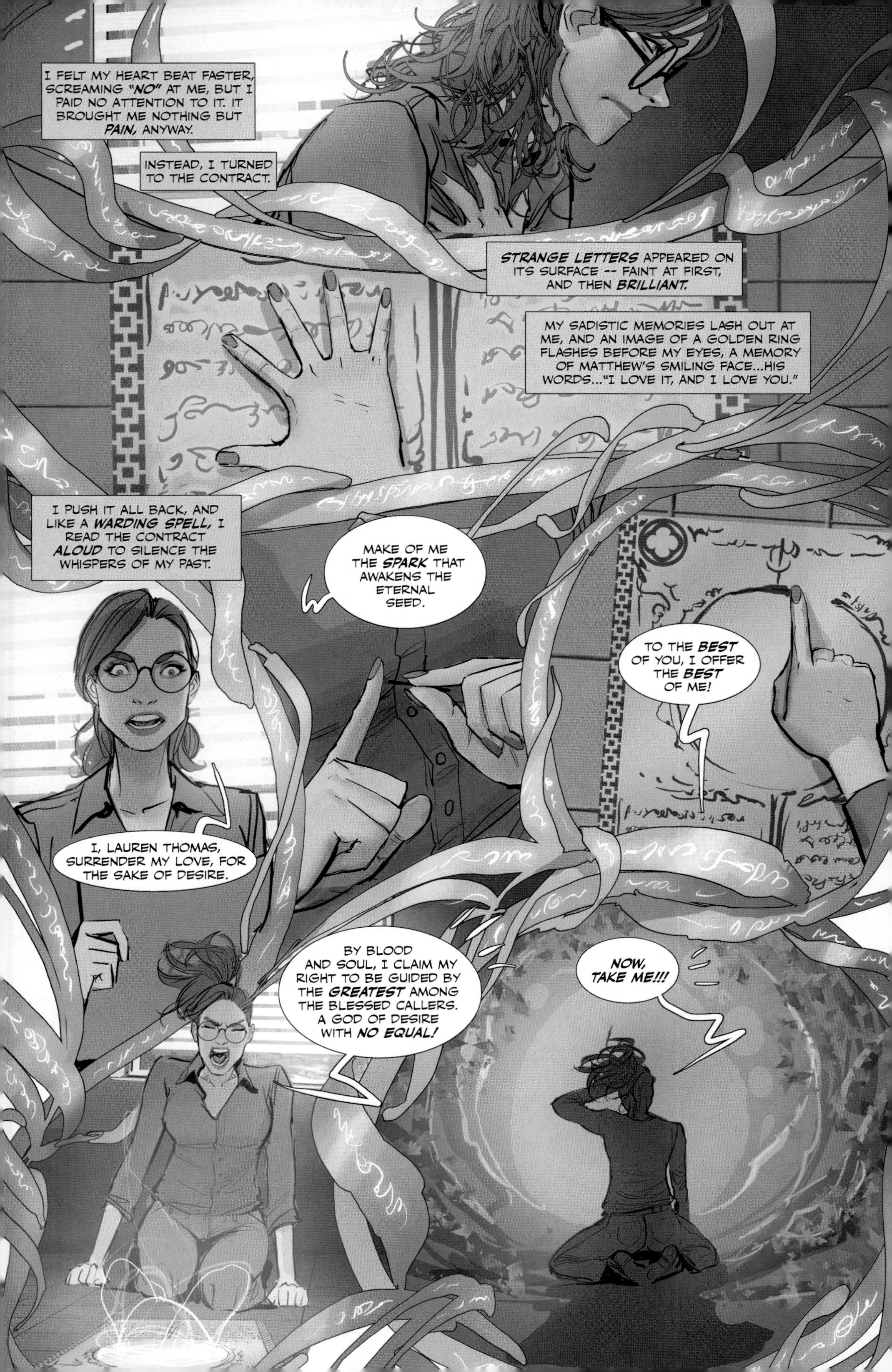

I FELT MY HEART BEAT FASTER, SCREAMING "NO" AT ME, BUT I PAID NO ATTENTION TO IT. IT BROUGHT ME NOTHING BUT PAIN, ANYWAY.
INSTEAD, I TURNED TO THE CONTRACT.
STRANGE LETTERS APPEARED ON ITS SURFACE -- FAINT AT FIRST, AND THEN BRILLIANT.
MY SADISTIC MEMORIES LASH OUT AT ME, AND AN IMAGE OF A GOLDEN RING FLASHES BEFORE MY EYES, A MEMORY OF MATTHEW'S SMILING FACE...HIS WORDS..."I LOVE IT, AND I LOVE YOU."
I PUSH IT ALL BACK, AND LIKE A WARDING SPELL, I READ THE CONTRACT ALOUD TO SILENCE THE WHISPERS OF MY PAST.
MAKE OF ME THE SPARK THAT AWAKENS THE ETERNAL SEED.
TO THE BEST OF YOU, I OFFER THE BEST OF ME!
I, LAUREN THOMAS, SURRENDER MY LOVE, FOR THE SAKE OF DESIRE.
BY BLOOD AND SOUL, I CLAIM MY RIGHT TO BE GUIDED BY THE GREATEST AMONG THE BLESSED CALLERS. A GOD OF DESIRE WITH NO EQUAL!
NOW, TAKE ME!!!

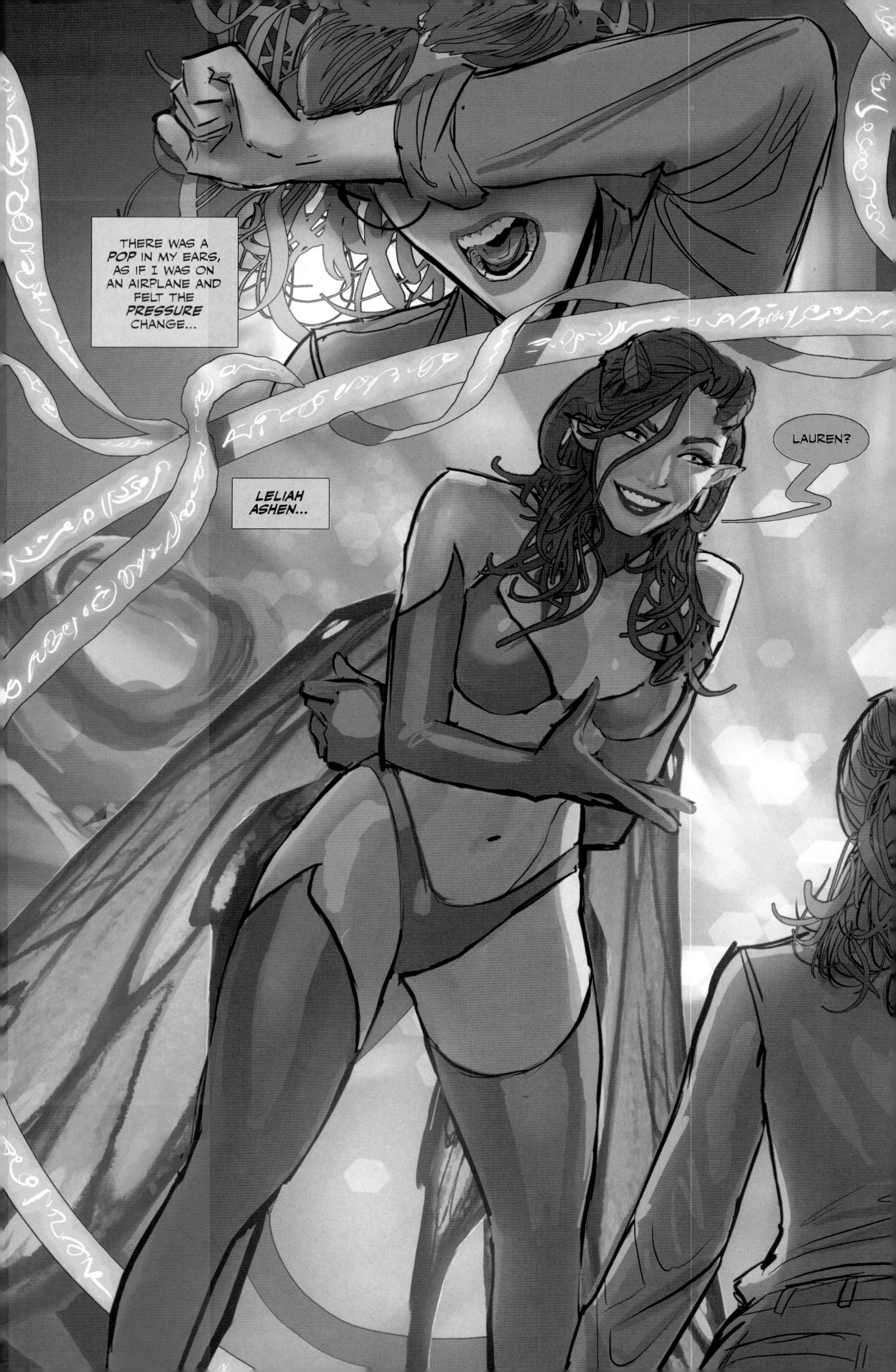
THERE WAS A POP IN MY EARS, AS IF I WAS ON AN AIRPLANE AND FELT THE PRESSURE CHANGE...
LELIAH ASHEN...
LAUREN?

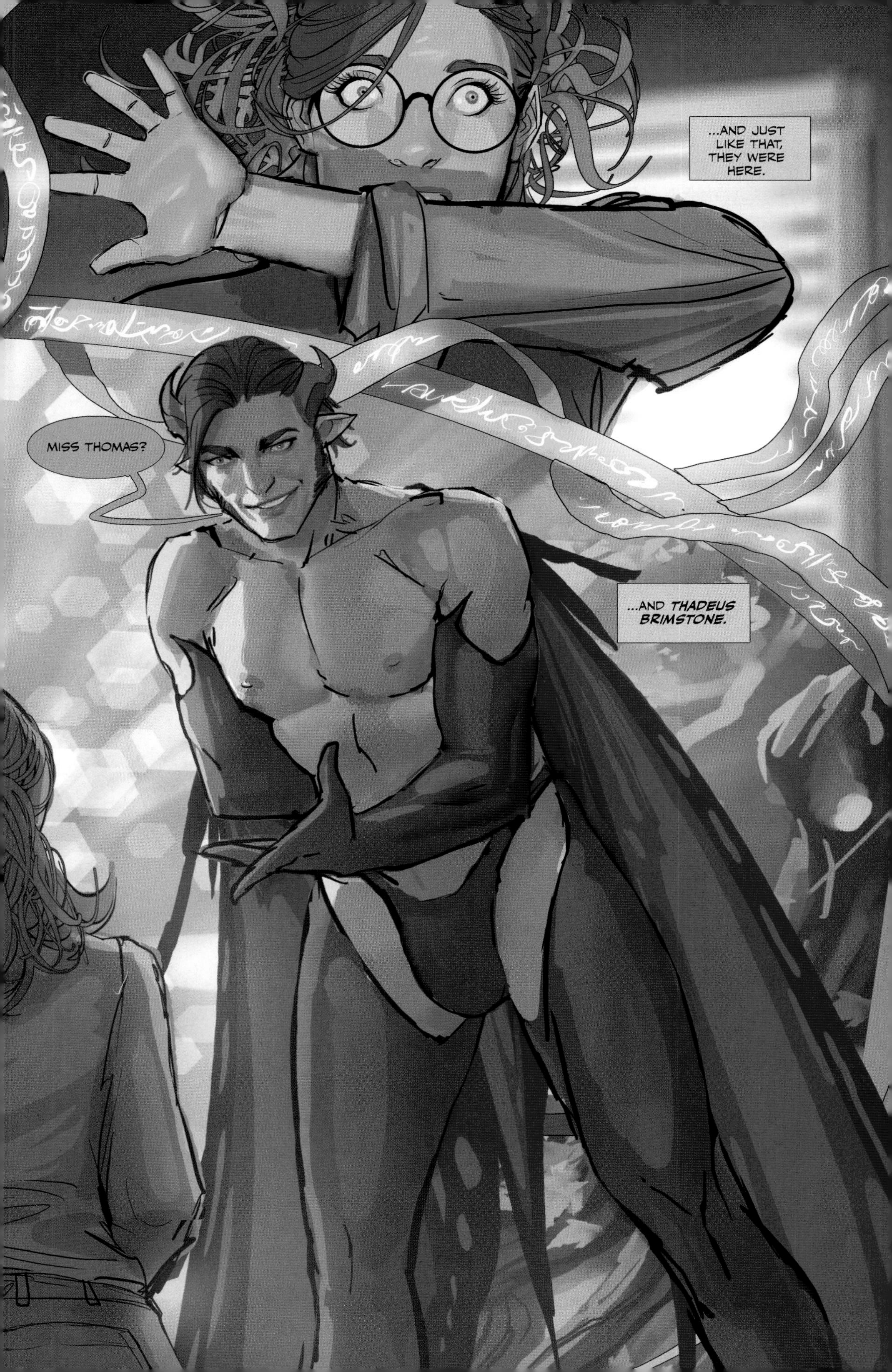
...AND JUST LIKE THAT, THEY WERE HERE.
MISS THOMAS?
...AND *THADEUS BRIMSTONE.*

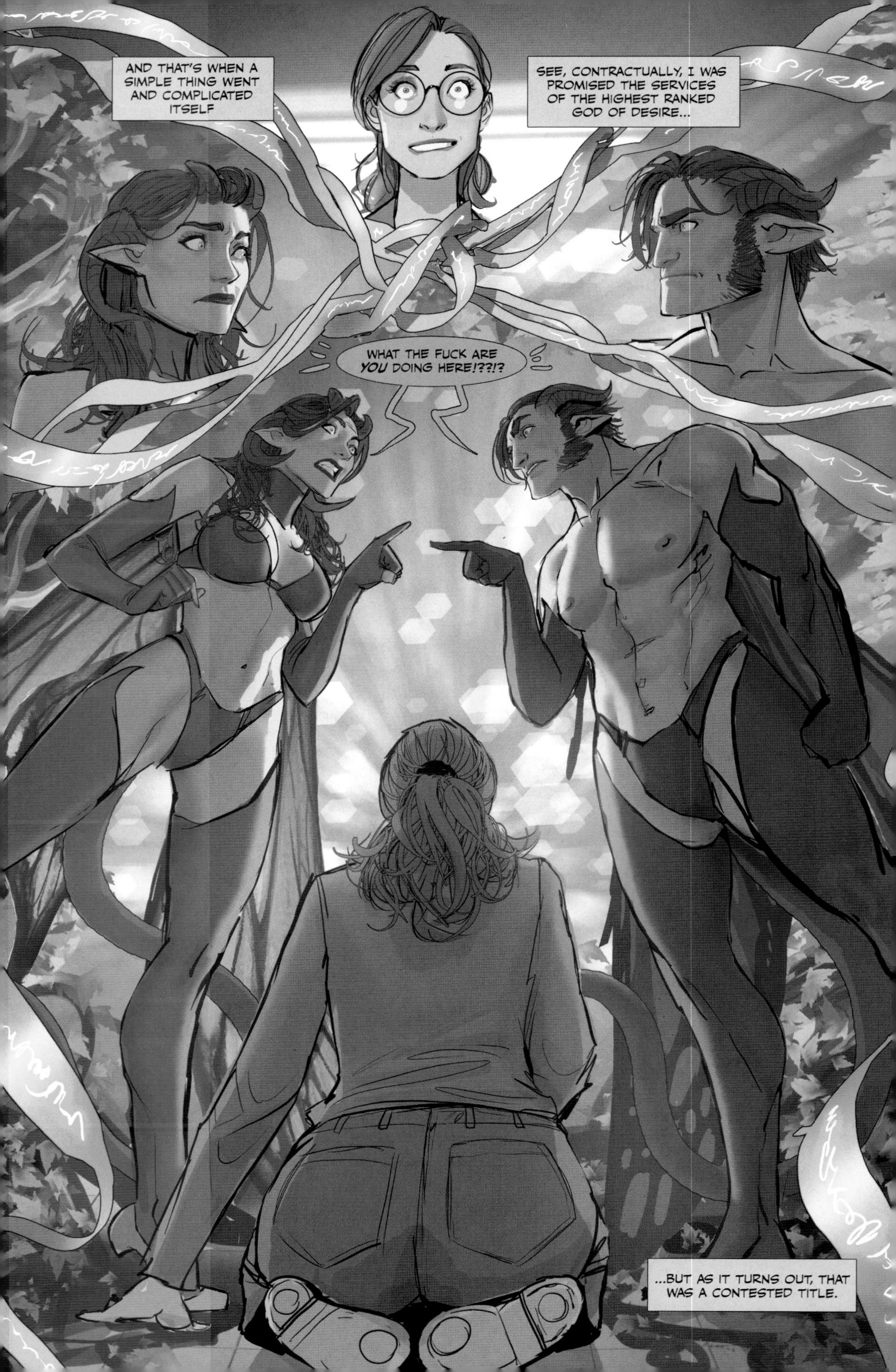
AND THAT'S WHEN A SIMPLE THING WENT AND COMPLICATED ITSELF
SEE, CONTRACTUALLY, I WAS PROMISED THE SERVICES OF THE HIGHEST RANKED GOD OF DESIRE...
WHAT THE FUCK ARE *YOU* DOING HERE!??!?
...BUT AS IT TURNS OUT, THAT WAS A CONTESTED TITLE.

Chapter 6

The last moments of calm...

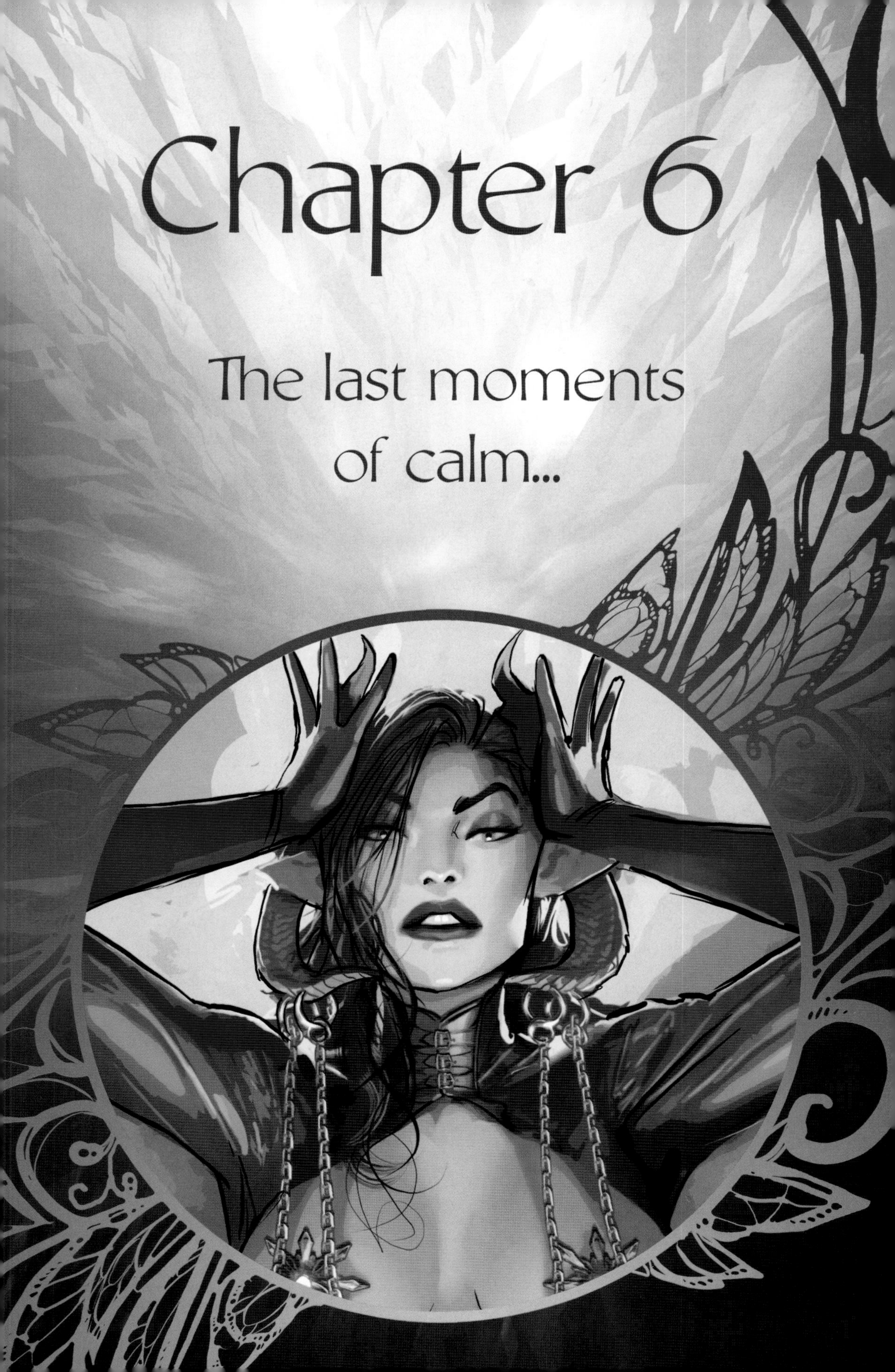

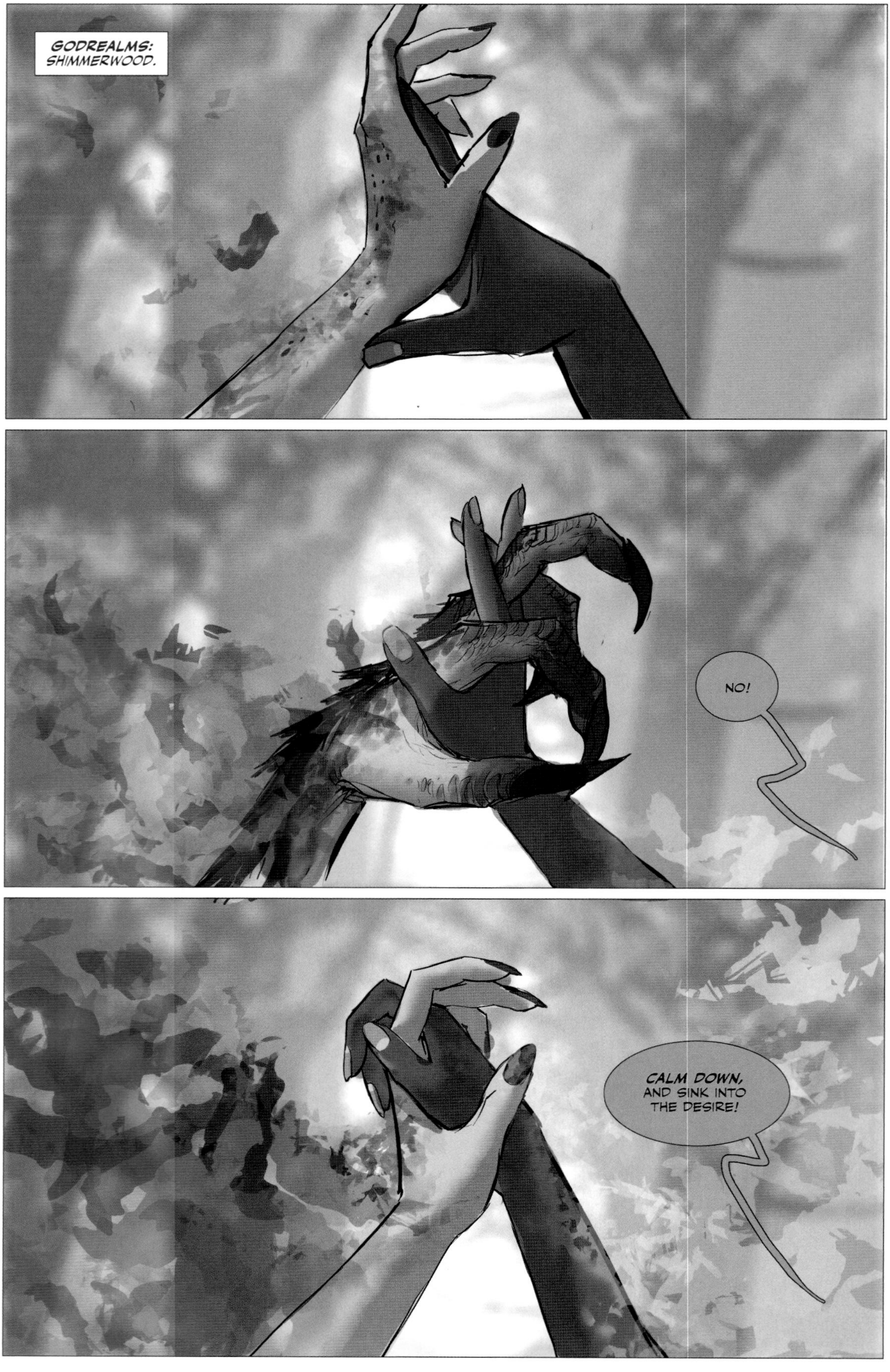
GODREALMS: SHIMMERWOOD.
NO!
CALM DOWN, AND SINK INTO THE DESIRE!

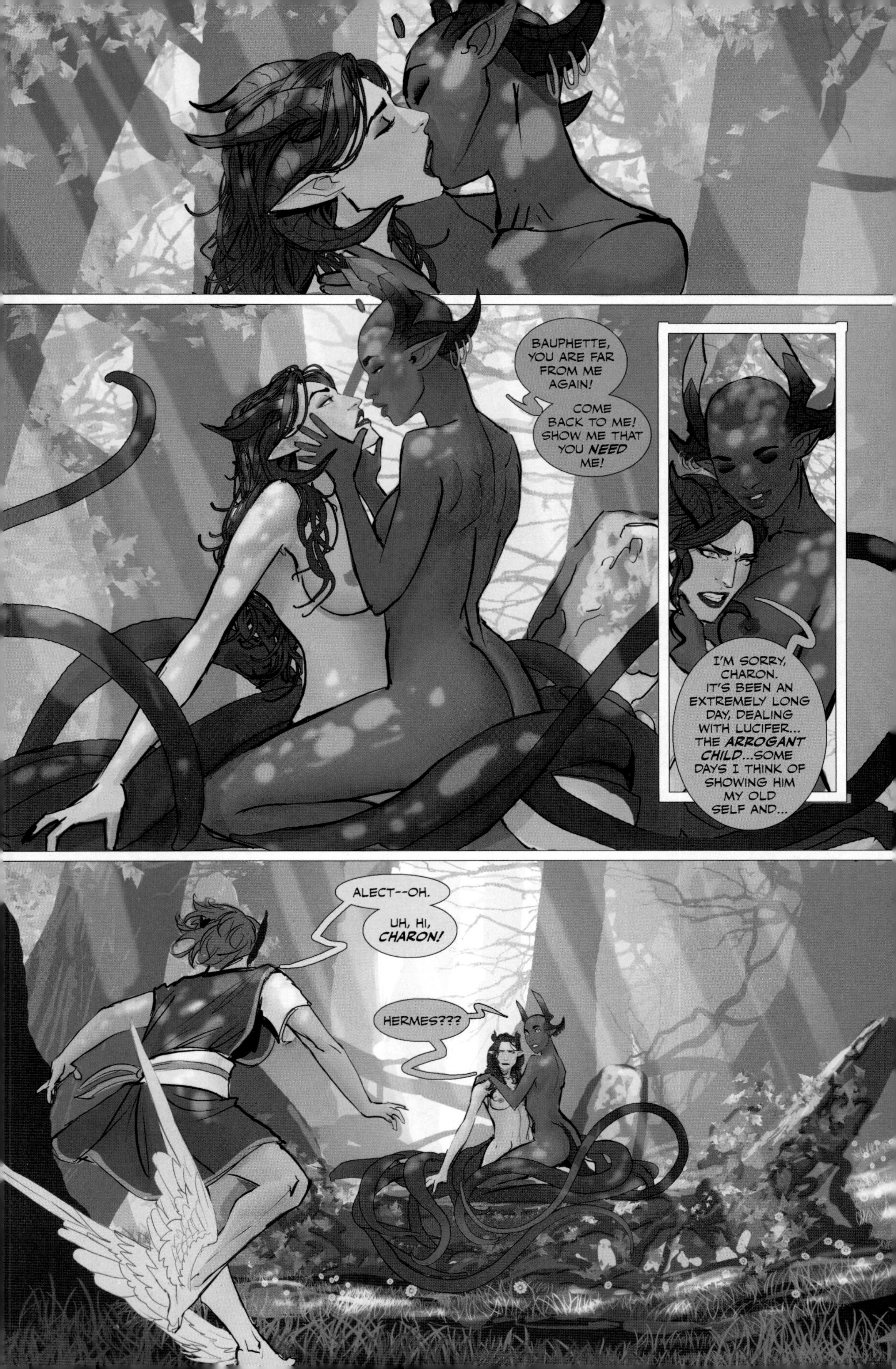
BAUPHETTE, YOU ARE FAR FROM ME AGAIN!
COME BACK TO ME! SHOW ME THAT YOU **NEED** ME!
I'M SORRY, CHARON. IT'S BEEN AN EXTREMELY LONG DAY, DEALING WITH LUCIFER... THE ***ARROGANT CHILD***...SOME DAYS I THINK OF SHOWING HIM MY OLD SELF AND...
ALECT--OH.
UH, HI, ***CHARON!***
HERMES???

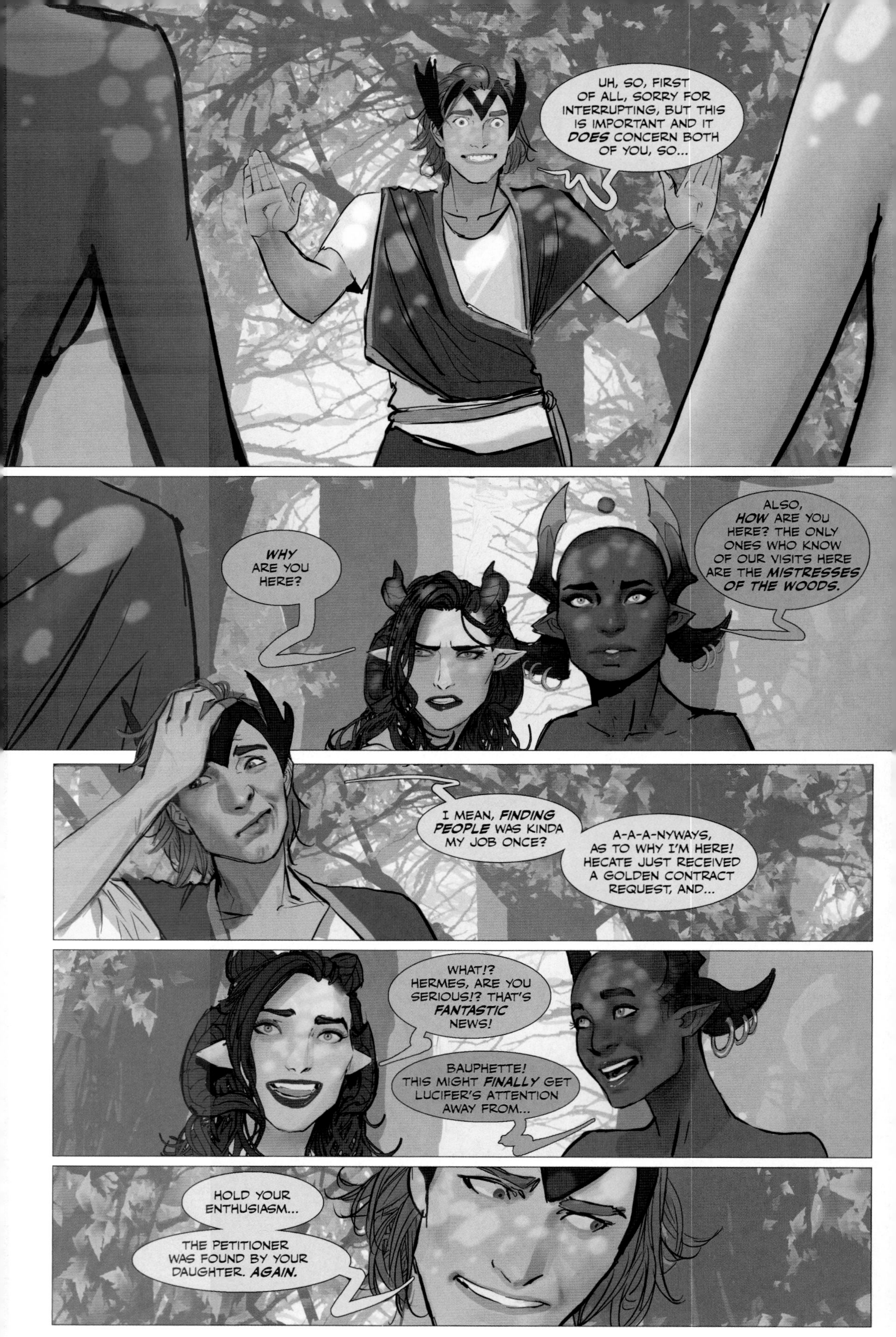
UH, SO, FIRST OF ALL, SORRY FOR INTERRUPTING, BUT THIS IS IMPORTANT AND IT *DOES* CONCERN BOTH OF YOU, SO...
WHY ARE YOU HERE?
ALSO, *HOW* ARE YOU HERE? THE ONLY ONES WHO KNOW OF OUR VISITS HERE ARE THE *MISTRESSES OF THE WOODS.*
I MEAN, *FINDING PEOPLE* WAS KINDA MY JOB ONCE?
A-A-A-NYWAYS, AS TO WHY I'M HERE! HECATE JUST RECEIVED A GOLDEN CONTRACT REQUEST, AND...
WHAT!? HERMES, ARE YOU SERIOUS!? THAT'S *FANTASTIC* NEWS!
BAUPHETTE! THIS MIGHT *FINALLY* GET LUCIFER'S ATTENTION AWAY FROM...
HOLD YOUR ENTHUSIASM...
THE PETITIONER WAS FOUND BY YOUR DAUGHTER. *AGAIN.*

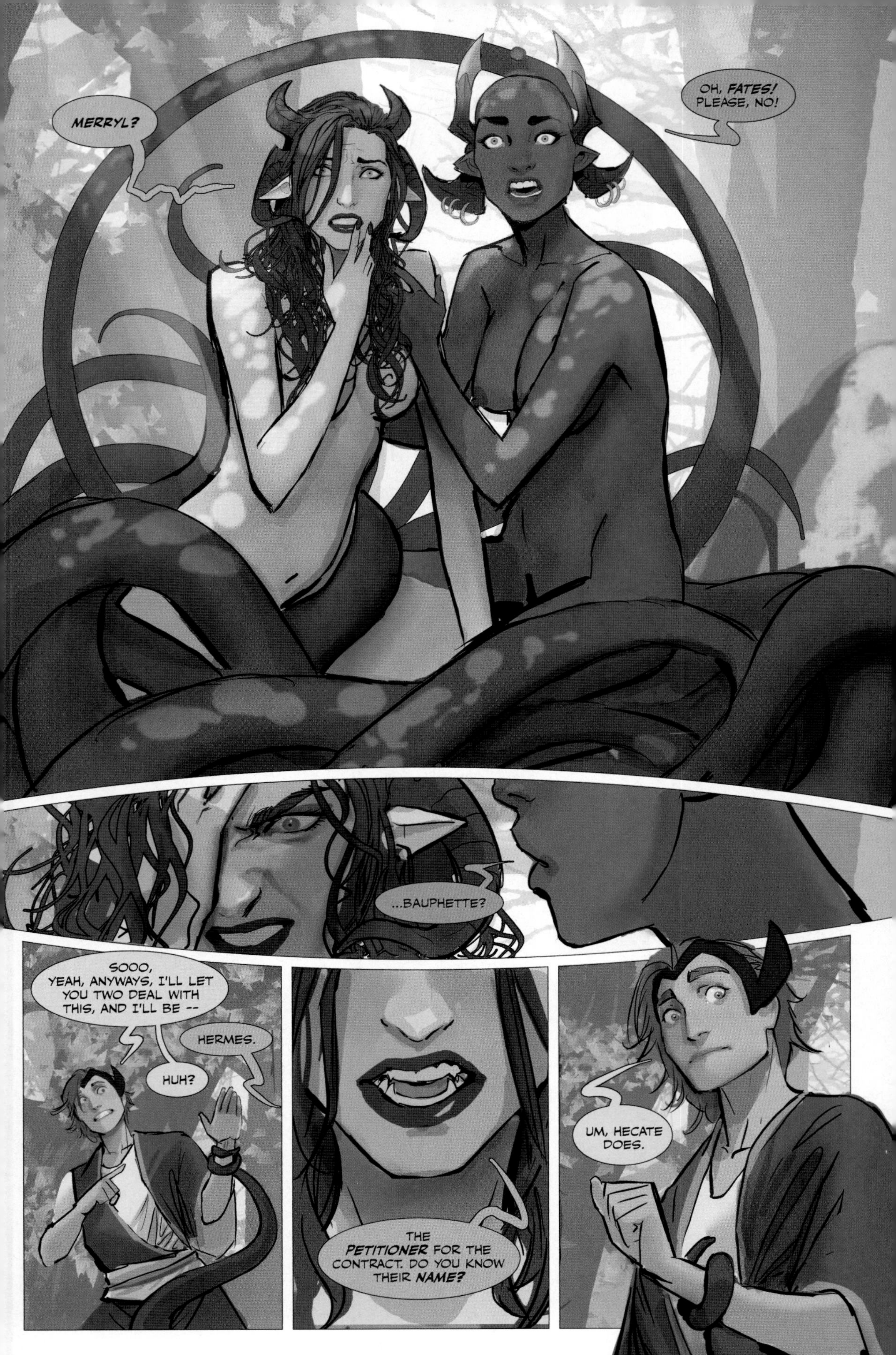
MERRYL?
OH, FATES! PLEASE, NO!
...BAUPHETTE?
SOOO, YEAH, ANYWAYS, I'LL LET YOU TWO DEAL WITH THIS, AND I'LL BE --
HERMES.
HUH?
THE PETITIONER FOR THE CONTRACT. DO YOU KNOW THEIR NAME?
UM, HECATE DOES.

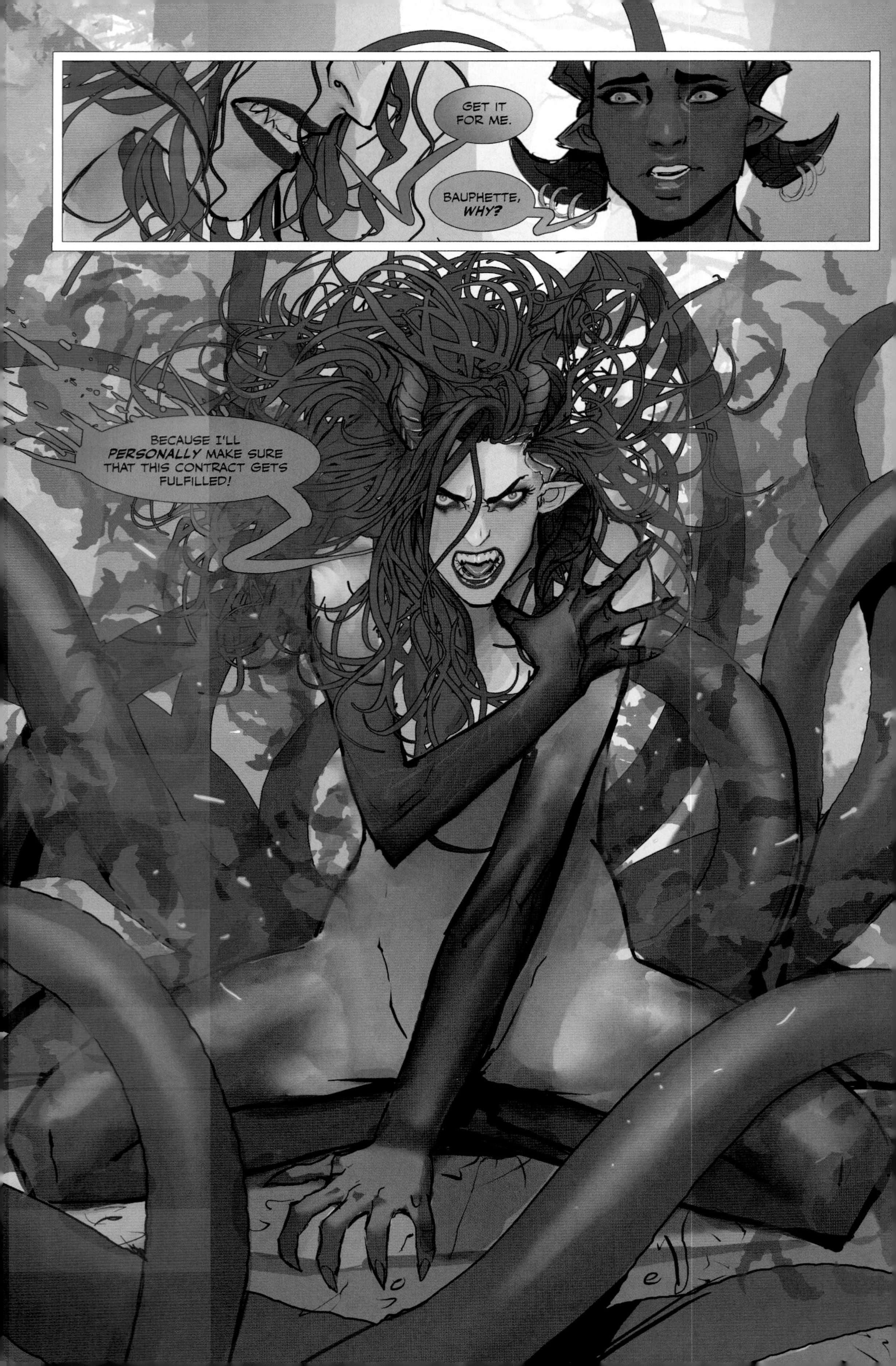
GET IT FOR ME.
BAUPHETTE, WHY?
BECAUSE I'LL PERSONALLY MAKE SURE THAT THIS CONTRACT GETS FULFILLED!

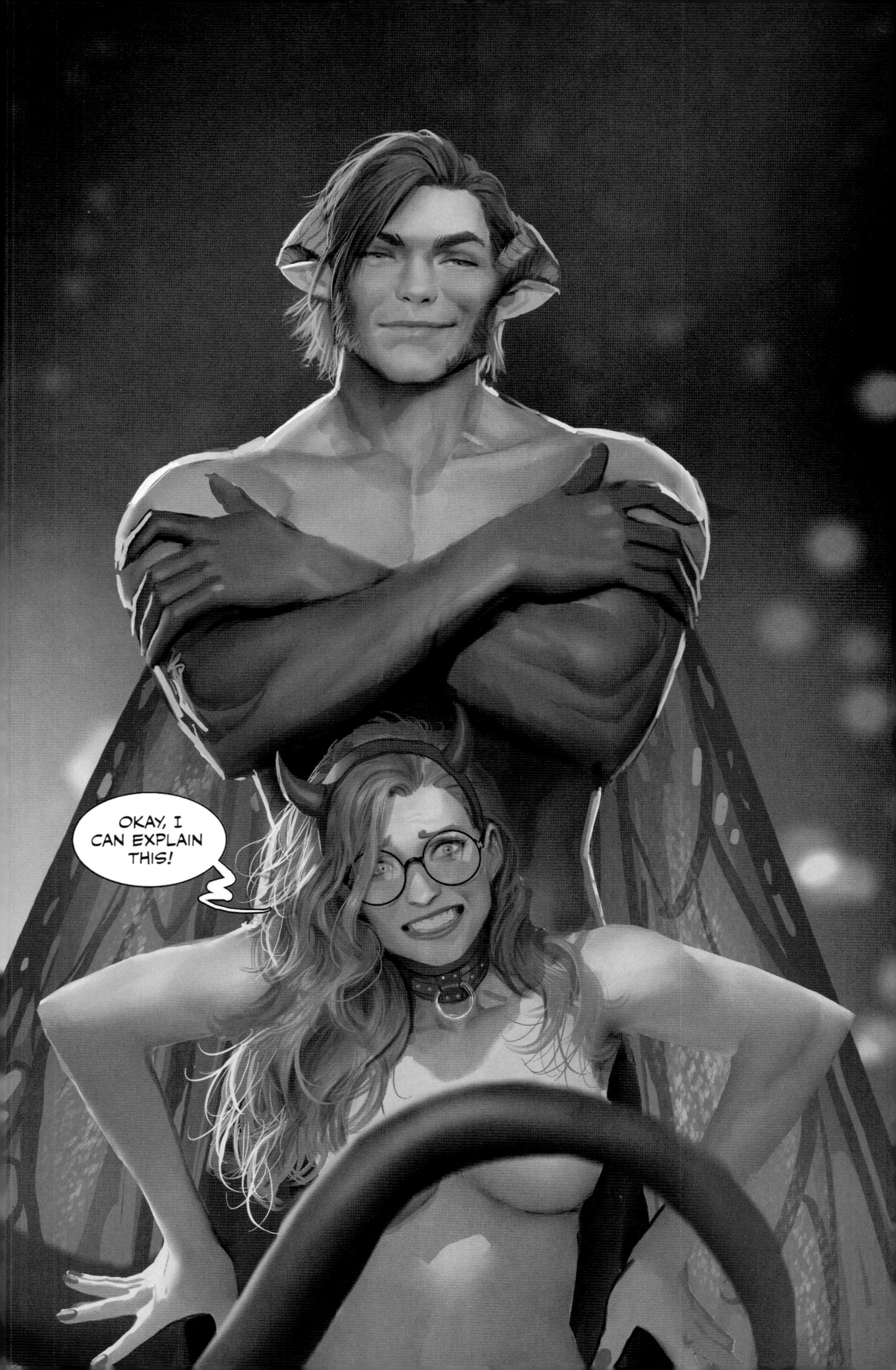
OKAY, I CAN EXPLAIN THIS!

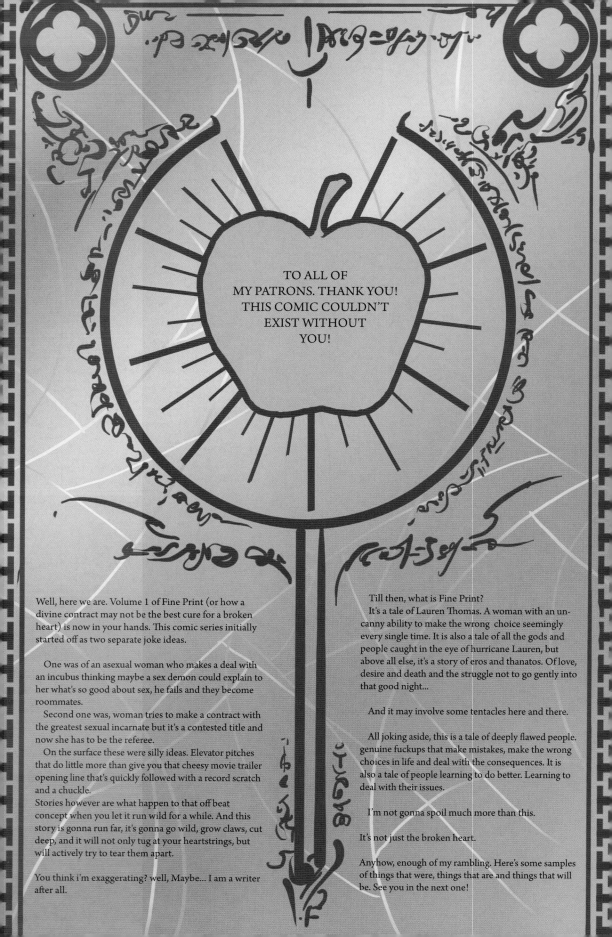

TO ALL OF
MY PATRONS. THANK YOU!
THIS COMIC COULDN'T
EXIST WITHOUT
YOU!

Well, here we are. Volume 1 of Fine Print (or how a divine contract may not be the best cure for a broken heart) is now in your hands. This comic series initially started off as two separate joke ideas.

One was of an asexual woman who makes a deal with an incubus thinking maybe a sex demon could explain to her what's so good about sex, he fails and they become roommates.

Second one was, woman tries to make a contract with the greatest sexual incarnate but it's a contested title and now she has to be the referee.

On the surface these were silly ideas. Elevator pitches that do little more than give you that cheesy movie trailer opening line that's quickly followed with a record scratch and a chuckle.

Stories however are what happen to that off beat concept when you let it run wild for a while. And this story is gonna run far, it's gonna go wild, grow claws, cut deep, and it will not only tug at your heartstrings, but will actively try to tear them apart.

You think i'm exaggerating? well, Maybe... I am a writer after all.

Till then, what is Fine Print?

It's a tale of Lauren Thomas. A woman with an uncanny ability to make the wrong choice seemingly every single time. It is also a tale of all the gods and people caught in the eye of hurricane Lauren, but above all else, it's a story of eros and thanatos. Of love, desire and death and the struggle not to go gently into that good night...

And it may involve some tentacles here and there.

All joking aside, this is a tale of deeply flawed people. genuine fuckups that make mistakes, make the wrong choices in life and deal with the consequences. It is also a tale of people learning to do better. Learning to deal with their issues.

I'm not gonna spoil much more than this.

It's not just the broken heart.

Anyhow, enough of my rambling. Here's some samples of things that were, things that are and things that will be. See you in the next one!

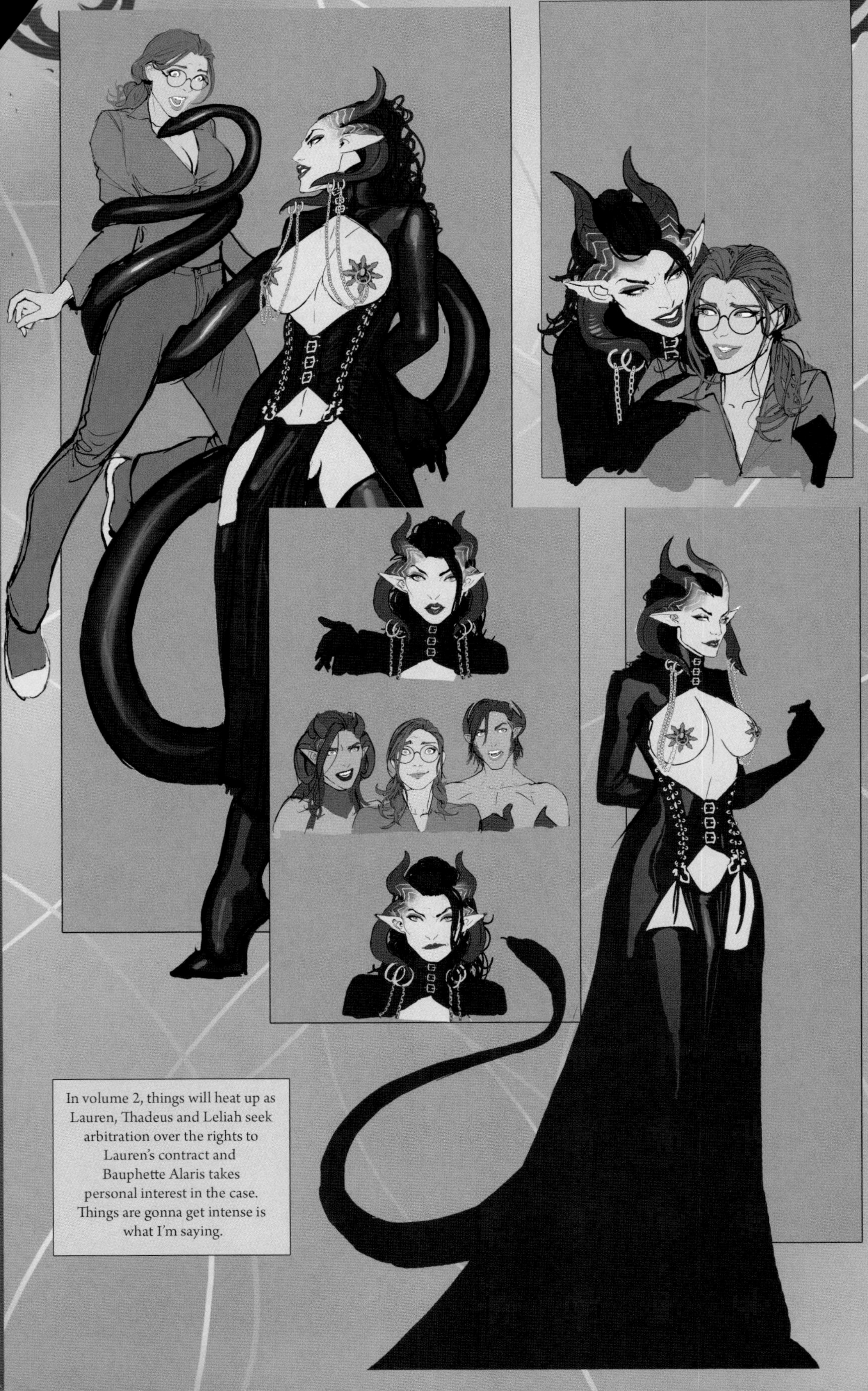

In volume 2, things will heat up as Lauren, Thadeus and Leliah seek arbitration over the rights to Lauren's contract and Bauphette Alaris takes personal interest in the case. Things are gonna get intense is what I'm saying.

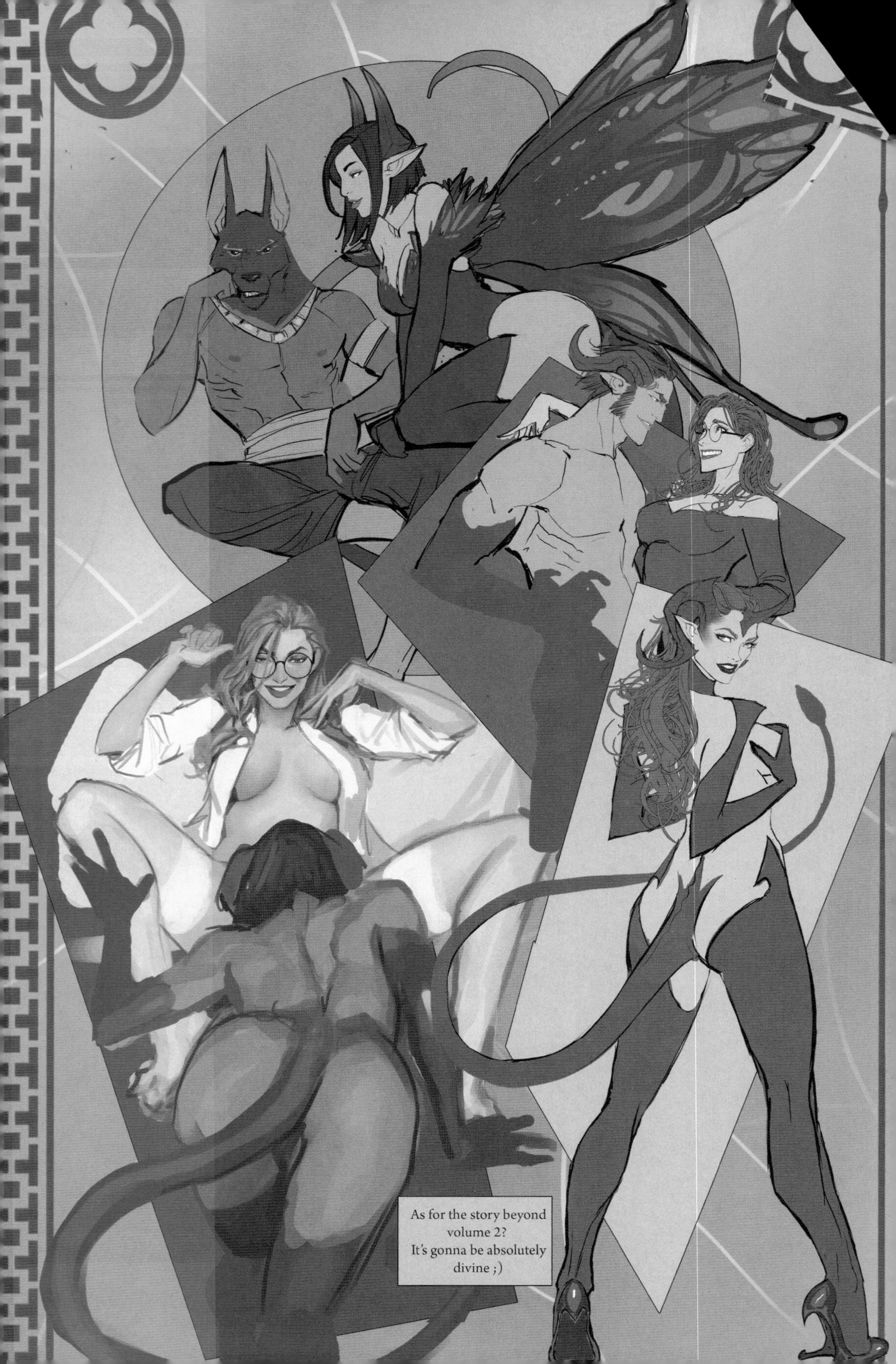
As for the story beyond volume 2?
It's gonna be absolutely divine ;)

One of my favorite aspects of Fine Print is that the series is a part of a shared universe of stories. Some mine, some by my wife, Linda Sejic. We have a simple rule with our stories. While they are in continuity you don't need to read one to undestand another.

With that out of the way, here are some samples of Linda's comic, Punderworld. Volume 1 is already in print and it's a story of Hades and Persephone's romantic adventures. It may involve some familiar faces.

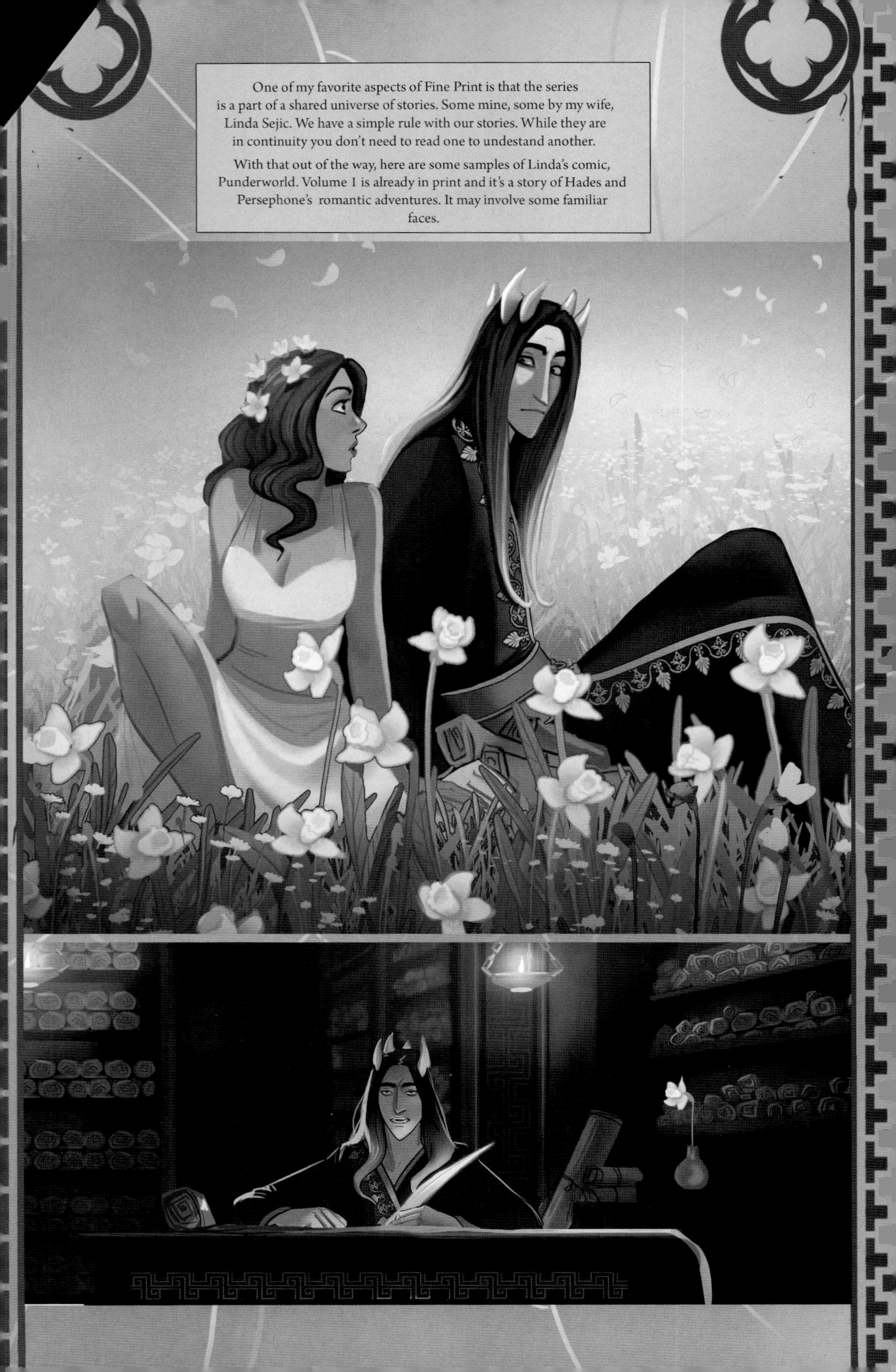

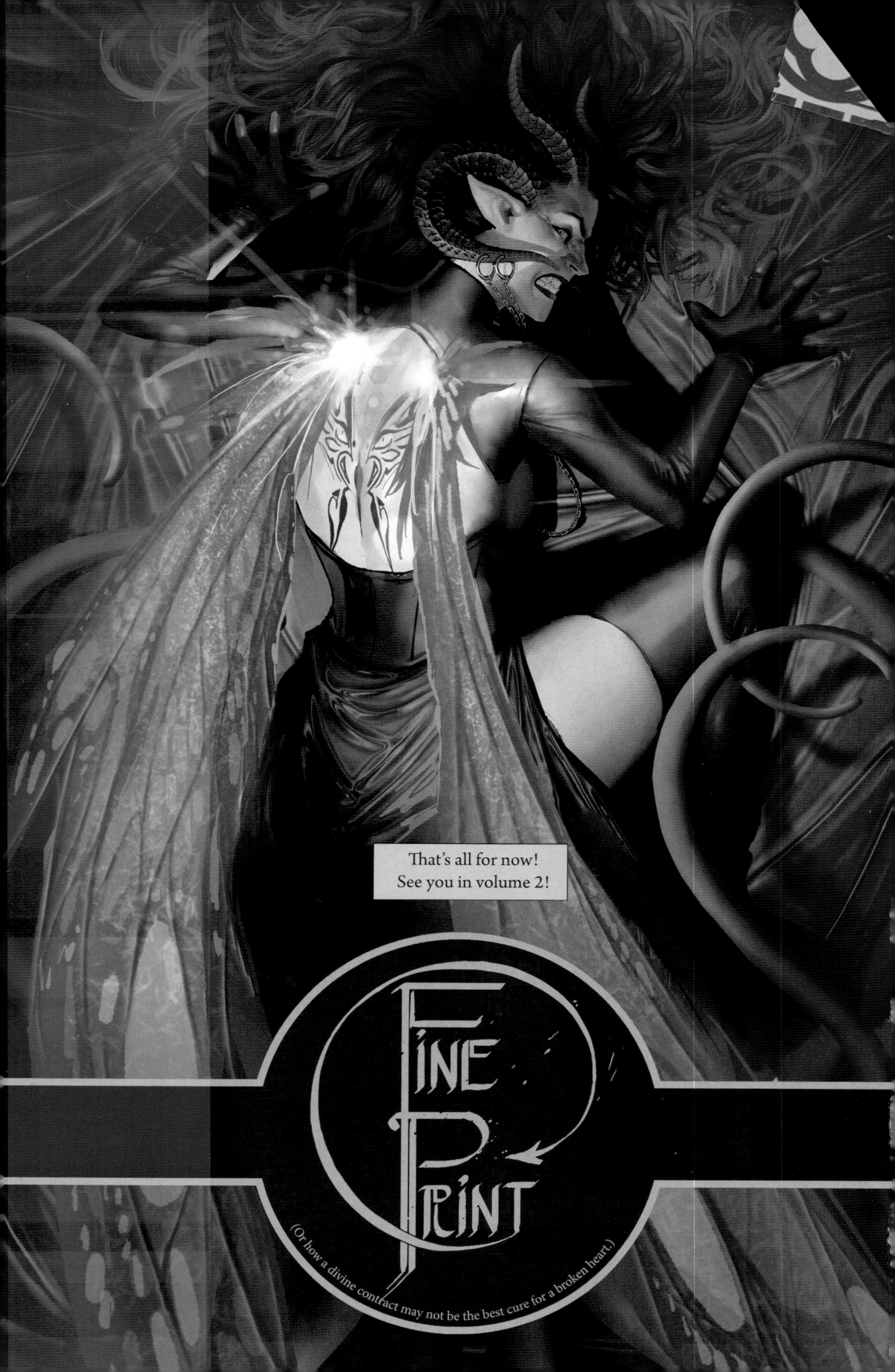
That's all for now!
See you in volume 2!
FINE PRINT
(Or how a divine contract may not be the best cure for a broken heart.)